THE RIPPLING EFFECT

A Novel

The "Spencer's Mill" series

Cherie Harbridge Williams

This is a work of fiction. Names, characters, places, and incidents either are the product of the author's imagination or are used fictitiously. Any resemblance to actual persons, living or dead, events, or locales is entirely coincidental.

All scriptures referenced in this book are from the King James Version.

First paperback edition December 2022

Book design and map by Cherie Williams

ISBN 979-8-9874296-0-0

www.CherieHarbridgeWilliams.com

DEDICATION

This story is dedicated to everyone who has ever been betrayed,

to every victim of betrayal who has failed to forgive,

and to everyone who has been the betrayer.

ACKNOWLEDGMENTS

With special thanks to Gail Anderson, Jeanne Boyce, Janice Shoe, Jerry Nebergall, and Sarah Mae for feedback from the reader's point of view,
and to Nancy Mills and Renee Pearison,
cover consultants.

Photos and fonts used in the cover artwork from
Envato.com

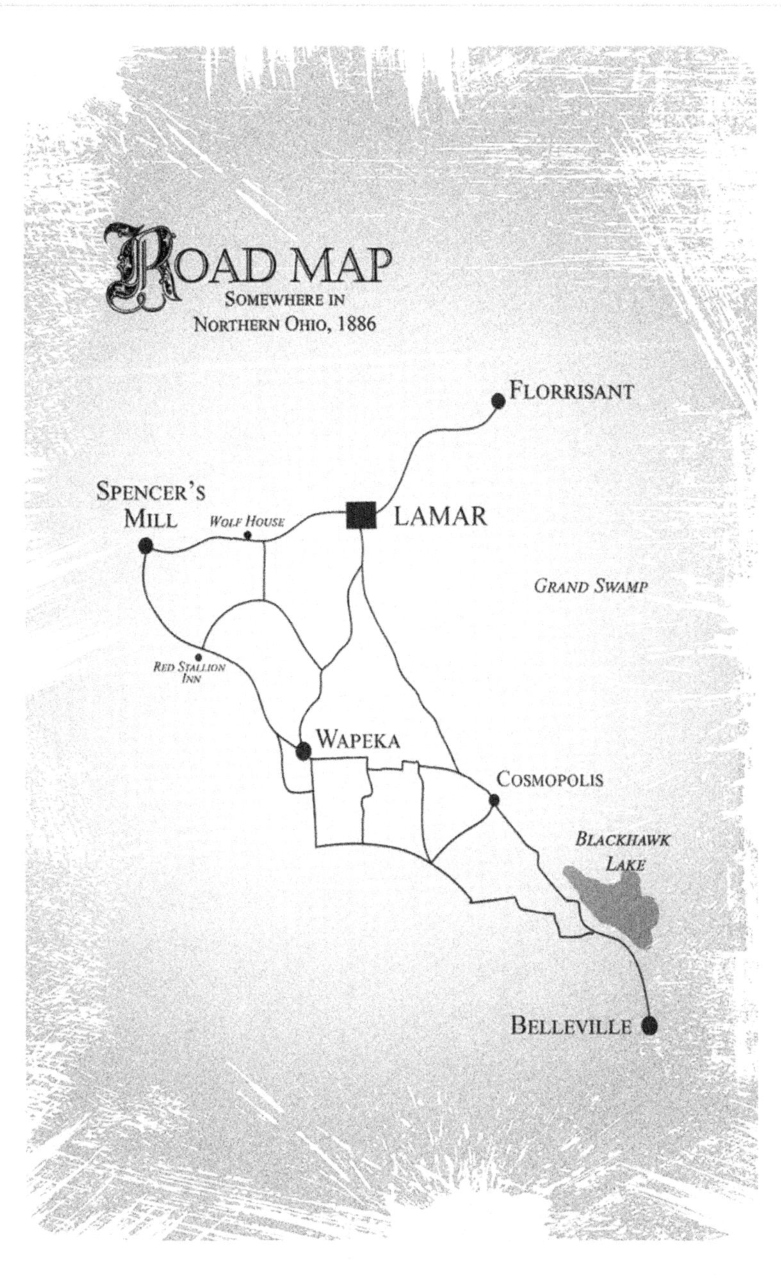
ROAD MAP
SOMEWHERE IN
NORTHERN OHIO, 1886
FLORRISANT
SPENCER'S
MILL
WOLF HOUSE
LAMAR
GRAND SWAMP
RED STALLION
INN
WAPEKA
COSMOPOLIS
BLACKHAWK
LAKE
BELLEVILLE

TABLE OF CONTENTS

IT ALL STARTED SIX MONTHS AGO

In the earlier story, *Teacups and Lies,* John Reese was the eldest son of ten children of Daniel and Susannah Reese. In 1886, after a sudden heart attack took his father, John became the estate's executor, charged with administering his father's fortune in cash and real estate. However, temptation overcame him. He made the mistake of thinking he would never get caught diverting some of the estate's rental income to his personal account.

When his mother's attorney investigated secretly and found proof of the theft, he gave John an ultimatum: replace the stolen funds and resign as executor of the will or have his theft made public. John was trapped. He signed the resignation only to keep his larceny a secret from his family. His financial plans for the future had just been thwarted, and he was furious. Even worse, after a five-month courtship, his mother married the attorney.

He tried to get revenge by sabotaging his new stepfather with lies and slander. When that didn't work, he devised an elaborate scheme to regain control of his siblings' inheritance. He successfully persuaded most of them to sign a bogus agreement, but one of his brothers suspected John's dishonesty and filed a lawsuit to block his plans. At the hearing, John's lies and deceit were revealed. His mother and other siblings were shocked, and John's employer fired him because of his dishonesty.

John realized he had hit bottom. In the face of his family's anger and mistrust, he was forced to see himself as God saw him. His only reasonable option was to repent and ask forgiveness, a step not taken lightly. Most of the family forgave him, except Eli, his closest brother.

John began the long, arduous task of rebuilding his life and earning back his family's trust. But even though there is forgiveness, there are also consequences.

His Ma warned him of the rippling effect of sin . . .

Chapter 1: UNEMPLOYMENT

Monday, January 10, 1887
Spencer's Mill, Ohio

Unemployment was a new experience for John Reese and his family—and he was to blame. His lucrative job at Johnson's Oil Company had ended after last week's court hearing exposing his lies—the lies he had hoped would convince his nine siblings to let him manage their inheritance. The knowledge that his actions had created this crisis weighed like a stone around his neck.

John was an ambitious twenty-nine-year-old man with brownish-blonde hair, a mustache and beard, and serious eyes. He had achieved notable success at a young age. Friends knew he was accustomed to a handsome salary because he often told them. Unfortunately, that had come to a sudden and unpleasant end.

He had been out in the winter cold all morning looking for work, first at the nearby mill. After that, he journeyed fifteen miles on horseback to the railroad office in Lamar, where they advertised for a clerk. Then he applied at the trolley company, hoping for a job as a driver. He even tried at the livery stable. He would have been glad to clean the stalls. Anything to feed his family. But nothing. Most prospective employers had read the story in the newspaper and treated him with contempt. When they found out who he was, they didn't even bother to talk to him. They just shook their heads. He couldn't hold up under any more scorn today, so he came home in defeat, chilled to the bone.

He dropped into a kitchen chair, his hands trembling and his heart thumping rapidly. It had been five days since the court hearing—five long, stressful days. Sweat ran down his face and dampened his shirt. He turned to his wife with wild eyes. "What's wrong with me, Kate? I feel something horrible is about to happen, but I don't know what."

Kate was a petite woman of about twenty-eight years who could have been considered plain. She had long brown hair and hazel eyes. She only owned two old dresses, thanks to her husband's tight hold on his money. But she had battled through her emotions and decided to forgive him.

"Something horrible has already happened, John—the court hearing. That was only a few days ago. I think you're having a delayed reaction."

"I feel sick to my stomach."

Kate nodded and rubbed his shoulders, but her efforts didn't do much to calm him. "Why don't I go get Danny? He'll come over and sit with you." Danny was John's younger brother, but they had been on opposite sides of the lawsuit. Still, he had expressed forgiveness, and John had few friends left.

"No. Not Danny. Not anybody. All I want is to be alone. Please, Kate, leave me alone." He sank his head into his hands, sobbing.

John and Kate had been praying over John's lack of employment. In 1887, there would be no money coming in without regular work. Besides being financially disastrous, the experience was emotionally devastating. John had taken the situation in stride until today when he went to pieces suddenly. He didn't know why he was falling apart now. The term 'panic attack' was not familiar to him.

"John," she said, "it's frightening to be out of work. I understand that. Not only do we have no income, but you've just come through the trauma of having all of your lies exposed. We have to expect there will be suffering from this, but God is merciful as well as just. You've repented, and He surely has a way for our family to survive."

John hung his head, hands still shaking.

Even though most of his family had forgiven him—except his closest brother, Eli—they still didn't trust him. His shame stung so sharply he could barely think. All those lies he told about his new stepfather stealing a man's inheritance, being involved with a young woman behind his mother's back, and a lucrative investment opportunity that didn't exist—all had been revealed to everyone. They had seen it unfold in the courtroom: his Ma and her new husband, his nine siblings, their spouses, his former employer, and all the courtroom witnesses. And now it had been reported in the Lamar newspaper. No one would ever forget any detail, he was sure. That was especially true of Eli, who was most hurt by his betrayal.

He was fortunate that Kate had forgiven him, even though their marriage would never be the same. Today, he was at home with her, still healing from a courtroom assault on his jaw, trying to figure out the future.

But John's life had taken on a new focus. Of course, he had always believed there was a God. He had even gone to church for a while to please his wife. But at his lowest point, right after the court hearing, he recognized there was nothing he could do to fix this mess. He couldn't talk his way out of this one. There was nowhere to turn. So, after struggling with his decision, he finally turned to God in desperation. Now, he was living the life God intended. But the process would not be quick or easy.

His actions weren't without their consequences. . . oh, the consequences. They would be difficult to survive. Ma had warned him about the ripples flowing from a life of lies and selfishness. Now that he was experiencing it, he thought it was more than ripples. It was almost like a tidal wave.

Kate pulled a chair beside her husband and fastened her eyes on him. "John, look at me." Her hand went to his shoulder, and he raised his eyes to meet hers. "Just for today, I think you should rest. Do nothing but relax. Sleep. This has been hard on you. Then tomorrow, when you're more alert, we'll think together. How does that sound?

Without even replying, John rose from the kitchen chair, shoulders slumping. He was so weary that his feet moved automatically, heading for the bedroom. He lay across the bed without turning back the quilt and fell asleep.

Kate unfolded a spare quilt over him. He hadn't been the only one affected. This whole episode had been tough on her, too...discovering that her husband was a liar—and an accomplished one, at that...finding that her family had no income...having to struggle with the forgiveness issue...learning that forgiveness is hard work. She wanted nothing more than to nap on the sofa, but she had the children to look after.

As she tiptoed back into the parlor, someone rapped on the door. *This is the wrong time for visitors,* she thought as she grasped the doorknob.

A young lady stood on the porch wearing a dress with a fashionable bustle, a warm cloak topped by a chinchilla boa, a feathered hat, and the latest style of pointed shoes—Kate's cousin.

"Francie, what a surprise," Kate said in a low voice, not wanting to invite her in. She was already weary and didn't want to deal with a busybody. Besides, she needed to keep the house quiet for John. "John's not well today, and he's in bed. We'll have to be quiet if you come in so he can rest."

"I don't mind, Katie. I'll keep my voice low." She stepped over the threshold.

"All right." Kate's heart sank. "Well, let me get you a cup of tea, and we'll whisper in the kitchen." She led Francie into her kitchen, which was usually bright and sunny but now reflected the gray atmosphere outside and the gray mood inside.

Francie pulled out a chair and planted herself, waiting for her tea. "I've been out of town for a few days, Katie. I had the chance to take a train trip with Mother. She wanted to go shopping in Chicago." Francie and her mother spent a lot of time shopping. "I'll have to show you the new dress I bought."

Kate sighed. A new dress was not even a distant possibility for her. She put the kettle on, took the saucers and teacups from the sideboard, and then sat at the table waiting for the kettle to boil.

Francie leaned forward and dropped her voice to a whisper. "Someone told me a rumor about John. How is he doing? I didn't know whether to believe it."

So that's why Francie is here. The fallout from the hearing had already consumed Kate's day. She sighed again. "I don't know if I can talk about this anymore, Francie. It's wearing me out."

Francie grabbed her hand across the table. "They said things went badly for John—he got caught lying and taking some of the family money. If that's true, it's an awful thing for you."

"Well, it's true." Kate might as well admit it. "But he returned the money before the family knew it was gone. They didn't know about it until it came out at the hearing."

The water simmered in the copper kettle. She poured it over the tea leaves before the kettle could whistle and disturb John.

"What happened?" Francie wanted details.

Kate sighed, then relented. "I'll give you the short version." She took a chair at the table to wait for the tea to steep. "When John's Pa died suddenly last July, John became the estate executor. His Ma had no experience handling money, so he wanted to take control and administer the assets for her and his brothers and sisters."

"I guess she objected to that?"

"I'd say. She hired a lawyer to help her manage her finances. He blocked John from making decisions concerning her share of the funds. Later, when John tried to have the attorney removed, well, it involved spreading some rumors that weren't true. I must admit that."

Kate rose and poured the tea into her best cups. She brought them to the table with the sugar bowl.

"Care for any cream?"

"No thanks . . . What kind of rumors?"

"There's no sense going into details. They involved casting doubt on the attorney's character. Of course, I believed everything he said. He's my husband." She sighed deeply. "I haven't wanted to believe the truth. But there's something I need to say out loud. If I hear myself say it, I'll have to deal with the truth."

After a pause, Francie urged her on. Her eyes were riveted on Kate, who continued. "Let me say that when the first rumor backfired, the next one had to be bigger and more convincing, and the third one, well—I guess even the devil must have been impressed. It's time I came to terms with the truth."

Francie giggled despite herself. "You'll have to fill me in on the details."

"No, I won't. The details aren't important. To make matters worse, his mother married her attorney last month."

Francie sat with her mouth open. "That must have made John crazy," she said in a stage whisper, and Kate put her finger to her lips. Francie continued, "In Aunt Susannah's defense, a woman just about has to be married these days to get along financially. And she still has the three younger ones at home."

"That's true," Kate said. "It was just her choice of husbands. It couldn't have been worse, as far as John was concerned. We didn't even go to the wedding. John's brother said it was beautiful. I'm sorry we missed it. Of course, we're on better terms now that John has confessed and asked for forgiveness. But that was painful for everyone."

"So, what was the lawsuit about?"

Kate stirred a spoonful of sugar into her tea and blew the steam off.

"The judge ruled that none of the brothers and sisters could control the inheritance of the others."

Francie sipped her tea and peered at Kate over the cup's rim. "That doesn't sound so bad."

Kate was torn between not wanting to share anything more with Francie and a strong desire to purge herself. "Well, he's lost the trust of his family. But Francie, John wasn't himself while he was doing all that. He's always been a good man and started with good intentions. He just snapped, that's all. He wanted to be in charge of his Pa's affairs, and his Ma had other ideas."

"I know he's a good man," Francie said, reaching across the table to pat Kate's hand.

Kate ignored what she took as a patronizing attitude and continued. "But now he has two problems. John's employer testified against him, and so did a big, angry woman who owned the Red Stallion Inn. She believed the last lie. She must have borrowed money to cash in on a false opportunity John invented. After the gavel came down at the end of the hearing, she came at John like a steam locomotive and attacked him before he left the courtroom.

"Are you serious? Did she hit him?"

"Left him unconscious on the floor with a swollen jaw."

"Kate, how awful. How are you holding up?"

"And then John was dismissed from his job."

Francie sucked in a breath, and her hand went to her mouth.

"Oh, no, Katie, that means you're without income. What are you going to do to feed your family?"

"I don't know, except God will take care of us." She spoke confidently, sipped her tea, and looked straight into Francie's eyes.

Francie fiddled with her teacup and stared at the table. She rubbed her neck and glanced up. "You sound so sure of yourself, but that sounds like wishful thinking."

"It's not. It's what He does."

"How can you know that for sure?"

"I trust Him," Kate said. "He's always taken care of us one way or another."

Francie's lips were pressed together, and she studied her hands. Kate regarded her silence as an indication of her doubt. *How sad,* she thought.

Her cousin picked up her teacup, drained it, and said she needed to get home.

"I'll come back for another visit later, Katie. Good to see you again. And good luck to John as he looks for a new job."

Kate was relieved to close the door when Francie left.

She tiptoed in to check on John and readjusted his quilt. He snored softly, so it was time to get down to business. Four-year-old Gracie was napping, and six-year-old Steven was still at school. This was her opportunity.

She sat alone in the silence, praying for guidance and asking for opportunities to open for John. A random wisp of memory floated into her mind. Mentally, she traveled back to last November when Eli and Mary came for dinner. It had been the best dinner she had ever made. She remembered Mary saying, "You really know how to bake a pie. You should open a restaurant."

That comment had struck a chord in her heart. Baking was

something she loved to do. With John's business skills and her baking talent, she was sure they could make a living. That would be the answer to their lack of income. She had no idea how it could ever happen, but she was sure this would solve their problem.

She could hardly wait until John woke up to tell him she had a plan—maybe not a full restaurant. Perhaps just a bakery. But for now, let him sleep.

Chapter 2: THE INSPIRATION

Four hours later, John emerged from the bedroom unshaven, his hair disheveled and his stomach growling. Kate grinned as she put a steaming plate of beans and buttered cornbread before him.

"Kate, you look excited about something, but we're in trouble. What happened while I was sleeping?"

Kate giggled. "I know you'll think I've lost my mind, but as I prayed this afternoon, I got a wonderful idea. Let me tell you about it, and we'll think it over together."

John shoveled a spoonful of beans into his mouth and glanced at her. His face showed deep stress lines. She had never seen him so haggard, but at least he had stopped trembling and sweating.

Her words tumbled out. "Here's the idea. You have business skills, and I'm well-known in town as a good cook. I've been told my pies are better than anyone else's, and my bread is top-rate, too. I believe the women of Spencer's Mill would rather buy my bread in the morning than bake it themselves. John, we could open a bakery. Mary even suggested it once. We could call it 'Reese's Bakery.' My reputation in town should give us a good start in sales. What do you think?" She was almost dancing around the kitchen as she brought him a mug of coffee to drink with his meal.

He shook his head. "That's a foolish idea. You forgot about

my reputation." His tone was flat. It was clear he didn't share her excitement. "If we had a sign that said, 'Reese's Bakery,' people would know it was me and walk the other way. Besides, what would we do for money?"

Kate refused to be put off.

"For one thing, we don't have to call it Reese's Bakery. There are other names. And I don't know what we'd do for money because you never confided in me with any financial information." Her tone was firm, almost accusing. "How much do we have, exactly?"

She had never spoken like that to him. He stared at her as if he didn't know her.

"Now is the time, John."

He hesitated. Kate sensed that the old John was struggling to maintain control of all the money and decision-making power in the family. But he wasn't the only one who had changed. Kate had undergone a profound transition since the court hearing. She wouldn't live in unquestioning loyalty any longer. She was a bright, thinking wife who wanted to take on a more active role in their financial crisis. He needed help, and she could give it. So she pressed on. "John, you can try to handle this crisis yourself, or we can do it together. Which is it?"

John continued to tuck into his beans and cornbread. Kate took a chair across from him, staring into his face. He pretended to ignore the heat of her steady gaze, but it was a mighty struggle.

After a few uncomfortable moments, he finally locked eyes with her. "You're backing me into a corner."

She continued to gaze at him.

He dug his spoon into the beans. "All right, Kate, even though it's the husband's responsibility to support his family, I'll agree to try this together. You and me and God. If it works, it works. If it doesn't, we'll have to do something else."

She jumped up and ran to his chair, throwing her arms around his neck and knocking his spoon out of his hand. Beans splatted on the pine tabletop. "This will be exciting," she said.

He managed a thin smile. "I hope so. But it won't be easy. I know from experience that hardly anything is as easy as expected. There are always wrinkles. Always."

Hot food in his belly and the afternoon's deep sleep had invigorated him. His panic attack was over. Little Gracie came in with her doll and wanted to sit in her Pa's lap. He picked her up and stroked her blonde curls as she told him about a tea party with her dolls.

"Papa, I had all my dolls at my tea party, but Mopsy spilled her cup, and I had to punish her and put her to bed. Would you come to our next tea party?"

"We'll see." He grinned and hugged her. His eyes took on life for the first time in days.

She clambered off his lap and ran into the next room to pester her brother.

"You know, this might be good," he said, warming to Kate's idea. "We would be the only bakery in Spencer's Mill."

Kate had raised the question of finances for the first time in their marriage. John rose from the table, entered the parlor, and unlocked his desk. He took out the bank book, a few sheets of paper, and a pen.

"Look at this bank book, Katie. Look at the balance here. This is all the money I have…we have. We'll have to rent a storefront, buy equipment and supplies, and make this money last until the bakery turns a profit. That'll take some doing."

"I've never seen that bank book before. That's a lot more than I thought we had, but I don't know what our costs will be." John's salary at Johnson's Oil Company had been greater than she realized. "Fortunately, I've learned to squeeze a dollar until it bleeds. I confess that I often resented your stingy attitude, but now I can see it's paying off. And we still have your inheritance once your Pa's property is sold. If we get into a hard place, maybe your family will help us."

John wagged his head. "I don't know how much my family will be willing to help after that court hearing. That was pretty rough."

"Most of them have forgiven you. Maybe not Eli. But even if they can't help, God is still in charge. We'll make it."

Chapter 3: THE SEARCH

John wondered if Kate's idea was a possibility. Was this the divine plan to move them out of their crisis? There were so many obstacles to surmount and so many decisions to make.

"We can't sell bread out of our house," he said. "We don't have enough cash for a down payment on a store, so our ideal situation would be a commercial rental."

Try as they might, they could find no commercial rental in Spencer's Mill. They were tempted to give up looking, but something urged them on. Finally, they decided to look at a property for sale next to the general store. It needed repairs, but the location was excellent. The biggest obstacle was that down payment. They needed to conserve their funds for living expenses and business equipment.

John dreaded talking to his brother Danny since he was the one who filed the lawsuit. Danny said he forgave him, but was that genuine, or did he say it to please Ma? He would rather take a beating than face scorn yet again. But since Danny worked at the general store next to the property they wanted, he may have the needed information. John saddled Ginger, his chestnut-colored quarter horse, and reluctantly went to face his brother.

Surprisingly, Danny welcomed him in. He was younger than John by eight years, a pleasant brown-haired young man who had taken a wife only two months ago. After an awkward start, he warmed to the idea of John and Kate opening a bakery.

"I'm sure you remember that storefront was a carpenter's shop," he said, "but the owner died a year ago with no heirs. He willed the property to Wesleyan Church. They want to sell it. Reverend Buchanan can show you the building."

"Thanks for the information, Danny. I'll share that with Kate."

"How did it go?" Kate asked, surprised that John had returned home so soon.

"Danny was friendly toward me and gave me the information we need. I'm so thankful he isn't still angry."

Kate tilted her head and spoke softly. "Try to see things from his side. You have a good family, but you should tread gently around them. Think about that punch to your jaw. It looks like it's almost healed, but it still hurts. That's probably how it is with Danny and the rest of your family. They've forgiven you for hurting them, but they still hurt. They still don't know if they can trust you. So it would be wise to tread gently."

John nodded.

Tuesday, January 11, 1887

After lunch the next day, they planned to visit Reverend Buchanan before Stevie came home from school.

At the front door, John pulled on Kate's arm to delay her stepping out. "We need to have a little chat before we go, Kate. I need to give you your first lesson in buying real estate."

"What's that?" She turned her face toward him.

"We may be able to look at the property today. When we go in, if there are things you don't like about it, feel free to say so. But if you do like it, even if you think it would be perfect for us, don't let the owner know, or it will be harder to negotiate a lower price."

She gave him a sly smile. "I can do that."

John hitched the horse, and the three set off for Wesleyan Church in the frigid January air. Gracie sat beside her Mama, clutching her doll and swinging her short legs under a lap blanket.

Arriving at the church, they opened one of the double doors and hurried inside. The winter air whooshed in ahead of them.

"May I help you folks?" Reverend Buchanan was in his office just off the main foyer. He rose from his chair, shivering from the sudden influx of cold air around his feet. As the Reeses came in, he grabbed a bookmark off his desk and marked his place in his Bible.

"Yes, sir. I'm John Reese, Danny's brother. This is my wife, Kate, and our daughter, Gracie. We're interested in looking at your property next to the general store. We're thinking of opening a business."

Reverend Buchanan beamed at them. "Wonderful! I have the key in my desk. Would you like to look at it now?"

"That would be helpful," John said. "If you like, we can take you in our carriage and bring you back afterward. We can talk along the way."

"Very good," said the pastor. He groped around his desk for the key, shuffling papers and files, then held it up triumphantly. They left the warmth of the pastor's study and returned to the cold.

Reverend Buchanan pulled his fur collar tighter around his neck to block the wind. "I know your brother. He married the Fletcher girl just a couple of months ago."

"Yes, he did."

"They've been attending church regularly since then. Fine couple."

"Yes."

"Did you know the carpenter lived in the apartment over

the store? I don't know if you folks would be interested in living up there, but if not, you could rent it out for extra income."

"I wasn't aware there was an apartment upstairs," John said. "That certainly expands the possibilities."

Rev. Buchanan smiled. "What kind of business will you be opening?"

Kate spoke up, bubbling with enthusiasm. "We want to open a bakery. John has sharp business skills, and I'll do the baking. The folks at our church know my reputation in the kitchen."

"Are you from Trinity Chapel, then?" inquired the pastor.

"Yes, sir."

Trinity Chapel was the only other church in town.

They arrived at the store and tied the horse to the rail. The pastor shivered as he jiggled the icy skeleton key into the lock with an ungloved hand. The door opened with a screech, the hinges rebelling against being opened in freezing temperatures.

The neglected interior was covered in dirt. It was littered with the remnants of projects unfinished when the carpenter died. A dusty Windsor chair without legs lay next to the treadle lathe. Frozen cans of varnish and paint with rusty lids were stacked against the wall. John and Kate took their time inspecting the layout and condition of the building, making mental notes of how they could use the space.

"How much are you asking for the property?" John asked.

"I believe the Board will entertain offers for a thousand dollars. Don't hold me to that," he said. "Our Board of Trustees has the final say over the price. If you're interested, you'll want to make an offer; then it will have to go to the Board for review."

"That sounds high for the condition of the building."

They were surprised to hear rapping on the front window. A tall, dark-haired gentleman in a top hat peered through the dirty glass.

"Excuse me," said Pastor Buchanan, glancing away. "Let me see what this fellow wants."

He opened the door, and the man entered, dressed in a pricey business suit, cloak, and expensive, imported shoes. "Sorry to intrude," he said. "I hoped someone was here. I thought I'd stop and ask how much you want for the building."

Buchanan brightened. "The Board of Trustees is asking a thousand dollars. Are you interested in buying?"

The man nodded. "I plan to open a shoe shop here in Spencer's Mill. This looks like it might be the perfect spot. A friend told me a church owns it, and there haven't been any offers for a long time. I'll look around, and if it suits me, I hope to pick it up at a good price."

The pastor stuck his hand out. "I'm Reverend Buchanan, the pastor of the church. And you are--"

"Pardon my manners. My name is Skinner. Roy Skinner."

"Well, Mr. Skinner, this is Mr. and Mrs. Reese. They're interested in the building for a bakery."

John and Kate glanced at each other, heartsick. "Thank you for showing us the building, Reverend. Kate and I will go home so you can show the building to Mr. Skinner. We'll talk this over, and I'll get back in touch with you. Will Mr. Skinner return you to your study?"

"Yes, I'll do that," Skinner said.

John and Kate stepped out onto the sidewalk with Gracie and studied the front. It was a handsome but tired-looking brick façade needing paint on the trim. The large multi-paned window area would be perfect for displaying baked goods. They hadn't said anything to each other in the pastor's presence, but John had mental notes of ideas for a later private discussion. That was before Skinner showed up.

"What do we do now, Kate?" John asked. His stomach was in knots.

"We pray."

John and Kate continued toward home, with Gracie hugging her mother for warmth. As they traveled, Kate giggled, which surprised John under the circumstances. "What are you thinking?" he asked.

"While we were looking at the front of the building, I imagined a banner sign over the window that said, 'Katie's Bakery,' or some name we'll decide on later."

She expected a comment from him, but John wasn't paying attention. He was preoccupied with his thoughts. "Imagine the church not getting any offers for a year; then someone else shows up just when we show some interest." John smacked his fist on the seat beside him. "This messes up our plans. It's like the devil sent him."

"This is a temporary trial, not a death sentence for our plans. After he inspects the building, Mr. Skinner may not like it. Maybe he doesn't have enough money. Maybe he won't be able to get a loan. Maybe the dirt and clutter will overwhelm him, and he'll back out."

The horse traveled at an easy trot. Kate continued with her thoughts. "What did you think of it? I was pleased with it, even though cleaning would take days of work. Of course, I don't have enough business savvy to know if a deal was good or bad. What did you think?"

"I think we could put that building to good use. Let me work on the price as if we had never met Skinner. I know real estate values in this area. The church is asking too much, but they'll come down to a reasonable price if they have a smart Board of Trustees. Let's see if they'll work with us on that. Of course, Skinner's presence complicates the matter."

The horse clip-clopped along while John held the reins loosely. He glanced at his wife. Her eyes twinkled, and her mouth turned up in a large grin. Her excitement worried him.

"Don't get your hopes up too high, Kate. That will only make the fall harder if things don't work out."

Kate smiled. "If things don't work out, it's not the end of the world. We'll do something else to meet our *real* goal."

"What's that?"

"Our real goal is to provide for our family. The bakery is only one possible path to getting there. There could be other ways, don't you agree? So if we don't open a bakery, we still have a chance at our real goal by doing something else."

"I see your point, and I agree. That's one goal, but I have another goal that's just as important as supporting the family."

"What's that?"

"I want my relationship with Eli to be healed. That one eats at me as much as our lack of income."

To John, losing Eli's companionship was one of his worst consequences. He didn't know what it would take to earn his brother's forgiveness, but he was willing to do whatever it took.

Chapter 4: A VISITOR BRINGS HOPE

Wednesday, January 12, 1887

John lay in bed during the night, tossing about uncomfortably and disturbing Kate's sleep. When the night was its blackest, John dreamed about his family's faces: his Ma, his stepfather, each of his nine siblings and their spouses. One by one, the faces passed before him, scowling, then distorted grotesquely and receded into blackness. Kate shook him awake when he began thrashing around in bed.

In the morning light, he shrugged off his dark mood and climbed out of bed just as Steven left for school. He hadn't slept well but was determined to work on building their business.

"Breakfast smells good, Katie," he said, giving her a good-morning kiss. The aroma of coffee filled the house.

"You're dressed in your business suit," Kate said with surprise.

"Yes, I'm going to Lamar today to talk to the bank manager about a loan on my share of Pa's estate. After I get the answers to some general questions, we'll know what kind of offer we can make."

"I'd like to go with you."

"I would enjoy having you and Gracie with me, but it's not a good idea. It would take us almost twice as long if we had to take the carriage, and we wouldn't be back before Steven came home from school."

Her face fell. She wanted to go, but he was right.

"I do hope we'll be successful. I don't think any other place in Spencer's Mill would be as good as that one."

Kate gave him a bowl of oatmeal with his coffee. "Eat this. It'll help keep you warm on the way."

The temperature was warmer than the day before but probably wouldn't get above the low forties on the Fahrenheit thermometer. John gulped his breakfast and left. He wanted to be in Lamar, a fifteen-mile journey, when the bank opened. That would give him a chance to get back home before lunch. He took off on horseback with only a canteen of hot coffee tucked into a thick, quilted bag Katie had made to keep the contents warm.

Gracie padded into the kitchen in her nightgown.

"Good morning, pumpkin," said Kate as someone knocked at the door. She went to see who would come calling this early. She was surprised to see her mother-in-law, Susannah Wolf.

"Mother Reese! I mean..."

Susannah laughed. She had married Christian Wolf only a month ago, and her name was no longer Reese. "Why don't you just call me 'Mother'? Mother Wolf still sounds a little strange to my ears."

Kate was relieved to see a family member, hopeful that healing had begun. "Please come in," she said. "Can I get you a cup of tea?"

"Grandma!" Gracie clasped her around the knees.

Susannah grinned and picked her up. "Hello, cutie. Yes, tea, please, Kate. The air is so cold outside. I came alone—can you believe it? Seven miles in the cold, all by myself, and I'm chilled to the bone."

"I'm sorry, but John isn't home." Kate put the kettle on to boil and filled the silver tea ball with orange pekoe. "What brings you here on a freezing day like this?"

Susannah put Gracie down and kissed her forehead. "Eli

said John lost his job. I was sorry to hear that, but I wasn't too surprised after that trouncing he got in court. So we thought you'd need some money. I'm returning the amount John gave me as my monthly allowance when I was a widow."

"No, that was a gift—"

"Yes, I know, dear, and now it's a gift back to you. Time has reversed our situations. Thanks to my dear husband, I'm comfortable financially, but now you're in need. Christian told me to give this to you." She left a small pile of banknotes on the table.

It was a godsend to Kate, and tears formed in her eyes. "I can't thank you enough."

Susannah continued, "I confess, bringing this money wasn't an easy decision after all John did to us, but we couldn't have you and the children suffering. It's hard to forgive completely. We're still praying our way through our feelings on this." She sighed. "Katie, if you need more, we want you to tell us. I'm praying for God to care for your financial needs, knowing He will. But part of His plan may be working through Christian and me."

Kate nodded and wiped her cheek with the back of her hand. She and Susannah kept their eyes on Gracie as she skipped into the bedroom and returned with wooden blocks. She sat at Susannah's feet and stacked them up.

"Now, dear, I want you to tell me how things are going with you."

Kate's face broke into a smile, her eyes twinkling with enthusiasm, much to Susannah's amazement. "I have something exciting to tell you. Wait, I think the water's boiling. . ."

The steaming water bubbled over the tea leaves, and the liquid began to steep, growing rich in color and flavor.

"I can hardly wait to hear what could be good news for someone without income," Susannah said. "Did John find another job already?"

Katie poured the tea into cups and took them to the table with the sugar bowl. She took her time, smiling with an impish glint, wanting to keep John's mother in suspense. The steam swirled into the air. Visible wisps rose and curled before evaporating.

"Well, we've been discussing the possibilities, and it turns out that John has been putting money away for quite a while."

"I suspected he was," Susannah said. "He always bragged about his income, but you haven't had a new dress in a long time, and you're the most frugal person I know. Before I married Christian, I promised myself I would help you and the children as soon as possible."

There was a crash at Susannah's feet. The toy blocks tumbled to the floor with a rattling noise. Gracie giggled and stacked them up again.

"Well, he didn't find another job, but God willing, we've decided to open a bakery here in Spencer's Mill." Katie laughed and clapped her hands in delight. Gracie, mimicking her mother, clapped her hands, too.

"You what?" Susannah's eyes opened wide. "Can you do that?"

"John is on his way to Lamar to talk to the bank manager about a loan on his share of the inheritance. We inspected that empty store downtown yesterday, the one beside the general store. It's for sale, and we think we could make it work for us. We'd have to sell this house and move in over the store. We'd use part of the downstairs as a sales area to sell bread and pastries."

Susannah's jaw dropped. "I think that might work," she said. The smile on her lips grew wider as she began to get excited along with Kate. "Wouldn't it be wonderful to see that store with a large sign reading 'Reese's Bakery' and people lined up to get in? Oh, Katie, that might work."

"But there's a problem. The building has been up for sale for a year with no one interested. Now, a man from Lamar suddenly wants to open a shoe shop there."

"Oh, no." Susannah's brow knitted. "We'll have to pray. If the store goes to the shoemaker, God has something better in mind for you. Remember, He said, 'I know the plans I have for you…plans to give you hope and a future.'"

"I remember. I got the idea when I was praying for direction. I'm sure it came from God. It's not something I would have thought of on my own."

Susannah smiled and nodded knowingly, then stirred a spoonful of sugar into her tea. "He does that, doesn't He?"

Sitting at the table, Kate leaned toward her mother-in-law. "John is a different man now. Yesterday, for the first time, he shared information with me about how much money we have, and we discussed a budget together for starting the business."

Susannah's chin dropped, and her eyebrows raised. "That was a big step. I know first-hand how controlling John has always been."

Gracie patted Susannah's leg. "Look at my blocks, Grandma. I stacked them so high."

Susannah lifted Gracie into her lap. "Tell me about that pretty doll over there. Is that a new one?"

Gracie hopped down and retrieved the doll. "I named her Claudia."

Susannah fussed over Claudia, smoothing her wrinkled dress. Turning to Katie, she said, "Tell me what we can do for you."

"At this point, I don't know. It's still early. We don't even know if we can get that building. Wesleyan Church owns it, and the sale is subject to approval by the Board of Trustees. We'd have to sell our house and get a loan from the bank. But if we can buy the store, we'll need help cleaning it and getting it ready for customers. It's pretty rough right now."

"I'm sure the family will rally around you and give you whatever help you need," said Susannah. "This is exciting news. I can't wait to tell Christian. I'll be praying for you both."

The two women sipped their tea, chatting happily about possible names for the bakery and tossing about ideas for the types of bread, cakes, and pastries that could be sold.

"Thank you for the tea, dear. I feel more optimistic about your future now." Susannah hugged Gracie and her daughter-in-law, and left.

Chapter 5: THE RIPPLES FLOW ON

John arrived in Lamar minutes after nine o'clock, stiff and weary from the ride. He tied his mount, Ginger, in front of the bank. Then he patted his pocket to ensure he had his bank book with him just in case—in case of what, he didn't know. It never hurts to be prepared. He walked into the bank lobby and stepped to the teller window. "I'd like to speak to Mr. McDonald about a loan."

"He left the bank for just a few minutes. If you like, you can wait for him at his desk." The ordinarily chatty teller was only as friendly as his job description required. John assumed that news about the court hearing had reached him.

As he crossed to McDonald's desk, John's boots tapped a hollow rhythm on the wood floor. He remembered how uncomfortable those chairs were. They tilted slightly forward, so customers were worried they would slide out. He took a seat, pressed his right boot to one of the legs on the desk to keep from sliding, and fidgeted until the manager returned.

Soon, McDonald entered the bank and strode to his desk. His features were grim, and his voice boomed with a challenging edge. "Mr. Reese. What can I do for you?"

John's stomach turned, but he kept his poise. "Good morning, Mr. McDonald. I came to talk about a loan."

McDonald lowered himself into his big, leather swivel chair with padded armrests and leaned back as far as the chair would allow. He clasped his hands behind his neck, crossed his legs, and made himself comfortable. John could have sworn that was a smirk on his face. "I heard you were fired from your job, John."

John lowered his head. "Yes, I was. I didn't realize word would get around so fast."

"Your brother Eli was here and told us about it. It was quite the news." There was a heavy pause while McDonald leaned forward, folded his hands on his desk, and stared at John with an amused smile. "How would you expect to repay a loan without an income?"

John's heart sank when he learned that Eli had been at the bank ahead of him. He squirmed uncomfortably in his seat, not only because of Eli. Something around his right ankle itched, but he didn't want to lean down to scratch it. "My wife and I have thought things through. Here's my bank book. You can see that we have quite a nest egg that will last us for a while. I also have my inheritance from Pa's estate that will come through as soon as all the property sells, and you can take my share as collateral."

"Mm-hmm."

John wiggled his right foot around, hoping to alleviate the itch. "Here's our plan," he said. "We want to open our own business, a bakery in Spencer's Mill, which will give us income to pay our bills. I have several years of business experience, and my wife is an extraordinary cook. Her pies are legendary in town. We can do this. We plan to sell our house and buy a store with an apartment over it, and we're going into business. We can probably do it without a loan from the bank, but we could do it faster with a loan. So what do you say? Do you think it's a possibility?"

The bank manager took a moment to look at John in a different light. He pursed his lips. "I must tell you that I thought the newspaper article might have been exaggerated, but Eli confirmed it. He even embellished it. My first thought was that I didn't want to do business with you after the bad reputation you earned, but I am intrigued by the plan for the bakery. The bank would profit from the interest, and our risk would be low since your late father's real estate would cover the loan."

John's attention was on the man's eyes, trying to read him.

"Let me study this for a moment," McDonald said. "You're not borrowing money to live on until you get a job. This is different. And if your bakery doesn't thrive for whatever reason, there are still enough assets to cover your loan." He nodded. "The proposal sounds interesting. I'd be willing to accept an application under those circumstances. Do you have any idea how much you'll be asking for?"

"No, sir. We haven't negotiated a price for the building yet. We're not even sure our offer will be accepted. Maybe you've seen the store, the old carpenter shop beside the general store in Spencer's Mill. There's an apartment upstairs where we'll live if we can get that building."

"I've been by there. I've seen it from the outside. Is that the building Wesleyan Church is holding right now?"

"Yes, it is, so we'll have to go through the Board of Trustees. That may stretch our timeline out a little longer."

"Well, we'll hope for the best." McDonald stood and stuck out his right hand. "Best of luck, John."

John stood and shook his hand. "Thank you, sir. I'll be in touch."

McDonald was now smiling.

John left the bank with his head higher than when he arrived. His joy was short-lived. As he stepped onto the brick sidewalk, Attorney Zedekiah Martin approached to take care of his banking business. Martin was a fresh-faced attorney just out of law school. He wore a heavy cloak with a fur collar. He glared, still angry that John had caused him two embarrassing experiences in court. The first was a lawsuit accusing Attorney Wolf of stealing a client's inheritance. That one backfired since Wolf had courthouse records proving his innocence. The second was the recent fiasco where John's lies were exposed, and the judge threw out the contract that Martin drew up.

"Good morning, Martin," John said.

"Mm-hmm," said Martin. His greeting was terse, and his lips were pressed together. He broke his stride to face John. "I expect you'll pay my bill promptly. I intend to see that you do."

John sighed. "Martin. I'm sorry for the grief I caused you in court. I sincerely apologize. I'll pay the bill as soon as I get it. It hasn't come in the mail yet."

"I can get you a copy at my office if you'll stop by this morning."

"I can be there in fifteen minutes. By the way, how much is the bill?"

Martin quoted the amount, which John believed to be excessive, but he decided not to object. He knew he deserved it. John returned to the bank, withdrew that amount, pocketed the cash, and then strolled to Martin's office. He was the first to arrive.

As he waited outside in the cold, John shoved his hands in his pockets and stomped his feet to keep warm. A sign hanging by two metal hooks in front of the office read "Zedekiah L. Martin, Attorney at Law" in ornate script. It squeaked as it swung in the wind. John had nothing to do but watch his breath form clouds, then evaporate and blow away. Squeak … squeak … squeak…

After a few minutes, Martin returned and unlocked the door. "Come on in, Reese," he said. His voice was as cold as the icicles hanging from the eaves.

The men entered Martin's sparsely furnished office, and John took the lone chair in front of the desk. The embers in the stove were dying, so the struggling attorney tossed in more wood and lit a new fire.

He turned to John. "I hope I never run into another person

like you. You made me look like a fool. You destroyed my chances of starting my legal career successfully. Now I'm nothing but a laughingstock."

"I don't know what to say except I'm sorry. I don't know how I can make it up to you."

"First off, you can pay your bill." He shoved a handwritten invoice at John, who pulled the money from his pocket and slid it across the desk.

"Paid in full, Martin. Would you write a receipt for the cash?"

Martin scrawled out a receipt and thrust it at John. "Can't say I'm sorry to see the last of you. If you ever need any more legal work . . . call someone else."

John stood, folded the receipt, and stuffed it in his pocket. "Best of luck with your law practice, Martin."

He went back out into the cold, closing the door behind him.

That encounter stung deeply, even though John fully recognized that he deserved it. He headed to the general store to buy an apple and some cheese for the road. He was hungrier than he thought he would be. He decided to stop worrying about his run-in with Martin. Even though it grated on him like sandpaper, he could hardly blame the attorney.

At the general store, it only grew worse. He ran into an acquaintance from his job at Johnson's Oil Company. The man was a salesman for the oil drum manufacturer and used to come into the office.

"Hello, Walter," John said. He couldn't remember Walter's last name, but he had always enjoyed chatting with him when he visited the office.

"John," said Walter, who barely nodded at him and kept walking.

I guess it will be this way for a while – people angry with me, John thought. He fought back his grief. Reality was sinking in. Even though there is divine forgiveness, there are still consequences. The emotional lift he had enjoyed at the bank was gone. Shoulders slumping, he mounted his horse and made for home.

At the stream, he stopped to let the horse have a drink and a short rest. Most of the ice was melted, and the stream bubbled freely. He stroked the horse's nose, speaking to her in gentle tones. "You're a good girl, Ginger." Ginger didn't care that he had blown it so badly for his family. That was worth something. He offered her a sugar cube.

Back in the saddle, he had time to think. The horse loped along the trail to Spencer's Mill, and John realized his solitude was a blessing.

His thoughts turned to Mr. Skinner, their competitor in bidding for the building. There was something off about him. Maybe it was the way he dressed. The more John thought about it, the more he was bothered by his flashy attire. That man was no shoemaker, or he couldn't afford a wardrobe like that. That meant he was probably not truthful about his reason for wanting the building.

Chapter 6: OLIVER HARDIN

Friday, January 14, 1887

Two days later, John lifted the brass door knocker – tap, tap, tap – and waited. He was at Oliver Hardin's house in Lamar. This was his next step toward buying the store on Main Street. Hardin had been an associate of his pa's in the real estate business, so John had heard his name mentioned often. But he had never met him face to face until that miserable experience in court.

A tall, lean man opened the door. He was dressed conservatively and carried himself in a calm, mild manner. Mr. Hardin stared at the man on his doorstep. His jaw dropped. "John Reese?" he asked.

"Yes, sir. May I come in? It's a real estate matter."

Hardin hesitated and swallowed hard. The only time he had ever seen this fellow was in court when John's dirty laundry was being aired. Hardin's testimony had even helped reveal what a scoundrel John was.

"Please, sir. I come in peace." John managed a weak smile.

Hardin eyed him suspiciously but relented. "Come in. You can sit there," he said, motioning to a well-worn leather chair.

John took his seat and glanced around the room. The house was in the average price range, belying the wealth of its owner, but it was comfortable. John figured that Hardin probably lived alone, as there were no pictures on the wall and no fancy bric-a-brac. The furnishings were clean but had seen better times. Most women wouldn't live that way for long if they could change it. They would put decorative touches on it.

"What can I do for you?"

John decided to begin by bringing up the issue on both of their minds. "You know of my history. I hope we can get beyond that. That experience in court was an eye-opener for me. I saw myself clearly for the first time and repented. If we can do business together, I believe you'll be able to see that."

"I congratulate you on that, sir," Hardin said. His voice was flat and unimpressed. "I hope that helps you, but I'm still curious about what you would like from me."

John paused, thinking he had made a mistake by beginning a business conversation that way, but he pressed on. "I know you used to consult with my father on real estate matters. He mentioned your name often. I want to hire you. My wife and I have an opportunity to buy a building in Spencer's Mill, and we need to know what the property is worth. Can you appraise that building for us?"

"Interesting," said Hardin, mentally slipping into appraiser mode. "Tell me about this building. Is it commercial or residential? And what's the background story?"

John told him about wanting to open a bakery. "We would have to sell our home and move into the apartment over the store, so we'll need your evaluation of our house, too. The empty store is next to the general store in Spencer's Mill. The Wesleyan Church owns it. Can you go over to take a look?"

"You have my interest. Can you schedule an appointment with the person in charge of the building?"

John smiled. "The pastor has the key. He's in his office every afternoon, studying for his sermon. Would you have time to come today?"

Hardin checked his pocket watch. "How about going right now?"

The two men mounted their horses and began the journey to Spencer's Mill together. Hardin was still guarded, but he asked questions about the real estate deal. It occurred to John that if he and Kate didn't buy this building, Hardin might look at it as a possible investment for himself.

Along the way, they became better acquainted. The horses trotted down the road in tandem.

"How long have you lived in Lamar?" asked John as they traveled.

"I was born there," responded Hardin, "so it's been over forty years. I grew up when Lamar was nothing but a little village. I inherited the real estate bug from my father. He loved buying and selling. He taught me the basics and the rest I picked up along the way. And what about you? What's your story?"

"I worked at Johnson's Oil Company for the past five years. After the court hearing, I was fired from my job. I can't blame Abner Johnson, but now we have to live on our savings. My wife suggested that we open a bakery to earn some income, and I have to tell you, I'm getting excited about it. We can make it work if we get a reasonably priced location."

"Well, maybe I can help you with that. And what about your house?"

"We'll go there first so you can look at it. I'd like you to tell us what we need to do to get the best price. I remember Pa doing a little painting, landscaping, or making certain repairs to increase a property's selling price."

"Yes, that's a whole science by itself. I enjoyed working with your Pa. He was a good mentor with sharp business instincts. He earned a small fortune with his investments and gave me advice that made me some money, too. It was a deep personal loss when he suddenly passed away."

When they arrived at Spencer's Mill, the men were conversing comfortably. John was overcome with gratitude that this man was treating him with respect. He used to take it for granted, but now it had become so rare. John invited Hardin to come in and look at the house before lunch.

"Katie, this is Oliver Hardin. He was Pa's friend and cohort in the real estate business, and now he's our friend, too. He's here to appraise our house and the store."

"Very nice to meet you, Mr. Hardin."

"And you, Mrs. Reese."

"While I'm showing Mr. Hardin around the house, can you make something for lunch?"

"Of course." Kate went to work in the kitchen, adding some herbs to a pot of soup to serve with rolls she had baked just that morning. She also had a pound cake she made to test the recipe, planning to add it to the menu at the bakery.

When the three adults and Gracie sat down to lunch, Hardin took his first mouthful of savory soup with chunks of potato, onion, celery, carrots, and ham. He smiled and nodded his approval. "Is that a hint of tarragon in there?" he asked.

Katie blushed and nodded. "I'm impressed that you noticed. That's my special touch."

"I taste cheese in there, too, and it's delicious," he said. Then he tried one of the fresh rolls, and his eyes opened wide. The roll was hot, crusty, brown on the outside, and melt-in-your-mouth tender on the inside, generously buttered, a perfect accompaniment to the soup.

"Mrs. Reese, I compliment you on your cooking skills. With good management, I'm sure your bakery will succeed."

Kate smiled. "Thank you, Mr. Hardin. Would you like another bowl of soup?"

He turned down seconds, but she put a liberal slice of pound cake in front of him, dusted with caster sugar, which he happily polished off.

Hardin was eager to get started. "John, do you think the pastor would be in his office now? I'm eager to see that store."

"Let's take my carriage to the church. You can leave your horse here."

John hitched his horse to the carriage, and the two men drove off together. On the way, John needed to clarify the situation. "We're not the only ones interested in this store. There's another prospective buyer, a man from Lamar, who says he wants to put a shoe shop in there."

"Mm, that does complicate things. That tends to raise the price. I'd gladly discuss it with you if you need advice during the negotiation. Your Pa and I talked over deals often."

"Thank you for offering to advise me. What do you think of the house's value now that you've seen it?"

"I'd say, as it stands, and for its location in Spencer's Mill, you should aim for about $650. You might get a little more if you whitewash the fence as soon as the weather turns warm, and you need to clean up the walls in the children's bedroom. Children are hard on real estate prices." He grinned knowingly at John.

"I'll do that."

At the church, they found the pastor in his study.

"Reverend Buchanan, I'd like you to meet Oliver Hardin," John said. "He's a real estate investor and appraiser from Lamar, consulting with me on buying the store. Do you have time to let us into the store again?"

The pastor stood and extended his hand to Hardin. "Good to meet you, Hardin. Folks speak well of you. Let's all go over to the store. I want to get that building sold. I thought we had another live buyer, but he hasn't submitted his offer."

Once they were all in the carriage, Reverend Buchanan brought up the price. "I talked to the chairman of the Board. He confirmed that they are asking a thousand dollars for the building."

John's heart dropped. "You mentioned that figure before, but I hoped it would be less. Let's see what Mr. Hardin says. He consulted with my Pa for years on his real estate deals, so I trust his judgment."

"Of course." They reached the store, climbed out of the carriage, and the pastor jiggled the key into the lock again. "Might need a little graphite here to loosen up the lock," he said apologetically.

Inside, Oliver took his first overview. "It'll take some time to clean up this greasy dirt and sawdust...All of this carpentry equipment is going to have to be moved out. It'll probably take two or three strong men to get rid of it."

He inspected the walls in each room, running his hand over them.

"These walls are pretty shabby. You'll need a heavy broom to clean the sawdust and cobwebs off, and then they need a couple of good coats of paint. You'll want to sand down some of those rough spots. And look at the windows. At least they're not cracked, but I don't envy the crew cleaning them. They probably haven't been cleaned in two or three years." He swiped a finger over the glass, leaving a visible track in the heavy dust. Then he paused, casting his eyes down. "I'd say this floor should be refinished or painted before you open the bakery to customers, John. Look at the spilled shellac and splattered paint. Seeing those ugly spots would kill the appetites of customers trying to buy bread and pastries."

The pastor had a suggestion. "You could cover up those stains with an oilcloth rug."

"Mmm, not a good idea," said Hardin. "The edges would curl, and customers would trip on them. Bad for business."

John and Reverend Buchanan followed Hardin as he made his inspection. He tested the pump in the kitchen and made sure water came out. "You'll have to put in stoves, expand the cupboards, larder, a big work table, and storage space for all the equipment Kate will need to do her baking. That'll set you back. Don't forget to include all those things in your budget."

"Maybe I could get volunteers from the church to do some of the work," said the pastor. He squirmed every time Hardin found fault with the building. "We could save you having to hire someone to do the work. Maybe we could both benefit that way."

"Maybe," John mumbled, trying to be vague.

Hardin ignored the pastor and continued with his observations. "I'd have that chimney checked out before you light a fire," he said. "You don't want to smoke yourself out if it's clogged, or worse yet, burn the building down. Let's check the living quarters upstairs."

Hardin took the stairs quickly, and John was on his heels, but it took the pastor longer. He gasped for air when he reached the top and needed to lean against the wall to catch his breath.

"The stairs seem to be in good condition. Why, John, the size of this apartment is not nearly as big as the house you live in now. How do you think you could manage that?"

"We thought about partitioning off the downstairs so Katie could use the same kitchen for family meals as for the bakery. The partitioned part would double as a playroom and dining room, so there would be no need to carry meals up and down the stairs."

"That would work, but it'll add to your costs."

"Yes, we're aware we'll have to add that into our budget."

Hardin checked out the three rooms accessible from the parlor space. "How do you plan to use these rooms?"

"They'll be bedrooms," John said.

"Where will your office be? You'll need a private office with a door you can close. Otherwise, your children could be a real distraction while you work."

John hadn't thought of that. "Hmm. I see what you're saying. I'll have to work on that. I could put a desk and filing cabinet at the end of that large bedroom. The bedroom door could be kept closed while I work."

"That would solve your problem if you didn't need to be closer to the salesroom."

The trio walked out back, inspecting the small outbuildings. "Well, I think I've seen enough now," Oliver said. "We'll return you to your study, Reverend, then John and I will discuss value."

"I'd be interested in your evaluation, too," Buchanan said. "I don't think our Board members have much real estate experience, but they can be tough negotiators with crops and other goods. I hope they won't hold out and keep the church hanging on to a property we can't use."

After delivering the pastor back to his church, John and Oliver continued to the house.

"What was your impression of the building?" asked John.

"I believe it's workable for you, but it will take a lot of money and even more work to get it ready. Here's my initial thought—you shouldn't pay more than $850 for that store. I hope you can get it for something less. But if they leave all those tools there, you may be able to sell them to offset some of the cost of the building. I'll think on it and mail you a written appraisal with an invoice."

"Thank you for your time and expertise."

"That still doesn't address the problem of the shoemaker. If you're still interested, you'll want to put in the highest bid that makes sense. You don't want to offer more than you can afford. You can't survive in business doing that. But you certainly don't want to offer anything too low, either. It's a tricky decision."

They arrived back at the house, and Hardin mounted his

horse.

"Just one more thing, John. This morning, when you told me about your change of heart, you must have seen I didn't believe you. But you're not the same belligerent John Reese in the courtroom. I've enjoyed getting to know you." He waved and turned toward Lamar.

As he rode away, John said softly, "Thank you, friend."

Chapter 7: A DIFFICULT SUNDAY

Sunday, January 16, 1887

On Sunday morning, Kate was the first to awaken. She had fed and dressed the children alone every Sunday since John stopped attending church, but today, he got up to help her.

"Is Pa going to church with us today?" Steven asked, wide-eyed, when his father was dressed in his Sunday clothes.

"Yes, I am, Stevie," John replied.

"I want to sit beside you."

"I'll save you the spot right next to me."

The entire family piled into the carriage and drove to the church, with Steven clinging to his father.

As they stepped out of the carriage and tied the horse to the rail, there were mixed reactions from the other worshippers. Some folks spoke to one another in hushed tones and glanced at the family. The church members had read the newspaper article about what happened in court. The gossip had spread through their social circle like wildfire.

Now, as they were confronted with the man behind the rumors, some weren't sure how to respond. Should they shun him as someone giving the church a bad name? Or rather, should they demonstrate Christlike forgiveness and acceptance? Each person was left to decide that question individually and behave accordingly.

Some of the gentlemen were more forgiving than their wives. Ben Beavey, one of the men of his Pa's generation, made a point to shake John's hand and slap him on the back. "It's good to see you again, John. How've you been?"

"It's been a hard road, but we're much better now, Mr. Beavey. Thanks for asking. How about you and your wife?"

Mrs. Beavey, his mother's closest friend, had reluctantly testified against John in court.

"We're doing fine, thanks. Why don't you and your family come to our house later this afternoon for tea? It would give us a chance to catch up."

"I'd like that. Thanks. We'll see you later."

The Reese family made their way into the church. The people outside melted away from their path as they entered. John and Kate were aware of it but only smiled at the folks staring at them. Inside, John's brother Eli and his wife Mary sat in their accustomed seats on the right side of the aisle. Eli nodded at John without smiling, acknowledging his presence, but didn't make a move to get any closer to him. John recognized the snub. It stung. Before the court hearing, he and Eli had always had a special bond, more than the other brothers.

Shortly, his mother and her new husband came in with three of John's younger siblings, William, Amos, and Lizbeth, who were still in school. His mother, a graceful, well-dressed woman with graying hair, approached her oldest son with a smile and threw her arms around him. "John, you're back."

"Morning, Ma," John said with a smile.

"Good to see you, son. And you too, Katie."

Kate grinned at her.

"What's happening with your business plans?"

"Well, to give you the quick version," John began, "I had Oliver Hardin look at the building we're interested in. He gave us a good idea of the price we should be looking at. I'll have to give you the details later. The service is about to start."

Several of the church folks observed the interaction between mother and son. She smiled and waved at them. She crossed the aisle and patted Eli on the shoulder, then returned to her seat with her husband.

After the service, John made a point of seeking out Eli. The meeting was awkward. Eli glanced around for an escape, but John happened to reach him and his wife when they were near a corner of the room.

"Eli, I can see you still haven't forgiven me. I can't blame you. I just wanted to tell you again how sorry I am."

"You betrayed me, John. Me, a lot more than the others. I don't want to get myself in that position again."

"I can't say that I blame you. I'll give you some distance in hopes that someday… Oh, so you'll know—Katie and I plan to open a bakery in Spencer's Mill. If you could be praying for us, we would appreciate it."

Eli frowned, and Mary stood at his side quietly. "We have to go now."

John moved aside to let them pass, choked back his grief, and watched their backs as they left the building.

Later that day, after Gracie's nap, John and Kate took their children to the Beavey home for tea. The men sat in the parlor while the women prepared tea in the kitchen. As the ladies entered the room with a tea tray, Ben said, "Tell me, John, do you have any work yet? Rumor has it that you lost your job."

"Yes, I did, but here's our plan, God willing. Katie had the idea of opening a bakery here in town, and the more I thought about it, the more enthused I became. We went through the old carpenter's shop beside the general store. It's up for sale now. If we can buy it, we'll move our family upstairs and run a bakery from the ground floor. It's a perfect location."

A delighted grin spread over Ben's face. "Why, this town could use a bakery. And you could sell other things besides bread. What about cakes, pastries, and cookies?"

John enjoyed Ben's enthusiastic reaction to his news. It sounded like he was almost as excited as they were.

Steven spotted a bowl of nuts on the table and reached for it. John slid the bowl away from the boy's eager hands without interrupting his sentence. "We're thinking about what items could be offered for sale."

"And what about a name for the bakery?" asked Mrs. Beavey.

"We haven't figured that out yet," said John. "We just don't want to call it Reese's Bakery."

"What about Katie's Bakery?" Mrs. Beavey offered.

Kate grinned. "I once thought of that myself. But no, it needs to be something more creative."

"What about The Sweet Shop?" Mrs. Beavey was fascinated with the challenge of naming a bakery. "Or here's another one—what about Our Daily Bread?"

"Well, we need something to include bread, pies, cakes, and whatever other goodies we think up," John said. "But I suspect bread and rolls will be our biggest sellers."

The conversation continued until the children became restless. John and Kate thanked the Beaveys for an enjoyable afternoon.

Chapter 8: KATE'S ENCOUNTER

Wednesday, January 19, 1887

A few days later, Kate's pantry was low on staples. It was time to go to the general store. Her brother-in-law was still working there, and she was eager to see him. Even when Danny filed a suit against the whole family, she had always liked him. She realized he did it to save their inheritance, not harm them.

"I need some things from the general store, John," said Kate. "I'll have to go today. We're running out of quite a few things."

"Where are you going to get the money?" John asked. "You'll have to wait until I get to the bank. I'm out of cash."

Kate blushed and lowered her head. "I forgot to tell you your mother was here the other day. She brought back all the money you gave her after your Pa died. I have enough money to hold us in groceries for a long time. I'm sorry. I should've told you."

John cringed and sat down heavily.

"John, what's wrong? I just gave you good news."

"That news made me relive the memory of how stingy I was after Pa died. I never wanted to give her the money I promised; now, look how generous she is. I'll have to make a special point of thanking her."

"I don't need to carry all that money with me. I only need

three or four dollars right now. That would be plenty to buy all the supplies we need. With five dollars, I could stock up and have enough supplies to experiment with recipes for the bakery. Let me give you the rest." She retrieved the cash from her purse and handed it to her husband.

John put it in his pocket with tears in his eyes. "Thank you, Katie. This is humbling."

Her heart was overwhelmed at the change in his attitude. She smiled softly and locked eyes with him in admiration. "John…you're getting to be sort of wonderful."

After Steven went to school that morning, John said he would stay home with Gracie while Kate went grocery shopping. "I want to do more work on our budget figures. And something about that shoemaker is nagging at the back of my mind. There's something wrong about him."

"Good luck with that."

John hitched the horse to the carriage for Kate. She left for the general store with her list and the handsome sum of five dollars in her purse. Even though they had no current income, she was wealthy today. She smiled, her gratitude overflowing.

The general store was the largest in town, jammed with everything a body could need for daily living. Canned goods lined the shelves with bags of flour and sugar, giant dill pickles were stored in a barrel of brine, and jars of tantalizing candy were lined up at child height. They also stocked cleaning supplies, farm tools, hunting equipment, and other necessities.

When Kate arrived, Danny was helping another customer, Agatha Brown, a gaunt, stern, humorless woman. Katie's heart sank. She tried to be charitable toward her, but Agatha had a well-deserved reputation as the town gossip. She had gleefully spread the news about John's disastrous courtroom experience to everyone around her. Kate understood that John had earned a poor reputation, which would be difficult to overcome. Still, she was confident that things would slowly change when people got to know the new John—unless Agatha kept the gossip going.

"Good morning, Mrs. Reese," Agatha said.

"Morning, Mrs. Brown."

Agatha moved closer to Kate to speak to her in low tones as if she were an intimate friend. "Mrs. Reese, if there is anything I can do to help, please let me know."

Kate thought she was speaking of John's loss of employment. "Thank you, Mrs. Brown, but we're doing fine."

"But I know what's going on, and it's just a shame," Agatha continued. "John can't support his family, so he's making you do it. Opening a bakery and making you do all the work. Hmph. The very idea."

Anger rose from the pit of Kate's stomach. So, the news was getting around, but in a twisted way. "Mrs. Brown, I'm afraid you have it wrong. Opening the bakery was my idea, and we're both excited about it. I love to bake. I can't imagine a better way to spend my time. And if John and I can partner in a business, how wonderful will that be?"

"You're a brave girl," said Agatha, patting Kate's arm.

Kate realized that Agatha was only interested in juicy gossip, but she was determined to make her point.

"Mrs. Brown, you're dead wrong about our situation. And I'd appreciate it if you didn't tell people that John is forcing me to support the family. There's not a bit of truth in that." Kate turned abruptly and walked away before Agatha could say anything else. The woman was insulted, but Kate's heart bore no guilt. She had said what she needed to say.

"Danny, I have a list of things I need," she said to her brother-in-law as Agatha huffed out the door, jingling the bell as she left.

Danny grinned at her. "When did you get your backbone, Katie?"

A sheepish smile crossed her face, and they went about collecting her supplies.

A few minutes later, Eli entered the store to buy supplies. His appearance had changed since learning that John had deceived the family. He didn't look like the same Eli. His eyes were dull, and his clothing had seen several days' wear.

Kate was startled at his disheveled appearance but managed a smile. "Eli, it's good to see you. We've been missing you."

Danny smiled. "You've been missing some family time, Eli. We wish you'd come to visit."

Eli's expression turned bitter. "I'd visit either of you, but I'm not going anywhere that John might show up. When I'm around him, I feel like I'm withering inside, like I'm sucking lemons. I don't want any part of him."

Danny's face fell. "I know you're hurt and angry, Eli. I can't say that I blame you. I was, too, before I filed suit. But you need to forgive for the sake of your health."

Eli replied as if Danny hadn't said that last part. "What he did to me eats at me day after day, without stopping. Sometimes, I'd like to leave town so I'd never have to see him again. But I'm a grown man with responsibilities, so I can't do that."

His face was red, and the veins in his neck began to show themselves, so Danny and Kate decided to leave that topic alone.

"What's my total, Danny?" she asked, pulling the money out of her purse. Once the bill was paid, she took a breath and sighed. "Goodbye, you two. I hope to see you later."

She decided not to mention that encounter to John.

Chapter 9: THE OFFER

In the Reese home, bright hope coexisted with gut-wrenching uncertainty. John's brow was covered with sweat as he juggled numbers, broke the lead in his pencil, sharpened it, and started again.

"I've been revising budget numbers this morning," John said when Kate returned home with her groceries. "The postman came. He brought Mr. Hardin's written estimate of the value of the store. Look, he appraised the building in as-is condition at $825. He told us verbally that we shouldn't pay more than $850 for it, so he gave us a little negotiating room. Good man."

Kate peered at the letter and nodded.

"Here's what I think," John said. "I think we should show the Board this letter and give them an opening offer of $800 based on the cleaning and necessary remodeling. If Skinner hasn't already beat us to the deal, they'll come back with a counteroffer higher than we want to pay, and we'll keep talking until we get the price down to $850 or less. If we have to, we could squeeze out a few more dollars, but I think we should stick to $850 as our top bid. What do you think?"

"What you said sounds like a good plan. But what about the other buyer? What if he offers more?"

"That's a possibility. But if we have to pay much more than that, we won't be able to stay within our budget. We'll run out of money too soon and end up destitute. That doesn't make sense. We can only offer what we can afford."

"All right. Be sure and tell them our offer depends on selling our house and getting a loan from the bank."

Quite right, we should tell them that," he said, "but just between you and me, it may be possible to buy the building before we sell the house. It'll depend on how the numbers fall."

Together, they asked God to lead them in the right direction and bless them as they tried to navigate the future together. They had never been so united in purpose.

"Steven will be home from school soon," John said, "so one of us needs to stay here. I'll present our offer to the pastor now. He'll pass it on to the Board of Trustees. Let's get this thing in motion."

Katie's eyes were sparkling, full of hope. She kissed her husband as he went out the door.

John led Ginger from the barn, saddled her, and mounted up. On his way to see Reverend Buchanan, he mentally rehearsed what he would say. He had always been confident in his ability to persuade, but this time, he wasn't pushing his own agenda first. Even though he thought the building would be perfect for them, he determined to accept God's will if that wasn't in His plan.

He entered the church through the double front doors and went to the pastor's office. Reverend Buchanan glanced up from his reading. "Mr. Reese. How are you?"

"I'm fine, Reverend. I came to make an offer on the building today."

"You're just in time, John. Come in. Mr. Skinner has put in an offer, too, so this will make for an interesting negotiation."

The news came as a gut punch to John. "Oh? How much did he offer?

"I believe he offered full price. Do you still want to put in your offer?"

"Yes, I do." John's stomach was in his throat. Was there any point in continuing? He desperately wanted to increase his offer, but Kate wasn't here to discuss it. Besides, there was no way they could match Skinner's offer. He chose to submit the proposal as they had initially discussed. "I have a letter from Mr. Oliver Hardin, the man you met the other day. He's an expert in Bledsoe County real estate. That's why I consulted him on the value. He says in his letter that the store is worth $825 as it sits in today's market. However, Katie and I would have to put in considerable time and work to make it suit our purposes, so we would like to offer $800."

He laid the written proposal on the desk, feeling foolish. He somehow found the courage to look Rev. Buchanan in the eye.

Buchanan's eyebrows raised. "Well, sir, I'm sorry that your offer will make the Board's decision easy. We'll have to wait and see the outcome, but I think I already know." He regarded John with a sympathetic look.

"I understand that, sir. I want to offer more. I do. But Katie and I have prayed over this. This is what we can afford. And the Board needs to understand that this offer is good only if we can sell our house and get a loan from the bank."

The pastor stood and extended his hand. "I'll pass that offer on to the Board and give you official notification of what they decide. They're meeting—" he checked his calendar "—one week from today."

John shook his hand. *This is a death knoll over our plans. How can I break the news to Katie?*

He had never been a person to give up control of a situation easily, but now it was in God's hands, not his. It would be a tough week.

When John returned home in a subdued mood, he found Kate

on her hands and knees happily scrubbing floors, humming a cheerful tune, and Gracie sitting at the table eating an apple.

He blurted out the bad news. "Katie, Skinner has made an offer higher than we can match. It's a thousand dollars."

She straightened up on her knees with the soapy sponge in her hand. "Oh, no. Is he paying cash, or does he need a loan?" Water ran to her elbow and dripped on the floor. She brushed a stray hair away from her face.

"I was so sick over the whole thing that I didn't even ask."

Katie's heart sank. "We'll have to keep praying for God's will to be done." She went back to scrubbing but less enthusiastically. "Do we put the house up for sale or wait until we see what's happening with the store?"

John sat at the table with Gracie. "I say we put the house up for sale and keep looking for a backup property for a bakery. It will take some time to find a buyer for the house, and even if someone wants it, we don't have to sell if we don't have a place to go."

Gracie interrupted. "Mama, can I have another apple?"

"No, not right now. You'll spoil your dinner."

Gracie hopped down from her chair with sticky hands, leaving her wet apple core on the table.

John realized his wife wouldn't be able to catch the child in time to keep her from transferring messy apple residue if she touched anything. He jumped up and grabbed Gracie around the waist with his right arm. "Let's wash your hands, baby." He pumped a squirt of water and cleaned up his daughter.

"You've never done that before," said Kate, fascinated by the scene that had just played out. "John . . . how much are we going to ask for the house?" She wrung out her sponge.

"Well, Oliver says it's worth $650," John said, "so we'll set the price at $695. That way, someone can talk us down to $650 and feel like they got a bargain."

Katie chuckled. "I'm beginning to understand how this works."

John was cheered by her laugh. "Setbacks are to be expected," he said. "We'll get through this."

That night, Kate couldn't sleep. She sank into her pillow beside John, listening to his slow, steady breathing. She realized that during the early years of their marriage, she had been treated more like a servant than a wife. Now, for the first time, she was in partnership with him, a valuable part of a team of two. It was a wonderful new position, and she was deeply grateful.

Chapter 10: HOUSE FOR SALE

Friday, January 21, 1887

John woke full of energy. "Katie, now that we have a For Sale sign in the yard, I'm going to Lamar to advertise the house. I'll put an ad in the paper. While I'm there, I'll visit a few people I know and tell them the house is for sale. They'll help pass the word for us."

"All right, John. Be careful."

John kissed his wife, mounted old Ginger, and took off for Lamar with a handful of sugar cubes and a carrot in his pocket. Ginger had plenty of energy, so they made good speed on the road.

Reaching town, he went directly to the newspaper office. He told the blue-eyed young woman at the front desk that he wanted to place an ad for a house for sale in Spencer's Mill. The ad was to tell prospective buyers to contact John Reese.

"Most of our readers are in Lamar," Miss Blue Eyes said. "Do you have an alternate contact here that would make it easier for a buyer to reach you?"

"Good suggestion," said John. "The alternate contact would be Christian Wolf. I'll verify with him today that he doesn't mind forwarding messages to me."

"Christian Wolf, the attorney?"

"Yes. He married my mother last month."

He paid cash to run the ad for three weeks and left.

His next stop was the First Ohio Bank to tell Mr. McDonald they wanted to sell the house. Then, he steeled himself against possible scorn and went to Johnson's Oil Company, his old employer. He met Peter, his replacement. A wave of nostalgia flowed over John and tugged at his heart as he recognized the familiar journals and files spread on Peter's desk.

"Hello, Peter. I'm John Reese."

Peter gripped his pencil so hard it nearly snapped. He tapped out a staccato rhythm with it on his desk. "I thought Abner said he canned you. Was I wrong? Are you here to take your job back?"

John smiled. "No, you were right. I don't work here anymore."

Peter relaxed and laid his pencil down. "You must have had a reason for coming."

"Yes, I'm telling everyone I know that my house in Spencer's Mill is up for sale. If you know anyone looking for a nice house with two bedrooms, a barn, and a chicken coop, would you tell them to contact Attorney Christian Wolf?"

"Sure thing. I'm sorry you lost your job and have to sell your house."

"Oh, no, that's not the way it is. My wife and I are opening a bakery in Spencer's Mill. We hope to buy a storefront with an apartment over the bakery and live there. Can you pass the word on to Mr. Johnson?"

"Yes, I'll be glad to. Good luck with the house."

"Thanks. Good to meet you, Peter." The two men shook hands, and John left his old office for the last time. It was a bittersweet moment.

While in town, he also visited the general store, the Old English Tea Room, and Attorney Ross. He even dared to venture into Zedekiah Martin's office. He talked to everyone he could think of. He also needed to stop by the office of Christian Wolf, his new stepfather. He hoped Christian would be at least cordial.

"John, how are you?" Christian seemed hospitable but guarded. "Are you and Kate getting along so far without an income?"

"Yes, sir. Thank you for sending the money over to the house with Ma." He lowered his eyes and shuffled his feet. "It forced me to think of how I withheld it from her when she needed it. I've had to do an awful lot of thinking lately."

"Adjusting to the recent events has been hard for all of us, and we're still working at it. I've had to ask for God's help in forgiving you several times when I slip back and un-forgive you. It's a process. I hear you've made some major changes in your life. Your mother says you're on the right path."

"I know what you mean about it being a process. I grieve, get encouraged, and then grieve some more. I want you to know that I am very sorry for what I did to you."

"We'll all make it eventually, son. Even Eli. Now, what's this I hear about opening a bakery?"

John smiled and nodded. "It was Katie's idea originally, but I think it's good. We found a commercial building we're trying to buy. Unfortunately, someone else has bid more for the property, so it's unlikely we'll get it. In the meantime, we're selling our house and looking for an alternate property."

"Hmm. Let me think. It seems like someone told me about a property recently. It might have been outside Spencer's Mill. If I remember where it was, I'll let you know."

"Thank you, sir. Oh, and there is one more thing. I placed an ad for our house in the paper today. The young lady there suggested that I put the name of a contact person in Lamar to make things easy for prospective buyers. Would you mind if I used your name?"

Christian chuckled. "Of course not. For me, that's free

advertising. It'll make readers familiar with my name. It might even lead to more business. I'll contact you if anyone asks about the ad."

John hesitated, then decided to open up to Christian. "Do you have a few minutes to discuss something puzzling me?"

"Certainly."

"The other buyer has raised my suspicion. He was dressed like a dandy and claimed to be a shoemaker. Then he offered a thousand dollars for a property that Oliver Hardin appraised at $825."

"I agree. Something isn't right. What's this fellow's name?"

"He said his name is Roy Skinner."

Christian's brow wrinkled into a confused expression. "Hmm. That sounds vaguely familiar, but I can't bring any details to mind. Why don't you go over to the courthouse and search his name? Find out if he owns other property. Find out if he has a record of having been before the judge. You can do all that without Skinner ever finding out you were looking into his past."

"Those are good suggestions."

"If you don't mind if gossip gets back to him, you could ask about him at the newspaper office and ask the sheriff if he knows him. But I wouldn't count on any confidentiality there."

John nodded and smiled. "Thank you, sir."

"Good luck to you, John."

Chapter 11: THE INVESTIGATION

John was grateful for the advice Christian gave him. He turned his horse toward the courthouse. He had never been at the County Clerk's office in that building before, but it was where his Pa died of a heart attack last July. It was a white-walled room with a long counter across most of the room, providing a barrier and work surface between the clerk and customers. Record books were lined up along shelves on the side wall. Light flowed in through double windows at the back. Inside, he stood before the counter, studying his surroundings, wondering exactly where Pa was in his final moments.

"May I help you, sir?"

He shook those thoughts out of his head and turned his attention to the clerk.

"My name is John Reese," he said. "I'm looking for any property owned by Roy Skinner. Can you give me that information?"

The young man pulled a giant, cloth-bound ledger from the shelf under his countertop. He flipped through the pages, looking alphabetically until he reached the listings of property owners whose initial was S.

The man ran his finger down the entries but found no one named Skinner.

"Sorry," he said. "I don't think Mr. Skinner owns any property in Bledsoe County."

"Does he appear in the court records?"

"Do you know when he would have been arrested or sued?"

"No, I'm sorry. I'm not even sure he'll be listed."

"It could take some time to find something, then. Would you like to look by yourself? I could put the book on a table behind me."

"I would appreciate that."

The clerk carried the weighty book to the table behind the front desk and offered John a straight-backed wooden chair. He took his seat and scanned the records, beginning with the most recent court cases and working backward. He passed over the entry where Danny had sued the entire Reese family, shook his head to erase the memory, and kept going.

He found his first sign of trouble when he came to the October court cases. Mr. Skinner had been arrested for running illegal gambling in his rented house. The name of the man charged with him was Simon Beadle.

John continued to search. Going back to February 1886, he found a record of Roy Skinner's arrest for theft of the cash box at the trolley company. Could this be an indication of a gambling problem? He closed the book, thanked the clerk, and left.

As he mounted his horse, he didn't know what to do with the information he had just learned. He decided to revisit the newspaper office.

Once there, he entered the door and asked Miss Blue Eyes to speak to a reporter or editor. She showed him to the back office. The reporter was at his desk working on a news article but glanced up with his pen poised over the paper.

"Have a seat, sir. What can I do for you?"

"I'm looking for any information you may have on Roy Skinner and Simon Beadle."

The reporter scrunched his brow and tilted his head. His eyes snapped back to John. "Oh, yes, I remember. There was something about the two of them last year. One of them was running illegal gambling in his parlor. He wouldn't have been caught except for selling liquor to his patrons. There was heavy drinking, and the drunks got loud and boisterous. Yes . . . I remember. The neighbors complained to the sheriff after this went on night after night. I believe both fellows spent some time in jail. I'm glad I wasn't the owner of the house they rented. I heard they left it in shambles."

John wagged his head. "Skinner says he's a shoe cobbler now and wants to buy an empty store to open his shop. Do you have any idea where his shoe shop is? I got the feeling it was in Lamar."

"The only shoe shop I know of is on Market Street. It's called Bonaccini's. The fellow came over from Italy. He makes beautiful shoes and boots."

"Thanks," John said. "I'll check and see if Skinner works there."

The reporter smiled. "You know my business is snooping information. Would you mind telling me why you're looking for him?"

"Because I want to buy the same property he's interested in. He's offered much more than it's worth. I'm just curious why."

"Hmm. I agree that sounds suspicious. Good luck, friend. By the way, what did you say your name is?"

"Reese. John Reese."

A flicker of recognition crossed the newsman's face, and John's heart sank. *Here we go again.*

The reporter tapped on his desk with his pencil, lips pressed together, and stared at his hand. Then he raised his eyes and smiled. "Well, good luck, Reese. If this turns out to be a story, I may want to talk to you again."

John left the newspaper office, thankful the reporter hadn't mentioned the court hearing. He hoped he hadn't caused a problem for himself or his family if Skinner learned he was digging for information. But John was determined to continue his quest to discover all he could. He mounted Ginger and rode to Bonaccini's Bootery.

When he entered the store, the suggestion of fine quality was everywhere. Comfortable chairs waited for customers. Expensive gentlemen's boots and ladies' shoes were artfully displayed on tables. John browsed the brogans, Oxfords, kid slippers, Hessian boots, pumps, and ladies' sandals with ribbon straps.

As he surveyed the footwear on display, a friendly, conservatively dressed man of about fifty years came from the back of the store. He spoke with a heavy Italian accent. "Good morning, sir. May I help you with a pair of fine boots?"

John extended his hand for a shake. "I can see that you have well-made boots here. And one day, I hope to be a customer, but I can't do it today. I'm looking for a cobbler named Roy Skinner. I wonder if he works for you?"

"Oh, no. Bootmaking is a refined art that takes years to perfect. I don't employ anyone else. All the work is done by me alone." He made a little bow. "I am a boot artist, you might say." He picked up a brogan. "Do you see this fine stitching? And look at the soles. They are made of the finest leather, comfortable to wear, but sturdy enough to last for years." He turned the boot over for John's inspection.

"I see. I want you to make my next pair of boots. This is excellent work."

Mr. Bonaccini beamed. "Whenever you're ready."

"I must go take care of my next errand, sir. Thank you for the information. I'll pass the word about the quality of your work."

John left the store, thinking that if bootmaking took years to learn, as Bonaccini said, chances were that Skinner didn't have the necessary skills. He decided to return to Christian's office.

Christian had just left to get lunch at the Old English Tea Room, his favorite restaurant. John didn't have enough money in his pocket for a meal, but he could get a cup of coffee, so he walked to the Tea Room to find Christian. He found him sitting at a table alone.

"John," Christian said when he spotted his stepson approaching. "Come join me, won't you?"

John smiled and made his way to the table.

"What will you have?" Christian asked.

"Just a cup of coffee. I'm not hungry."

"Nonsense. If I order a bowl of beef stew for you, would you eat it?" He didn't even wait for a reply. He signaled the waitress, who came to the table and took the order.

"What did you find out this morning?" Christian asked.

John told him about Skinner's arrest for hosting illegal gambling, selling liquor in his house, and the earlier arrest for theft. He also said he couldn't find anywhere that Skinner was selling shoes. Further, Bonaccini said it takes years to learn the craft. A man can't decide to be a cobbler and open a store with no apprenticeship.

The waitress brought their lunch. Christian stared into the distance, thinking. He punched the air with his spoon to emphasize his point. "There's a good chance that Skinner intends to turn the Spencer's Mill property into a bar with illegal gambling in a back room somewhere."

"I thought something like that, too." John stirred some sugar into his coffee and took a sip. "I don't know what to do with this information. If I approach Reverend Buchanan with it, he'll think I'm spreading ugly rumors to get a chance at buying that building."

"Since there's no proof yet, I would agree with you. Let me

think about it, and we'll pray for guidance. Maybe I can figure out a way to intervene. If an idea comes to me, I'll tell your mother what's going on, and she can drive to Spencer's Mill to keep you informed."

"Thank you, sir." His face fell as discouragement set in. "You know, without that building, I don't see any possibility of opening a bakery. That would leave us without prospects."

"If you can't open a bakery in Spencer's Mill, you could move your family to Lamar and open one here."

John's eyes brightened. "Sir, you don't know what a relief it is to realize there are other options. I hadn't thought of that. Moving wouldn't be my first choice; we love living in Spencer's Mill. But we'll do what we have to do."

"Let's work on the Spencer's Mill property first. Give me some time to think it over."

Christian and John finished their lunch and left the restaurant. John had one last errand to finish, but Christian decided to talk with Sheriff Beeler. When he arrived, he found Beeler at his desk.

"Attorney Wolf," said the sheriff. "What brings you here today?"

"I have concerns about two fellows who got into trouble about a year ago. They may be at it again, but this time in Spencer's Mill."

"Maybe you should talk to Sheriff Lane, then. That's out of my territory."

"But you'd have the information. Can't you give me a few minutes of your time?"

Beeler sighed. "All right, Wolf. Have a seat, and we'll talk. I know you. You'll badger me until you get what you want anyway."

Christian grinned. "You're probably right. This won't take long. It's a couple of fellows you're familiar with. Their names are Roy Skinner and Simon Beadle."

"Oh, yes. I didn't know they had branched out into Spencer's Mill."

"Skinner is trying to buy a building there from one of the churches. He told them he intends to open a shoe shop, but that's highly suspicious."

Beeler threw his head back and roared with laughter. "Skinner a cobbler? I don't think so." He dried his eyes with his handkerchief. "How did you come by this information?"

"My stepson has put in an offer on the same building. He wants to put in a bakery."

"Listen, you tell the young man to watch his step. Skinner and Beadle are vicious. If they find out he's opposing them, no telling what they might do to him or his family."

"Really? I wasn't aware they were in any danger."

"If Skinner doesn't get what he wants—without getting jailed first—yes, sir, they could be in real danger."

"I'm glad I came in, then. Thank you for letting me know."

Chapter 12: THE PINK DRESS

While Christian visited the sheriff's office, John made one more stop—the thrift store. He remembered his mother speaking of it. He found the shop on a side street.

"May I help you, sir?" The clerk was a pleasant, grandmotherly woman with silver hair.

"I'm looking for a nice dress for my wife. I don't know her size, but she's just a little thing. And she hasn't had a new dress in a long time."

The clerk smiled. "Let's see if we can find something pretty for her." She led John to a rack with ladies' dresses. He finally spotted one he liked. He guessed it to be about Katie's size. Tiny blue and white flowers were printed all over the light pink fabric. The dress had long puff sleeves with buttons near the wrist. It sported a fashionable peplum attached to the waist and was trimmed with an abundance of white lace.

"This is beautiful," he exclaimed. "It'll look good with Katie's brown hair. I wish I could buy her a new dress, but this will have to do for now. I'll take it. If it doesn't fit, can she exchange it?"

"Yes, sir. If it doesn't fit, return the dress with the receipt, and we'll exchange it for another size." She folded the dress carefully as if it were fit for a princess, wrapped it in a sheet of newsprint, and tied it with string. "I hope she likes it."

"I do, too." John smiled, placed the package under his arm, and headed home.

When he reached the house, he spotted Steven coming up the road, just getting home from school. John waited for him to catch up, and they filed into the house together.

"Mama! Papa and I are home," called the little guy. Kate appeared from another room with Gracie. John was astonished to see the angry fire in her eyes.

"What's wrong, Kate?"

"About a half hour ago, three older boys came by the house. They threw a shower of pebbles at the windows and yelled, "Liar, liar." Thank God the windows aren't broken. When I tried to see who it was, they ran away, laughing. At first, I was scared, thinking they wanted to hurt us. Now I'm just angry."

John, stung by guilt, put his arm around his wife. "I'm sorry, Katie. They were aiming their accusation at me. Do you know who the boys were?"

"No, they ran off before I got a look at their faces." She blew her nose and began to calm down. "Maybe that was just a one-time thing. Maybe they got it out of their system and will leave us alone now."

"I don't think they intended to hurt anyone. I think they just wanted to create mischief."

Kate brushed some hair from her face. "I hope you're right."

John held out the package. "Here, I brought you something," he said. "It's a promise of better things to come. Maybe it will help you forget those ruffians."

Kate rubbed her eyes and took the bundle from his hand. When she untied the string and pulled the paper aside, her mouth flew open, and she gazed at John with wide eyes. "John, we can't afford this."

He laughed. "I didn't want to tell you I bought it at the thrift shop. It's not new, but we'll get you a new one as soon as possible."

"May I try it on?" She held it up in front of her, and that particular shade of pink enhanced her skin color. Her eyes were dancing, her ire over the morning incident pushed aside.

"Of course. Go try it on now." John grinned at her excitement. She disappeared into their bedroom. In a few minutes, she appeared wearing the dress. It was exquisite on her. She had never been so lovely. John didn't know what to say.

"How does it look?" she asked.

He smiled and shook his head. "Gorgeous," he whispered while she bounced toward him and threw her arms around his neck.

Chapter 13: THE BOARD MEETING

Tuesday, January 25, 1887

A distinguished-looking group of men met for the Board of Trustees meeting at Wesleyan Church that Tuesday evening in late January. They were gathered in a side room around a rectangular table. Oil lamps on the table offered light, and a fire in the potbelly stove at the end of the room spread its warmth.

Anthony Whiddle served as Chairman of the Board, a businessman in his seventh decade of life, relatively short of stature, his belly overflowing his belt, wearing a suit and vest. The gold chain of his watch hung from his vest pocket.

Second, in order of influence and assertiveness, Marcus Donovan was a no-nonsense retired banker with gray hair and piercing eyes.

The third was Hiram Wells. A farmer in his forties, he was a sharp negotiator in corn and soybeans. His face was weathered for his relatively young age, his hands rough and muscular.

The fourth was sandy-haired James Jackson, about forty years old. He owned a sawmill and building supply store in Lamar and had twenty years of business experience.

Last was young Isaac Day, chosen to be on the Board only because they wanted to train someone more youthful should one of the older ones need to be replaced. Isaac was a tall, slender man in his late twenties, short on experience but brilliant and eager to learn. He showed great potential. The other men had welcomed him into their group. His opinions didn't seem to carry the same weight as the others, but he accepted that fact without resentment as long as his vote counted.

Whiddle, the Chairman, addressed the other four men at the table. "Let's call the meeting to order," he said. "What are we discussing this evening?"

Sitting to his right, Donovan said, "The ladies' missionary guild wants to schedule a regular day once a month where they work on quilts to send to foreign missions. They want to come on the second Thursday of every month."

Whiddle sighed. He didn't want to spend time on women's matters he deemed unimportant. "Do we have anything on the schedule already for that day? James?"

James Jackson, in charge of the church calendar, verified that the time slot was open.

"Anyone have any objections?"

"I don't object," said Wells, "as long as they don't try to store their sewing supplies in the church closet. We need to keep that free for hymnals and extra chairs."

There were no other objections, so Whiddle told Jackson he could tell the ladies to schedule their quilting day on the condition that they carry their supplies home each time. "What's next?" he asked.

Donovan said, "We finally have an offer on the Main Street property. In fact, we have two. We need to discuss whether to accept, counter, or reject them."

Whiddle smiled. "This is a stroke of good luck. Tell the group the details."

"One offer is from Mr. John Reese, a local man who wants to open a bakery with his wife. He's submitted a letter from Oliver Hardin, who appraised the property at $825. He's offering $800 because of the extensive cleaning and remodeling he would have to do before it could be ready for customers. The offer is pending the sale of his house and a loan from the bank. The bank manager says he'll have no trouble getting the loan since he's using his deceased father's real estate as collateral. Mr. Reese will inherit a substantial amount of that property."

"Thank you, Donovan. I hope the next offer is more favorable. Tell us about the second one."

"Mr. Roy Skinner from Lamar wants to open a shoe shop in Spencer's Mill. He's offering one thousand dollars, our asking price. It's a cash offer. He will close when his partners put in their share of the money. He anticipates that will be inside a week."

Hiram Wells spoke up first. "I don't think we even need to vote on that. The answer is obvious."

Isaac Day ventured an opinion. "Do we know anything about either of these men? We don't want to sell to any shady characters."

Donovan turned to him with a condescending smile. "Isaac, I hope you don't take this wrong, but I'm a realist. I don't think selling real estate involves any moral consideration. You own property; you sell it. It's all dollars. What happens to the property after that is the buyer's responsibility."

Day stared at him. "Are you serious? I'm shocked to hear you say that. Don't we have a responsibility to the village to protect the quality of life here? Especially since we're a church."

Donovan stuck to his opinion. "Do you want to discuss who has the more acceptable morals—a baker or a cobbler?"

Wells, the seasoned negotiator, fidgeted in his seat. "I don't think we should stall a response just because we don't know the personal views of the prospective buyers. Here's what I think we should do. Let's accept Skinner's offer but give him a definite closing date. We don't know if his partners will follow through or if he's only giving himself a little time to borrow money. If that deal falls through, we approach Reese and find out if he's still interested—at a more favorable price, of course."

Jackson sat with a puzzled look on his face. "The name of John Reese sounds familiar, but I can't place it."

Donovan asked the group to focus on the issue at hand. "How long should we give Skinner to come up with the money?"

Wells suggested ten days. "That gives him the week he requested, plus a few days in case one of his investors drags his feet."

Jackson's mouth flew open as he smacked the table with his hand. "Now I remember how I know the name of John Reese. There was a court case about three weeks ago. It was in the Lamar newspaper. His brother sued him, and he was defeated. The judge accused him of trying to take over the family inheritance. That must be the same John Reese."

"Really?" Whiddle was interested. "How did I ever miss that bit of news? Well, it's good we have another buyer. We wouldn't want to sell to anyone with a cloud over him."

Heads nodded all around.

"Then," Whiddle said, "are we in agreement that we'll accept Skinner's offer with a closing window of ten days? All in favor say 'Aye.'"

There were five ayes. Decision made. A bright smile lit Whiddle's face. He said he would write up the acceptance and contact Roy Skinner so the pastor didn't need to be bothered. However, he would give him a progress report.

"We'll meet again next month," he said. "We'll have decisions to make about what to do with all the money we're about to receive." The meeting was dismissed, and the board members congratulated each other that it hadn't taken as long as the last meeting.

Wednesday, January 26, 1887

The following day, as John patched a wall in the bedroom, he wondered about the outcome of last night's Board meeting. Even though there was no reason for optimism, he wanted official notification.

He put his trowel down and straightened to a standing position. "Katie, I can't stand this waiting any longer. I'm going to the pastor's office to ask about last night's meeting."

"All right, John. I'll stay here and wait for Steven."

John took off on horseback to the church and entered through the double doors.

"Ah, Mr. Reese," the pastor said. "Please have a seat."

John sat across from the pastor at his desk. "I came to find out how the board meeting went last night."

"You probably already know there's no good news for you. The Board accepted Skinner's offer. It was so much higher than yours; they felt they could not deprive the church of the extra money. I'm sorry, son. The bakery would have been a good addition to Spencer's Mill. I wish you luck in finding another property."

"I understand. It's what I expected, but I wanted to hear it from you."

"If I hear of another available property, I'll let you know."

John rose from his seat. "Thank you, sir." With shoulders slumping, he trudged to the door and rode home to give Kate the bad news.

All their planning…crushed in a moment.

Chapter 14: A FRATERNITY OF FELONS

Roy Skinner sat at a folding table in his rented room above the Mad Fox Tavern in Lamar. Three of his compatriots—Murdock, Beadle, and Houlahan—sat with him. Murdock was the only well-groomed man among them. He wore Levi's and a plaid shirt. His short dark hair was parted in the middle and slicked down with bear grease on both sides. Beadle's lack of concern about personal hygiene was evident in his unshaven face, dirty shirt, and body odor. Houlahan had recently joined the group to feel a sense of belonging, but he wasn't as quick-witted as the others. His hair was unkempt under his shabby bowler hat.

Beadle and Houlahan were both avid smokers, making the air in the room thick and gray. Each man had a pile of money and cards on the table. Skinner kept their glasses full. He had collected from them in advance to cover the cost of the liquor.

"Boys, you'll have to come up with $300 each, and quickly, if we're to get that building in Spencer's Mill. We need it to open a successful place away from the Lamar cops. I received word from the church today that our twelve hundred-dollar offer was accepted, but we need the money within ten days, or they'll sell to the other buyer."

"What? I thought they were asking a thousand." Houlahan stared at Skinner with a dark expression. "We should only need $250 each."

Skinner was quick. "Look, there was another interested buyer. I had to raise the offer, or the baker would have gotten it."

That satisfied the suspicious partners.

Beadle had a question. "Ten days isn't much time to get three hundred each. How are we going to do that?"

Murdock sat quietly, listening to the conversation. Finally, he spoke up. "I have another question. How did you get a church to agree to sell to someone wanting to turn it into a saloon?"

Skinner laughed, a dry cackle. "That didn't take much. I told them I wanted to open a shoe shop."

The other three burst into laughter, sharing glances and slapping their knees. "That's a good one," said Beadle, wiping his eyes, "but you didn't answer my question. How will we get three hundred each in a short time?"

Skinner leaned back in his chair and grinned. "We're going to withdraw it from the bank. Where else in Lamar can you find that much money in one place?"

"What do you mean, withdraw it from the bank? I don't have an account there," said Houlahan. "I don't suppose you fellows do, either."

Skinner leaned over the table toward his friend. "You don't have much of an imagination. You don't need an account. All you need is a mask and a revolver." He lifted his glass, drained the spirits with a smug expression, then tapped it smartly on the table.

The rest of them sat thinking and fingering their cards. "I never robbed a bank," said Murdock. "What's the plan?"

Skinner wagged his head. "It's easy. You put on your mask, walk into the bank holding your revolver, and demand money. Only a fool would refuse to cooperate."

Beadle's tongue went to his upper lip as he thought. "And what about the sheriff?"

"Even if someone sends for the sheriff, we'll be on our horses and long gone before he can get there. We'll head south toward Wapeka and hide in the woods before we circle back to Spencer's Mill and pay for our building."

Murdock seemed skittish. "I don't know about this. This sounds high risk. What if we're caught?"

"Don't be a pansy. We won't get caught. Think about that saloon we'll have. We'll put in a piano and hire working-class girls to entertain—you know the type. Silk stockings...feathers. Think about the money rolling in from the sale of liquor, and we'll make a profit on the gambling. We'll charge men for admittance to that special poker room upstairs. Then we'll fix the game so they don't win, except once in a while...sort of like salting a gold mine."

"And we'll split the earnings four equal ways. Right, Skinner?"

"I'll take my manager's salary and pay the expenses; then we'll split four equal ways. Boys, as soon as we get established, three hundred dollars will seem like nickels to us. We'll be rich."

Houlahan spoke. "Count me in. When do we do this?"

"It has to be quick. We don't have much time. Let's say Friday, right before the bank closes for the weekend. That will make it harder for the sheriff to investigate. Meet here at three o'clock on Friday and bring your loaded revolvers. I'll have the masks and a pillowcase for the money. Don't take any coins, just paper money. Coins would slow us down. Everybody agreed?"

The three men all nodded and clinked their glasses together.

Friday, January 28, 1887

At 3:00 on Friday afternoon, Skinner, Beadle, and Houlahan waited for Murdock. They were tense, sweating, drumming their fingers on the table, and jiggling their knees. Beadle and

Houlihan held lit cigarettes in their yellow-stained fingers. They were equipped with weapons and masks. Skinner carried the pillowcase to hold the money.

"I wonder where Murdock could be?" asked Houlihan. "He'll ruin everything."

"No, he won't, because we're going without him if he doesn't show up within ten minutes. That means we'll have to 'withdraw' four hundred each for a one-third share."

Beadle laughed, seeing an opportunity. "If the bank has twelve hundred dollars for four customers, it will have the same amount for three, won't it?"

"That's right." Skinner was smiling. He would have to shut up Murdock later, but that could be worked out. He had the same fate planned for Houlahan.

Ten minutes went by without Murdock making an appearance.

"I had a feeling he was getting cold feet," said Skinner. "Let's go. Beadle, you approach from the north like a regular customer, and Houlahan, you come in from the east the same way. I'll come in on Main Street from the south. When we're almost at the bank, put your bandanas over your face and draw your weapons. We'll enter the bank together. I'll take the lead and force the teller to give me the money from his drawer. You men hold the manager and customers at bay until I get the money."

"Got it."

They clambered down the stairs to the sidewalk, mounted their horses, and took off in their assigned directions. Fifteen minutes later, they approached the bank and tied their bandanas over their faces. Good fortune seemed to be with them—only two customers were inside.

Skinner burst through the bank door, shouting, "Everyone, turn around and face me with your hands up." Startled, the customers spun around and threw their hands into the air. Their faces were drained of color, and their mouths were agape. The teller ducked down so he couldn't be seen, but it was to no avail.

"Teller. Show yourself, or I'll come around there and empty my revolver into you."

The teller rose slowly. His eyes were wide, and he trembled violently.

McDonald, the bank manager, sat at his desk with his hands up.

Beadle and Houlahan were almost as nervous as the teller but held their guns on McDonald and the customers.

"Hurry up, Skinner," said Houlahan under his breath.

Skinner spun around and hissed, "Shut up, you idiot."

He turned his attention back to the teller. "Put all your money on the counter so I can see it."

The teller opened his drawer and pulled out bank notes. Without counting it, Skinner estimated it was less than a thousand dollars. He shoved it all in his pillowcase and started shouting again. "That's not enough. Get over to the safe and open it up. Right now. Hurry up."

"This is taking too much time, buddy," Houlahan hissed through his teeth.

"You shut up, or I'll shoot you. If you think I'm kidding, say something else. This is my last warning."

Houlahan believed him and kept his mouth shut.

The teller moved to the safe with its giant combination lock and began entering numbers. The first try didn't work because his hands were fluttering.

"Hurry up," screeched Skinner.

The heavy safe door swung open, revealing bags and boxes inside.

"Is there money in that bag?" Skinner pointed at the bag nearest the safe door. It was bulging. Even if the bills were singles, that would probably make up the thousand he needed to close on the building.

"Yes."

Skinner grabbed that bag and the one next to it to buy furnishings and inventory. He stuffed them both into his pillowcase, then backed toward the door. His friends had let their attention lapse. Greed turned their concentration to Skinner's pillowcase.

Seizing his opportunity, Murdock leaped up behind the teller's window with a revolver. "Drop your guns," he shouted.

The three robbers spun around to face him. In the confusion, the bank manager was able to jump Skinner, knock the gun out of his hand, and wrestle him to the floor.

"Which one of you boys wants to be first?" Murdock shouted, aiming his revolver in the general direction of his two card-playing friends.

"Don't be a fool, Murdock. There's still a share of it for you." From his belly-down position under McDonald's right knee, Skinner wasn't too convincing.

"It's Deputy Murdock to you, Skinner." He turned to the teller. "Go outside and get the sheriff. He's standing at the corner of the bank."

Once the three were in handcuffs, the sheriff pulled their bandanas down. "Are these the three you told me about?" he asked Murdock.

"Those are the three. I'll help you get them to jail."

The sheriff holstered his gun. "We'll have to transport them one by one in my carriage. Can you keep two of them under control while I take Skinner first?"

"I certainly can."

"Put a closed sign on the door," the sheriff said, and the bank manager moved into action, posted the sign, and snatched the pillowcase with the stolen money bags. The sheriff escorted Skinner from the bank. For all his planning and risk, Skinner's take was precisely zero.

Murdock tied Beadle and Houlahan to chairs. "You boys know Skinner never intended to cut you in on the business, don't you? You would have ended up dead."

"I don't believe you," Beadle said, anger flashing from his eyes.

Houlihan sat mute with his head down, a man defeated.

"He didn't offer twelve hundred for that building, either. He offered a thousand. The extra money collected from you would have gone into his pocket."

"You're lying." Beadle tried to come up at Murdock from his chair, but he was securely tied. He jerked violently to get loose without success. He and the chair slammed back down on the floor.

"And he was cheating you at cards."

Chapter 15: THE BOARD CONVENES AGAIN

Sunday, January 30, 1887

Whiddle called an emergency meeting of the Board of Trustees on Sunday afternoon after the worship service. Their families killed time in the church lobby, so the men were under pressure to hurry it up.

He brought the meeting to order. "Gentlemen, I've been informed by the sheriff that the buyer for our store has been arrested for bank robbery." He cleared his throat. "The sheriff also says that his true intent for the store was opening a saloon, not a shoe shop. His plan was for illegal gambling in the upstairs apartment."

Donovan folded his hands and dropped his head. "My, my. I must reverse my opinion. If we had sold it to someone who put a saloon in there, it would have attracted all kinds of shady characters and drunks to the village. The church would have been criticized without mercy."

Isaac Day shifted in his seat but was kind enough to let the apology go without comment.

Jackson raised his hand. "I'm for withdrawing our acceptance of Skinner's offer. I don't think we need to vote on it. He didn't give us a down payment, and he won't be able to close the sale within ten days if he's in jail."

"I agree, Jackson," Whiddle said. "Technically, our

acceptance of Skinner's offer doesn't expire until Wednesday, but we don't need to worry about that under the circumstances. We need to find out if Reese is still interested since we rejected his offer completely. I don't want to have to meet again this week. Let's proceed as if he still wants the building and decide what to do about his offer."

"All right, let's review," said Donovan. "John Reese wants to open a bakery with his wife. The building was appraised at $825, but he's offering $800 because of the extensive cleaning and remodeling necessary. The offer depends on a bank loan and the sale of his house."

"Thank you, Donovan. We're open for discussion."

Hiram Wells spoke up first. "We've already had one offer for a thousand dollars. Don't you think we should hold to that?"

Jackson shook his head. "No, Hiram, you need to consider that the man willing to pay that amount expected huge profits from crooked gambling and the sale of alcohol. A bakery won't make enough money to afford that much."

Donovan nodded. "That's right. When we first decided to ask for a thousand, we didn't know what the property was worth on the open market. We have an appraisal for $825. And let me mention that this is our first honest offer in a year."

Isaac Day ventured an opinion. "I'm in favor of holding out for top dollar. I don't think we should grab this offer so fast. What if someone else bids higher after we accept this one?"

Donovan smiled, knowing Isaac was young and had never bought or sold real estate. "Isaac, selling real estate is like tossing dice. If you wait until you're sure no one will bid higher, you'll be too late. By the time you decide, your high bidder will have tired of waiting and bought himself another property. You can only do your best and take your chances."

Jackson nodded and smiled. "Selling real estate has a lot in common with gambling."

Isaac nodded. "I understand your point."

Wells, the seasoned negotiator, was fidgeting in his seat. "I don't think we should delay taking action. If Reese loses interest, it may be another year before someone else wants it. Here's what I think we should do. Let's counter the offer with Mr. Reese. Maybe $800 is too low. Maybe we can get more out of him."

Wells suggested countering at $950. "We can't just give the property away," he said.

Jackson disagreed. "We have an appraisal value from a man who is an expert on local real estate values. Oliver Hardin's reputation is well known. He owns a lot of property in this county and knows what to pay for it. He says it's worth $825. I agree we should push for a little higher than that, but we need to be reasonable, or we'll never sell the property. And right now, it's sitting there depreciating and deteriorating. Have you seen it? It's a fright and gets worse the longer it sits there. There are piles of dirt everywhere. The floors and walls are stained, and it's full of junk that has to be removed. Fellas, if we want top dollar, we'll have to clean it up and get it in top shape. I don't have the time or the inclination to do that. Do you?"

Wells said, "Well, then what about $925?"

Isaac Day took a shot at airing an opinion. "I bow to you fellows' experience, but it seems we shouldn't go for more than $900. Just a feeling I have."

"Wait," Jackson said. "What about Reese's poor reputation? He lost a court challenge recently, remember."

"Since he has relatives in town, I can't believe he wants to do something illegal with the property," said Donovan. "His brother and sister-in-law are members here. That's something in his favor. We can put language in our counteroffer to protect the church if Reese can't complete the deal or if he tries to get cute with us somehow. I agree with Isaac on this one. Let's counter with $900."

"What kind of language are you talking about, Donovan?" asked Whiddle.

"Well, for one thing, we should give him a time limit for closing on the deal. We can give him a reasonable time to sell his house and get that loan. Say, forty-five days."

"No one can expect to sell a house around here in forty-five days," said Jackson.

"Despite that, we wouldn't want to tie up the church's options for longer than that, would we? If Reese can't close on our terms in forty-five days, we can either extend his time or work with another buyer if we've found one in the meantime."

The other four men understood that wisdom and nodded their heads.

"Then," Whiddle said, "are we in agreement that we'll draw up a counteroffer for $900 with a forty-five-day closing window? All in favor say 'Aye.'"

There were ayes all around. Decision made. Whiddle said he would write up the counteroffer and contact John Reese. The meeting was dismissed.

Chapter 16: HOPE AND DESPAIR

Monday, January 31, 1887

The following day, as John patched a wall in the children's bedroom, there was a knock at the door. "Can you get the door, Katie?" he called.

Kate wiped her hands on her apron and opened the door. There stood a short, rotund man dressed in business attire. "Yes?" she asked.

"My name is Anthony Whiddle, ma'am. I'm from the Board of Trustees at Wesleyan Church. Is Mr. John Reese at home?"

"Yes, of course. Come in, won't you?"

John put his trowel down and straightened to a standing position. He stretched to clear a kink in his back. "Be right there," he said. He brushed his hands on his dungarees and walked into the parlor. "I'm John Reese. Good to meet you, Mr. Whiddle." He extended his hand, and the two men shook. "Won't you sit down?"

They both took a seat, and John waited expectantly. He assumed Katie was listening from the kitchen.

Whiddle took an envelope from his pocket. "We had a meeting of the Board last evening and discussed your offer on the Main Street property. We hope you're still interested. We want to pursue a sale with you, but not at your suggested price."

"What? I thought you had signed another buyer."

"That one didn't work out as we expected."

Hope flickered in John's chest. "Do you have a counteroffer for us?"

"Yes, it's right here." He handed the envelope to John, who opened it and took out the folded paper. "We think $900 would be a fair price. After all, it's next to the general store, which would bring you a lot of walk-in traffic. It's probably the best business location available in Spencer's Mill. And I'd like to point out we are meeting you halfway."

John took a moment to read the letter in his hand and pressed his lips together, unimpressed. In an absent-minded gesture, he turned it over to look at the back, then turned to the front again. His eyes met Whiddle's.

Whiddle continued. "I must tell you that our offer is contingent on closing within forty-five days."

John laid the counteroffer on the coffee table. "Forty-five days is hardly enough."

"We thought about that," said Whiddle, "but in fairness to the church, we don't want to limit our options longer than that. Here's how it will work. If you haven't closed in forty-five days, we'll look at where you are in the process. We may decide to extend your time, or we may decide to go another direction."

"I'd like to know the situation with the other buyer. If he decides he can complete his deal, will you abandon your agreement with me to get more money from him?"

Whiddle shifted uncomfortably in his seat. "Please don't worry about our integrity, Mr. Reese. Once we sign an agreement, we will honor it. It was the buyer who abandoned that last contract. He couldn't come up with the cash he promised. Besides," he said with a broad smile, "our wives would like the option of buying bread instead of spending time baking it themselves."

"I appreciate that, Mr. Whiddle. My wife and I will pray

over this and let you know by tomorrow what we decide. How can I contact you?"

Whiddle began to stammer. "I . . . I thought . . . How disappointing. I thought you would jump at this offer. Well, John, I'll tell you what. Why don't you write your decision and deliver it to me by tomorrow evening? I'll give you my address." He jotted his address on the envelope.

"Sounds fine, Mr. Whiddle. Thank you." The two men shook hands again, and Whiddle left.

After the door closed behind him, Kate came out of the kitchen smiling. John, on the other hand, had his stomach in knots. "We may yet have a chance at that property, Katie, but it's still very uncertain."

"Well," she said, "it looks like things are going just as you said. They countered a higher price than we want to pay, so we'll come back with another price."

"Everything in me wanted to accept that counteroffer. But I realize we can't afford to pay $900 and stay within our budget. We would be ruined financially."

"John, we don't have to manage this ourselves. This is a matter of prayer. Move over, and let me sit beside you."

In the quiet of the parlor, they bowed their heads and asked for wisdom so they could negotiate with confidence.

In the courtroom in Lamar, three men stood before Judge Noonan, holding their hats in their cuffed hands. Skinner and Beadle stared at the judge defiantly while Houlahan's head hung low, staring at the floor. The judge glared at them with a critical eye, then opened the file folder before him. "So, you fellows were trying to rob a bank and threatening people with firearms. Do you have a lawyer?"

"We don't need one," said Skinner. "The truth is on our side."

The judge rolled his eyes. He and his bailiff glanced at each other. "Very well. We have a statement from the sheriff's deputy that he was present when you discussed your robbery plans, and the bank manager is in the courtroom, ready to testify. Do we need to continue with these proceedings or go directly to sentencing? What do you have to say for yourselves?"

The most imaginative of the three, Skinner said, "You can't believe anything Deputy Murdock says. He was in on it with us. He wanted his cut, but the bank manager found out, so he pretended to be on the level. He's crooked, your honor. There's nothing worse than a crooked lawman. If we get locked up, he should get locked up longer."

The judge turned his attention to the deputy. "Do you want to comment on that, Murdock?"

"Yes. That's nonsense. Sheriff Beeler will tell you that he and I have been watching Skinner and Beadle since their last arrest. Houlahan is a latecomer to their group. I managed to gain their trust and join them. They would never have trusted me had they known I was a deputy."

"That's a lie," Skinner said. "We knew all along. He said he would keep the sheriff away from us. Besides, your honor, I only wanted to pull that bank job to make sure my Ma is taken care of. She's an old lady living in poverty with no one to help her. If you put me in jail, she'll be destitute … homeless. She'll be begging from door to door."

"Where does your mother live?"

"Columbus, sir."

"Deputy Murdock, do you have any information I need to hear?"

"Yes, sir. I can't confirm that his mother is living in poverty in Columbus. Maybe she is, or maybe she's wealthy, or maybe she's already in her grave. Skinner is such a liar that there's no way of knowing. I know he signed a contract with Wesleyan

Church in Spencer's Mill to buy a commercial property from them. The price was one thousand dollars. He didn't plan to spend that money on his dear old Ma."

Beadle and Houlahan shot glances at each other, slack-jawed. Beadle glared at Skinner. "You said it was twelve hundred."

Skinner shook his head and whispered back. "He's trying to turn us against each other. Trust me; it was twelve hundred."

The judge pounded the bench. "Quiet."

The deputy continued. "I was there when they talked about using the stolen bank money to open a saloon in the Spencer's Mill property and promote illegal gambling in the upstairs rooms. They planned to charge men to get to the gambling tables and then cheat them. They would occasionally allow someone to win to keep them all interested."

"Mr. McDonald, tell me the story as you see it."

"Yes, sir. Deputy Murdock told me in advance that the robbery was planned for late afternoon, sometime after three o'clock, but we weren't sure exactly when. We decided to risk letting customers in the bank to take care of their business. We hoped we could get them in and out quickly before anything happened.

"Well, sir, Murdock took a position in hiding behind the teller's window at about a quarter of three in the afternoon. He waited while the sheriff holed up outside. It was sometime around half past three when the robbers came in. Beadle held a gun on me, and Houlahan held his gun on my two customers. I've never been so frightened in my life. I didn't think we'd come out of it alive. Skinner took all my teller's money from his drawer, then forced him to open the safe. He grabbed two bags of money and stuffed them in a pillowcase. While Beadle and Houlahan had their attention distracted by the bags of cash, I was able to jump Skinner and kick his gun away. I held him down while Murdock got the jump on Beadle and Houlahan. Then the sheriff came in and locked them in cuffs."

"Murdock, you say you had been watching Skinner and Beadle, but Houlahan was new to the group?"

"Yes, sir."

"Does Houlahan have a criminal record?"

"No, sir, at least not in Bledsoe County."

"I'm going to sentence Skinner and Beadle to seven years in the Ohio Penitentiary in Columbus. Skinner, you'll be happy to know you'll be close to your Mama. As for Houlahan, since this is the first offense we know of, he'll have one year in the county jail. Mr. Houlahan, you spend the year thinking about what you could do if you weren't locked in a little cell. And choose your companions more wisely. Case dismissed." He whacked the gavel on the bench.

Skinner spoke up quickly. "Sir, could I at least send a telegram to my Ma and let her know where I'll be?"

The judge stared hard at him, then spoke to the deputy. "Murdock, I need you to send a telegram to the warden at the prison, telling him to expect two prisoners. While you're at the telegraph office, can you escort Skinner inside? Let him telegraph his Mama, then take him to jail."

"Yes, sir. Will the bailiff take care of Beadle and Houlahan?"

"Yes."

Murdock took Skinner by the arm and escorted him to the carriage waiting in the street.

"What a fool you are, Murdock. You could have been a wealthy man."

"I already am. I have a wife, three kids, my integrity, and my freedom. That's all I want." Murdock slapped the reins and began the short trip to the telegraph office. "You're lucky the judge let you have this privilege. I was surprised you didn't go directly to jail."

Seemingly, out of nowhere, a large dog chased a cat into the road right in front of them, barking ferociously. The barking startled the horse, who reared and whinnied. While Murdock's attention was distracted, Skinner leaned over with his two cuffed hands and pulled Murdock's gun from its holster. The horse finally settled, but Murdock found himself at the mercy of a desperate criminal.

"All right, Murdock, quietly now, unlock my cuffs."

"I don't have the key."

"Liar. You put keys in your pocket back at the courthouse. Now, uncuff me, or I'll shoot. You'll never walk again." The barrel of the gun was pressed against Murdock's knee.

He reluctantly brought the horse to a stop, then reached into his pocket for the keys. With the gun held on him, he slid the key into the lock on his prisoner's handcuffs, and they snapped open.

Skinner was giddy with glee, giggling like a little girl. "Now, give me the key and snap the cuffs on yourself. You drive to the jail, and I'm sure someone will free your hands. That is if they still believe you weren't conspiring with me." Skinner hopped out of the carriage, grinning broadly.

Murdock drove away, knowing the gun was still pointed in his direction until he was out of range. He had no choice but to go to the jailhouse, where the sheriff would free his wrists.

Skinner couldn't believe his good fortune. His mind went into high gear. He was near the telegraph office and decided he had enough time to send a telegram before anyone caught him, then he would figure out a way to disappear.

He strode to the telegraph office, blending in with other pedestrians as if he had a right to be among them. Entering the door, he smiled at the gentleman at the desk. "I'd like to send a telegram."

"Yes, sir." The clerk pulled out his pencil. "Who is it going to?"

"It's going to Anthony Beadle at 2734 Wimpole Street in Columbus."

"And what do you want to say?"

Skinner thought quickly. The number of words didn't matter since he didn't plan to pay.

"Say: Ran into trouble. Stop. Send boys to Lamar Hotel with funds. Stop."

The telegraph clerk counted the words to calculate the total cost.

Skinner raised Murdock's gun. "There won't be any charge today," he said. "Send the telegram. And don't try anything cute. I know Morse code as well as you."

The clerk began to object, then thought better of it. He turned to his telegraph and began tapping the key.

Chapter 17: A COMPLICATED TRANSACTION

Tuesday, February 1, 1887

When John entered the kitchen hungry for breakfast, Kate was cooking and trying to get Steven ready for school. "Kate, I've been praying, and I think I know what we should do."

"I do, too. You first."

That wasn't the response he expected, but he decided to continue. "I think we should stick to our plan and not offer more than $850."

"That wasn't quite what I thought we should do, but almost. I was praying, too, and thought we should offer $825. That was what Mr. Hardin thought it was worth."

"If we do that, they may reject our offer completely. We may lose our chance at it."

"Yes, I know. The final decision is yours, but that's what I believe God told me. Not in my ears; in my spirit."

John smiled sheepishly and nodded. "All right, that's what I believed God told me, too, but I was too cowardly to go with it. I had to add twenty-five dollars to make our chances better. I guess I thought I was helping God." He lowered his head, and then his eyes met hers. "You're a brave woman. I admire your courage. Since God spoke to us both with the same message, that's what we'll do. We'll counter with $825 and plan to close the sale within forty-five days."

They were amazed at how peaceful they felt as they wrote their new offer. John stashed it in his pocket, then took it to Whiddle's house. They would have to wait until the Board of Trustees could meet one more time to find out whether it would be accepted.

Wednesday, February 2, 1887

Whiddle arrived home from work on Wednesday afternoon, looking forward to a hot meal with his wife. Instead, he found two gentlemen waiting in a carriage in front of his house. They were both large men, between thirty and forty years old, wearing expensive Inverness coats. The older one had heavily pocked skin behind his mustache.

"Are you gentlemen waiting for me?"

"Yes, if you're Whiddle."

"Would you like to come inside?"

The three men went into the house. It was a comfortable, well-appointed home with stylish furniture and a thick Oriental rug. Whiddle took them into his study and invited them to be seated across from his desk.

"Now, what can I do for you?"

"We represent Roy Skinner. We're here with the thousand dollars to pay for the building you agreed to sell him."

Whiddle went pale. "I...I understood Mr. Skinner was arrested for bank robbery and would be in prison for a while."

"Unfortunately, he was falsely accused and is in jail temporarily until the appeal. We're here to represent him. Now, you sign the deed to us, and we'll pay you."

Whiddle stalled and cleared his throat. "Gentlemen, I'm sorry to tell you that the Board of Trustees decided that in the absence of a down payment—and the absence of Mr. Skinner—

we would pursue a sale with another buyer. That building is no longer available."

One of the men raised an eyebrow and leaned forward over the desk. He stared into Whiddle's eyes. "What other buyer?"

"A man named John Reese wants the building for a bakery. We're negotiating with him right now."

The man continued to drill into Whiddle with his eyes. "John Reese, you say? I wouldn't count on a sale with him. Mr. Reese is about to change his mind."

The two men rose from their seats and left the house, leaving Whiddle trembling in fear. He recognized they had just threatened John Reese. He waited at the window until they were out of sight, climbed on his horse, and headed to the sheriff's office at a gallop.

"My name is Whiddle," he said and sat opposite the sheriff. Sheriff Lane was a tall, muscular man with a prominent cowlick and a telltale impression in his hair where his hat had pressed down. A tattered Wanted poster was tacked to the wall beside the hook that held a ring of keys for the jail cells. His desk was disorganized with unfinished paperwork. Whiddle continued. "I just had two very nasty characters visit my home, and there's trouble afoot. You need to know about it in advance."

Lane closed the file he was working on. "What kind of trouble?"

"I'm the chairman of the Board of Trustees at Wesleyan Church. A fellow named Roy Skinner offered us a thousand dollars for the building we own next to the general store. He said he wanted to open a shoe store. However, he has since been convicted of bank robbery. We found out he wasn't putting in a shoe store. He wanted to open a saloon. Naturally, we wouldn't allow a saloon to be opened in our quiet village."

"Naturally."

"Well, we approached our other interested party who wants to open a bakery, and we are currently negotiating. Two fellows came to my door today with a thousand dollars in cash. They claimed to represent Skinner, our first buyer, and wanted me to sign the deed to them."

"You turned them down, of course."

"Of course. But they wanted to know who our other buyer was. Foolishly, I gave them his name. They told me not to worry because that buyer was about to change his mind. That's a threat, sir."

"It does sound like it. What is the name of the buyer?"

"John Reese."

"That name is familiar. Isn't that the fellow who told all those lies and was sued by his brother?"

"So I've been told. I've met Mr. Reese in person. I believe he's made a big change in his life. But that doesn't matter. Whether he's a liar or honest, he's still in danger. And so is his family."

"I apologize for my careless remark. So what can you tell me about those two visitors?"

"I can't tell you much. I didn't get their names. They knew the details of Skinner's plans and how much he had promised to pay for the building. They were both big guys, probably around forty or younger. One of them had a mustache and a bad complexion."

"I wonder where they came from. They're not local, for sure. Maybe they're staying in a hotel."

"Oh, and they were wearing expensive coats and angry expressions."

"I'll keep an eye out for them. And I'll send word to Sheriff Beeler in Lamar. They may be staying there."

"Thank you." Whiddle picked up his coat and left.

The bell over the door at the general store rang, and Danny Reese greeted the customer. It was a stocky man he didn't recognize. "What can I do for you, sir?"

"I suppose you know a lot of people in town."

"I know a lot of them."

"Do you know a man named John Reese?"

Danny chuckled. "You've come to the right place. He's my brother."

The stranger smiled. "That's a stroke of good luck for me. I understand he's opening a bakery. I sell products for commercial kitchens. Can you tell me where he lives?"

"Yes, he lives on Lincoln Street. You'll see his name on the letterbox."

"Thanks, buddy."

A few minutes later, there was heavy rapping on the door on Lincoln Street. Startled, Kate answered while Gracie sat on the Chesterfield with her doll. A strange, unpleasant man asked, "Is Mr. Reese home?"

"Just a moment."

John heard the conversation from the kitchen. Something was wrong; he could feel it in his gut. He came in from the kitchen and sized up the visitor. He could almost hear the alarm bells in his head. This was not a friendly visit. "I'm John Reese. What can I do for you?"

The man pushed past John and stepped inside without being invited, followed by another large man. "Nice family you have here." He reached out boldly and stroked Kate's hair. She recoiled from his touch, shocked at that brazen violation, and slapped his arm.

The man roared with laughter.

John's anger flared. He blocked the man's extended arm with his fist. "Do not touch my wife. I've never known anyone to be that vulgar." He inserted himself between the rude strangers and Kate but didn't throw any punches, seeing that he would be overpowered in a fight.

The man laughed again. He had no fear, no sense of decency. "We want to discuss purchasing that building beside the general store."

"What about it?"

"You don't want it, understand? We're going to complete the sale the church promised to Roy Skinner. You tell the church you changed your mind."

Kate pulled Gracie close to her. "You don't determine who buys that building," she said defiantly. "God makes that decision."

"Kate, let me handle this, please," John said, turning to her. "You and Gracie go back to the bedroom and wait."

An unusual boldness overcame Kate, and she defied his instruction. "I'm taking Gracie out for a walk." She took her daughter by the hand, grabbed their cloaks, and led her out the kitchen door.

"Who are those men, Mama?" asked Gracie.

"They're bad men, and we must go for help so they don't hurt Papa."

She continued around the side of the house, not knowing what she would do, but she had to protect John from those dangerous characters somehow. Her heart pounded. The strangers' carriage was out by the street, harnessed to two horses. With a flash of inspiration, she stepped into the waiting carriage with her daughter and slapped the reins. The horses took off, and she urged them to a gallop, heading for the sheriff's office. *What am I doing?* she thought. *I've just stolen a carriage and two horses.*

Her heart was in a panic. She didn't know how those men

might harm John. She had to get the sheriff before Steven came home from school. If those men would molest a woman in front of her husband, what might they do to an innocent little boy? She leaped out of the carriage in front of the sheriff's office and ran in the door. "Sheriff, come quick," she shouted. "Two men are attacking my husband at home."

"By any chance, is your husband's name John Reese?"

"Yes. Hurry."

"Get back in your carriage," he said. "I'll follow you."

He strapped on his weapon as he ran for his horse. "Let's go," he shouted, and Kate took off again.

"Hang on, Gracie," she shouted. Gracie hung on tightly, bouncing on the seat as they raced over the streets. The horses panted as they galloped at top speed, hooves pounding and wheels clattering.

The sheriff burst into the house with his weapon drawn.

John sat calmly on the Chesterfield, alone.

Kate rushed into the room, confusion written on her face, as the sheriff holstered his gun. "Where are those men?"

"Have a seat, Sheriff," John said. "Shortly after you left, Kate, after you stole their rig"--he grinned—"a third man showed up. They realized you had their carriage and had probably gone for help. So all three ran out of here and took off in the third man's carriage."

"They'll no doubt be back," the sheriff said. "What did they want?"

"They tried to bully me into giving up the purchase of the old carpenter's shop beside the general store. Katie and I want to buy it and open a bakery."

"But you're fine for now?"

"Yes."

"Those first two could be accomplices of Roy Skinner, an escaped convict. The church originally agreed to sell him the building. The third could have been Roy Skinner himself. I had a bulletin about them from Sheriff Beeler in Lamar, saying that Skinner had escaped custody. Well, if everyone is safe, I'll return to my office. Keep me informed if those men show up again."

"Wait," Kate said, "has Steven come home yet? He should have been home by now." Her face paled. "Where is Steven?"

"I'll go get him," John said, fear rising in the pit of his stomach. "You stay here in case he shows up. Those three men might have grabbed him."

"I'll follow you," said the sheriff and ran for his horse.

They left Katie in tears, pacing frantically.

John jumped into the carriage that Katie had commandeered and took off like a madman, with the sheriff close behind. They followed Steven's route to school, but he wasn't anywhere to be seen.

John was hysterical. "My son," he shouted. "They have my son."

The sheriff pulled up beside him. "Try to remain calm, Mr. Reese. We don't know if they have him. Maybe he just wandered off his normal school route. We'll probably find the boy soon."

John would not be consoled. "God is punishing me. I should have known something like this would happen." He sat in the carriage, bent forward, and held his head, sobbing.

"Mr. Reese, God didn't kidnap Steven. Those two men might have him, but we have an excellent chance of finding him. Go home to your wife. I'll look for him."

"You must be joking," John said. "Do you think I'd sit at home while somebody is holding my boy? They're probably on their way to Lamar. I'm going after them."

"What will you do when you find them? Are you armed?"

"No, but you are. Come on!"'

The two men took off down the road at a gallop. The sheriff, on horseback, outpaced the carriage. Ten minutes passed as the chase continued. Twenty minutes ... thirty minutes. As they tore down the road, John's thoughts raced just as fast. He died inside a hundred times, thinking he had lost his son and blaming himself. But he kept going. The horses were spent when they caught sight of three men and a boy in a carriage ahead.

"Halt," the sheriff shouted at them. They kept going, so he fired a shot into the air.

"Whoa, whoa," one of the men shouted. "They can't get all three of us at once. Scatter!" Three of them jumped from the carriage and ran into the woods in three different directions, leaving the boy in the carriage. Steven ducked down on the floor. Gunfire came at John and the sheriff from all directions, missing their targets.

John and the sheriff stopped behind the kidnappers' carriage. John ran toward a large tree and crouched down for cover while the sheriff concealed himself behind one of the carriages.

"Papa," cried Steven.

"Stevie, get down," John shouted. "Lay on the floor."

"I am."

The three lawbreakers continued crashing through the frozen underbrush, turning to fire occasionally, until finally, there was silence in the woods.

"Papa," called the boy. John ran to the carriage and swooped him up. Steven clung to him as if his life depended on it.

"Thank God, thank God, thank God," John said with tears running freely down his face. He stroked Steven's hair and kissed his cheeks.

"I'm all right, Papa. I knew you'd come to get me."

"That's what papas do."

The sheriff eyeballed the woods from the road, but all three men had disappeared into the underbrush. "Thankfully, those weapons aren't known for accuracy." He held his position for a moment longer. "Upon my word, I thought they would continue firing," said Lane. "They must have run out of ammunition. Well, we're not going to help them get home." He took a rope from his saddle and tied his horse to the escapees' carriage. Then he climbed in and turned back toward Spencer's Mill.

John laughed. "Now we have both of their carriages. They'll be hard put to get back to Lamar on foot. It'll be dark before they can walk that far."

"This probably isn't over. You know that, don't you, Reese?"

"I don't want to think about that right now. Anyway, I don't think there will be any more trouble tonight."

The sheriff sighed and kept traveling. "You might want to look for another place to stay until this blows over."

Later, Lamar's Sheriff Beeler and Deputy Murdock responded to a complaint by a farmer that three men had stolen his wagon and two horses and had taken off in the direction of Lamar. Beeler and Murdock threw glances at each other.

Murdock snorted. "Three men? I'll bet we know who they are."

"Can you describe your wagon? Was there anything about it that would be different from others?"

"Yes, sir. It's blue and has 'Howard's Dairy' painted on both sides."

The two lawmen grinned. "They must have thought even a stolen blue milk wagon would be better than going to town on foot," Lane said. "There's a good chance we'll be able to get your wagon back for you in time for tomorrow's deliveries, Mr. Howard. Let's go, Murdock. They're probably at the hotel or renting a room over the saloon."

Sunday, February 6, 1887

Whiddle called a special meeting of the Board on Sunday afternoon right after the church service. He wanted to finalize the ongoing issue of their inherited building. That building was getting to be more trouble than it was worth.

Whiddle brought the meeting to order. "Gentlemen, we have two issues to deal with today. The first is our original agreement to sell the building to Roy Skinner. That agreement hadn't yet expired when we submitted a counteroffer to John Reese."

The other board members nodded in acknowledgment.

"However," Whiddle continued, "on the day the first contract was to expire, I was visited by two aggressive men who tried to give me the thousand dollars to pay for the building. I refused. They told me not to worry about John Reese because he was about to change his mind. That, men, sounded like a threat to me. I have been in contact with Sheriff Lane about this matter."

"What does he have to say?" Jackson asked.

"He tells me they were representatives of Roy Skinner, our first buyer, who escaped the sheriff's custody. He's now at large and dangerous."

"Is he a threat to Mr. Reese, then?"

"Yes, and he's a threat to me if I complete the sale to Reese."

Donovan spoke up. "Then this is a problem with deadly serious consequences. We need to find out where we stand legally while we do everything to protect ourselves. Do we have an attorney in the church?"

"I don't know of anyone," Whiddle said. "I've used Attorney Wolf before. He lives between here and Lamar. Maybe we could contact him. He has a good reputation."

"That's half of the problem," Donovan said. "I'll contact him myself if you don't object. He's an old friend of mine. The other problem is how we might protect ourselves and Mr. Reese from those hoodlums."

"All we can do is warn Reese he's in danger. I'll ask Sheriff Lane to look out for him."

Isaac spoke up. "Now we need to discuss what to do about Reese's offer if he hasn't changed his mind."

"Mr. Reese has countered our counteroffer," Whiddle said. "He has raised his offer to $825, the exact value of the appraisal, and agreed to close within forty-five days. We need to decide how to respond."

Donovan asked, "Has anyone else shown interest in the building?"

"No, not a soul."

Jackson spoke up. "That building has been on the market for over a year. My Pa used to say that a bird in the hand is worth two in the bush. That never meant anything to me until now. I say we accept Reese's offer. If he doesn't close in forty-five days, we'll still have the option of selling to another buyer. We don't have to take down the For Sale sign until we have the cash in hand."

Wells disagreed. "Don't you think we could squeeze another twenty-five out of him? If he's willing to pay $825, he'll probably pay $850."

Jackson was reluctant to push the price. "We don't know this man or how he thinks. Trying to push the price above the appraised value might be the final aggravation, and he'd walk away. His desire to buy this building may be more fragile now. I don't want to lose this sale."

Isaac spoke up. "If my opinion counts, I agree with Mr. Jackson."

"Gentlemen," said Whiddle, "my wife has dinner ready at

home. Can we vote on this? All in favor of countering at $850, raise your hand."

Wells' hand went up, but he was alone.

"All in favor of accepting Reese's offer as it is; raise your hand."

Four hands went up.

"I'll write up our acceptance this afternoon and have it to Reese by evening. Meeting dismissed. Thank you, gentlemen."

After dark that winter evening, Kate put the children to bed. John was alarmed to hear a knock at the door. No one ever came that late.

"Kate, go hide in the bedroom with the children. This could be the men who snatched Steven." He pulled his revolver out of the desk drawer and loaded it while Kate concealed herself. Then he called, "Who's there?"

The voice on the other side of the door answered, "It's Whiddle."

John's shoulders relaxed, and he opened the door. Mr. Whiddle stood there with another envelope in his hand. The weather had turned much colder. Large, wet snowflakes were falling heavily.

"Mr. Whiddle, come in. What are you doing out this late in this horrible weather?"

Whiddle brushed the snow off his topcoat. "May I sit down?"

"Of course. Let me take your coat. Katie, would you make a cup of tea for Mr. Whiddle? He's about to freeze."

"Do you have any coffee?" Whiddle asked. "I hate to impose, but I never developed a taste for tea."

Kate passed through the parlor on her way to the kitchen. "Of course, Mr. Whiddle. Give me just a few minutes. I'll brew some coffee to warm you up."

"Thank you, Mrs. Reese."

The two men sat facing each other. "I hope there isn't bad news," said John.

"No, not at all," said Whiddle. "I came to tell you we've voted to accept your offer of $825. You have forty-five days to close the deal." He smiled at John.

Katie dropped a spoon in the kitchen. It clattered to the floor.

A huge grin spread over John's face. His mind calculated the days. "Today is February 6th, so forty-five days from today is—let's see—twenty-eight days in February—that makes it March 23rd. Is that right?"

"That's what I figured. Since it's late tonight and you can't do anything about this until tomorrow, let's say you have until March 24th to close. We want to be fair and open."

Katie soon came in with a hot cup of coffee and handed it to Whiddle. "Drink this before you go back into the cold, sir."

"Thank you, Mrs. Reese."

He turned to John and hesitated. "There's something else we need to talk about."

"What is that?"

"I was visited by two horrible men who said they represented our original buyer. They tried to pay me for the building. They wanted me to sign the deed. But I refused, and they made threats against you."

"I'm already aware of those fellows. Those two and a third man molested my wife and kidnapped my son today. The sheriff and I went after them and got Steven back."

Whiddle stared at him in shock. "Then they were quite serious about their threats."

"Deadly serious."

Whiddle lifted his coffee cup to his lips and blew gently. "Since this has become a legal problem, the board has decided to approach Attorney Wolf to find out what we have to do to get out of the contract with Skinner."

John smiled. "Attorney Wolf is my stepfather."

"Are you serious? That's quite a coincidence." Whiddle sipped his coffee.

"Let me ask why you want out of that agreement since he was willing to pay much more than I was."

Whiddle blushed. He explained about the buyer being convicted of bank robbery and wanting to open a saloon in the building, not a shoe store, as he led them to believe.

John's lips formed an O. He grinned and nodded his understanding.

"John, I'd like to ask you a question that's none of my business, so I won't be offended if you'd rather not answer. What was that rumor about you in a court hearing a few weeks ago? You seem like a man who wouldn't be involved in anything underhanded."

It was John's turn to blush. He dropped his head. "I wonder how long I'll have to deal with this," he said. "Sin doesn't want to disappear so easily."

"If you'd rather not talk about it…."

He decided to confess to his guest. "I'm afraid it's true, Mr. Whiddle, but I'm not the same man I was then. The old John Reese used some pretty ugly tactics to make extra money off my father's estate, but during the court hearing, I was forced to look at myself realistically. It wasn't pretty. Faced with that, I repented, and God is changing me every day. But I'm still suffering the consequences of what I did."

Kate reached over and put her hand on his. "He's telling the truth, Mr. Whiddle. John is a different man now than even a month ago." Whiddle peered at her over his spectacles and smiled.

"Thank you for telling me that. I believe you. I'll keep you informed about what Attorney Wolf has to say. And I do wish you the best of luck getting your finances in order so we can close on that building. I promise my wife will be one of your best customers."

He finished his coffee and left, then John grabbed Kate around the waist and spun her around. "We did it. We did it."

"Yes, all three of us," she said. "You, me, and God." She stepped away from him and became serious. "Now we only have to deal with those dangerous criminals."

Chapter 18: THE THREAT

Marcus Donovan entered the office of Attorney Christian Wolf. The attorney rose from his chair and extended his hand with a grin. "Marcus, I haven't seen you in years. What brings you to my office?"

"I wish this was a social call, Christian. I'm here on behalf of Wesleyan Church in Spencer's Mill. We have a legal problem involving your stepson, John."

Christian's face fell. "Has he done something to offend you?"

"Oh, my, no," said Donovan. "He's made an offer on our building, and we wish him every success in getting his finances ready to open that new bakery in town. But there's a wrinkle."

He explained the whole situation. Christian didn't know that the original buyers had already abducted Steven to get John's cooperation.

Christian gasped, and his knees went weak. "Oh, my. That will upset my wife. I dread telling her that. What would you like me to do for you?"

"We need some advice. Can we legally continue our sale with Mr. Reese? Or do we need to hold off until the problem with Skinner is resolved?"

Christian leaned back and thought for a moment. "I know saloons operate openly in Lamar, but since Ohio is a home-rule state, the village of Spencer's Mill has the right to pass laws independent of the rest of the county. I'll do a review. If a saloon is illegal in the village, that nullifies your agreement—unless Skinner were to open a shoe shop." He snickered at that far-fetched idea.

"What can we do to protect ourselves in the meantime?"

"Keep your eyes open, your doors locked, and your weapons loaded. I'll work as quickly as I can."

"We appreciate that."

"You're not completely out of danger," Christian cautioned him. "If Skinner has two buddies willing to travel from Columbus to Spencer's Mill to do his bidding, there could be more." He leaned forward and folded his hands on his desk.

"Isn't there court testimony that he intended to open a saloon?"

"Yes, and that will be a helpful piece of information."

"I'd be very grateful for whatever you can do, Christian. And it's good to see you again."

That afternoon, Christian conferred with Sheriff Beeler. He learned that the three men had been recaptured. They were charged with kidnapping and stealing a milk wagon and two horses. Skinner and Beadle were on their way to the Ohio state prison. Skinner was awaiting a second court appearance on the new charges. Houlahan was in the county jail to begin serving his sentence for bank robbery. The two thugs hired by Skinner were also in the county jail, awaiting an appearance before the judge on the charges of kidnapping and theft.

Christian exhaled slowly through pursed lips. John's family was safe.

At the courthouse the following day, he found a copy of the statutes of Spencer's Mill. No business selling liquor was permitted within the village. Christian smiled. He would tell John and Kate that they were legally cleared to buy that building. If Skinner ever filed a lawsuit—unlikely since he was a guest of the State of Ohio for the next seven years—it would be a case easy to defeat.

Chapter 19: GEORGE AND SALLY

Monday, February 7, 1887

At the general store, Danny Reese was behind the counter, waiting on a customer. As he worked on her order, an older couple came in and stomped the snow off their boots. The lady pulled off a red knitted scarf that protected her neck and shook it, sending a gentle cascade of snow to the floor.

"Be with you in a minute, folks," Danny said and finished with the first customer.

The couple shivered. It was too cold outside to be on a pleasure trip. A team of draft horses was pulling their canvas-covered wagon. Danny guessed they were hauling a lot of weight.

"I can help you now," he said.

"We need directions to Lamar," said the man. "We think we're lost."

"No, sir, you're on exactly the right road. Just keep going for fifteen miles. You'll see some pointing signs along the way. Are you looking for any place in particular?"

"We're looking to buy a home there," said the man. He was tall, balding, and had the hands of a man who worked the fields for a living. "We're from Indiana. We were there caring for my wife's sick mother, but she passed away five months ago. We sold her farm and want to be near our daughter. From what she told us, she lives on the west side of Lamar. By the way, my name is George Evans. This is my wife, Sally."

"It's a pleasure to meet you. I'm Danny Reese. Coincidentally, my wife and I plan to move out west this summer after school is out. We learned you can buy good farmland there at a low price."

"That's true," said George. "Land goes cheap in Indiana and Illinois. We're concerned that with the price we got for our house, we might be unable to find a suitable place we can afford. Prices seem much higher here, so we may have to get a smaller house than we're used to. I don't know where we'll put all the furniture in our wagon. We brought it with us only because we didn't want to leave it behind in the house for somebody we didn't know."

An idea flashed into Danny's head. "If you have anything you want to sell, I could look at what you have. I might be able to buy it from you and put it up for sale here in the store."

"Say, we do have some extra things we won't need. Sally, what do you think about letting some of our excess go?

Sally was a plump woman in her fifties. Her hair was snow-white, and her cheeks were red from the cold. Danny thought that if Santa Claus had a wife, she might look like Mrs. Evans.

"There might be something if we could agree on a price," she said. "Let's take a look."

Danny threw on his coat and walked outside with them. The three went to the back of the wagon, and Mr. Evans lifted the canvas. The wagon was jammed with furniture, bedding, kitchen supplies, and farming tools. It was in such a jumble that it was difficult to look through.

Sally apologized for the confusion in their wagon. "It was packed neatly when we left Indiana, but over the miles of bumpy road...."

Danny nodded. "Of course."

"We have an extra bedstead that was my Ma's and some of her kitchen pots we packed up when I moved my things into the house. And there's that tall curio cabinet with glass doors. It's so big I wouldn't know what to do with it, but it was too good to leave behind."

She showed Danny where all the items were. The household goods they showed him were usable, but the best part was the curio cabinet. It was about six feet high, made of polished walnut with decorative carvings up the two front corners. Its claw feet were beautifully carved. Glassed-in double doors protected the deep shelves. George showed him the carved cornice that would sit on top. One of the door knobs was missing, but that could be replaced. Danny thought Mr. Link might want to use that to display merchandise.

"I think we could sell these things in the store. What are you asking?"

The friendly dickering began. After the appropriate back-and-forth, they agreed on a price, and both sides were pleased.

Danny paid them out of the cash drawer. After struggling with boxes and that large cabinet, everything was inside the store.

"Mr. Evans, if you're looking for a house in Lamar, let me give you the name of a man you should talk to. His name is Oliver Hardin. He's well known as the expert on Bledsoe County real estate and can steer you in the right direction." He wrote down Hardin's address on a scrap of paper.

"Much obliged, Reese," said Evans. "We'll get in touch with him."

"It was good to meet you folks. I hope to see you again sometime. Welcome to Ohio."

They shook hands and parted, both delighted with their good fortune. The wagon pulled away and headed east toward Lamar.

A few minutes later, Mr. Link, the store owner, came in from lunch and stopped short. "What in the world—?"

The curio cabinet dominated his sales area, along with the bedframe and the crates of kitchenware. His forehead wrinkled, and his eyes narrowed. "Why have you cluttered up the store?"

Danny beamed with pride. "Mr. Link, I bought these items from a couple moving to Lamar from Indiana. And I know where to sell them at a profit—well, maybe not the bed. If you want to keep the cabinet to display items for sale, you can keep it, but I think I can sell it at a profit, too."

Mr. Link put his angst on hold long enough to hear Danny out. The boy had never done him wrong before. "Where can you sell it?"

"My brother John. He and his wife are opening a bakery, and they'll need all those kitchen supplies. And if you don't want that curio cabinet, look at those nice deep shelves. Perfect for displaying fresh bread and cakes, don't you think?"

A slow smile crossed Mr. Link's face. "Good thinking, Danny. I hope your brother agrees."

"I'll see him after work today and tell him about this stuff. Do you mind if we keep the cabinet in the storeroom temporarily until they close on the purchase of their store?"

"Where did you say their store is going to be?"

"Why, right next door in the old carpenter's shop."

Chapter 20: SUCCESS AND DISASTER

John enjoyed bursts of energy and optimism as he approached Lamar. Things were working out well. His family was safe, and he was legally cleared to buy the store. His main reason for today's journey was applying for a bank loan. Ginger trotted along, and they made good time.

But fortunes can change at a moment's notice. He didn't see the hole in the road until Ginger stumbled. John's eyes bulged, and he pulled on the reins, shouting, "Whoa, whoa!" Ginger went down with a sickening crunch, neighing in fright, as John was thrown from the saddle. He landed heavily on his shoulder in the mud and snow, stunned and in pain. Ginger thrashed around with wild, glassy eyes.

John got up as quickly as his pain allowed but took a moment for his head to clear. He stroked Ginger's neck to calm her down. She couldn't be calmed; one of her legs was broken. It flopped wildly as she kicked. This wasn't good. John's heart was grieved to realize he would have to put her down. For several years, she had been a faithful horse. She had taken him back and forth to work hundreds of times.

He freed her from the saddle and duffel, and tossed them under the nearby tree. He continued petting her neck, speaking gently to her, but he couldn't allow her to continue suffering. He covered her shoulder with the saddle blanket, then offered her some sugar cubes, putting off the inevitable.

He was heartsick, but the time had come. His soft words had calmed her only a little. He reached for his Pa's old percussion muzzleloader he carried on road trips and filled it with black powder and a ball. Then he approached his beloved horse from behind her head, hoping she wouldn't see him. With tears pouring down his face, he raised his weapon and pulled the trigger. It was a heavy pull. The ball shot out the barrel with a blaze of fire and a thunderous boom echoing through the woods. White smoke filled the air. As the haze cleared, Ginger twitched, then became still. John knelt and petted her neck one last time, shaking with grief. He knelt by her side for several minutes, tears streaming down his cheeks.

It would be a mile's walk to Lamar. He was cold, muddy, distraught, and in pain. In addition, he had to carry his rifle. Why do these things happen? He had such grand plans for today. He could only hope someone would come by and give him a ride. He needed to find some way to take care of Ginger's carcass. He remembered a rendering plant south of town. He would ask Christian to borrow his horse long enough to visit the renderer.

The walk was grueling. Every step jarred his injured shoulder, but he finally reached Christian's law office. He walked in, injured, wet, and muddy. Christian was busy with a client, so John stood in the lobby to wait for him. He couldn't soil those expensive chairs with his dirty clothes. It took all his strength to stand and wait.

Finally, the client left, giving John a sideways look as he passed through the reception area.

When Christian came out of his office, his mouth flew open. "John, what in the world happened to you? Take your coat off, man, and let's clean you up."

John wiggled out of his coat, favoring the sore shoulder. Christian took it outside and tried to knock some of the mud off.

Some clods dropped off, but the rest was still too wet. He took the coat back inside and laid it over the back of a wooden chair near the potbelly stove.

"Now, man, tell me what happened."

John shook his head slowly. "The church agreed to sell us the store at the price we wanted, so I was on my way to the bank to apply for a loan. But a mile back, my horse stepped into a hole and broke her leg. I was thrown from the saddle into the mud. I put her out of her suffering and walked the rest of the way, but she's still lying in the road."

Wolf jumped into action. "I don't have any client appointments for a while. Let's take my carriage to the rendering plant and tell them where they can pick up your horse. We need to find you another one to get you home."

"I need to go to the bank to get the money to buy another horse. I don't have that much cash with me."

"Let me tell my clerk where I'll be. He'll take care of the office."

As Wolf gave instructions to his clerk down the hall, John struggled to get his wet coat back on. Wolf returned to the reception area. "Take that coat off, John. I've borrowed my clerk's coat for the afternoon. You can use mine."

John smiled with relief. "That's quite a blessing. Thank you." He took the coat offered him and slowly wiggled into it. "I'm afraid I wrenched my shoulder when I hit the ground."

Wolf nodded. "We'll be careful of it as we travel. Let's go to the bank first and take care of your business there. Then we'll head to the rendering plant and tell them where they can pick up the horse."

He remembered something. "Give me a moment to pick up some papers from my desk. We may need them if you're applying for a loan."

The men climbed into Christian's carriage and headed

toward First Ohio Bank. The temperature had risen, and the snow had turned to slush, but the air was still nippy. John was relieved to be under the wing of someone willing to give him aid. And to think, this was the same man he had tried to sabotage last year to get control of his father's estate. He blushed at the thought.

Reaching the bank, they went inside, stomping the snow off their boots. The warmth from the potbelly stove was a welcome relief.

"Good morning, Mr. Reese…Mr. Wolf," said the teller. "I presume you want to talk to Mr. McDonald. Go on over to his desk."

"Thank you."

The men exchanged pleasantries with the bank manager; then, John and Christian made themselves as comfortable as possible in those chairs at McDonald's desk.

"Christian. How nice to see you. I see you're here on a mission to help John. That's good."

"Nice to see you, too, but Frederick, when will you replace these chairs? These are awful." Christian wiggled his chair and tried to make it more comfortable.

McDonald's eyebrows drew together, and he cocked his head. "Really?" He walked around his desk. "Stand up, Christian, and let me try it myself."

John's muscles tensed, and he rubbed the nape of his neck as he witnessed the exchange between the other two men. This was no time to insult someone in a position to loan him money.

McDonald sat in the chair himself.

"This is miserable," he said and turned the chair upside down to inspect the bottom. "Why has no one told me this before? Maybe a shim right there would fix them up. If not, I'll have to replace them."

He returned to his side of the desk. John's mouth was agape

when he realized McDonald hadn't been offended.

"What's the good word, John? Are you buying that building?"

John's attention snapped back to his business. "Yes, we negotiated a purchase with the church for $825. Here's the signed contract."

McDonald studied the document. "Very good. I assume you're here to borrow enough money to buy the building."

"Yes, sir. I want to borrow $825 using my share of Pa's estate as collateral. We plan to sell our house and repay the loan as quickly as possible."

"I see. Well, the bank's policy prevents us from loaning one hundred percent of the real estate value. We can loan up to seventy-five percent."

John's heart sank. This may put them in an impossible situation. He would have to revise the budget again. "That's only – let's see – about $620. I don't know if we can tighten down that much. This may cancel our plans." His head throbbed. The day, which had already gone wrong, was turning worse.

"No, not seventy-five percent of the value of the property you're buying," said McDonald, smiling. "We'll do seventy-five percent of the value of the property you use as collateral. Let me have the appraisal figures on your father's holdings. We'll have to total it, deduct your mother's half, and take ten percent of the rest as your share. We can loan you seventy-five percent of that number."

Christian smiled. "I have the figures here. I picked them up before we left the office. The total appraised value comes to $20,500." He spread the appraisals out on the desk. McDonald added them to verify the figures and came to the same conclusion.

"Excellent. Half of $20,500 is $10,250. Mrs. Reese gets

$10,250, and ten children will share the other half equally."

Christian corrected him. "Mrs. Wolf, now. I married her."

McDonald continued without missing a beat. "Mrs. Wolf, then. That's $1,025 each, and we can loan seventy-five percent of that... round it off to $770. We'll take your loan application for $770, John."

"I appreciate that." It was a more workable figure.

Wolf intervened. "Would you do a personal favor for me, Frederick? John is in a temporary crunch until his house is sold. Can you move back the first payment for sixty days? That would help him and Kate a lot."

McDonald smiled. "For you, Christian, I'll do that. But don't let it get around. I'm not doing that for anyone else."

"Are you finished with those appraisal papers, Frederick? I'm going to need them myself."

McDonald handed the papers over to Christian. John leaned forward, propping himself on the edge of the desk. He answered some questions as a formality and signed over his share of his father's property as collateral. The last step was signing the loan agreement.

"What happens now?" asked John.

"I'll take this paperwork to the courthouse and file it, and as soon as that's done, we'll put the $770 into your bank account. It should be there by tomorrow."

John wanted to jump up and down for joy, temporarily forgetting the loss of his horse and the pain in his shoulder, but he maintained his dignity and kept his boots on the floor. He stood to shake the banker's hand and thanked Christian profusely. At the teller's window, he withdrew enough money from his savings to buy a horse to get himself back home.

John couldn't wait to give Katie the news. The loan was short of what he wanted, but he trusted the Lord to see them through that.

Christian put a hand on his shoulder. "Let's get to the rendering plant. Then we'll come back and look for another horse."

They traveled south on Main Street and into the outlying area. As they approached the rendering plant, the stench of waste animal tissue became more pronounced. How could anyone work in a facility like that?

They reported the death of Ginger and told the renderer where he could find the horse. John was naïve enough to think someone would sympathize with his loss of a beloved animal, but there was no such luck. This business dealt with dead animals every day, so it was just another transaction to them. John had a hollow, numb feeling in his gut. There should have been more ceremony to Ginger's final journey.

He would miss his horse. Maybe he would see her in heaven. He would have to find out if the Lord had animals there.

John and Christian headed back toward Lamar and went to the livery stable, where he bought another good horse. John was alarmed at the price—this wasn't in their budget.

"Trust God to take care of this for you, John," Christian said. "Last year, when I was in an impossible situation, He protected me and helped me find the solution. He'll do the same for you."

John nodded. He realized that Christian was kind enough not to mention that the cause of his impossible situation … was John.

They tethered the new horse to the back of Wolf's carriage and led him back to the office.

"I'll be closing the office at five o'clock," said Wolf. "If you want to wait until then, I'll take you to where you left your saddle. But if you're in a hurry, you could go bareback."

"Sir, if you don't mind, I'd like to stay here and wait for you. Since I don't know the horse, I don't want to jump on, especially with my hurt shoulder."

Wolf grinned. "I see your point. Feel free to make yourself comfortable."

John took a seat and fidgeted. If only he could contact Kate and tell her where he was. She would worry. He finally settled in and occupied his mind with thoughts of the bakery. He had missed lunch, and his stomach complained. The afternoon dragged on slowly, but the advantage was that his coat dried from the heat of the potbelly stove before he had to put it on and go out in the weather.

When Wolf was ready to leave, they closed the office and took off together, leading the new horse behind them. It didn't take long to reach John's saddle. The men from the rendering plant had already taken Ginger's body.

"Looks like there's no serious damage to your saddle," said Wolf. "Just a few scuffs. Let's get it on the horse. You haven't had anything to eat all day. Why don't you stop by the house? I'm sure your mother would love to feed you."

John grinned. "I could use a bowl of soup. Thank you, sir. I'll need to eat quickly because Katie doesn't know where I am. I'm sure she's worried. . . By the way, I want you to know I'm grateful for what you did. I don't know what I would have done if you hadn't offered to help me."

"No problem with that, son. And I think you need to start calling me Christian. We're family, you know."

"Thank you, sir."

Christian clucked his tongue, slapped the reigns, and headed home, following John on his horse. John stopped at the house with Christian long enough to have a bowl of hot soup and coffee; then, he was on the road again.

Earlier that afternoon, Kate wondered when John would return. He was later than she expected. He still wasn't home when Danny rapped on the door.

"Come on in," she said. "John's not here. He went to Lamar to apply for a loan. I expected him home hours ago. He must have run into some delay. Anyway, the church accepted our offer on the property."

"That's exciting news. And I have more exciting news for you." His eyes sparkled.

"Please, sit down and warm yourself for a few minutes. Would you like some tea while you tell me about it?"

Danny laughed. "You're just like Ma with the tea. No, thanks, I won't be that long. Here's the news: I met some people today with a wagon full of household goods. I bought some things from them—paid for them out of the store's cash box, and everything is for sale now. I thought you'd want to be the one to see it first. There are crates full of kitchen supplies—baking pans, at least two Dutch ovens, mixing bowls, and several pots—all kinds of stuff. I got it at a good price, so we can sell it to you cheap and still make a profit for Mr. Link."

Kate became increasingly excited as she thought about the equipment he could sell her. "Danny, that sounds wonderful. I would come right this minute before someone else buys it, but Steven isn't home from school yet, and John isn't home from the bank."

"Don't worry. I set aside the crates of kitchenware in the storeroom for you. No one else will see any of it until you look it over. But there's one other thing, too."

"What?"

"There's a big walnut curio cabinet, six feet tall, not counting the cornice on top, with deep shelves and glass doors. It's beautiful, Katie. Mr. Link is still deciding whether to keep it for himself, but it would make a perfect display case for fresh bread."

Kate's eyes lit up. "We're going to need a display case."

"Yes, I know. We're all looking out for you." He grinned at

her.

"John and I will look at everything in the morning after Steven goes to school."

"I'll look forward to seeing you there."

After Danny left, Kate snuggled onto the Chesterfield and tried to calm herself. Her swinging emotions—the low of this morning and now the high—were wearing her out. Maybe a good cup of tea would help.

Her nerves were tightly strung until Steven was home, remembering he had been grabbed the other day. John was still not there. She checked the window every few minutes to see if he was coming. The longer time stretched on, the more she worried. What if those thugs had held him up?

Later she cooked a meal and fed the children. The evening sun had already gone down, but there was still no sign of John. She was eager to tell him about the used kitchen equipment, and she wanted to find out if he was able to get a loan.

An hour later, John put his new horse away and then came into the house.

"John, I was worried sick. Where have you been?"

"It's a long story. Give me a few minutes to rest. Then I'll tell you the whole thing."

"Do you have good news?"

"Yes and no. Sort of," he said. He sounded weary. "We got a loan approved, but not for $825. I could only get $770. That will leave us in a serious budget pinch. But the other good news is, Christian went with me to the bank and convinced the bank manager to put off our first loan payment for sixty days."

"That's good, isn't it?" She wasn't sure what that meant.

"Yes, we won't have to make any payments until the bakery makes a profit. The bank doesn't generally do this for people. He only did it as a favor for Christian. Now I need to tell you the bad news."

Her head turned toward him in alarm. "There's bad news?"

"I had to put Ginger down. There was an accident on the way to Lamar. Ginger broke her leg, and I was thrown off. I landed on my shoulder. Healing may take some time."

"Let me see your shoulder."

He pulled off his coat and shirt. Some swelling and tenderness made it difficult to move his arm. The puffy skin was purple.

"I'd put a cold cloth on it, except you've been out in the cold, so it would probably have no effect. How did you get home?"

John told her about Christian's help, taking him to the bank, the rendering plant, and the livery stable to buy a horse. "The cost of the horse will take another bite out of our budget."

"That can't be helped. I'm sorry about Ginger. She's been with us for several years. That must have been a real blow to you. I know how you loved that horse." She paused and shook her head sadly. "Are you hungry?"

"No, I stopped by Ma and Christian's house. She gave me a bowl of vegetable soup."

Even though Kate wore a smile, her eyes were dull, and she was slow to move. John recognized the signs of fatigue.

"I have some good news," she said. "Danny was able to buy a lot of used kitchen supplies today—pots and pans, that sort of thing—and he's willing to sell them all to us cheap. They're at the general store in the back room. He says we can look at them before anyone else."

John grinned. "Wonderful. When can we take a look?"

"Tomorrow after Steven goes to school. And there's another thing that may be available if Mr. Link doesn't want it for himself. It's a big walnut cabinet with deep shelves and glass doors that Danny says would be a perfect display case for loaves of bread."

"His good luck must have been running high today. We'll

go over there first thing in the morning."

That night, lying beside John, Kate was restless. There were exciting visions of a fully operating bakery running through her head, stocked with loaves of sourdough bread, rolls of all kinds, pastries, and cakes. She imagined the bakery full of customers and the cash box springing open, then slamming shut with money bulging out almost non-stop. Her thoughts kept her from sleeping. She let her mind wander to the kitchen items that Danny had waiting for them and wondered how much more they would have to buy.

John slept soundly beside her.

Chapter 21: MAKING PROGRESS

Tuesday, February 8, 1887

The following morning, John and Kate bought all the kitchen equipment Danny had acquired from George and Sally Evans. At the sight of the curio cabinet, Kate moved toward it, sucking in a breath. She reached out and ran her hands over the contours of the carving on the corners. Later, she laughingly told a friend at church that she thought the angels sang when she first saw that cabinet.

Only one of the doors had a knob, so she pulled that one open to feel the depth of the shelves. "This is a beautiful piece of furniture, John. Do you think it would make a good display case?"

"It depends on how much the general store wants for it."

"Well, work it out with Danny. I love it. I hope we can afford it."

Danny took a moment to consider the price. He finally quoted a figure as favorable to his brother as possible, still being fair to Mr. Link.

John pursed his lips, then nodded. "We'll take the cabinet, Danny. I'll bring you the money after I go to the bank this afternoon. Can you hold our things until then?"

"I sure can, John. I'm glad you'll be able to use it."

"All right, brother. We'll see you later today. Hopefully, when I return, I'll have the key to the store next door, and we can move everything in."

"Sounds good. See you then. So long, Kate."

Kate's heart sang. That elegant cabinet was going to be their new display case.

John found himself traveling to Lamar for the second time in two days. He would be glad when all this riding back and forth was over. He wanted to clean up the store and get the supplies in. He was concerned about whether Kate could take the physical and emotional strain. She had been unusually pale lately, and her energy had been low.

Mile after mile, John passed landmarks as familiar as his street in Spencer's Mill. He prayed that yesterday's disaster wouldn't repeat itself. Finally reaching the bank after the long ride, he went inside to see Mr. McDonald.

"John, good to see you. Have a seat, and we'll finish up your loan."

John took a seat.

"We were able to fund the loan. Give me your bank book, and I'll make the entry."

John handed over the book, and McDonald added $770 to the existing balance, adding his initials with a flourish to make it official.

"How are things going with the bakery plans?"

"So far, so good," John said. "We bought some used equipment at a bargain price, and tomorrow we'll start cleaning up the store. We need to sell our house so I can pay down this loan. If you hear of anyone who needs a nice two-bedroom wood-frame house in Spencer's Mill, let them know about it, will you?"

"I will certainly remember to do that. And good luck with your new endeavor." He stood and grasped John's hand, shaking it with enthusiasm.

John walked to the teller's window and withdrew enough cash from his account to pay for the store and the supplies bought from Danny. That left the balance uncomfortably low. He counted the bills and slid them into the pouch he brought, tucking it into his shirt for safekeeping. That money was their whole future.

John started for home, urging the horse as fast as he dared. He didn't like carrying that much cash, especially after his recent experience with the kidnappers. He wouldn't have worried a month ago, but times change. Arriving in Spencer's Mill, he went straight to the church, hoping to find the pastor still there. He was in luck.

"Good afternoon, John," said Reverend Buchanan. "Whiddle tells me you're buying our Main Street building. Congratulations, and best wishes for a successful business."

"Thank you, sir. I have the money with me to complete the purchase. I want to pay you and get the key to start cleaning the place."

"Oh, no, please; I can't have that much cash in the office. I'd much rather you went to Mr. Whiddle's home and paid it to him. But I can give you the key. You're welcome to go in and clean it up. I trust you to finish the transaction with Whiddle."

John accepted the key but was grieved that he couldn't relieve himself of that cash. He didn't feel safe carrying it.

"I hope the building is all that you need it to be for years to come."

"Thank you, sir. And we'd appreciate it if you'd pass the word that there will be a new bakery in town in a few weeks." John shook his hand and left the bulging pouch under his shirt. He turned his horse to the general store to pay Danny for the kitchen supplies and cabinet, but Danny had already gone home for the day, so John went home to Kate.

"How did it go, John?"

"Not quite the way I expected," he said, peeling off his coat. "I got the money, but Reverend Buchanan wouldn't take it. He didn't want to be responsible for that much cash in his office. I have to take it to Whiddle's house after he gets home from work. And I went by the general store to pay for the kitchen equipment, but Danny wasn't there, so I came here. I do have the key to our bakery." He grinned and dangled the key in front of her.

She giggled with delight. "So tomorrow we can start work?"

"Absolutely."

"Let's sit down and have some dinner. I have a pot of stew ready."

After dinner, the winter sky was already dark, but John needed to visit the Whiddles anyway. He took a lantern, saddled up, and rode to their house with the precious package under his shirt. His eyes darted from one side of the road to the other, checking for signs of movement. He was sharply aware of everything around him. He had vivid memories of the thugs who kidnapped Steven, who would gladly relieve him of the money he carried.

Light from the lantern illuminated the large, wet snowflakes coming down heavily. Snow piled up on John's hat and coat sleeves and blew about the horse's hooves as he traveled.

When he knocked on the door of the Whiddle home, Mrs. Whiddle opened the door. It was a beautifully appointed home with a fireplace spreading its warmth.

"Yes?" she asked.

"I'm here to see Mr. Whiddle, please," said John.

"Let the young man in, dear," said a strong voice in the background. "Come in, Mr. Reese. It's good to see you."

"Thank you, sir." He stepped into the foyer and shook the snow off his hat. "I came to let you know that I got the loan from the bank, and I'd like to pay you for the building. Do you have time to complete the sale tonight?"

"Yes, we can do that," Whiddle said. "You brought the money?"

"Yes, sir."

"Come into my study down the hall. We can do business there."

"I need a receipt for the money, and you can record the deed at your earliest convenience."

"I'll do better than that, son. I'll sign the deed and give it to you. Will that be as good as a receipt? You can record it yourself. That way, you'll know the job has been done."

"That would be just fine," said John with a smile.

Whiddle's study walls were lined with bookcases full of important-looking volumes. The desk was polished mahogany, and the floor was covered with a Persian rug. When the two men completed the paperwork, John reached into his shirt, pulled out his pouch, and passed over the cash. Whiddle signed the deed and handed it to John.

John grinned and took a deep breath. "I feel like a load has been lifted now that I don't have to carry that money around. Thank you, sir." They shook hands, and he went home with a clearer mind and a thankful heart. He and Kate were the owners of a store and a new apartment. That was a little scary now that it was a reality.

Chapter 22: GEORGE AND SALLY'S PREDICAMENT

That same day, George and Sally Evans visited Oliver Hardin.

"Can I help you folks?" asked Hardin when he opened the door to strangers.

"I hope so," said Evans. "Danny Reese gave us your name. We're moving to this area from Indiana and need to buy a home. Danny said you could help us."

Hardin smiled. "Come on in. I believe I can. Please take off your coats and have a seat. What specifically are you looking for?"

"We want to be near our daughter, who lives on the west side of Lamar. We want two bedrooms. We drove around Lamar a bit and were disappointed that it was full of those noisy oil wells and dirty steam locomotives. We thought this would be a cleaner place to live."

Hardin chuckled. "Yes, those of us living in Lamar overlook the dirt and noise after it becomes such a part of daily life. I suppose we consider it a minor annoyance necessary for our prosperity. But I can show you a few houses out on the edge of town that might suit you better. What's your budget?"

"We're afraid our cash may not go very far. We only have $600," said Evans.

Hardin sucked in his breath. "You're right. That won't go very far around here," he said. "But let's see if we can find something. If you want to return in a couple of days, I'll make some inquiries. Where are you staying if I need to contact you?"

"We're staying with our daughter," Mrs. Evans said and gave him the address on McDonnell Street.

Chapter 23: FAMILY TIME WITHOUT ELI

Wednesday, February 9, 1887

The following day after Steven went to school, John and Kate sprang into action. They loaded Gracie, some firewood, and cleaning supplies. Then John guided the carriage to their new store and tied the horse to the rail. They stood in the slush at the street's edge, facing their store, and looked at each other, grinning. This was a significant moment in their lives, one they would never forget.

John pulled the key out of his pocket and jiggled it before Kate's face. They giggled like children and shared a heady moment as he worked the key into the lock for the first time. John turned the doorknob and pushed. The door resisted but finally yielded to his pressure and opened with a long squeak. This was it-- their new store, their new home.

They stepped inside, holding hands with Gracie and surveying their property. Funny, it had a different feel now that it was theirs. It held real promise.

The day went quickly. John enlisted Danny's help to bring their purchases over from the general store next door; then, he went to work cleaning the future sales room. Gracie helped by picking up wood scraps scattered around the work area. Kate scrubbed the kitchen cabinets and floor while John swept all the dirt and sawdust from the front room where the customers would come in. He had to work around the treadle lathe, band saw, planing bench, and other tools.

Later in the morning, Susannah entered the store carrying a picnic basket.

John welcomed her with a hug. "Ma, how did you know where to find us?"

"It was easy, son," she said. "Christian said you'd be closing on the sale of the building. I made lunch and thought I would probably find you here." She gazed all around, her face betraying dismay at the condition of the walls and ceiling.

"So. . . look at all this. Look at how dirty it is."

"It's filthy," John said. "Can you believe the carpenter died without cleaning it up first?" John said it lightly to be funny, but Susannah didn't recognize his flash of wit.

"Hello," Kate called from the kitchen. "Come see what we have in here."

Susannah carried her casserole dish into the kitchen. "This is amazing. Look at that huge pantry and the big fireplace. But you'll need some help cleaning this up, won't you?" she asked. "Why don't you all take a break? We'll have some lunch. Then I'll help with the work."

John leaned around the doorway. "What do you think, Ma? Do you think we can sell bread in here?"

"John, I think you could sell firewood in the jungle with your sales skills."

He laughed. "I'm glad you brought some food. Let's eat."

After a quick lunch, John took his mother on a tour of the upper floor. "This room will be the parlor, and here is our bedroom. As long as the children are small, they can share another room, and I'll keep one room for my office."

"It looks like it will work," said Susannah. "But John, this is such a small space for your family."

"We thought of that. So we plan to partition off a section of the downstairs to use as our private dining room with plenty of extra room for the children to play."

Susannah smiled and nodded. "That will increase your living area. I'll ask Christian if we can come on Saturday," she said. "Maybe we'll be able to help."

Saturday, February 12, 1887

It was the second Saturday in February, three weeks before the grand opening. The pressure was mounting, and there was still an overwhelming amount of cleaning and painting. John and Kate sat at the table in the kitchen and outlined the day's projects. John glanced at his wife. Her face was pale, and her eyes lacked that spark he loved to see.

"I'm concerned about you, Katie. You look weary, and the day's work hasn't even begun."

"I am tired, John. I'm tired clear to my bones, and my stomach is in an uproar. But I'll find some way to keep going. It's just that I still have all the work I had before, cooking and doing laundry for the family's daily needs while trying to get the store ready to open."

He grasped her hand. "We'll get you some help soon, I promise. You're working hard, and overdoing it is asking for trouble. I don't want you pushing yourself so hard you get sick."

"I need you to solve this problem quickly, John. I'm already sick."

"This is a priority, but I don't know anyone qualified."

Kate pushed her point. "I'm getting desperate, John. This is a serious situation."

"I hear what you're saying. I'll keep working on it."

She nodded.

John had laid out his plans in writing. It was a detailed schedule leading up to the Grand Opening, so he wouldn't miss anything. According to his schedule, it was time to order a Grand Opening banner from the print shop. It would announce free cinnamon bread knots on opening day. He planned to have it stretch across the storefront, which was being cleaned, and the trim freshly painted. The problem holding them up was that they still didn't have a name for the bakery, and that was a detail that needed prompt attention. Until they named it, they couldn't print the sign, put the ad in the paper, or have fliers made to be posted all over town. He hoped to address that issue today.

John and Kate were at the store with their children by 8:30 on Saturday morning. Kate had already lost her breakfast and felt ill, but she was determined to carry on. She sent Steven out back to get some wood for heat.

As she was sponging grime off the inside of the front windows, Susannah and Christian's carriage rolled toward the bakery, followed by Danny and Charlotte. John's sister Matilda and her husband Joshua came from the other direction and tied their horses to the rail.

Kate said, "John, look who's coming."

John welcomed them all as they filed in. "Did you come to see the new store?"

"No," Matilda told him, an amused smile playing around her lips. "We came to clean the store and help get it ready for business." She pulled John aside to speak to him privately. "John, it's been a battle to forgive you, but Josh and I finally worked through it. We wish you the best with the bakery."

John was profoundly grateful, considering how recently they had discovered his betrayal. They were there by an act of mercy and grace.

Susannah had enough food to supply lunch for the entire group.

Christian brought paint with him to cover the downstairs walls and went to work with his paintbrush. "This isn't my regular line of work," he said, "but I had plenty of experience at this in my younger days trying to work my way through law school." His labor slowly turned a shabby-looking room into a bright, inviting sales area.

John asked Danny and Josh to help him move the old carpenter's tools to the barn. Within a half-hour, all the tools were moved out of the store. Only the carved walnut display case was left, an imposing piece of furniture against the freshly painted wall.

After working through the morning, Susannah spread out lunch for her family. They sat down together to eat.

"I wish Eli and Mary were here," she said. "They're missing a family experience, and I miss them."

"I do, too, Ma," John said. "Eli has changed since the court hearing. I can't say that I blame him. It's my fault."

"It was your fault that he became angry," his mother told him, "but you made the hard changes in your life. Your life in the weeks since then has been different. Give Eli some time. Then, if he doesn't forgive, it's his fault. We'll keep praying for him and treat him gently."

John nodded. She was right, but guilt stabbed his heart. He had hurt his brother deeply. Eli had been too eager to accept his lies at face value and was devastated when he learned his brother had been deceiving all of them. This was a family problem that could only be healed by divine intervention.

As they conversed over the meal, the subject of the bakery's name came up.

"We haven't decided what to call the bakery," said Kate, who had begun to feel well enough to eat something. "Does anyone have any suggestions?"

Charlotte said, "How about The Staff of Life?"

"That sounds like bread. We need something to describe both bread and pastries," said John.

Danny had a mouthful of ham sandwich. "Wait a minute," he said. Then he swallowed. "I have an idea. What about 'The Baguette'?"

"Aw, that's too fussy. It would sound fine in Philadelphia, but I don't think it would fit Spencer's Mill very well. Any other ideas?"

Christian said, "You could call it the Spencer's Mill Bakery." He was a practical man.

"What about 'Bread and Cakes'?—Just tossing out ideas," said Matilda.

Joshua laughed. "Here's a funny one. Instead of Bread and Cakes, you could call it 'Crust and Crumb.'"

No one else laughed. There was a brief silence as they all studied one another's smiling faces, and finally, their eyes met in mutual agreement.

"The Crust and Crumb?" Kate repeated. "That's delightful. What do you think, John?"

"It might just grow on me," he said. "I can visualize it painted on the front of the store."

"I think you hit on something, Josh," said Susannah. "I like it."

They all liked it. The Crust and Crumb Bakery. It was a consensus.

After lunch, the family tackled the upstairs, mopping floors and painting. When they left later that afternoon, the upstairs apartment was ready to have furniture moved in. As Christian cleaned up his brushes, he told John, "Your mother said something about putting up a partition."

"Yes, it'll go right over there along the stairs. We'll put a door in it, so we'll have access to the apartment from the store and still be able to go up and down the stairs in privacy."

"That idea sounds workable. When are you planning to do that?"

"I hope to get it done this week so we can move in. I want a grand opening for the bakery by the first Saturday in March. Our money will run thin if we don't start generating some income."

"If you get the materials, I'll come to help you some afternoon. I can leave the office early one day."

"I appreciate the offer. I'll buy the wood for the studs, lath, and plaster. How does next Wednesday sound?"

"Sounds fine. I'll leave the office at noon. If I come on horseback, I can be here by about 2:00 or 2:30. Then we can work for a few hours."

It was a good day's work. Except for the partition, the bakery stood ready for the family to move in. A sign needed to be painted on the front, and Kate needed to stock the pantry. John's most urgent task was hiring some help. It was already the 13th of February, and they wanted to open in three weeks. The pressure was mounting.

Chapter 24: FIRST NIGHT OVER THE BAKERY

Monday, February 14, 1887

On Monday morning, John hitched up a wagon borrowed from Christian. He had errands in Lamar and worried it would take most of the day. His first stop would be the sawmill. He also needed to run an errand at the bank, order fliers at the print shop, and record his deed at the courthouse.

At the sawmill, John talked with the owner about his needs. "My wife and I just bought a building we want to remodel. I need to put up a twelve-foot wall with a door about midway. Can you tell me what I'll need to frame it in and put in the lath and plaster?"

"Come into my office. Let's sit down and figure this out," said Mr. Jackson. As he started his estimate, he made small talk. "Where's your building?" he asked.

"It's on Main Street in Spencer's Mill. My wife and I are opening a bakery there."

Jackson's head raised to get a good look at John. "You don't say. You must be John Reese."

John's chin dropped. "How did you know?"

Jackson grinned. "I'm on the Board of Trustees at Wesleyan Church. I voted to accept your offer."

"Let me shake your hand, sir," John said, thrusting out his hand. The two men shook like they had been friends for years.

"Okay, back to your project." Jackson finished his calculations and pushed his paper over to John. "Does this look about right to you?" He had priced the studs, nails, lath, powdered limestone, sand, and a bag of horsehair for the plaster. There was also an interior door, doorknobs, and hinges.

"One more thing I just remembered," John told him. "Do you have two matching knobs? I need them for doors on the front of a display case."

"Yes, I have them in plain brass or faceted glass."

"Give me the glass ones."

John took his load of wood and other supplies and drove to the bank to make a withdrawal. That was where he ran into Oliver Hardin, who greeted him with a grin and clapped him on the back.

"How did you ever make out with that store?" Oliver asked.

John smiled. "Kate and I bought that store at your appraised price, and it's cleaned up, ready to move in. We still have a lot of work to do, but we hope to have a grand opening by the first Saturday of March."

"Congratulations, John. I wish you the best of luck."

"Thanks." John turned to leave.

"Wait a minute, Reese," called Hardin. "Let me ask you about your house. Is it still for sale?"

John sighed. "Yes, unfortunately, we haven't found a buyer yet."

"I ran into a couple a few days ago, just moving to the area. They're looking for a two-bedroom. I've searched all over Lamar and can't find anything in their price range. I was wondering about yours. They might be ready to look at something further out."

"How much are they looking to spend?"

"Six hundred."

John's eyebrows went up. "That's too low. I don't think we

can do that. You appraised our house at $650. I couldn't get a loan for as much as I had hoped, so our cash is tight. We need everything we can get out of the house. We still have to stock supplies and hire help to run the bakery."

"That's tough. I'm sorry to hear that. Well, good luck."

"Thanks, Oliver. Stop by the bakery and see what we've done to the building the next time you're in Spencer's Mill."

"I'll do that." Hardin turned and left with a grin and a wave.

John's next stop was the print shop to order the Grand Opening banner and fliers. They would announce the opening of the Crust and Crumb Bakery and offer free cinnamon bread knots to everyone who came in on Grand Opening day. He would pick up the fliers in a week. After a final stop at the courthouse to record the deed, he turned his horses toward Spencer's Mill and took his building supplies to the bakery.

That day, after Danny's shift at the general store, he came next door and helped his brother unload his wood and supplies. Later, the two brothers moved the bedroom furniture and parlor chairs from the house to the bakery apartment.

That night, John's family spent their first night in their new home. It was a special family time. The children explored every corner of the apartment while Kate spread the sheets and quilts over the mattresses. Her strength nearly failed her. She was desperately weary and relieved to at last get under the covers.

John's muscles ached from the strenuous activity of the past few days. He burrowed under the sheets and quickly went into a deep sleep.

In the morning, John and Kate were hard at it again. The following two weeks would be full of frantic activity. The family loaded into the wagon, dropped Steven off at school, and went to the old house to finish loading their furniture from the parlor and the kitchen.

Again, they discussed Kate's immediate need for help, but neither could think of anyone suitable. The problem was becoming critical. John was fearful that Kate's health would break down.

Chapter 25: BUILDING THE PARTITION

Wednesday, February 16, 1887

On Wednesday afternoon, Christian came as promised, and Gracie ran to him. "Grandpa!" He laughed and picked her up, swinging her high above his head. That was the first time that one of Susannah's grandchildren called him Grandpa.

The girl giggled and ran to her mother. "Mama, Grandpa made me fly up high."

Kate grinned. "You need to leave Grandpa alone now. He has work to do with Papa."

"Let's get busy with that wall, John," said Christian. "I brought my tools with me."

The two men busied themselves measuring and cutting the wall studs. The work went about as fast as molasses dripping from a long-neck bottle.

After a while, John stopped. "This cutting is taking too long, and I just remembered the carpenter's treadle saw out in the horse barn. Why don't we bring that in and use it?"

Christian shook his head and laughed. "We were fools not to think of that earlier." It took two of them to bring it in, and within a couple of hours, they had the beginnings of a wall. They framed where the door would go and put a transom window over it.

"I don't know how much time you have to spend here, sir. Is it time to put away our tools, or can we start the lath?" John asked.

"Let me have a few minutes to take a break," Christian said. "I'm not used to this kind of physical work. Oh, by the way, your mother will be here soon with some dinner."

Kate was relieved to learn she wouldn't have to cook. She was unbelievably weary, almost to the point of tears. The demanding work of the last few weeks had caught up with her. She was putting up a good front for John's sake. He didn't know she was on the very edge of breaking down.

John smiled. "Please take a break, Christian. I'll cut a few four-foot pieces of lath so we can start tacking them to the wall studs. Kate, do you think you could get some tea for us?"

"Of course." She moved around the kitchen mechanically, tears dampening her cheeks, longing only to lie down. Silently, she begged the Lord for help.

The Evanses had no luck finding a home in their price range. Even though they didn't care for Lamar's dirt and oil wells, they determined to stay there to be close to their daughter. But to do that, they would need jobs to pay for a mortgage. They couldn't find immediate work in Lamar, so they drove back to Spencer's Mill.

The bell over the door at the general store tinkled.

"Hello, Danny."

"Well, friends, I'm surprised to see you back in Spencer's Mill. What brings you? Have you found a house yet?" Danny asked. He was working a few extra hours for Mr. Link.

George Evans shook his head. "We didn't realize how expensive real estate was around here," he said. "We're getting pretty discouraged. We only have $600. We haven't found anything less than $700, and that was a small house way outside

Lamar. We talked to your friend Oliver Hardin, but he hasn't been able to help."

"We don't know what to do," said Sally. "Our daughter is gracious enough to let us stay with her, but that can only be temporary. We know we're making things crowded in her little house."

"I'm sorry to hear that," Danny said. "I completely understand. I'm fortunate that life with my father-in-law is going well."

"We're looking for work to afford mortgage payments since we'll have to spend more than we have. We're going to need jobs pretty quickly. Do you need any help here in the store?"

"I'm sorry, we don't, at least not until June. That's four months from now. What kind of experience do you have?"

"I'm a retired farmer, and Sally here used to waitress in a restaurant back in Indiana."

"My brother is looking for help in the bakery if you can wait until the end of the month."

"We were hoping for something before that."

"Why don't you ask around at the other merchants here in town? Maybe the butcher would need some help."

"I'll check."

"Wait, why don't you go next door anyway? Tell my brother John that you're available for work. He's remodeling the store, and he's under pressure to get it done before Grand Opening."

Evans brightened. "I can do construction work. It would be something to fill in, anyway. Thanks, Danny. We'll see you later."

Sally gave him a little wave as they turned to leave. The bell tinkled again, and they were gone.

"What do you think, Sally?" asked George as they stood on the sidewalk. "Do you think we should introduce ourselves to Danny's brother next door?"

"It can't hurt," she replied. "Then we'll have to head back to Lamar. We're already too late for dinner. Maybe Jennie will save us a bite to eat."

They went next door to the bakery-in-progress. They found themselves in a sawdust-laden work area with a young man busy cutting lath, a tall older man sitting on a crate drinking tea, and Sally's mother's cabinet standing proudly against one wall.

"Look, George, it's Mother's curio cabinet." Sally was irresistibly drawn to it, running her hands over the trim. "I didn't think I'd ever see it again. And it has new knobs."

John turned toward the newcomers. He tilted his head as he peered at them. "I hope I haven't caused trouble by buying that cabinet. I paid a fair price for it."

"Not at all. We didn't think we'd ever see it again. We're looking for John Reese," said George. "Danny next door sent us over."

John brushed his hands on his pants and approached George with an outstretched hand. "I'm John Reese," he said. They shook hands while Sally, still looking like Mrs. Claus, stood by with a smile on her cherubic face.

"Danny says you might be looking for some help. We're looking for a little work. We're here from Indiana, needing a house in Lamar, but we don't have enough money to buy a decent place. We're staying with our daughter Jennie until we can save enough money to buy a home."

"I might be able to find some temporary work for you until we get the store open in two weeks. You can see we still have a lot to do."

"We'd be grateful for anything," George said. "I'm a retired farmer. I'm strong and can do construction work. You still have a long way to go with that wall. I can see you need to cut and nail on the lath; then, it'll need three coats of plaster. That'll take some time, and I've done many a wall in my day."

"Well, sir, you're right. It's going to take some work, and I have other chores to attend to. Let's work out a wage acceptable to both of us and see what you can do."

Sally found a crate and sat on it. Kate peeked at her through the kitchen door. In her weary state, she shrank from the very thought of being sociable, but her conscience got the best of her. She went out and introduced herself.

"Hello, I'm Mrs. Reese, John's wife. Could I get you a cup of tea while you're waiting?"

"That would be lovely, dear. I'm Mrs. Evans. Would you mind if I came into the kitchen to help?"

"You would be most welcome. I've been so tired lately with all the work we have to do here, watching the children, doing the laundry, and cooking." The two women moved into the kitchen.

"My mother-in-law will be here soon with dinner," Kate continued. "She always brings enough for a platoon, too much food for us. Would you like to stay? It looks like your husband will be helping John for a while."

"I think we would both love to stay, thank you. You mentioned children. Tell me about them. We don't have any grandchildren yet, but we hope to have some eventually."

Kate smiled. She liked this lady on first impression. There was something grandmotherly and calming about her. "My children will be here soon, I'm sure. They're in our apartment upstairs, which is why the partition is going up. Our family will need some privacy." She put the water back on to boil. "There's Steven, age six. He's in his first year of school. And there's Gracie, age four, whose main job now is playing with dolls and having tea parties."

Mrs. Evans smiled. "I look forward to meeting them." Her eyes scanned the kitchen. She marveled at all the cake pans, pie tins, and Dutch ovens. She admired the copper utensils hung on the walls. "What will you be selling in your bakery?"

"I'm told pies are my specialty, and I love to bake pies, but I think our biggest selling products will be bread and rolls. I'm hoping that the women of Spencer's Mill will prefer to buy bread rather than make their own every day."

"If I had that convenience available, I would certainly want to take advantage."

The front door opened again, and Susannah came in carrying a chicken and dumpling dish.

She greeted them cheerfully. "Hello, everyone."

John introduced her to George, then told her that Mrs. Evans was in the kitchen with Kate, so Susannah joined them.

"Katie, can we heat these dumplings? They got cold on the trip."

"Of course, Mother. Let me introduce you to Mrs. Evans. She and her husband came to Ohio from Indiana, and her husband is helping John put up the partition."

"Very nice to meet you, Mrs. Evans. I'm Susannah Wolf, John's mother."

"Nice to meet you, Mrs. Wolf."

"I've invited Mrs. Evans and her husband to stay for dinner. I hope there's enough to go around. If not, I'll get something from the root cellar."

"Oh, there's plenty," Susannah said. "Where are the children?"

Just then, two pairs of small feet clattered down the stairs. "Grandma? Is Grandma here?" It was Steven and Gracie. Gracie carried her poor, worn-out doll with her. They ran into the kitchen, then stopped short at the sight of Mrs. Evans.

Gracie asked, "Who are you?" Steven only stared with wide eyes.

Kate's face turned red, but Sally just chuckled. "That's a fair question," she said. "You can call me Mrs. Evans. Let me see your doll."

Gracie brought her doll, and Sally made a fuss over it. "Look at her pretty hair. Do you comb it every day for her?"

"Yes," Gracie lied innocently. "And we have tea parties. Sometimes Grandma has tea parties with us."

"That sounds like a lot of fun."

The children ran to their grandmother for hugs while the teakettle whistled. "Let me do that for you, dear. You look so tired." Mrs. Evans poured the tea for herself and the other two women. They sat together and had a good chat while the dumplings were heating. Kate was still desperately weary and relieved that her visitor made herself at home so quickly.

Mrs. Evans entertained the ladies with stories of her life growing up—about how she came from a family of seven children, then married Mr. Evans, and could have only one child. "So what about you, dear? This bakery will be a heavy load for you, doing all that baking every day and trying to care for your family."

"John's going to hire some help for me. Unfortunately, we don't know anyone who would be right for the work."

The dumplings were heated by then, and it was time to put the meal on the table. There weren't enough kitchen chairs, so they all filled their plates and found crates and chairs wherever they could.

It was well after dinner when everyone went home. Kate and John were both exhausted, but she had enjoyed the company of both Mrs. Evans and her mother-in-law. The young family took their oil lamps, went through the open door frame in the new wall, and climbed the stairs to their bedrooms.

Chapter 26: TWO SOLUTIONS AND A WRINKLE

Thursday, February 17, 1887

Mrs. Evans came into Spencer's Mill in the morning with her husband, not wanting to spend the day alone while her daughter went to work.

Kate was pleased to have her company and even more delighted when she fell naturally into occupying the children, helping clean up the kitchen, and making meals. *What a blessing,* Kate thought. *I wish I could have her here with me all the time. I wish she didn't have her heart set on living in Lamar.*

The two women passed the day pleasantly.

That afternoon, while George worked on the wall, John went to the general store next door.

"The steel cash drawer you ordered for us, Danny - has it come in yet?" he asked.

"Came in yesterday afternoon. It's in the back. Let me get it for you."

When John returned to the bakery, he carried the prized steel cash drawer.

"Look at this, Kate," he said. "We'll build a display for pies and such, and this cash drawer will get attached under the top counter. Then the cash will be out of the reach of pilferers and villainous pie-eaters."

Kate giggled.

Evans took a look at it. "I can build that counter for you if you'll just give me a drawing of what you want," he said.

"Let's sit down and do the drawing now. Will you help me, George? I could use your expertise. Then you build it. But this might be the last project I can afford to pay you for."

"I understand," George said. "I'm grateful for the work you've been able to give me so far."

The two men sat at the kitchen table and devised a three-shelf sales counter with a glassed-in display area.

"If you can advance me some cash," George said, "I'll go to the sawmill in the morning on my way here and pick up the necessary supplies. I'll bring you the receipt and the change."

"That's an offer I appreciate, George. It will save me a good deal of time and trouble."

At the day's end, when they were alone, John took his wife's hand. "Come over here to the table with me, Kate. I've been praying for wisdom, and I have an idea. Let's see what you think."

Kate allowed herself to be led to the table and focused on him. "I'm afraid I'm not thinking clearly," she said. "The days have been so full of frantic activity that I've neglected my Bible reading and prayer. I feel physically exhausted and spiritually dry. This is no way to live."

He studied her face. "I may have found an answer."

"What's your idea?"

"We need to hire some help for store opening and daily operations. We really can't afford that until we sell the house. The Evanses could help us, but they need a house and can't afford one. What if we put those two problems together and came up with a solution?"

"How would that work?"

"We could sell them our house if they're agreeable. They

would pay us their $600, and we would give them a mortgage for the balance. They would agree to work off the mortgage in our bakery. We would keep track of their work as if they were being paid cash, but they would be paid by crediting their unpaid mortgage. By the time their mortgage gets paid off, we should be able to pay their salaries in cash from our profits."

Kate's eyes lit up. "Do you think that would work?" she asked. "I would love having Sally here to help me."

"It would work if the Evanses agreed to it. I'll talk to George in the morning. But Katie, I'm worried about you. You don't seem able to get your strength back."

"John, we need to talk. I've had my suspicions recently, and now I'm sure. We're going to have another baby."

John shook his head. "No, we can't," he said firmly, as if he had a choice. "This isn't a good time."

"You're telling me." She broke down in tears. "Frankly, John, I never expected a reaction as insensitive as that after the way I've been pushing myself through morning sickness. I've been sick and still kept up with my regular work and did all the work to move and get the bakery ready to open." She pounded a fist against his chest as she sobbed. John recovered his good sense and put his arms around her, letting her cry. Shortly, when she was all cried out, he gave her a handkerchief to wipe her eyes.

Her eyes were still angry. "Remember, I didn't do this by myself."

"I know. I said something stupid, and I'm sorry. You caught me off guard," he said, trying to redeem himself. He took her face in his hands and gazed into her eyes. "It will be all right. This child will be a blessing. Why, he'll even be someone else to help in the bakery when he's old enough. We'll get through this. Kate…will you forgive me?

Kate nodded as her tension relaxed. They went upstairs to

sleep.

Friday, February 18, 1887

The following day, John and George unloaded the lumber he brought for the sales counter and display case. "I'd like you to put the second coat of plaster on the wall, then cut lumber for the case," John said, "but first, sit down here with me for a couple of minutes, George. I have a proposition for you."

George's ears perked up. "Always glad to listen to a proposition."

"Here's my idea," John began. "I know you wanted to buy a house in Lamar to be close to your daughter, but you haven't found anything in your price range. If you could see living in Spencer's Mill, we could sell you our house. I think you'd like it, and I can show it to you today. We're asking $695."

"John, you know I don't have – "

"Wait, listen to the whole plan. You could use your $600 for a down payment. We would give you a mortgage for the balance, which you and Sally could pay off by working for us every day. Once the mortgage was paid, we would convert your pay to cash."

George mulled over the idea. A slow smile spread across his face. "That might work," he said. "Of course, Sally will need to be involved in the decision, but it might work. When can we look at your house?"

"We can go now if you like."

"Let's get that second coat of plaster on the wall. Then we can go after lunch while the plaster dries."

After the noon meal, the two men rode to John and Kate's old house. John gave George a tour, pointing out the ample kitchen, the parlor and two bedrooms, the root cellar, the chicken coop, and the barn in the rear. George opened kitchen cabinets to look in, checked out the pantry for mold and insects, and ran his hands over the windowsills, checking for rot and splinters. He opened and closed the horse stall doors to ensure they were in good order.

"John, do you have a ladder?"

"I think there's one still in the barn." Together, they fetched the ladder, and George clambered onto the roof to inspect it thoroughly.

"I'll ask Sally to look at this tomorrow," he said. "I like this house a lot, and if we have a reason to live in Spencer's Mill, like having jobs here, I think this would be a very workable situation."

Back at the store, as the second coat of plaster dried, George measured and cut lumber for the sales counter, whistling a cheerful tune.

Saturday, February 19, 1887

On Saturday, Sally was eager to see the house. She made herself useful by playing with Gracie and Steven. She rolled a canvas ball with Steven, stacked blocks, and then played tea party with Gracie and her dolls. She chatted with Kate while George put the third coat of plaster on the wall. Then she went with John and George to look at the house. They were back at the store in an hour, and Sally was alive with excitement.

"That's a very nice house, better than anything in Lamar in that price range," she said. "I think we would be happy spending the rest of our lives there, and we would still be close enough to Jennie to make it a day trip. There's even enough room for her to come live with us if she'd like."

"Let's talk about price, John," said George. "I'd like to buy the house for $675. Would you accept that offer?"

John was taken aback that George wanted to dicker but

quickly realized that this should be handled like any other transaction. "Normally, I would counter your offer with a bunch of blah-blah-blah," he said with a grin, "but I think $675 would be acceptable. You'll give us the $600 down, and we'll get my stepfather to draw up a legal contract for the mortgage, which will be paid in labor. Is that the way you understand it?"

"Yes, sir. I'll bring the $600 on Monday." The two men shook hands, and the house was sold. They also had competent help for the bakery.

John and Kate remembered the words of the Apostle Paul: "And we know that all things work together for good to them that love God….."

Chapter 27: FEAR CONQUERED

When George went home for the day, Kate gave the family a quick supper.

John dressed for traveling in the cold evening. "I'm going to Ma's house tonight to see Christian," he said. "I'm going to hire him to draw up that contract. I'm sorry to leave you like that overnight, but time is short. Can you take care of yourself?"

"Do you have to go tonight?"

"It's only a one-hour ride on horseback to their house. If Christian can draw up that contract while I'm there, I'll sleep there tonight and come back with him and Ma when they come into town for church tomorrow. But if I wait until Monday when he's at his office in Lamar, it will be a two-hour ride each way, and I'll have to wait until he's finished the contract. It would take the entire day. I'd rather go tonight and have Monday to do other things. Will you be safe here with Steven and Gracie if I do that?"

Kate shuddered. Since their wedding, she had never spent the night without him. She would miss that feeling of security, especially now that her emotions were swinging wildly in pregnancy, but this would save John an entire day. Time was a precious commodity. With an uncomfortable feeling in her stomach, she said, "Yes, go. I'll be fine. But be careful, John. It's already dark and cold out there, and you have a long way to go."

As Kate cleaned the kitchen, John mounted his horse and left quickly. She still had time to relax before bedtime. She wished he hadn't gone, but she understood the need.

She lit the oil lamps and read her Bible in the warm glow as the children played at her feet. Soon, it was time to tuck the children into bed, leaving her alone in the parlor. She thought about John, traveling at night, and prayed for his safety.

When it was time to go to bed herself, she changed into her nightgown, extinguished the lamps, and crawled under the quilts alone.

All was silent except for two or three stray branches of the oak tree outside the bedroom window. They rubbed against the house as the wind blew. Skritch…Skritch…Skritch… She had not paid any attention to the sounds of this house before. There was the quiet crackling of the fireplace as the embers died for the night and the scurry of a mouse somewhere. The walls creaked slightly under the pressure of the wind, scaring her to death. With every new noise, her anxiety grew. Then, a shadow crossed the bedroom window. *It was probably only an owl,* she thought, *but what if it wasn't? I wish John would come home.*

She drew her knees up and wrapped her arms around them under the quilt, hoping to feel more protected. Finally, she gave in to fear. She began to tremble, and tears ran down her cheeks, dampening the pillow. What if someone broke in? She had no way to protect herself or the children.

That was when a strong impression formed in her mind, or maybe it was a whisper in her spirit. She didn't know how to describe it, but there it was, as real as anything. 'Praise the Lord,' it said. Then again, more insistently, 'Katie, praise the Lord.' She understood this whisper to be an instruction. She pulled the quilt up over her head. There it was again. Yes, it was very clearly an instruction.

Obediently, huddled under the quilt, she began to praise the

Lord in whispers. She started hesitantly, gripped with panic. She began to recite the Psalm that came to her memory, "Praise the Lord. Praise Him in his sanctuary." As she continued, her fright reduced with every worshipful declaration—"Praise Him for His mighty acts. Praise Him according to His excellent greatness." She continued until she was finally worshiping and praising joyously. She entered into a calm peace, and her heart swelled with gratitude.

Thank you, Father, for looking out for me and teaching me your ways, she prayed. *This is a lesson I will never forget. Fear does not coexist with praise.*

How often had she read the Biblical admonition to "Fear not?" The Lord does not want His people to live in fear.

With her heart calmed, she slipped out of bed, unable to still her mind. She stood by the bare window, looking at countless stars dotting the cloudless sky. The oak tree just outside the window stretched out its cold branches, backlit by the pale moonlight. Their horse barn was on the other side of the tree, and the alley stretched along the other side of that. She realized her children wouldn't have much space to play unless they walked to the park, but by living downtown, they may have experiences other children couldn't.

She wondered what the future held for all of them. She didn't know the answer, but God had it all in His hands. Her eyes grew heavy, and she climbed back into bed. Soon, she dropped off into peaceful slumber.

Chapter 28: THE INTRUDER

Monday, February 21, 1887

Early on Monday morning, John and George completed the sale of the house. John saddled his horse and left to take the $600 cash to the bank in Lamar. The Evanses took the day off to move, and Steven was at school, leaving Kate at the bakery alone with Gracie. Her stomach was sour, and she feared losing her breakfast.

I'll be so relieved when this morning sickness is over. I'm barely hanging on, and there's still much to be done.

As Kate worked on the laundry downstairs in the kitchen, she became aware of a strange young man standing outside the window. His hand, shading his eyes, rested on the window glass. He leaned forward to peer inside. She wouldn't have minded if he just took a peek and moved on, as one satisfying a passing curiosity. He stayed in that position far too long. He was oddly out of place, not moving, just looking in, minute by minute. His manner was intrusive and unnerving to Kate, but she tried to ignore him. She continued her work in the kitchen, hating his presence but unwilling to chase away someone who may later become a customer. Finally, he left, much to her relief.

An hour later, she carried another basket of laundry from their upstairs apartment to the kitchen. There he was again, forehead pressed to the window, just looking in. This time,

Kate's anger rose. She had a queasy stomach and was short on patience. She put down her basket and strode purposefully to the door.

"What are you doing here?" She studied him with a keen eye. She took him to be in his late twenties, smaller than most men, with brown hair and a thin mustache. He wore rough brown pants and a coat with sleeves that were too long. His shoes were unpolished and worn down with ground-in dirt like he had been tromping in mud.

"What do you want?" she demanded. "The bakery isn't open yet."

He pushed right past her through the door without being invited, raising her fear.

Despite her angst, she kept a firm voice and turned to face him. "I said, the bakery isn't open yet. You need to leave. Now."

The stranger made no move to comply. He stood there examining everything, floor to ceiling. "I have a right to be here. This is mine," he said.

Kate stared at him for a moment. "What did you say?"

"I said, this is mine." He picked up confidence. "This building belonged to my Uncle Brigham Taylor. He had a carpentry shop here. I just learned of his passing, and I'm his only heir. So this building is mine."

Kate feared she would faint but tried her best to maintain her demeanor.

"You're too late. The carpenter who used to own this property willed it to his church, and we bought it from them legally. So no, this is not yours."

"I say it is, and I'm going to prove it. You're going to have to leave. Where is your husband?"

"He'll be back very shortly. You need to go outside if you're going to wait." She turned to her daughter. "Gracie, run next door and get Uncle Danny. Tell him it's an emergency." Her hands trembled, but she kept them out of sight underneath her apron.

When she called for reinforcements, the stranger decided to make a strategic retreat. He stepped out onto the brick sidewalk in front of the store. In a moment, Danny rushed into the bakery right behind Gracie.

"Katie, what's wrong?" he shouted.

Kate was almost hysterical. "It's that man out there, Danny. He says the store is his, not ours, and we have to move out. He plans to stick around here until John gets back."

"He says what? I'll talk to him. You stay here."

"Do you think he's working with that Skinner fellow?"

"I don't know."

Danny dashed outside, where the stranger was backing away. "You come here. You have some questions to answer."

Danny ran and grabbed the young man by the arm and pushed him to the door of the general store.

"Ow. You're hurting me." He raised a ruckus, hoping that someone would hear. While Danny tried to push him inside, the stranger continued making as much noise as possible. "Help! Help! I'm being kidnapped! Help me!"

The butcher came out of his shop across the street to find out what the commotion was about. "Do you have a problem, Danny?" he called.

"Under control, Harmon. This scoundrel is harassing Katie at the bakery." He pushed the young man into the general store. "Now, what is this, you upsetting Katie by telling her you own the store?"

"Look," said the interloper, whining. "My name is Noah Taylor. I'm from Florissant. It took me a long time to get here."

"Where is Florissant?"

"It's about thirty miles from here. I came to claim my property. It was my Uncle Brigham Taylor's store, and I'm his only heir. I just learned he died a few days ago, and I want what's rightfully mine."

"My brother bought that property from Wesleyan Church and paid hard cash. It belongs to him and his wife. You need to forget this nonsense and get out of here."

Noah sneered. "I'll wait for Mr. Reese. He'll listen to me."

"You get out of here now. If you don't, I'll send for the sheriff."

Noah glared at Danny but slowly turned and ambled out of the store, casually fingering merchandise on his way out, taunting Danny with defiant eyes.

What an arrogant lowlife, Danny thought. He observed him go down the street a short distance and loiter in front of the milliner's shop.

After an hour or so, John returned to the store in good spirits. His trip to Lamar had been successful. "I'm back, Katie," he said.

She ran to him in tears. Her face was ghostly pale, and her eyes were red from crying. "John, a horrible little man came in here and claimed to own the store. He pushed his way in and wouldn't leave until I sent Gracie to get Danny. He says we have to move or pay him for it."

"He what?"

"He said he owns the store because he's the only heir of the carpenter. Danny came over and ran him off. What are we going to do if he presses a claim?"

"I'll talk to Danny," John said and went next door.

Danny was still keeping surveillance on Noah down the street.

"That fellow down there," Danny said, pointing at Noah. "He went into the bakery and told Kate the store belonged to him. She's all upset. He says his name is Noah Taylor, the nephew of Brigham Taylor, and he says he's the rightful heir. I told him to leave or I'd send for the sheriff. He's been down there for about an hour, waiting for you."

John's face flushed, and he flexed his fists. "I don't want Katie getting upset. She's had too much to deal with lately," he said. He paused and groped around in his mind for a sensible response.

"I'm sorry, man. I know you don't need this aggravation while you're trying to get the store ready to open."

John frowned. "The real issue here isn't who owns the building. Kate and I do. That's easy enough to prove in court. The real issue is this guy's aggressive nature and obsession with the building. I'm afraid he might try to hurt Katie when I'm not home. I can't ignore this problem. What if he's one of Roy Skinner's thugs, trying to take the building by force? The sheriff said there might be more of them."

"You need to know if he's with Skinner, and I just had an idea," Danny said. "That man says he's from Florissant. I could ask my father-in-law to go there and do some research on him. He could check out his story and find out if he has a criminal record and if he runs with Skinner's pack. Mr. Fletcher is retired. He likes traveling and has nothing else to do right now."

"I'll pay his expenses if he'll do that."

"Well, I already told you everything I know about that fellow." Danny pointed at Taylor, loitering down the street. "Right down there. If you want more detailed information—he's right in front of the milliner's."

John nodded and headed out to the sidewalk. He approached Noah.

"Are you Noah Taylor?" he asked.

Noah eyed him suspiciously.

"I'm John Reese." He offered his hand, catching Noah off guard. He shook John's hand.

"You were right. I'm Noah Taylor, and that's my building

down there."

"Then you and I disagree, friend. Why don't you come back to my office, and we'll discuss this."

Noah decided to go with him, even though John had the advantage of height and weight, should it come to fisticuffs.

The two men returned to the bakery and seated themselves on opposite sides of John's desk. As John locked eyes with the interloper, a snippet of scripture popped into his mind: "Be ye therefore wise as serpents, and harmless as doves." Ah, yes. He could use some serpent-style tactics here.

"Now," John began, "what can you tell me about this claim you're trying to make on our bakery?"

"It's not your bakery," said Noah. "It's mine. You'll have to move out unless you want to buy it from me. I'm the nephew and sole heir of Brigham Taylor, the carpenter who owned this store. I live in Florissant, so I just found out my uncle passed away. I'm here to claim what's mine."

"Where do you live in Florissant?"

Noah gave him an address. "Catalpa Street. 578 Catalpa, to be exact."

John wrote that down. "Do you live alone?"

"Yes. There's nobody but me. I'm the only heir. The *only* heir, understand?"

"Do you have other friends in Florissant? Go to a church?"

Noah got defensive. "What business is that of yours?"

"I'm just trying to find out who I'm dealing with. How do I know you are who you say you are?"

"Trust me; I'm Noah Taylor. I'm giving you a week to either move out of here or get me my cash. I'd say this property is worth about a thousand dollars. That's what you owe me."

At the mention of that figure, chills went down John's spine. That was the figure Skinner had offered. Could this man be working for him? "Do you know Roy Skinner or a man named

Beadle?"

"No. Are they tough guys you're going to send after me? Don't bother. I can handle myself."

"Look, if you have a legitimate claim, you'll have to prove it in court. I have no intention of ever moving out of here, and I certainly don't plan to give you any money."

"If you want to do it the hard way, fine. You'll see me later."

"Do you have anything to prove you're Noah Taylor?"

"Nothing with me. I have a pistol in my room to prove it."

"What if I want to contact you?" John asked. "Where are you staying locally?"

"The closest place I could find was the Lamar Hotel. Since this is my building, I should bring my pallet here and sleep on the floor."

"If you try it, you'll see the open end of my gun barrel. You stay away from my store and my family."

Noah stood. "You've been warned," he said. He rose from his chair and left with a smirk.

Chapter 29: PHINEAS FLETCHER

John walked into the kitchen as Kate tried to relieve her stress by diving into her work. "John, when the Lord honored our request for this building, I had no idea it would come with threats and problems."

"I didn't, either. But we're not the first people to experience this. Think about King David, running for his life even after he was anointed king of Israel."

Kate sighed. "We're in good company."

"Kate, I'm going to Danny's house to talk to his father-in-law. I'm going to ask his help with this problem."

"I want to go with you, John. Please don't leave me here without you. I remembered my lesson about praising through fear, and I've been doing that, but it would be foolish to ignore the ongoing danger. That young man is as bold as they come. If he sees you leave, he might come back." She was near tears again.

"It's probably a good idea for you to come along. Get Gracie ready to go with us. We'll pick up Stevie from school on our way back home." While Katie prepared her daughter, John went out back to hitch the horse to the carriage.

She double-checked the front door, latched it, then took her daughter out the alley door to join John.

Since it would be a quick visit, Kate and Gracie stayed bundled up in the carriage while John walked up to his mother's old house. It was a large two-story currently occupied by Danny, his wife, and her Pa. He rapped on the door. Danny's father-in-law was there alone. Mr. Fletcher was a widower in his early fifties, full of life, with graying hair and a lively interest in everything around him.

"John, come on in," he said with a sweeping motion. "Danny isn't home yet."

"Yes, I know, Mr. Fletcher. I came to see you. Danny said you might be interested in doing some research for me if I would pay your travel expenses."

Fletcher brightened. "He must have told you how I love to travel, and it's a rare day that someone offers to pay my expenses. It sounds interesting, John. Come in. What's the assignment?"

John stepped inside and explained about Noah Taylor from Florissant. "It would be quite a long day's ride to get there by carriage," he said. "You may have to leave before dawn. What I would like you to do, if you're interested, is find out everything you can about this man. Go to 578 Catalpa Street and make sure he lives there. Visit his neighbors, ask them for a physical description to make sure this is Noah Taylor, and ask them for any information on his background. What kind of person is he? Does he have friends? Do they know any gossip they would like to share? That kind of thing. Try to find out if he has a criminal record. Especially find out if he's associated with Roy Skinner."

Mr. Fletcher was smiling broadly. "That sounds like it's business well-suited for a snoopy old man like me. When do you want me to leave?"

"The sooner, the better. Can you leave tomorrow morning?"

"Yes, sir, I can. I should be back in about three days with some useful information, or my name isn't Phineas Fletcher." He was delighted to have something interesting to do. He was tired of sitting in his bedroom reading books. "Excuse me, John. I have some packing to do." He turned abruptly with the energy born of enthusiasm, then headed up the stairs, leaving John to see himself out.

Tuesday, February 22, 1887

At dawn the following day, Phineas dressed in his best trousers, vest, Inverness coat, and bowler. He hadn't worn those clothes since he retired from his business. He was glad to see they still fit, except for the bottom button on the vest. It had to strain a little harder than before. He climbed into his carriage, slapped the reins, and started the long trip to Florissant. He had never been there. It would be a new adventure.

His route took him through Lamar, where he stopped for an egg, toast, and cup of coffee at the Old English Tea Room. He smiled to himself as he slipped the receipt into his pocket. This would be on John's bill. Then he asked the locals for directions to Florissant and turned to the northeast. It was a long day's ride past farms and fields with no good place to stop. Still, he enjoyed the scenic ride through rolling farmland, imagining how beautiful it would be in the summer when the crops were growing.

His stomach was complaining when he rolled into town late in the afternoon. At a roadside diner, he stopped for a meal. There was nothing fancy about the restaurant, but it was clean and well-kept. Blue and white checkered cloths covered each table.

"I'd like your dinner special," he told the young waitress, "and bring me a cup of coffee with sugar."

"Yes, sir." She smiled at her well-dressed customer, who would be dining alone. She brought the coffee, making sure it was good and hot.

"Ma'am, could you tell me where I could find a room for the night?" he asked.

"I believe you could go to Mrs. Courtney's Rooming House down the street about five blocks," she said. "She nearly always has an extra room. Will you be staying in town long?"

"Maybe only a night or two. It depends on how much I can get done tomorrow."

"Are you in town on business?"

"I'm a private investigator doing work for a client." Technically it was the truth, even if this was the first day of his career. He sipped his coffee and peered at her sideways over the rim of the cup to see her reaction. She was properly impressed, looking down at him, smiling, her hand resting on her hip. She was a pretty thing.

"That's exciting," she said with a grin. "I'll check and see if your dinner is ready yet."

In a few minutes, she returned with a plate of ham, mashed potatoes, and green beans. "Would you like a splash of vinegar on those beans?"

"Yes, please," he said and waited while she tipped a bottle of the pungent liquid over his plate, using her thumb to release measured drops onto his beans. He dug into his meal with gusto. He treated himself to a piece of apple pie, then paid the tab, leaving a nice tip. He added that to his receipts. He hoped John wouldn't mind.

Mrs. Courtney's Rooming House was a pleasant place to stay. It was a Civil War-era two-story house with richly carved crown molding and dark walnut floors in the lobby. Red flowered carpet covered the stairs. He checked in and was assigned to Room 5, then carried his bag upstairs to his room.

A finely-stitched blue quilt covered a comfortable bed. For washing and shaving, the dresser held a matching bowl and pitcher beside a neatly folded towel and a washrag. A shiny brass chamber pot sat on the floor near the bed, awaiting the guest's convenience.

Phineas parted the lace curtains and took in the view of the street. Mature blue spruce trees graced the front lawn, and bright yellow witch hazel bloomed beside the stone fence.

Just beautiful, he thought. He went downstairs to the lobby to chat with the establishment's owner.

"Mrs. Courtney, this is a lovely place you have here. I enjoy looking at all of those trees out on the lawn. And your witch hazels—my, such a nice accent. It must be even more beautiful in the summer."

"Thank you, Mr. Fletcher. It's not often that people remark on my gardening. Have you had a long journey?"

"I left Spencer's Mill today before dawn. It was quite a long drive. Can you give me directions to an address here in Florissant?"

"I can try."

He pulled his note out of his pocket. "It's 578 Catalpa Street."

"Mm, I'm not familiar with that address," she said. "But I can point you to the sheriff's office. He must know every address in town."

"Good idea," he said and wrote down the address she gave him for the sheriff.

"Breakfast is at seven in the morning. Will that suit you?"

"Perfectly, and thank you, Mrs. Courtney."

Wednesday, February 23, 1887

Breakfast in the morning was outstanding, and Phineas enjoyed chatting with Mrs. Courtney while he ate. She served him two eggs with a slice of bacon, coffee, and a sweet roll. He hadn't had such a breakfast in a long time.

Mrs. Courtney was a genial lady about his age, average height, with her brown hair layered in curls on the back of her head by some mysterious force. Since he was the only registered guest that day, he invited her to sit at his table and chat. They swapped information about their children and their late spouses.

"I'd like to stay one more night if my room is available," he told her. She opened her logbook, marked off his room as occupied for another night, and wished him a good day.

Phineas' first stop was to see the sheriff. The small office was in a brick building that included a jail with three cells, all unoccupied. The three cells were on a corridor separated from the office by a heavy wood paneled door. The sheriff, a muscular fellow in his forties, was seated at his desk.

"I'm looking for the nephew of an old gentleman who recently died," Phineas said. "The address is 578 Catalpa Street."

"Hmm," Sheriff Milligan said. "I know where Catalpa Street is, but I don't know if there's anything in the five hundred block. You'll have to go look." He pointed to the town map on the wall, showing Phineas where he was and how to get to where he wanted to go.

"Thank you very much, sir," said Phineas. He tipped his hat and made the trip to his assigned destination, enjoying the quaint architecture of the town along the way. Some homes were lavishly decorated with the gingerbread style so much in favor: scroll-sawn brackets, balusters and cornice trim.

Even though the air was chilly, the sun shone brightly, and Phineas reveled in his freedom. This was much better than reading "The Old Curiosity Shop" for the second time in his bedroom at home.

As he turned onto Catalpa Street, the frame houses were neat and well-tended, even though they were plain. Phineas took most of them to be one-bedroom homes, each with an outbuilding of one kind or other. He rode to the five-hundred block at the end of the street. At the 578 address, he found a slightly run-down property with a lawn showing large patches of mud. In obvious need of painting, the door and window frames gave the property a general air of neglect. He walked up the uneven brick walk and knocked on the door.

When no one answered, he turned to the house next to it and rapped with the door knocker. A tiny wisp of a lady with white hair answered the door. "May I help you?"

"Ma'am, my name is Phineas Fletcher, and I'm trying to find your neighbor, Noah Taylor. He's the nephew of a carpenter in Spencer's Mill. Can you tell me about him?"

"I'm sorry, sir. I'm a bit hard of hearing. Can you speak up?"

"I'm trying to find your neighbor, Noah Taylor," Phineas shouted. "He's the nephew of a friend. Can you tell me about him?"

"I hate to speak poorly of someone related to your friend, but Mr. Taylor, he's an odd one," she said. "I don't know where he is now. He ain't been around for two or three weeks."

"I wonder if you could describe him to me." Phineas was still loud. "There's a man claiming to be him, but I'm not sure that fellow is who he says he is."

"Why yes, I can describe him. He's about fifty years old, big and muscular, but he dresses in shabby old clothes and goes about with his hair uncut. He always looks like a bum."

Phineas made a note on his paper. "Is there anything else you can tell me about him? What does he do for a living?"

"Nothing, as far as I can tell. I don't know how he gets along."

"Does he live alone?"

"What?"

Phineas ramped up his volume again. "I say, does he live

alone?"

"Oh, yes, at least he did until recently. Then a younger man moved in with him; I'd say about a month ago—a skinny little guy with a mustache. I don't know who that man is. He's not a nice man. I can tell you that. After he moved in, I didn't see Mr. Taylor much."

"Ma'am, would you mind telling me your name so I can take complete notes? This sounds more serious than I had first imagined, and the sheriff may want to ask you some of the same questions."

"My name, you say?"

Phineas nodded.

"Yes, sir. My name is Polly Pringle."

"Thank you, Miss Pringle. I'll be talking to some of the other neighbors now. You've been a tremendous help."

She smiled and waited until he was at the fence. When Phineas took a last glance at her house, she was standing in the doorway, smiling and wiggling her fingers goodbye.

So, our young friend is posing as Mr. Taylor. I wonder who he is. Phineas decided to check with another neighbor.

He sized up the houses on the block and chose to knock on a door across the street.

The neighbor, a man about Phineas' age, answered his knock. Phineas again introduced himself and stated his business.

"Come in, sir. I'm glad to tell you what I can about Mr. Taylor and his young companion," he said. "Mr. Taylor lays about with no apparent income. I suspect he goes out at night to commit burglaries, or maybe he gambles. How else could he survive? He was always out at night, God knows where. Then, that young man came to live with him. Come to think of it, I haven't seen Taylor around too much since then. But the young guy was just creepy. He never was friendly at all, just kind of sneaky-like. Maybe Taylor moved out when the young guy moved in. They were in there arguing one time. Bad argument. Loud."

"By any chance, did you hear Taylor refer to him by name?"

"Maybe. Let me think... Oh, yes. He called him Carl."

"That helps. Thank you." Phineas scribbled another note on his paper.

The neighbor chuckled. "To be exact, he called him 'Carl, you traitorous miscreant.'"

Phineas smiled at the colorful insult. "One more thing, sir. To make sure the man calling himself Mr. Taylor is actually Carl, would you mind describing both men?"

"Certainly. Taylor lived there for a long time, so I know what he looks like. He's in his fifties or thereabouts. Big guy, about six feet tall. The man he called Carl was much younger...thin...shorter than Taylor. He had brown hair and wore a mustache. I swear, Mr. Fletcher, the expression on that guy's face made you want to slap him."

Phineas grinned and nodded. "I'll make a note of that," he said. "That may be significant. Oh, one more question. Were there other visitors ever there? I'm thinking specifically of a man named Roy Skinner."

"No, I don't believe I saw other visitors there."

"Thank you." He made a few more hasty scribbles on his notepaper. "Sir, I thank you for your time. I'll be on my way."

He took his leave and went to another home. One more interview should be enough.

The third neighbor was a pretty young wife with a small boy hanging on her skirt. "What can I do for you, sir?" she asked.

"Madam, I don't mean to intrude, but I'm here on an errand of some importance. May I ask you some questions about your neighbors at the end of the street?"

She motioned him in. She had a mouthful of information to tell him about those two men. "Have a seat there, please, and let me tell you what I know."

"I'll get my paper and pencil to make notes while you talk." He pulled his paper from his pocket, unfolded it, and began writing as she passed over information. He had to write small. He was running out of room.

"There used to be a Mr. Taylor who lived there. He used to be around all day but never came out of the house too much until evening; then, he would leave. I don't know when he returned, but it was after we were in bed. I can't imagine what he was doing at all hours."

"Mm-hm," Phineas said, moving his pencil as fast as he could.

"Then that other man moved in, and there was no peace for a few days. They yelled at each other and carried on something fierce. But then Mr. Taylor went away."

"Do you know what the fighting was about?"

"No. They made a lot of noise, but I couldn't understand the words."

"Can you describe the two men?"

"Mr. Taylor had gray hair and a ruddy complexion. He was tall and big." She spread her arms to show how big Mr. Taylor was. "The younger man was short and thin. He was doing most of the yelling, but not all of it."

"Do you know what his name is?"

"I thought it was Carl, but I'm not sure where I got that idea." Her little boy raised his hands, wanting to be picked up, so she put him in her lap.

"How did they make their living? Do you know?"

"I don't think either of them had a job. They didn't go to any workplace regularly like other folks. And they couldn't have done any farming on that property full of trees. Frankly, I don't know where they got their money. I'm sorry I can't help you there."

The boy squirmed off his mother's lap and toddled over to Phineas. Drool ran down his chin and onto Phineas' knee. His mother took it in stride, casually handing her guest a handkerchief to wipe off his pants.

"Thank you, ma'am."

Phineas waited for an apology, but none came. He cringed at the sticky, wet feeling and the spot on the only trousers he had with him, but his only choice was to continue the interview.

"Do you think they did much drinking?"

"I should say—both of them. You should ask for information from the sheriff. He was over there once. He probably knows something about them."

"That's interesting. I'll do that." Phineas patted her little son on the head. "Precious boy," he said. "You've given me some helpful information, ma'am. Thank you so much."

Phineas decided it would be worthwhile to revisit Sheriff Milligan.

"Mr. Fletcher," the sheriff greeted him. "Were you successful in finding the nephew?"

"No, I'm afraid not. No one was home, but I spoke to some of the neighbors. They said you might have some information for me."

"Really?"

"Yes, sir. It turns out that you were there for some reason. One of the neighbors told me about it."

"What address did you say that was?" the sheriff asked.

"That was 578 Catalpa Street. It would have been in the past two to three weeks."

The sheriff flipped through his journal. "Oh, yes, here it is," he said. "One of the neighbors complained about a disturbance one night. It was between a Mr. Noah Taylor and Mr. Carl Young. They had been punching one another and knocking over furniture. Neither of them would admit to the reason for the scuffle, but they promised to stop it, so I left. I haven't had any more complaints from the neighbors."

"That's because Mr. Taylor has disappeared. No one knows where he went."

"That's odd. Well, he probably got fed up and left."

Phineas pondered for a moment. "I wonder who owns that house."

"You could find out at the courthouse."

"Yes, I'll go over there, but let me share some information I learned from the neighbors. From their descriptions, the man calling himself Noah Taylor back in Spencer's Mill is actually Carl Young."

The sheriff raised his eyebrows. "Really? I wonder why he's pretending to be someone he's not."

"He's claiming to have inherited property from an uncle named Brigham Taylor. My daughter's brother-in-law owns the property he's claiming, and Mr. Young is trying to flimflam him for either cash or the building." With a voice full of sarcasm, he said, "He's kind enough to give him a choice."

"That's a criminal offense," said the sheriff. "Will you inform your sheriff?"

"I will. Now, can you direct me to the courthouse?"

With the directions in his pocket, Phineas stopped at the general store to buy more notepaper. He collected more information than expected and needed to compile his notes neatly.

He walked up the wide stairs to Florissant's new Blanchard County courthouse. He found the recorder's office and asked about the ownership of 578 Catalpa Street.

The clerk was accommodating. "That property is owned by Mr. Noah Taylor, sir." He pointed at a hand-written entry in a large book recording real estate transfers. He slid the heavy book around on top of the counter so Mr. Fletcher could get a good look for himself. Phineas scribbled the book and page number in his notes.

"Thank you," he said and went directly back to the sheriff's office.

"Mr. Fletcher, you're back again," said the surprised sheriff. "You must have found something significant."

"Yes, I did, and I suspect something is seriously amiss here in Florissant." Phineas pulled out his notes. "The owner of that house is Mr. Noah Taylor. Now, sir, if Carl Young is passing himself off as Noah Taylor, and the actual Noah Taylor has disappeared from his own house, doesn't that suggest foul play? And if the same Carl Young is down there in Spencer's Mill claiming property by virtue of being Noah Taylor, doesn't that strengthen my suspicions?"

"Yes, sir, it does. Here's what I'll do. I'll go by that address occasionally until I find someone at home. As soon as I find Carl Young, I'll bring him in for questioning. But from what you say, he's still in Spencer's Mill. Would you tell your sheriff that I will cooperate in any investigation? You can have him write to me or send a telegram as he wishes."

"Thank you, sir. I'm sure this fellow is more dangerous than we thought. He probably thinks he'll never be caught."

"Hopefully, we'll be able to prove him wrong."

Phineas left and returned to the rooming house. It had been a good day's work.

Mrs. Courtney was at the front desk when he arrived. "Mrs. Courtney, do you serve dinner here?" he asked.

"No, I'm sorry, Mr. Fletcher. You're on your own for dinner.

Only breakfast is included in the price of the room."

"Then, madam, would you do me the honor of accompanying me to dinner? You name the place. I don't know where to find the best restaurant around here."

Her eyes lit up. "Mr. Fletcher, I would love to. There's a pub about a mile from here where we could have a lovely dinner and a pint."

He grinned. "Give me some time to freshen up, and I'll come down for you at six. How does that sound?"

"That will give me enough time to change into something more presentable. I'll see you at six."

At the appointed time, Phineas came downstairs to find Mrs. Courtney in a fresh dress. A sign on the front desk said, 'Be Back Soon.'

Alone in his office, the sheriff pondered the information that Mr. Fletcher had brought him. Why would the property owner leave his home because a guest annoyed him? There was something very wrong with that. Any property owner would demand that the offender leave. He decided to visit that address and have a look around.

He mounted his horse and rode to Catalpa Street. The house at the 578 address had signs of being vacant, but he knocked on the door anyway. He waited. When there was no answer, he walked around the back of the property. He stood in the soft dirt on his toes, leaning over the bushes, trying to see through the windows, but the curtains had been drawn.

The back lawn extended to a wooded area. He walked back among the trees, crashing around in the cold, brittle underbrush. He stepped over a fallen log, pushed back some wet leaves, and found something he had hoped not to see. It was a fresh mound of dirt, quite large. His heart sank, and he swore to himself. He would have to get a shovel.

The sheriff's office was well-equipped with firearms but no tools for digging. He rode to the general store.

"McGinty, I have an official favor to ask of you on behalf of the sheriff's office," he said to the shopkeeper. "Could I borrow a shovel? It's of grave importance. I'll get it back to you tomorrow."

The shopkeeper was reluctant but had civic pride. "Take care of it, Sheriff. I don't want no dings and chips in it when you bring it back. I need to make a profit. I can't be giving the merchandise away."

"I understand. I'll be as careful as I can."

He left with the shiny new shovel and returned to the Taylor property. He wished he had that Fletcher fellow to help him with this unpleasant job. After stomping about in the woods and relocating the hill of disturbed dirt, he began digging. He wasn't a young man anymore and was soon short of breath. He rested a few seconds, then dug again. The skies were darkening. He was obliged to light his lantern to keep working.

After a few more minutes of digging, he struck something denser than dirt. He threw the shovel down and dropped to his knees on the cold, wet earth, scooping the dirt carefully with his gloved hands. He soon uncovered a man's shirt. The man was still in it. He scrambled to his feet in horror. This kind of thing didn't happen in a little village like Florissant. Ever.

He ran to his horse and rode as fast as he could to get the undertaker.

Later that evening, the decaying body of a tall, muscular man was pulled up from the dirt. The winter temperatures had slowed decomposition, so the sheriff quickly recognized the body as Mr. Taylor from the night he fought with Mr. Young. The undertaker took charge of the body. He would need to measure him for a coffin.

"I'll come tomorrow and find out what caused his death,"

Sheriff Milligan said. "It's hard to tell until he gets all that mud cleaned off him. I don't know the cause, but I know who did it."

"I'll let you know as soon as I figure it out," said the undertaker.

"When I get the official word, I'll somehow notify the sheriff in Spencer's Mill to arrest Young. Man, I am sick about this whole situation."

"I'll keep this from the newspaper as long as possible."

"I appreciate that. If they find out, they'll make a big splash of it. Florissant will have a black reputation. There's never been a murder here before."

Mr. Fletcher and Mrs. Courtney climbed into his carriage. They were dressed for a night on the town, as much as could be had in a village like Florissant and anticipated an enjoyable evening. Then they drove to the pub, getting better acquainted along the way.

Inside, energy was high, with folks talking and laughing. The clink of glasses and tableware added to the noise. Oil lamps at each table and along the bar lit the room. Taking a table near the back wall, they studied the menu and ordered chicken dinners, smiling at each other and chatting over mugs of ale through the candlelight. Dinner probably tasted delicious, but they were immersed in one another's company too much to notice.

The waitress came to clear away their dishes. "The cook has a warm, tasty vanilla pudding if you'd like dessert."

Phineas took the opportunity to extend the evening a little longer. "We'll have two of those puddings. Do you have any whipped cream to put on top?"

The young lady grinned. "Yes, sir. Coming up."

Phineas put the receipt in his pocket as they left, hoping John wouldn't mind paying for Mrs. Courtney. On the way back to the rooming house, he decided to detour along the river since the moon shone brightly. They drove slowly along the brick-paved street, enjoying the moonlight sparkling on the water. It was a delightful time together.

When they returned late to the rooming house, they found the sheriff sitting in the lobby.

"Sheriff Milligan. Are you waiting for me?" Phineas said. "This is a surprise."

"Mr. Fletcher, something has happened. I need you to get a message to the sheriff in Spencer's Mill." He glanced nervously at Mrs. Courtney and turned his back to her.

"Of course. What is it?"

The sheriff lowered his voice and drew nearer to Phineas. "I found Taylor's body buried in the backyard among the trees."

Behind him, Mrs. Courtney gasped.

Milligan glanced at her, then turned to Phineas, who stood open-mouthed. "There's every reason to believe that Young murdered him," he continued in an even lower tone. "Would you ask your sheriff to arrest him? I'll come to pick him up as soon as I get a telegram telling me he's in custody."

"I'll be home by tomorrow this time," said Phineas. "I'll deliver the message as soon as I get into town."

"Everyone in your town will be in danger until he's in shackles."

"That's quite likely, sir. Shouldn't you send a telegram?"

"The telegraph operator is at home with the flu. I won't be able to get a telegram out until he recovers."

"Sheriff, there's a question I forgot to ask you. Have you had any dealings with a criminal named Roy Skinner?"

"No … That name isn't familiar to me."

"He has a friend named Beadle. What about him?"

"No, sorry."

"I only asked because Skinner and his sidekick, Beadle, had

already sent some thugs to threaten my client over his building. I wanted to make sure Young wasn't connected with them."

"It's always possible, I suppose, but not to my knowledge."

The two men shook hands, and the sheriff left.

"Mr. Fletcher," said Mrs. Courtney, "was he talking about that investigation you were telling me about?" she asked. Her eyes betrayed her eagerness to hear the details.

"I'm afraid so. I must sit down." Reality was beginning to settle in on Phineas. His knees were shaking. He realized that his poking around for information had uncovered a crime of the most severe magnitude. He lowered himself into a leather wingback chair in the lobby. Mrs. Courtney took the chair beside him.

"I shall never forget this evening," she said. "It was the best evening I've had in years. And it was even topped off by murder." She leaned her head on the back of her chair and smiled contentedly.

He leaned over and reached for her hand. "Mrs. Courtney, I thank you for a wonderful evening. I will never forget you."

She blushed. "I share that feeling, Mr. Fletcher. Please, would you call me Adelaide?"

"Only if you'll call me Phineas."

She dropped her eyes for a moment, then raised them and smiled. "Well, I must say goodnight, Phineas. It's late. I'll have breakfast for you at seven."

They lingered for a moment, smiling fondly at each other. "Good night, Adelaide," he said. He turned and trudged upstairs to his room. It would not be easy to get to sleep. He was quite taken with that woman. He felt like a boy who had just had his first date.

Chapter 30: PURSUIT AND CAPTURE

Thursday, February 24, 1887

In the morning, Phineas woke after a restless night. He barely had enough time to pack his bag before breakfast. He went downstairs to the inviting aromas of bacon, coffee, and cinnamon. This was luxurious living. Too bad it was ending.

"Good morning, Adelaide."

"Good morning, Phineas." She beamed at him, still enjoying the memory of the previous evening. She served his breakfast: three eggs instead of two, buttered toast, two strips of crispy bacon, and a cinnamon roll with a cup of steaming coffee. She didn't serve this much to the other guests who had come in, but he was grateful for every crumb, knowing he had a long trip before there would be anything else to eat.

"I'm sorry to be checking out this morning," he said. "This has been a remarkable experience."

She smiled and gave him a receipt for his room fee; then, she put a bag with two cinnamon rolls in his hands for the trip, a personal gift.

"I'm sorry to see you go," she said. "Perhaps you'll come back another time?"

He took her hand. "I certainly hope so." He toted his valise to the carriage, waved at her one last time, and headed home.

It was a long, long day. Phineas drove the horses as fast as he dared, stopping to give them feed, water, and rest only when necessary. All day he mulled over the interviews he had with the neighbors of the Taylor property and his conversations with the sheriff. Often his thoughts traveled to Adelaide Courtney. What a charming woman. And then he thought of John and Kate. He hoped they were not in danger from that charlatan.

At that moment in Spencer's Mill, Carl Young was loitering down the street from the bakery, still claiming to be Noah Taylor. John was concerned that once all the shop owners on the street locked up and went home, he and Kate would be there to handle Young alone if he made good on his threats. Before that could happen, John went next door to the general store and asked Danny to fetch the sheriff after he closed.

Sheriff Lane came by and dealt sharply with the loiterer.

"Why are you hanging around this area of town, sir?" Lane asked him. All the shops are closed."

Young took a belligerent attitude. "Is it illegal to stand on the sidewalk?"

"Not usually, but I've had complaints from both the general store and the bakery. They say you're threatening them. We don't tolerate that kind of behavior in Spencer's Mill."

"I'll keep that in mind," said Young with a sneer. He was going to be tough to convince.

"Where are you staying?" the sheriff asked.

"The Lamar Hotel, if it's any of your business."

"Then there's no reason for you to be in Spencer's Mill. You leave here now. When I return, you will spend the night in jail if I find you still here."

The assailant gave him a dirty look and ambled down the street at a deliberately slow pace. The sheriff, weary from a full day's work, hoped the man would keep going, so he went to his own home. Young waited around the corner until the sheriff left, then returned.

Kate and John went to the window every few minutes to see what he was doing. Their nerves were about to snap, having endured this fellow's harassment for three days. The family was more vulnerable now that the neighboring shopkeepers had gone home—especially since Katie was in a delicate condition. John opened his desk drawer and took out the pistol he kept there. He carefully loaded it and tucked it into his belt.

Once again, he peered out the window into the darkness from a concealed position. There was Carl Young's silhouette creeping closer to the bakery. The entire block was deserted of people, except for John and his family. Danny had gone home to his wife, thinking the problem was solved. But it wasn't.

John sent the children upstairs with strict instructions not to come down without his permission, no matter what. "Steven, you take care of your sister. You have to be the big brother tonight," he said.

"Yes, sir," said Steven and escorted his little sister and her rag doll up the stairs.

Kate's heart went with the children, but she stayed downstairs in the kitchen should John need her.

"John, we could escape if we all slipped out the back and took the carriage to the sheriff's office."

"I don't think he'll hurt us, but what would he do to the property if he found out we weren't here? I think it's important to stay here and defend the bakery."

Late that evening, Phineas knocked on Sheriff Lane's door in Spencer's Mill.

"Who the devil is beating on my door at this hour?" bellowed the sheriff from inside.

"It's Phineas Fletcher, sir, and I'm sorry to bother you, but I have an urgent message from the sheriff in Florissant, Ohio."

The sheriff pulled the door open. He was in his nightgown. "Sorry about my foul mood. I had just gone to sleep when you knocked."

"Quite understandable. This is a matter of murder, and the murderer is here in Spencer's Mill."

"This is unheard of. We don't have murderers in Spencer's Mill. This is a quiet town."

"Well, you do right now, and he's harassing some of our citizens. I'm afraid their lives may be in danger if he's not arrested."

Phineas launched into a quick explanation of the story about a man named Carl Young, claiming to be Noah Taylor, insisting he was the rightful owner of the storefront property that John Reese had just bought. Then, as briefly as possible, he laid out the information he obtained from all the neighbors in Florissant. He told him about Sheriff Milligan investigating and finding the body of Noah Taylor. "He strongly suspects that Carl Young was the man who committed the murder and would like you to arrest him if he's still in Spencer's Mill."

Lane changed his attitude. His eyebrows raised. "I believe he is still here, Mr. Fletcher. I had to go to the new bakery this evening and throw him out for harassing the Reeses."

"Oh, no. Are they safe?"

"They're shaken, of course, but physically well. The blighter was yelling that he was the rightful owner of the property, but the Reeses showed me their deed. There didn't seem to be any question but what they are the proper owners."

"How long ago was that?"

"Oh, an hour or two ago. It was my second trip over there tonight."

"Do you think there's any chance he would go back there?"

"Heavens, I hope not. But I don't know. Do you think we should go check now?"

"Yes, sir, I surely do."

The sheriff slipped out of his nightgown and put his day clothes on. He mounted his horse and took off for the bakery at a gallop, with Phineas following as fast as he could in his carriage, his wheels clattering on the bumpy road.

The lamps were lit at the bakery, throwing yellow light into the street from the front window, which had been smashed. Someone was shouting inside. There was a crash and more screaming. The sheriff dismounted and ran into the bakery with his revolver drawn. The shouting and crashing stopped abruptly. He didn't see anyone, but they were still there.

"John Reese! Are you all right?"

Silence. "John? It's the sheriff."

John's muffled voice called out, "In the kitchen, sheriff. Watch out for Taylor."

The sheriff detected movement in the next room as the man calling himself Taylor took a quick peek around the door frame. "Carl Young! Come out of that room. You're under arrest for the murder of Noah Taylor."

Young slowly appeared in the doorway, holding one hand behind the doorframe to conceal his weapon. Then, in one sudden move, he spun to face the sheriff, crouched in an attack stance, and brandished the bat he had used to break the glass window. He charged at the sheriff, trying to swing the bat at his knees, but the sheriff sidestepped him, and Young lost his balance. He went flying and ended up with his skinny arms and legs spread-eagled on the pine floor in the middle of the broken window glass. His face, arms, and chest were full of glass splinters. The sheriff was on him in a flash, tying his hands behind his back with the rope from his belt. Young screamed that he was hurt, but Sheriff Lane ignored his pleas.

John and Kate came out of hiding in the kitchen, white-faced and wide-eyed.

"Mr. Fletcher, would you allow me to drive this gentleman to jail in your carriage?" asked Sheriff Lane. "I'll bring it back soon."

"Be my guest," Phineas said. "I might be able to get a cup of tea from Mrs. Reese while I wait. I'm sure they'll want to hear the whole story of my trip to Florissant."

The officer shoved his prisoner out the door. Young yelled about how badly he was hurt. Rivulets of blood dribbled down his face and arms. His shirt was splotched red. He shouted that he needed a doctor.

"I'll go for the doctor after you're behind bars. You're not going to get much sympathy from me," Lane growled.

"You came just in time, Mr. Fletcher," said John. "He was ready to bust up the store because we wouldn't move out and turn it over to him. I've never seen anything like it."

"You were lucky. He murdered the last guy who wouldn't turn his property over to him."

John's eyes grew wide, and his chin dropped. "Is he part of Roy Skinner's mob?"

"We didn't find any evidence of that. He was working independently in that twisted scheme. Once he killed the owner of a house in Florissant, it wouldn't have taken that much to drive you out or even kill you to gain your property. He could have sold it for a good price."

Kate shuddered at the thought. "I need to clean that blood off the floor before the children see it." She cleaned up the blood with wet towels. John came behind her with the broom to sweep up the glass. It was slow going on a damp floor.

"I'll make the tea," Phineas said. He was thirsty from his long drive.

When the evidence of violence had been cleaned as best they could, Katie shouted, "Children, you can come down now."

Steven shouted back. "Pa said to stay here until he says it's time to come down."

Kate chuckled and turned toward John. "You need to release your children," she said and pulled cups out of the cupboard.

"Come on down, Stevie," called John. "Bring Gracie with you. We're safe now."

The two crept down the stairs, wide-eyed.

"Come on in, children," Katie said. "I'll give you a glass of milk."

Phineas told them the whole story in detail. Their attention was riveted on every word. When he finished, Kate said, "John, I didn't realize how close we were to being . . ."

She didn't want to say the word in front of the children.

Phineas smacked his fist on the table. "Nuts. I forgot to tell Sheriff Lane to wire Sheriff Milligan in Florissant to pick up the prisoner. He'll stand trial for murder there. I wonder if Lane would want to deliver him in my carriage. I would volunteer to go along as extra security to watch the prisoner. I made a friend in Florissant I would like to see again."

Chapter 31: ELI'S DEFIANCE

Sunday, February 27, 1887

That Sunday after church, Danny and Charlotte stopped by the bakery to see the progress being made. The unfinished sales counter that George was building sat in the middle of the room. Danny asked, "John, do you plan to paint that?"

"I would like to do that eventually, but I need to economize wherever I can until we start making a profit."

"Pa had some paint. It's still at the house. I don't know what he used it for, but I'll bet there's enough to do that piece. If you come over, I'll show you where it is. Kate, why don't you and the children come with him? We'll all have lunch together. I think Charlotte can scrounge up enough food for all of us."

John and Kate were eager for a change of scenery, so they took an afternoon's break and went home with Danny and Charlotte. Kate shared kitchen duty with Charlotte to finish preparing the meal. As they worked, she thought Charlotte had something on her mind.

"Charlotte, you seem to be bothered with something."

Charlotte hesitated, then asked the question that had been on her mind. "Is your health good? You haven't been looking well lately."

"Oh, I'm fine," Kate said. "Just tired."

Charlotte put her hands on her hips with a twisted grin.

"Since we're family, I hope you'll forgive my rudeness, but I guess I'll have to ask this question directly. Katherine Reese, are you expecting another baby?

Kate blushed. "Quiet, Charlotte. Only John knows. I wanted to wait until I was sure before telling anyone else."

Charlotte giggled. "We all suspected it. You seem exhausted all the time. And by the way you sit, we predict it will be a boy."

"That's an old wives' tale."

Charlotte grinned. "Sometimes old wives are right. Never mind, I won't say anything to anyone until you're ready to make it official. Go over there to the table and relax. I can finish getting lunch ready."

The family sat down to a delicious turkey lunch. The conversation turned to God's grace in protecting John and Kate from a dangerous situation. Then they began to talk about Eli.

Danny said, "I wish Eli and Mary would join the family events. They haven't been with us in quite a while."

"It's my fault," John said. "I'd give anything to turn back the clock and do things differently. Do you remember Ma talking about the rippling effect of sin? This is it." He wagged his head slowly.

Danny had a suggestion. "Maybe you and I could go talk to him together."

Kate intervened. "Be careful about getting ahead of God on this. You need to make sure Eli is ready before you approach him."

"That's one point of view," said John. "But we can't just ignore this. We have to get this resolved. It wouldn't hurt for Danny and me to talk to Eli together."

Kate sighed. There was no talking him out of this.

After the meal, John and Danny took the carriage to Eli's house. Mary and Eli had missed church again that morning, but by all appearances, nothing else had changed. The chickens were in the coop, and the horse and carriage were in the barn. The place was quiet. John tied the horse to the rail, and the brothers walked to the door.

John knocked. Presently, Eli answered. He hesitated when he found his brothers standing there and finally asked, "What do you want?"

"Could we come in?" John asked.

"If Danny had come alone, he could come in. But no. Tell me what you want, then go away."

"Eli, we've been missing you at family functions." Danny hoped to appeal to Eli's sense of family, but his brother still nursed the hurt of betrayal. He wasn't having any of it.

"Danny, I'm sorry to be rude to you, but John should know he's not welcome here, and now you know it, too." He closed the door firmly. John and Danny stood on the porch with their faces mere inches from the closed door, not knowing what to do. The latch dropped into its slot on the inside.

Danny put his arm around John's shoulder. "Let's go."

John's spirit was so crushed he could barely breathe. He didn't expect that severe a rejection. His brother might as well have killed him. "We shouldn't have come, should we?"

"I guess not."

The following two weeks went quickly. The broken window at the bakery was replaced, remodeling was finished, the floors painted, and furnishings put into place. The new sign was installed across the front of the store, and a large banner hung in the newly replaced window, announcing a Grand Opening. "Free Cinnamon Bread Knots on Opening Day," it declared. Work schedules were finalized, prices were set for the baked goods, and supplies were in place.

George and Sally had their assignments. George would be

staffing the sales counter and taking care of small maintenance jobs. Sally would watch Gracie and Steven, take care of the laundry and cleaning, and possibly help Kate in the kitchen if she had time. Kate's job would be baking, and John would manage the business—ordering supplies, paying the bills, depositing the revenue, advertising, and evaluating which items were the best money-makers. If John's careful planning was correct, everything would be covered.

Chapter 32: DELIVERING THE PRISONER

Monday, February 28, 1887

On Monday morning, after Danny and Charlotte left for their jobs, Phineas was home in his kitchen enjoying a hot cup of coffee. He read a copy of the Lamar newspaper Danny brought home from the general store. The headline was, of course, the apprehension of a murderer in Spencer's Mill. The article reported that he had tried to extort a commercial building from John Reese, the man who had recently bought it. It cited the investigative work of Phineas Fletcher and the brilliant skills of Sheriff Lane in capturing the criminal. The newspaper said the Grand Opening of the bakery in that building would be on March 6th. That was free publicity for John and Kate. For them, the timing couldn't be better.

Phineas grinned. He wondered if he could get more copies. He would send one to his sister in Delphos and keep one in his dresser upstairs so he could revisit it from time to time, savoring the memory of his most remarkable adventure.

He was enjoying himself immensely when someone rapped on the front door. It was Sheriff Lane with his hat in his hand.

"Come in, sir," said Phineas, grabbing the sheriff's hand and pumping it up and down. "I'm surprised to see you again so soon. Let me get you a cup of coffee."

"No, thank you, Phineas." He clapped him on the shoulder.

"May I sit down?"

"You bet. Take the Chesterfield. It's the best seat in the house."

Lane took a seat. "Have you seen the paper?" He perched his hat on the arm of the sofa.

Phineas plopped into the wing chair, grinning. "Yes, I have. The reporter did an excellent job."

The sheriff smiled. "Well, I still have that scoundrel in my jail. I can hardly wait to get rid of him. Sheriff Milligan in Florissant telegraphed, asking if I could deliver him. I'm in a spot. My budget doesn't allow for a deputy, but the county would pay for your food and lodging if you would agree to some volunteer service. Do you think you could go along?"

Phineas grinned. "That would be quite an adventure. I would like that."

"Actually..." Lane hesitated. "Actually, could we use your carriage? I don't have any other way to deliver him."

"Certainly. We could work out a small per-mile fee for the carriage to cover wear and tear. And you'll need to feed my horses." Phineas was not one to miss an opportunity. "And if we break a spoke or something on the trip, I expect you to pay for repairs."

"I think that's reasonable. If you drive the carriage, I'll guard the prisoner. Do you understand there is some personal risk involved?"

Phineas nodded. "Yes. I'll take my pistol. If the blighter tries to escape, one of us will shoot him."

"No, no," Lane said, waving his hands back and forth. "We'll shoot him only if he attacks one of us, but if he tries to escape, we'll chase him down and tighten the shackles." Lane chuckled. "You'll not be too eager to use your pistol, will you? I hope I don't have an aspiring gunslinger on my hands."

Phineas leaned back in a hearty laugh. "I promise to go easy on the trigger. Just so you know, I'm not up to chasing him at my age," Phineas said. "You're on your own there."

The two men agreed to leave at dawn the following day. They planned to deliver the prisoner to Sheriff Milligan, then stay overnight at Mrs. Courtney's Rooming House.

Tuesday, March 1, 1887

Just before sunrise, in a heavy fog, Phineas hitched two horses to the carriage. The air was cold and damp. He hoped the sun would come out and burn off the haze early. He drove to the jail to meet Sheriff Lane. When he arrived, Lane bound the prisoner's wrists behind him for safe transport to Florissant. The unruly felon still had bandages on his head, arms, and chest where the doctor had treated his lacerations. Defiant as ever, kicking and thrashing about, he was complicating the sheriff's efforts to shackle his ankles.

"This will probably not be a pleasant ride," said Lane. "I'm bringing a gag with us in case he won't shut his mouth. If he behaves, I'll give him the freedom to speak, but if he abuses the privilege, the gag goes on. I'm short on mercy today."

Phineas chuckled. "It's a long ride. We'll have to see how that works out."

"I'm hungry," said Carl. "I need something to eat. I'm diabetic."

"Sure you are," said Lane, "and I'm the king of France. You already had breakfast in your cell. You'll get something to eat when we get to Lamar."

Phineas slapped the reins, and off they went. Carl started early, complaining that he was uncomfortable. He was cold. He was hungry. He was hot. His nose itched. He needed something to drink.

When they got to Lamar three and a half hours later, they

stopped outside the Tea Room. Phineas went inside and ordered three lunches to be eaten in the carriage. The proprietor balked at that unusual request, but Phineas explained they were transporting a murderer to Florissant. It wasn't safe for the restaurant patrons to have a murderer in their presence.

The proprietor had read the story in the newspaper. That changed her mind. "I'll send the food on a tray with three bowls and spoons. I'll give you a canteen of coffee and three cups. You make sure you get those things back to me."

"I promise that faithfully, madam. One tray, three bowls, three spoons, one canteen, and three cups." He left the restaurant with the food balanced on the tray.

They started down the road again. The sheriff had the job of spoon-feeding the prisoner his meal. Carl complained. "This is inhuman. Any decent person would loosen my hands long enough to let me eat by myself."

"Any decent person would not murder his host, either, or attack a family in their bakery," said the sheriff. "You'd better shut up, or you'll find yourself gagged."

He remembered something amusing he wanted to share.

"Say, Phineas, did I tell you I got a letter from Sheriff Milligan?"

"No."

"He told me about how he dug up the body."

"What happened?"

"Well, he didn't have a shovel to dig with, so he went to the general store and told the storekeeper what he had to do. He begged for the use of a shovel. The owner didn't want to let him use one because he was afraid he'd ruin it, and it couldn't be sold after that. But he finally relented. Civic duty and all. Milligan told him he'd bring it back."

He put another spoonful of stew in the prisoner's mouth.

"What happened then?"

"Well, sir, after he dug up the body, he took the shovel back to the general store with mud all over it. He apologized but told the shopkeeper he'd used it to find the body. I have to admit, the store owner is a smarter man than I am. He left the mud on it, doubled the price, and advertised it as the shovel that found the dead body. Sold it within a day's time."

He laughed and slapped his knee. Phineas had a good laugh, too, but the prisoner only glared at them. The sheriff spooned more stew into Carl's mouth.

The three men rode on and on, past wheat fields and corn stubble, up gently sloping rises and down again. The prisoner said he had to relieve himself, so they stopped the carriage beside a field full of dead cornstalks. Carl hobbled off into the field with his hands bound in front of him and legs in shackles.

Phineas and the sheriff were chatting back and forth when Phineas glanced over at the cornfield. The prisoner was tugging frantically at his shackles and trying to hop away. "Lane, look sharp. Carl is doing his best to escape over there."

The sheriff cursed under his breath. "Phineas, I believe I'll have to chase that wretch." He climbed out of the carriage and bolted into the cornfield, snagging the prisoner in no time.

"Back to the carriage," he commanded. As soon as they got in, Lane bound the prisoner's hands behind him as tightly as before. "You can't be trusted, so we won't make any more stops. I don't care if you explode. I'm also taking your boots, so if you manage to run off, you won't get far in your socks."

"I don't mean to interfere," said Phineas, "but be careful taking his boots off. He has small feet, so he may be able to slide out of those ankle irons more easily."

Lane reconsidered. "Quite right. You'll be keeping your boots on, Young."

The hours passed very slowly. Shortly after the cornfield incident, the prisoner became mouthy and belligerent, so he endured a gag for the rest of the trip. At times, he thrashed around on the carriage seat, bellowing through his gag, trying to escape his bonds. His antics wore on the nerves of Phineas and the sheriff.

Upon reaching Florissant, they were relieved to discharge him to the care of Sheriff Milligan.

"Nice to see you again, Fletcher," said Milligan. "I hear you had a part in the capture."

"I can't claim that, sir. It was all Sheriff Lane here. If he hadn't jumped into quick action when I told him about Young, my daughter's brother-in-law and his whole family might be dead by now. I hope the judge throws the book at this son of Beelzebub."

"He'll probably be hanged," said Milligan casually.

The prisoner fought every effort to escort him into the jail section of the building, so Milligan was forced to drag him in. He released his shackles and shut the iron door to the cell with a heavy clang. Carl shouted and shook the iron bars as hard as he could, but Milligan walked away and closed the door between his office and the jail section. The door muffled the sound.

"Whew," he said. "He must have been raised by monkeys."

"Good seeing you again, sir, and good luck getting the prisoner convicted."

"Thanks for bringing him in," Milligan said. "You'll likely be called to testify at his trial, you know."

"I never considered that," said Phineas. "That means one more trip back to Florissant." At that thought, he broke into a smile, then he and Sheriff Lane left to go the few blocks to the boarding house, enjoying the peace and freedom of being released from their difficult assignment. Thinking back, it had been like transporting the devil himself.

Mrs. Courtney was at the front desk when they walked in. Her eyes twinkled. "Phineas," she said, as a huge smile lit her face. "You came back."

"Yes, I did, Adelaide. My, it's good to see you again. Let me introduce you to Sheriff Lane from Spencer's Mill. We just delivered the prisoner to Sheriff Milligan."

"Oh, the murderer you told me about. The news story was in the paper this week. I told all my friends at church. I was so proud because I'm a friend of the man who caught the murderer."

"Well, it wasn't exactly like that," Phineas said, blushing, "but I did have a part in it. Do you have two rooms for tonight?"

"I believe I do."

"And would you like to go to the pub for dinner?" His teasing eyes peered at her over his spectacles.

She giggled. "Meet me here in the lobby at six?"

"Sure thing. You'll have dinner with two gentlemen tonight."

Phineas smiled an apology and took the keys from her. He thought she was a little disappointed that they would have a third person joining them. He preferred a more private arrangement, but he couldn't be rude to Lane.

The two men toted their overnight bags up the stairs and settled into their rooms. They had a short rest, then returned downstairs at the appointed time. Sheriff Lane, Phineas, and Adelaide rode to the pub and had an excellent dinner with fascinating conversation. They lingered over a piece of pecan pie and tea.

It wasn't as magical for Phineas as when he and Adelaide had a private dinner together, but at least he could give her a free meal cooked by someone else.

Back at the boarding house, the sheriff went up to his bed, leaving Phineas and Adelaide to continue their conversation in hushed tones in the lobby. Eventually, it was time for them to say good night.

"Do you think you'll ever be back in Florissant?" she asked him in parting. "I have so enjoyed our time together."

"It's likely that I will need to come back to testify in court. After that, who knows? I want to say yes, but I can't make a promise. I live with my daughter and her husband, who plan to move to Illinois in June. If they do that, I'll be going with them. Then it would be impossible to visit. I'll stay in touch with a letter."

She sighed. "Well . . . good night, Phineas."

"Good night, Adelaide."

In the morning, after one of Adelaide's delectable breakfasts, Phineas and the sheriff traveled back to Spencer's Mill.

Chapter 33: GRAND OPENING

Friday, March 4, 1887

Friday was the Day Before—the day before the widely advertised day when the bakery would open. A successful grand opening now depended on Kate. Fortunately, she was just about past her morning sickness. She gathered her ingredients, mixed up large quantities of bread dough, and set the bowls aside to rise. It would be ready by early morning to go into the Dutch ovens.

Sally peeled and sliced a large pan of apples while Kate rolled out dough and filled several small pans, finishing about five apple pies for the next day. Oatmeal cookies and sugar cookies came out of the oven. She baked four chocolate cakes while Sally lent a hand by mixing the icing with Kate's recipe. They worked together like the cogs of a Swiss watch, all while Gracie walked in and out of the kitchen, chatting tirelessly.

Saturday, March 5, 1887

Early in the morning, Kate rose and went downstairs to the kitchen. Early daylight crept in through the front windows. The kitchen was in perfect order, with bowls of dough ready to be put in the pans. She tied on her apron and took a deep breath. "It's time to launch the business, Father," she prayed. "This is

Your bakery, and I ask for success in sales today, and I pray that You will be honored in whatever happens."

The bread dough had risen nicely. Her hands moved quickly, forming some into loaves and some into rolls, some with a sprinkle of sesame seed. She formed the rest of the dough into bread knots topped with icing made of butter, caster sugar, and cinnamon. She needed about a hundred of those because John had advertised all over town that they were handing out free cinnamon bread knots on opening day. He wanted to get those customers in there.

As she concentrated on her baking tasks, breakfast completely slipped her mind. John and the children got up a little later and came downstairs looking for something to eat.

"John, can you make breakfast for the children?"

"This is one detail that slipped my list. I wonder what else I forgot. Well, sit down, children, and I'll have breakfast ready in a few minutes."

He cracked some eggs, dropped one on the floor with a splat, and fried the rest quickly while he grabbed a rag and cleaned up the gooey mess. The children sat at the table giggling over the egg accident. Kate smiled at them and continued to work, dividing the raised dough and placing loaf-sized portions into the Dutch ovens.

George and Sally arrived at seven-thirty, excited that the bakery was finally opening. Sally arranged all the baked goods in the two display cases. John took the coins and bank notes he had brought for making change and sorted them into the cash drawer for George. The first loaves of bread came out of the ovens, more went in, and the first customer arrived a little after eight o'clock.

In the kitchen, Kate strained to hear the activity on the sales floor. George's voice boomed. "Welcome to the Crust and Crumb, madam. Would you like to try a frosted bread knot?"

A woman's voice answered, "Yes, thank you. Is Kate here?"

It was the voice of Agatha Brown, that dreaded gossip.

"She's working in the kitchen, madam, and quite busy, as you can imagine. I don't know if she can come out right now."

Kate smoothed back her hair, took off her apron, and sailed into the salesroom with a bright smile. She was on a mission to defuse any trouble Mrs. Brown intended to cause. "Good morning, Mrs. Brown. You're our first customer. Congratulations. You win a free apple pie." She picked up one of the apple desserts, fragrant with cinnamon, and placed it in Mrs. Brown's basket. "There's normally a two-cent deposit on the pan, but that's free for you today. When you bring the pan back, we'll give you two cents toward purchasing any product in our bakery."

Mrs. Brown was taken aback by Kate's apparent delight in her work situation. She stumbled for words. "Thank you," was all she could say.

"Do you need any bread today?" Kate continued. George stood aside quietly, his mouth agape and his hands hanging loosely.

Mrs. Brown bought one loaf, paid Mr. Evans, and left the store.

Kate turned to George with a sheepish grin. "I'm sorry to interfere, Mr. Evans. That woman needed special treatment. She's a hateful gossip, and I wanted to shower her with goodies so she wouldn't have anything nasty to say. She's already done her share of damage."

George burst out in a belly laugh. "I wondered what was going on. I thought maybe you wanted to handle my job, too."

Kate grinned. "No, I don't. So don't give away any more pies today. That was a special situation."

Another customer came in. "All yours, Mr. Evans," said Kate and returned to the kitchen.

The bread knots ran short by ten o'clock since customers brought their children in for treats. While Gracie entertained herself upstairs, Sally came down to help in the kitchen again, passing through the sales area.

"How are things going in the salesroom?" Kate asked.

"There are two customers out there right now. They say they love the aroma of baking bread and cinnamon when they walk through the door. You're down to two pies and one cake. What can I do to help?"

"It would be a good idea to go to the root cellar for more apples," Kate said. "I'll mix more dough while the bread is baking."

Sally returned with the apples and put the knife to them.

"I wonder if every day will be this busy or if this is a big day because it's Grand Opening," Kate said.

"Part of it is due to those bread knots flying off the shelf. I suspect there have been some children in here more than once."

"I'm sure you're right."

"It will probably be less hectic as time passes, but hopefully, your sales will be steady."

"If this keeps up, I don't know how I'll manage dinner for the family."

"Well," said Sally, "you're making the crust for the pies. Why don't you use some of it to make a meat and potato pie for the family?"

"Good idea, Sally. That'll take care of today's problem."

After Kate took a short break for lunch, she asked Sally to wash some bowls and began to mix up more bread dough. Another customer came in asking for her. In the kitchen, Kate sighed. *Why do people want to interrupt me on a day like this?*

She washed her hands and walked out to the sales floor. "Francie," she said. "I'm surprised to see you today. I'm sorry I can't chat. We're working frantically back in the kitchen."

"No problem, Katie." She clasped her hands in front of her and lowered her eyes. "I just wanted to tell you that when you said God was going to take care of you, I didn't believe you."

Katie's eyes were full of compassion. "I knew you didn't."

"I can see that I was wrong."

Kate smiled and opened her arms for a hug. Francie walked toward her, throwing her arms around her cousin. Kate was careful not to get flour on the back of Francie's expensive new shirtwaist dress. "Thanks for letting me know."

She turned back to the kitchen as Francie asked George the price of a chocolate cake.

Kate discovered that the time of day affected sales. In the morning, loaves of bread sold best, but as the day wore on, folks came in for desserts to take home for dinner. The pies and cakes sold in the afternoon. Children walking home from school requested cookies for snacks. *Good to know,* Kate thought. *We'll have to adjust our baking schedule.*

The day was full of activity. One by one, the members of the Board of Trustees came by with best wishes. John gave them tours of the building so they could see how it had changed.

Susannah couldn't help coming by to see how things were going on Grand Opening Day. She brought a casserole to feed the family for dinner. "I'd love to stay, John, but I need to get back home to feed Christian. He'll be home late today."

"All right, Ma. Thanks for coming by."

Kate was especially relieved she wouldn't have to cook the family dinner after all the time she spent in the kitchen already.

The biggest surprise was a visit by the reporter from the local newspaper, looking to write a story on the opening of the bakery. He spent time with John, asking questions about how the bakery came to be. He had heard rumors about a man trying to extort the building, and someone else kidnapping the Reeses' son. John was delighted to give him all the details. This would be good free publicity.

Baked goods came out of the ovens all day, and the customers kept coming.

That evening, after the bakery closed and the family sat down to eat, they thanked God for His blessings on the day. It looked like the bakery was off to a successful start.

Chapter 34: JOHN'S BIG IDEA

Saturday, June 25, 1889

Two years passed quickly, with the bakery business doing quite well. The new baby, Davy, had grown to be a sturdy toddler. John's relationship with Eli was still broken, with no sign of change.

Sales in the store had leveled off, and John was restless again. He didn't want to be satisfied with living at that level for the rest of their lives. The responsibility for raising the profits would be on his shoulders. He re-evaluated the business, knowing Kate was doing her part in making the bakery successful. Fortunately, the Evanses had fit in well, taking a heavy load off Kate.

He ran the cost numbers one more time to figure out where to shave expenses. He kept statistics on how many items were baked daily, how many had been sold, and how much was wasted. He invented elaborate charts, trying to determine why sales fluctuated each day and how they could more accurately anticipate each day's needs. The numbers weren't speaking to him the way he wanted. He shook his head in frustration.

What if they branched out? They could use their dining area as seating for a restaurant, but without that room, the upstairs apartment wasn't big enough for a family of five. They would have to move into a house somewhere else. Was that even possible? He needed to brainstorm with his business partners—his wife and God.

"Kate?" He brought up the idea with her at lunch while they sat in the kitchen with bowls of ham and beans. "I want to talk to you about an idea I had about changing how we do business."

"Why is that, John? The way we run the bakery works well, and we're making a comfortable living."

"Yes, I know," he said, "but we can do better. This would have to be a matter of prayer, and we'd have to agree on taking a new direction. So let me tell you what I think, and then you tell me what you think."

She nodded. "All right, John, start talking."

He took a folded paper from his pocket and spread it on the table. "Here's my idea. We buy another house to live in, somewhere near here. We rent out the upstairs apartment here with some modifications, giving the renters a private entrance at the back. That would give us extra income to pay for the house. We fill the dining room with tables and chairs and decorate it fancy, like the Tea Room in Lamar. We offer a lunch menu of soups and sandwiches. What do you think of that?"

Kate sat stunned, with her hand resting on her chest. "That's quite a major change."

"Yes, but I think we could do it. We would have to hire waitresses."

"And cooks. I can't cook all that food and still keep the bakery stocked." Kate shook her head. "I have to say that this idea is overwhelming to me. I don't think I'm up to it."

"You don't have to have any increased responsibility. Profits are up. We'll hire people."

"Well, John, if you feel this is possible, I'm open to exploring it. Not saying yes, just saying maybe, because the idea scares me."

"'Maybe' is good enough," said John, leaning over to kiss

her cheek. "I'll work on cost and revenue projections and see if it's practical. And we'll pray for guidance."

She forced a thin smile and finished her beans while he jumped up and ran to his desk to work on numbers. Her eyes flooded, and tears began to roll down her cheeks. She wiped them away with the back of her hand. *He'll never be happy at one level if he sees a possibility of jumping to another,* she thought. *God help us.*

Chapter 35: A FAMILY DINNER

Sunday, June 26, 1889

Next Sunday after church, John's family was invited to visit his mother and Christian. Eli and Mary would also be there. When John learned that Eli had agreed to come, he was overjoyed. Perhaps all his prayers for his brother's change of heart were finally being answered.

They all relaxed over a delicious lunch and swapped family chatter. Eventually, Eli stood with a smile and tapped his glass with his spoon. "Could I have your attention?" he asked. "We have some big news to share."

The family conversation stopped, and everyone turned their attention toward Eli.

"We're finally going to be parents." He grinned and put his hand on Mary's shoulder. "We think the baby will probably be born sometime around Thanksgiving."

"Eli, that's wonderful," Susannah said, clapping her hands with the rest of the family. "You've wanted a baby for several years. God is certainly showing you His favor."

Mary blushed. "Eli, we weren't going to tell anyone for a while."

"I know, Mary, but I couldn't keep it in. This is such great news. I'm sorry, I should have let you tell it in your own time."

"No, it's fine, Eli. I've been eager to tell them, too."

"We have something to share, too," John said. "We're considering expanding the bakery to include a lunch restaurant."

Eli returned to his seat with lips pressed together, glaring at his brother. John was confused to see he was angry. He didn't know why.

"That's a big step, isn't it?" Christian asked.

"Yes, there's a lot to think about. Our first thought is that we'd have to move to another house to make more room. We're thinking of turning our dining room into the restaurant dining room."

"And that would involve closing off the upper floor and giving it an outside entrance?"

"Yes, sir. I haven't worked that out yet, but that was my thought. We hope to find a home nearby, even if we rent for a while."

"Sounds interesting," Christian said. "What kind of menu would you plan for the restaurant?"

"Soup, sandwiches, that kind of thing. We'd have to hire waitresses and another cook, but my projections show we could increase our income if we make these changes."

Susannah was captivated by this idea, but she was concerned about Kate. "How do you feel about all this, Katie?"

Kate shrugged and answered in a voice flat of emotion. "You know John. He was always ambitious. He does a good job managing the bakery, so I don't suppose he would fail at the restaurant business."

"But are you up for the extra work?"

Kate looked at her plate. "Well, frankly, I have all I can handle. I'm sure John will make room in his budget for enough help that the restaurant will be operated separately from the bakery."

Her mother-in-law gazed at her face with a keen eye, trying

to read her, but Kate turned away. She asked her sister-in-law, "I want to hear about the new baby, Mary. How are you feeling?"

Mary smiled. "Not so well in the morning. But later in the day..."

"Don't worry. It'll get better." Kate took a sip of her tea. "You need to get as much sleep as you can now because after the baby comes, your days and nights will run together. The little one will consume all your time."

Later in the afternoon, Christian drew John aside. "John, you know we have your mother's house in Spencer's Mill rented out. Our tenants said they'd be leaving at the end of July. They're buying a house in Lamar. Would you be interested in renting your mother's house?"

"I'll discuss that with Kate," John said. "That idea is very appealing to me. It would be like going home. My first thought was to buy a house, but renting Ma's house might work just as well. Thank you, sir. I'll let you know."

Chapter 36: JOHN'S ERROR

Tuesday, June 28, 1889

Later that week, John hitched up the horses to go to the lumber yard, wondering why Katie hadn't acted like herself for the past few days. She was ordinarily cheerful, the glue holding the family together and the center of the business. But her attitude had changed. He didn't know why and was starting to worry about her. He hoped she wasn't going to have another baby.

"Steven," he said, "I'd like you to go to the lumber yard with me. I need some help carrying the supplies."

Steven's eight-year-old chest puffed out. He had never been on a business errand with his Pa. He was being treated like a man and was going along to help. He hopped into the wagon. John sat beside him on the driver's seat when the boy asked a question.

"Why are we going to the lumber yard, Pa?"

"We're going to buy some wood for stairs, and we're going to buy a door so we can go outside from our apartment."

"Why do we want to do that?'

"So we can move to a new house, and someone else will live in our apartment. We don't want them to go through the bakery when they go outside."

"Oh. Mama doesn't want to move to a new house."

"What? Did she tell you that?"

"Yes. She was crying, and she told me that."

John's eyes grew large, and his jaw dropped.

"Are you sure, Steven?"

"Yes, Pa, I'm sure.

How could I have missed that? She never told me. How could I have been so unaware? "We're going to put off our trip, son," he said. "Hop down. I need to talk to Mama before we go."

Steven climbed out of the carriage, and John returned to the bakery. He found Kate in the kitchen, kneading bread.

"Kate, we need to talk. Can you put the dough down for a few minutes?"

She wiped her hands on her apron. "What do you want?"

"Sit with me for a few minutes. We need to have a meeting of the bakery owners."

She sat quietly, waiting for him to say something. "Well?"

John wasn't sure how to start. "Steven says you don't want to move to another house."

"That's right. I told you I didn't want to change the way we do business. I told you I didn't want to move, but you never mentioned it again. You kept making plans privately. As long as we live here, I can be around the children, and I don't have to worry about a menu for a restaurant or cleaning up after people's dirty dishes. Life is full already. I can't add another thing to my schedule and stay healthy. That's too much. And you didn't even ask me after our first conversation. You just told your Ma and Christian that we were opening a restaurant. We never talked it out. And I'm angry about that. This is not John Reese's decision. This is supposed to be John, Kate, and God." Tears squeezed out of her eyes.

Sally entered the kitchen, sensed something was going on between them, and backed out.

"Kate, I'm sorry." John stared at the floor. "I got so excited about the new plans..."

"Your new plans."

After an awkward pause, he continued. "I can cancel the plans. I need to tell Christian we won't be moving into Ma's old house."

"What? We were moving into your mother's house?"

John's face turned red. "I guess I didn't mention that to you, either. Christian says the tenants will move out at the end of July, and we could rent the house then if we want it."

Kate began to shift in her chair. "I didn't know that. That takes care of one big problem I dreaded: finding a new place. But what about all the extra work?"

"I promise you won't have any extra work. There's still room in the kitchen for another stove, and we'll hire a cook, waitresses, and people to clean up. I promise we won't open the restaurant until all the workers are lined up."

"John, it doesn't matter if you hire a whole crowd. I'll always end up with extra work, some detail that no one else can handle."

"Then we'll shift some of your other responsibilities to the staff."

"What about the children? I can't be here in the kitchen and at another house at the same time."

"I've worked the numbers. We can get someone, maybe a responsible single woman, to take care of the children at the house. Sally can help you here; if that isn't enough help with the baking, we'll hire someone else. Some young women in town would probably love to learn from you."

"And you won't rush to open the restaurant until we're fully staffed?"

"No. I promise. I have rushed into this too fast by myself; I admit that. I'm asking your forgiveness. And I'll slow down on it. We need to ask God's guidance on this thing, too."

Kate lifted her head and gazed into John's eyes. "If God says no, we'll stop. Agreed?"

"Yes. But if God says yes, we'll go ahead with it. Agreed?"

She nodded. "Now, why don't you get what you need at the lumber yard? Even if we don't move, it would be nice to have a private entrance."

For the second time that morning, John took Steven out to the wagon and climbed onto the driver's seat, this time with a clear head. The horses headed down the familiar road to Lamar. Fortunately, the lumber yard was on the near side of town, so they were there by noon.

John helped Steven down and went into the office with a list of supplies. "Good to see you again, Jackson," he said.

Mr. Jackson shook his hand and clapped him on the shoulder. "How is your business going, Reese? I'm sure you've met my wife. Whenever she gets anywhere near Spencer's Mill, she's a customer of yours."

"The business is going well. Yes, I've met your wife. Fine lady, and I appreciate her business. We're thinking of expanding, so I need some materials to make a private entrance to the upstairs. By the way, this is my son Steven. He's going to help carry supplies."

"Nice to meet you, young Mr. Reese," Jackson shook the boy's hand, making him grin. He had never had a handshake before.

Steven wandered the aisles while the men read the list, satisfying his curiosity about the different sizes of nails, small tools, and other mysterious items on the shelves so fascinating to a boy. Then, the men pulled the supplies John needed. Steven carried bags of nails, hinges, and doorknobs. He helped his father take boards to the wagon. As they headed back to Spencer's Mill, John reached into his pocket and pulled out four coppers. "This is payment for your work, son. And thanks for your help."

The boy's eyes lit up. "When we get home, can I go to the general store and spend it?"

"Only after you carry the bags into the bakery and put them by the alley door."

Steven carefully pocketed the coins, then sat beside his Pa, grinning and bouncing his knees to work off excess energy.

The children knew it would be time for the family to move into Susannah's house when the calendar turned to August. Gracie and Steven chatted about moving constantly. Little Davy caught their mood. This signaled a lifestyle change for the children. They would live in a big house and be able to play in the stream out back. They would have chickens and be able to collect eggs, and they might have friends their age in the neighborhood.

Kate was aware that for John this meant moving back to his childhood home, with its memories in every corner, but she was the least enthusiastic. Employee shuffling meant that Sally Evans would work at the house instead of the store, caring for the children, doing laundry, and cooking. She would no longer be able to slip into the bakery's kitchen whenever she had a few minutes to help. John had hired extra kitchen help, but it wouldn't be the same. Kate hoped that would work out for everyone.

There wouldn't be much heavy moving to do. Susannah's furnishings were still in the house, used by the tenants who were leaving. John and Kate would rent their bakery apartment furnished. All they had to move was their clothing.

This new lifestyle saddened Kate. She didn't know if the extra income was worth what they were giving up.

Chapter 37: ELI EXPLODES

July 1892

The bakery and restaurant thrived during the next three years leading up to 1892. They expanded the variety of products to their customers. As the town grew, so did their business.

John and Kate became generous as well as prosperous. If friends or neighbors ever needed help, they could find open hearts and hands from Mr. and Mrs. John Reese.

Life outside the village barely touched them. The newspapers printed stories about the upcoming presidential election. Former President Grover Cleveland was making another bid for the White House against the sitting president, Benjamin Harrison. A new elevated railway was up and running in Chicago, making a big splash in the news. But daily life went on as usual in Spencer's Mill, Ohio.

George and Sally Evans were with them for the first three years of the bakery and were considered family. It was a blow when they retired and were replaced by others, who came and went as their life situations changed. Kate trained other young women in her kitchen routine, using her recipes. Her equipment inventory had increased to cover many baking sheets, extra Dutch ovens, and an ample supply of pie and cake pans. They had even purchased two ice boxes that kept butter and milk fresh in the kitchen.

It was now five years since John's horrible courtroom experience. He had slowly gained back his good reputation and was even more respected than at first. The John Reese family was now well-known and well-loved in town...except by Eli.

There had been many changes in the extended family over the years. Danny and Charlotte no longer lived in Spencer's Mill, having followed their dream of farming. Gracie was in the fourth grade, and Steven was in the sixth. Davy wasn't quite five years old and hadn't started school yet. John's only siblings left in town—Matilda and Eli—had their own lives, and their families were no longer close.

Sunday, July 3, 1892

On a steamy Sunday after church, John and Kate relaxed on the veranda, drinking cold lemonade. Steven was restless. "Pa, can I take a walk to the park?" He was carrying a canvas ball and a bat.

"Yes, but be back before supper."

"All right, Pa."

Steven rolled his ball down the sidewalk, tapping it with his bat, and turned the corner toward the park. After he had walked a few blocks in the heat, he regretted not bringing a canteen. He was near Eli and Mary's house. Uncle Eli didn't like Pa, but maybe they would give him a glass of water anyway. He had always liked Uncle Eli.

He turned toward their house and knocked on the door. Aunt Mary opened it. "Why, it's Steven. Come in, Steven. It's hot out there. Would you like something to drink?"

The boy grinned. "Yes, please, Aunt Mary. It was a mistake to walk without a canteen on a day like this."

Eli walked in from the bedroom. "Steven, I haven't seen you

in a long time. What are you doing out in this heat?"

"I was bored. I thought I'd go to the park and hit my ball."

Mary brought him a glass of water, and he took a long, refreshing drink, wiping his mouth with the back of his dirty hand.

Eli studied his nephew. "It's probably just a coincidence, but I'm bored, too. Would you like some company on your walk?"

Mary objected. "Eli, you shouldn't. You promised Zach you'd play with him when he wakes up from his nap."

"I won't be long, Mary. Come on, Steven. Let's take a walk."

The two of them started down the path, chatting like best friends. Eli asked if Steven was eager to return to school in September and what games he liked to play with his friends. They spent several minutes getting caught up.

Then Steven remembered something he had been curious about.

"Uncle Eli, I never had a chance to ask you. Somebody told me you were mad at Pa for a long time. What was that about?"

What? Eli tensed and gasped as he stared at Steven. He had the sensation of being instantly sucked into the past. He flashed back nearly five years to that day in the courtroom when he learned that his closest brother had lied to the whole family and had exposed Eli as an unthinking fool. His head spun, and his anger flamed so unexpectedly that it consumed him. He tried to suppress it without success. He held his tongue for a minute but decided … Steven was old enough. He might as well know.

"There was a court hearing, Steven," he said, clenching his jaw. "I found out your Pa had lied to all his brothers and sisters to pad his pockets. And I was the one who believed him more than any of them. He made a fool out of me. Wouldn't that make you mad?"

"Pa did that? He lied?" Steven's mouth was wide open. His

eyebrows raised, and he shook his head as if to clear his brain of an idea that made no sense.

"You can ask anyone. Ask Aunt Matilda. Ask Grandma. They'll tell you."

"What kind of lie did he tell?"

Eli was really into it now. "It wasn't just one lie. It was many. One of his lies almost split up Grandma and Grandpa Wolf before they were married. Another lie almost made us all turn our inheritances over to your Pa until some imaginary oil refinery was built. He just made it all up. If we hadn't discovered the truth in time, your Pa would still be holding our money, and we wouldn't have any control over it."

Steven was shocked that he had upset Eli. He didn't realize things were so bad between Pa and his brother. "Maybe we should go back now."

"Well, let's go on a little farther first. I need to walk off some of this anger."

"So you're still mad. I didn't know that."

"I should say I am."

They walked on silently until they reached the park. "I'm sorry, Steve. I don't feel like playing ball."

"Me, either."

They sat on top of the picnic table in silence, with their feet resting on the seat. The shadow of a large oak shaded them. Two dogs ran through the park. An older woman shuffled along the sidewalk with her walking stick, fanning herself. Birds flitted through the trees. Finally, Eli put his arm around the boy's shoulders. "We should go back."

Eli stood and started to walk back, followed by Steven. In the silence, Steven had time to chew things over in his mind. "I had no idea Pa was that kind of man. He always told me never to lie…What's that word that means a person who says one thing and does another?"

"Hypocrite."

By the time they got back to Eli's house, Steven's heart had gone through a dark transformation. He went inside to get another drink of water, then started home.

Kate sipped her lemonade as Steven approached the house, but something had changed. His young shoulders slumped as he trudged along, and he wasn't rolling his ball.

"What's wrong, Stevie?" she asked. "Don't you feel well?"

"I feel fine. I'm going to my room. And I hate being called 'Stevie.'"

He marched off to his bedroom. Kate and John, wide-eyed, didn't know how to respond, so they let him go.

"I wonder what's gotten into him," John said. "Did something happen on that walk? He was perfectly normal before that."

"I have no idea."

Chapter 38: STEVEN LEARNS THE TRUTH

Monday, July 4, 1892

The next day began as usual. Like many village children, Steven and Gracie were enrolled in the new day camp program held by Trinity Chapel. The camp ran for three hours each afternoon at the park so children could do their morning chores at home. Today would be a special Independence Day celebration.

Steven was still silent as they were getting ready to leave the house.

"Do you want to talk to me about what's wrong, Steven?" asked Kate.

"No."

Kate sighed as the children struck off down the street.

It didn't get any better all week. Steven was the same sullen, uncommunicative young man. His attitude was wearing on the family.

The Reese family sat in their usual pew the following Sunday at church. Several people glanced at them from the corners of their eyes and whispered. It gave Kate a chill, but she didn't know what was happening. It had been a while since she had experienced that kind of treatment from her friends, so she was a little distracted during the service.

Afterward, her friend Cloris approached her. "Kate, some of

the ladies are saying awful things," she said in a low, confidential voice.

"What are you talking about?" Kate asked.

"There's a rumor going around that John has been telling lies. I'm not sure about the details, but there's something about a refinery in Lamar. That sounded familiar, but I couldn't put my finger on it. Do you know what's going on?"

Kate's hand went to the side of her face, and her eyes closed momentarily. "This is unbelievable," she said. "About six years ago, there were rumors about a refinery in Lamar. John was involved, but he repented, and he's been living a godly life since then. I wonder how that got started again. Where did you hear the rumor?"

"Peggy Larson told me."

"Peggy? Isn't she Howie Larson's mother?"

"Yes, I believe so."

Kate's eyebrows scrunched together. "Howie is one of Steven's friends. I wonder if there's any connection . . . Thanks, Cloris. I'll take it from here. If anyone else mentions that rumor, will you set them straight? I would hate to see John's reputation ruined when he has led such a godly life for six years."

"I'll sure do that, Kate. And good luck."

Steven's mood was unchanged the next day. John and Kate's long hours of demanding work to keep the business running made it challenging to take care of their children's needs immediately.

Kate said, "John, I'll let the staff run the kitchen tomorrow. I'm spending the day with Steven. He and I will have a serious talk."

"That sounds like a good plan."

By Tuesday, Steven's foul mood had lasted over a week. Kate had to do something about it. She laid out the day's work for her girls and told them they were in charge.

Steven got ready for his camp session and was his usual sullen self. When he started out the door, Kate said, "Sorry, son. You're staying home today. Gracie is going by herself."

Steven stopped short, confused. "Why?"

"You and I are going to spend some time together. I'll be ready in a few minutes."

Kate sat on her bed, praying about the day's events. "Father," she said, "only you know what Steven is going through. I don't. I ask you to reveal what is in Steven's heart and mind. Please give me the wisdom to know how to deal with it. Thank you for answering my prayer."

Her Bible was lying on her dresser. "James 1:5, Kate," she said to herself. "Remember James 1:5."

She left her bedroom and stood at the door to Steven's room. "Come with me, Steven. We're walking to the schoolyard and having your favorite for lunch—cherry pie." She had a picnic basket downstairs, covered with a bright red and white cloth.

His eyebrows were knitted in confusion. "Did you say we were having pie for lunch? At the schoolyard? There won't be anyone else there. All my friends will be at Bible camp at the park."

"Come on."

Steven left his ball on the bed and walked out behind his mother. They walked down the sidewalk and turned the corner onto the footpath heading for the school. "What's this all about, Ma?"

"You and I are going to have a heart-to-heart talk, Steven. You went through an abrupt change of attitude when you went for that walk, and I want to know what happened."

"Oh, that."

They walked on for several blocks without either of them saying another word. When they reached the schoolyard, Kate was overheated and perspiring. She spread a cloth on the grass under a large oak tree, and they sat on it. The shade was refreshing after their walk in the sun. She used a handkerchief to mop her face. "All right, young man. It's time to talk. So talk."

Steven had been thinking about it for a couple of blocks of walking. It had been building up in his mind the whole time. He shook his head with tears on his cheeks and blurted it out. "It's pretty bad when a guy finds out his Pa is a liar!"

Immediately, Kate realized what had happened. "Oh. Did you see Uncle Eli when you went for your walk?" She couldn't imagine anyone else who would have told him the history, and Steven had gone past Eli's house to get to the park that day.

"Yes."

"Well, Uncle Eli told you the truth."

Steven shot a glance at his mother, open-mouthed. "You know about it, then? You admit it?"

"Of course. Now, let me tell you the rest of the story. And I want you to pay close attention, Steven, because you must remember this for the rest of your life."

"What is it?" he asked. His eyes were angry, and his face was flushed.

"I will tell you the whole story, including the end, which Uncle Eli didn't tell you. Now listen to this. There was a time when you were a little guy, and your Pa worked for an oil company in Lamar. He was a hard worker and very ambitious, and he thought the most important thing in the world was making money to support our family. Even though he had a good salary at the oil company, he thought he could make extra money by doing other things on his own."

"Is there something wrong with that?" Steven asked.

"Not so far," Kate said. "But after your Grandpa Reese died—Pa's father—your Pa came up with a plan to make money by managing the inheritance of all his brothers and sisters. He wanted them to pay him to do it, but he was afraid they wouldn't unless he told them a lie. He made up a story about a new refinery being built in Lamar. He wanted them to agree to trust him with their inheritances until the refinery was built. He promised them they could double their money if they waited. Uncle Eli believed the lie because he trusted Pa. In fact, Uncle Eli was his biggest supporter. Naturally, the judge stopped Pa from doing it. If he hadn't, he would still control their inheritances because no refinery was ever planned."

"That was what Uncle Eli said. That sounds evil."

"Well, it was, but your Pa was so blinded by Satan he couldn't see it that way. Then Uncle Danny figured it out. He hired an attorney and filed a lawsuit, and the judge made Pa stop what he was doing. At the court hearing, everybody in the family learned about Pa's lies and what he was up to. You can imagine how mad they were."

Steven scratched his neck and sat thinking.

"That's the short story," Kate continued. "And there were other lies, too, but that was the biggest one. If you want to ask questions, I'll answer them when I finish telling you what I want you to hear."

"There's more?"

"Yes. There's the story's ending, the part Uncle Eli left out. During that court hearing, your Pa's eyes were opened—do you know what I mean by that? —and for the first time, he got a good look at himself as he really was. He was forced to stop fooling himself. That's a big problem, Steven, when people fool themselves and start believing the lies they tell. Remember that."

"So what happened after that?"

"When Pa finally realized how he had hurt people, he repented. He asked God and the whole family to forgive him. Everyone said they did, except Uncle Eli. He hasn't been able to let it go yet. You know Uncle Danny forgave your Pa. Those two brothers love each other. And Grandma and Grandpa Wolf forgave Pa, and so did your other aunts and uncles. Uncle Eli had a harder time because he felt stupid for believing the lie."

"What does 'repent' mean?"

"It means to agree with God that you've done wrong, ask Him for forgiveness, and trust Him to live in your heart and help you do right."

"And that's what Pa did?"

"Yes. And he's been changed ever since then. I think he's the best Pa you could ever ask for. Do you remember any time he ever lied to you?"

"No."

"Well, he didn't. Because God lives in his heart, he's been changed. He's not a liar anymore."

Steven ground the heel of his shoe into the dirt and mulled it all over. Tears squeezed from his eyes and ran down his sweaty face.

"Now, son, I think you owe your Pa an apology for your ugly behavior these past few days."

"I guess, Ma. I guess I owe you an apology, too."

Kate smiled. "You're forgiven, Steven." She hugged him and ruffled his hair, relishing that she could still do that. He might be too old for hair-ruffling in a year or so.

"The friends you told at camp—" she said, "can you set them straight, too?"

"I'll tell them tomorrow. But now I'm mad at Uncle Eli for not telling me everything."

"Uncle Eli's big problem is that he hasn't forgiven. Don't let that be your problem, too."

"All right, Ma."

"We need to treat Uncle Eli gently because he still hurts over that incident five years ago. Maybe we can help him let go of his anger."

She opened her picnic basket and took out the canteen of

cold water. She poured two glasses, and the two cooled their dry throats. Then she lifted the cherry pie, still warm and dripping with red, juicy goodness. They cut into it and celebrated Steven's new way of thinking with a decadent dessert.

Pie for lunch. This was probably a once-in-a-lifetime treat.

Chapter 39: THE DISAPPEARANCE

Tuesday, July 12, 1892

That night after Zach went to sleep, Mary slipped into bed beside Eli. She was concerned about her husband. He had something smoldering inside that he couldn't talk about. It had been going on for quite some time, but it had worsened over the past week. He was constantly in a dark mood, no matter how hard she tried to please him. Truth be told, she had given up, accepting that trying to please him was useless. She pulled the quilts up to her chin. Soon, she was deep in slumber.

When her breathing grew slower and more regular, Eli drew back the quilt and slid silently out of bed. He dressed quietly, then reached under the bed to retrieve the satchel he had prepared for himself. He slipped out the front door and closed it ever so gently.

After picking up a lantern from the barn, he mounted his horse and rode away. He wasn't sure where he was going, but he needed to go somewhere else to prove himself. He was worth nothing around here. His brothers were all more successful than he was, and his adult sisters had all married successful men. He couldn't tolerate being the dog's tail. And look how John had treated him, telling lies the way he did and upstaging him when he wanted to announce the new baby. If John didn't respect him, probably no one else in the family did, either.

These dark thoughts had worn a groove in his brain for so long that he was almost incapable of thinking about anything else.

He would miss Mary and Zach. He would send her a letter when he figured out where he was going and send her money whenever he could. If she left him, that's what he deserved. She needed a husband who could support her in a grander style. Maybe she would find one. He started sobbing at the thought of Mary with someone else, but he kept the horse on the road. He wanted to cover as much ground as possible before Mary realized he was gone.

It was slow going in the dark. The damp air pervaded his clothing and almost seemed to prevent the lamp light from spreading. He tried to hold his lantern high to light the road, but his arm got tired. It wasn't as bright as he wanted, anyway. He took the road east past his mother's house without stopping or leaving a note. When he reached Lamar, he turned south toward a small group of homes calling themselves Cosmopolis. He thought that was an unusually fancy name for a village with five houses. Maybe they put that sign up as a joke.

About that time, his lantern ran out of fuel and went dark. He tossed it to the side of the road. Fortunately, the branches of the trees outlined against the moonlit sky gave him some idea of where to guide the horse.

He passed through tiny Cosmopolis and was at the shores of Blackhawk Lake when the day began to break. Bone-tired and hungry, he yearned to lie down and sleep. When he came to a wooded area, he ducked into the trees, pulled his blanket out of his satchel, and stretched out on the ground for an exhausted nap.

Chapter 40: MARY'S ORDEAL

Wednesday, July 13, 1892

About that same time, Mary roused herself. She stretched out her arms, expecting to feel Eli beside her, but his side of the bed was empty. She rolled out of bed, padding barefoot into the kitchen. No Eli. Maybe he was in the barn. She slipped on her clothes and walked out without her shoes to find him. Eli wasn't there, and neither was the horse. Why would he have gone somewhere on horseback that early in the morning? Mary began to panic, suspecting the worst. She ran back into the house to get her son.

"Zach, wake up," she urged. "Let's go for a walk." She nudged him awake. Her hands shook as she dressed him.

She cooked a quick breakfast of eggs. Contrary to her routine, she left the dirty dishes in the sink and poured a canteen full of water. This was going to be a long walk.

"Where's Papa?" Zach asked.

"He's not here right now, baby," Mary said. "He'll be back later. We're going to see Uncle John. It's a long, long walk, so you'll have to be a big boy."

"All right, Mama."

Walking a mile with a two-year-old would usually be strenuous and trying, but Mary was emotionally distressed. It would be twice as hard.

Her mind was running at full speed. Had Eli run an errand

this early in the morning? Or, as she suspected, had he run away without saying anything? Would he come back? Surely, he would come back when he was hungry enough.

They struck out, heading toward the Crust & Crumb Bakery. Zach wandered off the path toward one side, then another, like a puppy seeing the world for the first time. Mary drew him back time after time. He grew tired, and finally, with his little-boy energy spent, he plopped down on the path. Mary was in tears. She picked him up and walked with him as far as she could, but he was too heavy. Finally, she sat on the ground with him to rest. They each had a long drink from the canteen.

At the point of exhaustion, Mary picked up her boy again and trudged forward. At last, as they turned the corner, the bakery was in sight. Mary wanted to hurry her steps, but she was too weary.

Finally, she reached her destination and stumbled inside with Zach. Her arms and back ached, and her feet were sore. The clerk, busy arranging the bread in the baskets for the day's sales, asked if he could help her. "I need to speak to John," she said quietly. Her eyes were swollen and red, and her face was wet with tears.

"Just a moment, I'll get him," said the clerk, leaving her alone in the sales area while he went to John's office at the back of the restaurant. He was gone for only a moment.

John rushed to the sales floor. "Mary—what's wrong?"

"It's Eli," was all she could say.

"Come to my office, and we'll talk there," he said. He took Zach from her and guided her through the adjoining room to his small desk area.

"Sit down, Mary. What's wrong with Eli?"

"He's gone."

"What do you mean?"

"When I woke this morning, he wasn't there. He's not in the

house or the barn, and the horse is gone. I don't know where he is, John."

John's back stiffened. "Let's not lose our heads," he said, taking a deep breath. His imagination went into high gear. "Maybe he went to see Ma. Maybe he'll be back later today. Or maybe he went to Matilda's house, or maybe he went fishing. I know he's been acting odd lately. And moody. He never wants to talk about anything."

"He didn't even leave me a note telling me where he went. He could have at least done that."

Mary realized she was not so panicked now as she was exhausted and angry. "What was Eli thinking?" she asked. "I've always believed that a wife should respect her husband and treat him with honor, but this is beyond the pale. I plan to speak to him sternly when he gets home, and if I'm so loud the neighbors hear it all, well...."

John stared at her. "I've never seen you angry before, Mary. I can't say that I blame you."

A moment passed while they each tried to process this shocking turn of events.

"Kate and I will be tied up trying to keep the bakery and restaurant running, so why don't I take you to our house today? You can rest and have lunch there. After the store closes this evening, we'll go to Ma's house and see if we can find him."

"Thank you, John. That would be such a relief to me."

"Of course. Sit and rest. You can go to the kitchen with Kate and have a cup of tea first. When you're ready, I'll take you to the house."

"Thank you."

When Kate heard the news, her eyes filled with tears, and she wrapped her arms around her sister-in-law. "I would give anything to stay with you today, Mary, but I can't. I need to keep up with a backlog of orders, but I know how to pray when my hands are busy."

After getting that tea and talking with Kate, she told John she was ready to go.

John drove away with Mary and Zach, leaving Kate with a heavy heart.

Chapter 41: ELI'S WANDERINGS

Eli had left home without much money, wanting to leave something in the desk drawer for Mary to buy what she needed until he could send her more. But he had brought enough to buy lunch at a diner in a small town whose name he didn't know. The eatery was between two larger businesses, a harness maker and a photographer's studio. He sat at the counter and ordered chicken and corn chowder with coffee. As he ate, he decided to travel further south. Maybe he could get to Cincinnati and find work on the river, loading cargo onto the riverboats. There would be enough to send Mary some money when he got paid.

At the village general store, he bought some horse feed and carrots. The carrots were for him and the horse.

He kept pressing south, hoping to find his way to the Ohio River. With no map, he wandered this way and that, trying to pick his way by the sun's location in the sky. Some roads that started in a southerly direction took unexpected turns around corn, turnip, or cucumber fields and curved along railroads and streams. When he took a route he believed went south, it often turned in another direction, so he wasn't sure where he would end up.

Hunger gnawed at his belly. He was out of money, so he was obliged to occasionally stop beside a field and pick a handful of vegetables. Strawberries growing beside a fence were as good as gold to him. He made a bag by tying knots in the corners of his handkerchief. It made a useful container for berries. They were a good snack as he rode along the dusty roads. At dinner time for most people, he found another resting spot in a wooded area. He dined on raw carrots and strawberries, drank water from the stream, and slept.

Chapter 42: SEARCHING FOR ELI

After closing the bakery and restaurant, John and Kate picked up their children with Mary and Zach and drove to Susannah's house. Mary was quiet during the trip. She didn't have high expectations.

"I agree with you, John, that Eli has been moody for quite a while," she said. "I thought maybe I'd made him angry, but he wouldn't talk to me about it. After a while, I gave up trying to talk and just avoided his moods whenever I could."

"Has this been going on long?" Kate asked.

"Quite a while, I guess," Mary said. "Maybe building up slowly for the past few years, but it's been much worse in the past week."

John thought back to the day Eli took a walk with Steven. Maybe old anger was resurfacing. Perhaps he wasn't mad at only John. Perhaps he was angry about a lot of things. Maybe he was mad at himself.

"I can't figure it out," he said. "Well, suppose he went to Ma's house for some emergency. We still don't know."

The horses traveled on until they finally reached the Wolfs' home.

The housekeeper greeted them at the door. "Mrs. Wolf, some of your children are here."

Susannah swept into the room, eager to find out what brought her family. "Hello, children," she said.

"Hi, Ma," said John. "Sorry to bother you so late, but we have a problem. We hope you can help us."

"What problem is that?"

"Eli's missing from home," Mary said. "We're hoping he's here with you. Have you seen him?"

Susannah was taken aback. "Eli's missing? I'm sorry, he hasn't been here. How long has he been gone?"

"He was asleep when I went to bed last night, but this morning when I woke up, he wasn't there, and the horse is gone, too."

Susannah stared at her for a moment, uncomprehending, then sunk back into the chair. "This is hard to take in. Why would Eli just up and leave without saying where he was going?"

"I walked to the bakery this morning with Zach to tell John and Kate. There was no other way to get there; Eli has the horse. It was a long, hard walk, so I stayed at their house all day."

"You haven't had any dinner yet, have you? We haven't, either. I'll have Hannah cook some extra for all of us. Problems don't look so bad when your stomach is full. We'll have dinner together tonight. Mary, did you say you've been gone from home all day? I'll bet Eli is at home waiting for you, wondering where you are." She smiled, hoping to encourage her daughter-in-law.

"He would have come to the bakery looking for me," said Mary in a flat voice.

"I guess he would have." That idea was quashed. "Do you suppose he was kidnapped?"

"Not likely, Ma," said John. "Think. If you were a kidnapper, would you grab a man in his bed with nothing of value for his wife to ransom him with?"

"I suppose not." Susannah turned and walked to the kitchen.

The entire family gathered at the dining room table when Christian arrived home. Over dinner, they speculated about where Eli might have gone. No one had any likely ideas, and soon it was time to head back to Spencer's Mill.

"Wait, I want to send some supplies back with Mary," Susannah said. "Since she doesn't have a good way to get anywhere to buy what she needs, let's make sure she has enough of everything."

Susannah went to her larder and packed up two baskets of staple foods. She collected milk and butter from the ice box and vegetables from the root cellar. It would feed Mary and her son for a week. They packed the supplies into John's carriage. "You check on Mary often, will you, John? And let me know as soon as you hear anything from Eli."

"I will, Ma." John hugged his mother, and the family headed back to Spencer's Mill.

It was after dark by the time they reached Mary's house.

"John, I hate being a coward, but I don't want to go in there alone. What if someone is hiding in there to hurt Zach and me?"

"I'm sure it's perfectly safe, but I'll go inside ahead of you and check the house." He picked up Zach and accompanied her inside. No one was there, including Eli. Mary was in tears.

John put his arm around his sister-in-law's shoulders. "God is watching over you, Mary," he said. "He's watching over Eli, too."

"Thank you for everything, John. We'll be fine. You and Kate need to get home."

"We'll check on you tomorrow after we close the store. We'll bring you some fresh bread. And you'll let us know if you need anything." It was more a statement than a question.

Sunday, July 17, 1892

On Sunday, Eli was still missing. John and Kate went to Mary's house to pick her up for church, but she wasn't ready.

"Please, Kate," she said. "I can't face anyone yet. I think Eli is gone for good. I'm so humiliated. A good wife would have been able to anticipate her husband's needs, but I was blind to what he needed. I'm sure it's my fault that he's gone."

John objected. "I'm sure it's *not* your fault, Mary. I think it's mine."

Kate put her arms around her sister-in-law's shoulders. Mary was sniffling. Kate realized she must have been doing a lot of crying this week.

John and Kate took their children and headed off to church. It was odd without Eli and Mary in their regular pew.

John's sister Matilda was there with her family. "Matilda," Kate said, putting her hand on her sister-in-law's arm, "we haven't had a chance to tell you that Eli is missing."

"What?" Matilda said. "Eli? Where is he?"

"We don't know. He's been gone since Tuesday. Mary said he disappeared in the middle of the night, taking their horse with him. She hasn't had any contact with him since."

Matilda's eyes were as round as saucers. "I haven't heard from him, either. Please keep me informed. He's been acting strange lately."

After the service, Christian and Susannah checked on Mary, leaving her with more food and supplies.

The next day, Christian turned in a missing person report at the police station in Lamar. He sat at the police chief's desk, holding his hat on his knee. "It makes sense that he would have come through Lamar, wherever he went."

"We'll take the report, but it's not hard if someone wants to disappear. I'll make inquiries wherever I can. I feel sorry for the little lady, being left alone with a two-year-old. That's tough."

"At least she has a good support group in our family," Christian replied. "Well, thanks, sir. I know you'll do your best."

Chapter 43: ELI FINDS REFUGE

Monday, July 18, 1892

Eli had been wandering about the farmland in Ohio for almost a week now, turning and twisting down one road after another, aiming in the general direction of Cincinnati as he guessed it to be, and he was long out of money. He and his horse were both getting weaker and needed some food. The horse grazed on whatever he could find when Eli stopped to rest, and Eli had sustained himself on raw vegetables pilfered from farmers' fields, berries gathered by the side of the road, and water from streams.

He slept each night in the woods, pillowing his head on his lumpy satchel and covering up with his thin blanket to ward off the mosquitos. His only baths had been in shallow streams, and he hadn't been able to wash his clothes. His odor was getting intense. Sweat ran off his head and into his beard stubble. Sticky days-old stink clung to his body. Even worse, he realized he was getting used to it. This was no way to live.

Mary would cook good, hot meals if he were home. He regretted leaving, but it was too late for that. She was probably so angry she would never want him back.

He worried that he had been wandering in circles in his frazzled state, but he wasn't sure. He often came across fields and farmhouses that were vaguely familiar. It was all beginning to look alike. He hoped he would get to Cincinnati soon.

On the horizon, he spotted a village with a population smaller than Lamar but larger than Spencer's Mill, shimmering in the heat. As he traveled closer, the reality of his situation pressed on him.

I can't go on like this, he thought. *My horse won't last if I don't get her something decent to eat, and I won't either. I'm at the end of what I can do.*

In desperation, he stopped in front of the first farmhouse on the edge of town. It was a good-sized house, neat and well-kept, except for the trim that needed to be touched up. There was a chicken coop and a large barn down a path, with woods behind the barn and a stream running through it. The entire farm was fenced off with a whitewashed wooden fence. He tied his horse to the rail and then knocked on the door. A plump lady in her sixties answered his knock. Her gray hair was wound into a bun on the back of her head. She wore a faded red apron and wiped her hands on a towel.

"May I help you, young man?"

Eli was relieved to talk to someone, a real, live human being. "Ma'am, I've been traveling for a few days and ran out of money for food for my horse and me. I wonder if you have any work I could do in exchange for something to eat."

She sized up the smelly, grubby fellow on her porch. "You look like you could use a bath, too."

"Yes, ma'am."

"Do you know how to mend a fence?"

"Yes, ma'am."

"Why don't you go on out to the barn? I'll bring you something to eat, and we'll get your horse fed. After you rest, you can mend that fence out there. Do you need a place to spend the night?"

He nodded.

"If you do a decent job, you can take a bath out there in private, then spend the night in the barn."

"Thank you, ma'am," Eli said with relief. He wiped a tear off his dirty face, and his shoulders relaxed. "Just one thing—can you tell me the name of this village?"

"Why, it's Belleville."

"Are we near Cincinnati?"

She tilted her head and peered at him. "Oh, my, no. Don't you know where you are?"

"I didn't know until just now. Thank you. I'll head out to the barn now."

Eli was so relieved that he was almost in tears. He led his horse to the barn and sat on a hay bale to wait for his meal.

How did I ever get into this mess? I must be out of my mind. This isn't even my life. I'm living someone else's life. I wonder how Mary and Zach are. I hope they haven't been suffering since I left.

The farmer's wife walked toward the barn with a steaming plate. Real food. He hadn't had a good meal in almost a week. He accepted it from her and ate it—no, he shoveled it down—with gratitude. She sat on a nearby stump and watched him.

"I'm curious about you," she said. "Do you mind if I ask why you're traveling and how you got to where you didn't even know where you were?"

He hoped she didn't mind if he talked with food in his mouth. "I'm embarrassed to tell you, but you deserve to know. I have a wife and son back home, but I haven't been a good provider. I could barely take care of my family. And my brother, well, he lied to me and didn't respect me. So I left, hoping to find something somewhere that I was good at."

"What did your wife say about that?"

He dropped his fork, not expecting that question. "I didn't tell her, ma'am."

"What? You just left?"

"Yes. She would have tried to talk me out of it."

"My dear Lord," she said under her breath. The words were spoken reverently as if she were sharing a private conversation with Him.

"Well, the tools are in the barn, and you'll find some wood there. The break in the fence is over there." She pointed in the direction of the road he had just traveled. "When you get it fixed, pump some water into a bucket and bathe yourself. I'll bring some of my husband's clothes out there. We'll burn the ones you're wearing."

"Yes, ma'am."

"Would you like a razor for that stubble?"

"Yes, please."

Eli's strength revived. He rounded up the necessary tools and nails and mended the fence. An hour later, with the job done, he pumped a bucket full of water. He found a change of clothes, a towel, a razor, and a bar of lye soap lying neatly by the bucket, just as the woman had said, so he stripped down, took his first honest-to-goodness bath in a week out behind the barn, and put on clean clothing.

A tiny flicker of hope sparked in his spirit. Maybe—just maybe—there could be a normal life after this fiasco.

Inside the farmhouse, Daisy Lloyd was talking with her Lord. "Jesus, you brought that young man to my door. I know you sent him to me for a reason. So now tell me what to do for him. I'm listening."

She kept an eye on him through her kitchen window. Eli wandered around the property in clean clothes, just exploring like a puppy in a new environment.

"Did he come here to rob me, Lord? I didn't get the impression that he was a dishonest man. Maybe a foolish one, but he doesn't strike me as dishonest. He looks like he needs

You."

Eli walked toward the woods, apparently unaware that he was under her watchful eye, and then turned back toward the little stream at the side of the property. When he finished his walk, he untied his satchel from his saddle and spread his blanket inside the barn door, stretching out for a nap.

Mrs. Lloyd put on a pot of stew, listening for God to speak to her as she worked. At dinner time, she went to the barn and woke him up.

"Looks like you did a good job, young man. Why don't you come into the house and have dinner with me?"

Eli roused himself and smiled. "I would be grateful. By the way, my name is Eli."

"You can call me Mrs. Lloyd, Eli. Nice to meet you."

The two of them walked into the kitchen, where bowls of hot stew waited.

"Is your husband joining us?" Eli asked.

"No, Mr. Lloyd passed away two years ago. It's just me now. Have a seat."

Eli settled into one of the chairs.

"We'll say grace before our meal," Mrs. Lloyd said. She bowed her head, and Eli followed suit.

"Dear Lord," Mrs. Lloyd said. "Thank you for sending Eli to help me with a couple of things, but you know he belongs with his wife and son. So I'm asking you for a miracle that only you can do, that you reconcile Eli with his wife. Please give him a spirit of confidence, a job that he can be proud of, and give his wife a spirit of forgiveness because he surely needs it. Oh, and thank you for this food. Amen."

Eli sat there red-faced, staring at his bowl. "Thank you, Mrs. Lloyd. I wish I had people back home praying for me like that."

"I'll bet you already do," she said. They dipped their spoons into their stew and enjoyed a good meal, engaging in gentle conversation.

"Let me help you clear the table and wash the dishes," Eli said.

As the two of them worked together, Mrs. Lloyd asked, "So your wife doesn't know where you are or when you're coming back?"

"No."

"Do you want to go back?"

"When I left, I didn't plan to go back, but yes, ma'am, I want to. When I go, I want to be successful at something. I don't know if she'll have me like this, especially now."

"Well, here's what I think you should do. You should write her a letter and tell her where you are. I'll give you the address here. Then you decide—you can either head back home to face her or stay here for a few days until you get a reply. But Eli, you need to send her some money. I'll give you two dollars, and you can work that off before you leave here."

"What happens if she doesn't want me to come home?"

"We won't worry about that until we have to," she said. "But until you leave, there'll be work to do here."

Eli didn't know how to express his gratitude. Tears formed in his eyes. "Thank you, ma'am," was all he could say.

"Sit there at the table, Eli. I'll bring you some paper, a pen, and an envelope, and you write her a letter right now."

Mrs. Lloyd disappeared into the next room and returned with the supplies he needed to write to Mary. She gave him an encouraging pat on the shoulder and left him alone in the kitchen.

Eli struggled over a letter for quite a while, imagining Mary opening his letter and reading it. Would she read it through tears of gratitude or rip it up in disgust? Eli bowed his head in prayer for the first time in a long time. How should he even start?

"God," he prayed, "I've messed up. I've hurt Mary and Zach, maybe more than I thought." He paused to choke back a sob. "Maybe they're worried about me. Maybe not. I don't know. I ask you to forgive me for leaving Mary that way and to pave the way for me to return home. I know I will have to face the consequences. But Lord, if you could just let me go home and get my wife and boy back ..." He broke down in tears. It took him quite a while to gather himself. Then, the letter flowed out of the pen.

As he tucked the flap into the envelope, he remembered his mother's words to John when she learned of his deception: "I can tell you that sin has a rippling effect, like throwing pebbles in a pond." Guilt stabbed his heart. He had rubbed his hands with glee to see John have to pay for his sins. Now, he was dealing with his own consequences.

Chapter 44: MARY'S RESCUE

Susannah's heart ached for her wayward son and his family. Eli had been gone for a week. His whereabouts were still unknown, but she could help Mary. She asked the caretaker to hitch up the carriage and drove to Spencer's Mill.

Mary opened the door to her. "Mother Wolf. I'm so grateful to have another grown-up to talk to."

"Do you know anything about Eli yet?" Susannah asked.

Mary shook her head. "I don't think he's coming back. I'm beginning to get used to the idea, so now I need to figure out what to do with myself. It's hard work taking care of Zach, doing all the household chores I used to, walking all that way with Zach to buy food, and carrying him and the food back home because he's too tired to walk. I don't know how long I can keep this up."

"Mary, I'd like you to stay with us for at least a few days. We have an extra bedroom now that William is away at medical school. We could set up a little pallet for Zach there, too. Would you like to do that?"

Mary smiled wearily and nodded. "When would be a convenient time for me to come?"

"This is as good a time as any. Go ahead and pack some things. We'll stop by the bakery and tell John what we're doing. And I'd like to spend a few minutes at Matilda's house before we go home. I don't get to spend much time with her anymore."

Mary didn't take long to pack a bag of clothes. She thought about the vegetables in the root cellar and decided they would be fine until she returned in a few days. She locked the front door, then she and little Zach climbed into Susannah's carriage.

Four days later, a letter arrived at Mary's house. It lay in the letterbox, unopened.

Friday, July 22, 1892

Susannah enjoyed Mary's presence in the house and delighted in her grandson. She urged Mary to stay longer, and that suited everyone. John checked Mary's place every other day to see if Eli had returned, but he never checked the letterbox.

Chapter 45: ELI's MISADVENTURE

Tuesday, August 2, 1892

Day after day passed. Mrs. Lloyd became fond of this strange young man who had stopped at her door. She enjoyed having someone to talk to. Eli was industrious and had a pleasant attitude. He had only been with her for two weeks, but he had already made quite a few repairs that had been neglected since Mr. Lloyd died. He took care of the horses and weeded the vegetable patch. The farm had gone fallow since her husband's death, but she thought if Eli were there long enough, maybe he could plant crops next year. She almost dared to hope that perhaps he would be around that long, even though he belonged with his family. She chided herself for getting attached to him as if he were a stray pup.

"Mrs. Lloyd, if you don't have any other work for me, there are some fallen trees in the woods. I'll take the axe and cut some firewood, so you'll have heat this winter."

"That's good thinking," she said. "Eli, have you gotten a letter from your wife yet?"

He shook his head. "She should have written by now. I don't think she wants me to come home." He choked back a sob.

"We'll keep praying. Maybe she's hurting so bad that she doesn't know how to respond. But until you hear from her, don't worry about a place to stay. You can stay here."

"Thank you. That's a great kindness. I do miss her so much."

That evening, Eli came into the house for dinner, filthy and exhausted. The size of the pile of firewood he had created gave him a sense of accomplishment, so he was wearing a satisfied smile.

"Eli, get yourself cleaned up before I put dinner on the table. You'll feel better."

He took an outdoor bath behind the barn, then returned, wearing more clean clothes he found laid out for him.

"Sit down here with me, son. We need to pray while the ham and beans are heating."

The two of them asked for God's protection over Mary and Zach. They asked Him to plant a desire in her heart to have her husband home again. Then they gave thanks for the food they were about to eat.

Thursday, August 18, 1892

Life fell into a routine for Eli. He took on more responsibility. He longed to see Mary and Zach, but his letter was still unanswered. He presumed Mary was so angry that she didn't want him anymore. He tried not to think of that.

"We're getting low on some staples," Mrs. Lloyd said after checking the supplies in her pantry. "If I give you a list, would you go into town and pick up what we need? I'll give you some money to take with you."

"Sure, just let me finish taking care of the chickens before I go," Eli said. It would be a welcome break in routine to get away from the house for a couple of hours, not that he was ungrateful for his current situation. But it would be nice to take a little side trip into town. It wouldn't take long.

The day was still young, and Eli gathered the eggs. He finished that job, fed the chickens, and went into the house to get the list.

"Better take the carriage for this order," Mrs. Lloyd said. "It's more bulk than you can carry on horseback."

He reviewed her list. It totaled about forty pounds of this and that—flour, cornmeal, beans, and the like. "That's quite a big order," he said.

"It will save having to go into town again, at least for a while. Do you need anything from town yourself?"

"I'll stop for a haircut if I can, but I should still be back within an hour or two."

He hitched the horse to the carriage. The list and money were safe in his pocket.

It was a pleasant day. As the horse pulled the carriage at a trot, Eli enjoyed the breeze blowing on his face, the sunshine warming his skin, and the easy rhythm of the horse. His thoughts went to Mary. He wondered how she was doing and how big Zach was growing. He wondered how many months had passed since he had seen them, but no, it had been less than six weeks.

It would be great if Zach could be here. He would have so much room to run and play. But there was no need to think about that. The thought only wrenched his heart.

He began to hum a tune to distract himself from his thoughts. The horse loped along in front of the carriage, its tail swishing back and forth and hooves raising dust in the road.

Within fifteen minutes, he arrived at the business area of Belleville and stopped the carriage in front of the general store. He tied the horse to the rail and went inside with Mrs. Lloyd's basket for the small items. The store was a tightly packed jumble of merchandise of every description, arranged in general categories according to the whim of the storekeeper. Everything you would need to keep your home running could be found there. A sign on the wall boasted, "If we don't have it, you don't need it."

Eli breathed in the tart aroma of vinegar from the pickle barrel, combined with licorice from one of the candy jars, cinnamon, and a vague musty smell. Sunlight flowed in from a side window, illuminating the dust floating in the air.

"Good morning, sir," he said to the clerk. "I'm here on an errand for Mrs. Lloyd. She would like these items on her list."

Mr. Peyton, the clerk, took the list from him. "I haven't seen Mrs. Lloyd for quite a while. Is she doing all right?"

"Oh, yes. She's fine."

"Are you kin? I didn't think she had any family."

"No, my name is Reese. I'm staying with her for a while to take care of some chores that have gone begging since Mr. Lloyd passed."

Another customer came in—a shirtless young man in bib dungarees and a straw hat. He breezed past the clerk's counter without speaking or looking at either man.

"Can I help you, young man?" the clerk asked as he passed.

"No, I want to look around."

Mr. Peyton glanced sideways at the boy. Eli got the feeling that something about him annoyed the clerk. He had to admit the fellow's social graces were lacking. He wasn't friendly like most folks.

The strange fellow slowed his pace, meandered around the store, picked up items off the shelf and inspected them while Peyton worked on Eli's order. The storekeeper occasionally glanced over at the odd young man. He had picked up random small items: matches and a spool of thread. He stood with his back to the other men and studied the rack of knives.

As Peyton filled Eli's basket, the young man strolled over to the counter.

"I'd like to pay for these matches and thread."

"Give me just a moment while I fill this gentleman's order,"

Peyton said with irritation.

Eli intervened. "I'm in no hurry," he said. "Go ahead and take care of him. I don't mind waiting." He stepped back, allowing the young man to approach the counter.

"As you wish," Peyton said. He told the young man how much he owed. The fellow turned over his coins and left the store.

"Now, the only thing I have left to get for you is the lamp oil." Peyton walked to the far end of the store where he kept the housekeeping products like shovels, nails, and the like and picked up a bottle of the oil. He returned to the counter and began tallying up the bill.

"Let's see; there's the flour, cornmeal, milk, butter...." Then he spotted the glint of metal in Eli's basket. His brow furrowed, and he glared at Eli over his spectacles.

"Say, are you trying to steal that knife?"

"What?" Eli was confused. "I didn't ask for a knife."

"That knife you're hiding in your basket. You're trying to steal it."

"No, sir, I assure you . . ."

The storekeeper raised his voice. "You're trying to steal that knife." He ran out to the sidewalk, shouting. "Someone get the sheriff."

Eli was frozen in place, not knowing what to do. He searched his basket, and there it was—a deadly-looking hunting knife with a nine-inch blade and a carved walnut handle. Where had that knife come from?

The other customer, the young man in the dungarees, loitered outside and motioned frantically at the window for Eli to come out. Someone else ran to the sheriff's office at the jail down the street.

Eli left his basket on the counter and walked to the door to ask the young man what he wanted. The fellow whispered,

"Bring me the knife, man, bring me the knife."

Eli recoiled in shock. "Are you crazy? Did you put that knife in my basket?"

As the sheriff raced toward the store, the young fellow decided to beat a hasty retreat. He ducked into the alley and disappeared without saying another word.

The sheriff dashed into the store with handcuffs, jerked Eli around, and cuffed his hands behind his back. "What do you mean by trying to steal from the shopkeeper? He works hard to make a living. Do you think you can steal his merchandise? You're getting locked up for a long time for this."

Eli began to tremble. He tried to explain, but Sheriff McCallum wouldn't listen. He pushed him out the door and down the street toward the jail. He was pushing so hard that Eli's feet could hardly move fast enough, and he thought he would trip over himself. Townspeople on the wood-planked sidewalk stepped aside to let them pass, mouths open in astonishment. The jail had been unoccupied for a long time, except for an occasional unruly drunk.

The sheriff shoved Eli into a cell, and the iron door clanged shut.

"Sir, please let me speak. I did not steal that knife. This is humiliating, especially since I'm innocent." Eli was gulping air so fast he was lightheaded.

"You had the knife in your basket. No denying that. It was at the bottom, partly hidden by the other things."

Eli fought to gain control of himself. "Yes, it was in my basket, but I didn't put it there. Ask the shopkeeper about the other customer who was in the store at the same time. While the clerk was filling my order, he acted weird and stood with his back to us while he inspected the rack of knives. He didn't pay for one when he left the store, but when the shopkeeper went to call for you, that same customer was outside the store window, motioning for me to come out. Then he told me to bring him the knife. I didn't do it. Please, check out my story with the shopkeeper."

McCallum's nervous energy was beginning to settle, and his breathing slowed. He lowered himself into the chair at his desk. He was more willing to listen, but his voice was still challenging and skeptical. "Describe this customer you're talking about."

Eli sat on the wooden bed in the cell. It consisted of two beams shoved into holes in the wall, fitted with legs and crossbeams, and padded with a thin corn husk mattress. Eli's mind wandered for just a moment. He patted the mattress. "This bed is miserable."

"This ain't the Astor Hotel. Describe the man."

"He was young, probably not even twenty years old. He was wearing dungarees, no shirt, and a straw hat. His shoes were filthy. I took him to be a farmhand because his arms were tanned by the sun. But I don't know his name."

"You say he was in the store at the same time as you?"

"Yes."

"What color was his hair?"

"Brown, I think."

"I'll check your story with Mr. Peyton. What's your name?"

"Eli Reese."

"You're not from Belleville."

"I'm staying with Mrs. Lloyd for a while, doing repairs around her farm. Please, I need to get back there. She needs the supplies I came to buy, and she'll be worried that I'm not there when she expects me."

"You'll stay put until I verify your story."

There was no sense arguing. Eli believed the sheriff was a man who liked to throw his weight around just because he could. He wondered why the good people of Belleville had voted for a man like that. He sighed. He had no choice but to calm down and sit on the edge of the lumpy mattress. What would Mrs. Lloyd think when he told her why he was late getting home? Would she believe his story? Or would she side with the sheriff and want him out of her house?

McCallum strode out the door, leaving his prisoner behind bars. Eli could only sink onto the rough bed in his cell and wait as the sheriff mounted his horse and left. Where was he going, and when would he be back?

The sheriff returned to the crime scene to speak to the shopkeeper, but oddly, a Closed sign hung on the locked door. That was very strange in the middle of a workday. Wasn't Peyton worried about losing his profits? The regular customers would be frustrated when they came in for their supplies.

The only thing to do now was to check out the suspect's story with Mrs. Lloyd. He had known her for years and had visited her home several times. He urged his horse to a trot and soon arrived at the Lloyd farm.

Mrs. Lloyd answered the knock on her door and found the sheriff on her porch.

"George, how are you? Come on in," she said.

"Hello, Daisy. May I sit down?" He took his hat off and held it with both hands.

"Of course. What's the reason for your visit? I'd be happy to get you a cup of tea."

"No, thanks." The sheriff took a seat on the Chesterfield. "I'm here on business. A gentleman in my jail says he lives with you."

"What?" Mrs. Lloyd's eyes opened wide, and she sunk into the armchair. "Why is Eli in your jail?"

"Well, that confirms that he lives here," said the sheriff. "It's a sketchy story. The shopkeeper at the general store accused him of stealing an expensive hunting knife, so I picked him up. Eli denies it, of course. They all do."

"Eli didn't steal anything, George. That's ridiculous. He's as honest as you are."

"Well, he was caught with the knife in his basket."

Mrs. Lloyd stared at the sheriff with fire in her eyes. "I'd stake my life that he didn't put it there."

"I'll go back and try to see the shopkeeper again. For some reason, he closed the store right after the incident. I'll have to find him."

"I want Eli home by this afternoon, George. I mean it. I need him."

"We'll see, Daisy. I can't release a suspect without good reason."

"George, I'm telling you that boy is innocent, and I want him back." Mrs. Lloyd's ire rose.

"I'll work it out as soon as I can. I'll keep you informed."

The sheriff took his hat and beat a retreat, glad to be out of there. He didn't want to lock horns with Mrs. Lloyd. She had a reputation as a fighter when she wanted something. He started his trip back to town at a gallop, thinking about that Closed sign on the general store. The more he thought about it, the more it didn't make sense. He needed to look into it.

When he arrived at the store, would-be customers milled around the window, trying to see inside. He tied his horse to the rail and pushed through the crowd to look in the window. "What are you people looking at?" he said.

"We're trying to figure out why the store is closed when we need to buy supplies," said one of the women. She didn't try to hide the fact that she was irritated.

The sheriff took another long look through the window, studying every inch. High in the sky, the sun reflected his face on the glass, making his efforts difficult, but he thought he spotted a pair of feet stuck out just beyond the counter's far end.

"Stand back," he said, instructing the crowd. They peeled back, one by one. He used the butt end of his sidearm to knock out a pane of glass in the door, reached in, and turned the handle, letting himself in.

"Don't anybody come in," he said, and no one did. But they didn't leave, either, hanging around in tight groups and murmuring among themselves.

The sheriff advanced slowly, weapon drawn, should someone be hiding in the store. He carefully approached the pair of feet and peered around the counter's edge. There was Peyton, the shopkeeper, alive but bound and gagged.

The sheriff quickly loosed his bonds. When the gag came out of his mouth, Peyton said, "Where the devil have you been? I've been tied up forever, unable to move while that rascal stole me blind. I could only sit here and watch him rob me."

The sheriff sighed. "It looks like we have the wrong suspect in jail."

Peyton stood, rubbed his wrists and stomped his feet to get the blood flowing. "It was that younger guy. He was in the store the same time Reese was—the one I accused. He must have dropped that knife into Reese's basket to divert suspicion from himself. The real thief returned to the store when you took your prisoner away. He pulled a knife on me—not the one he put in Reese's basket—and I could only let him tie me up or get cut up. What would you have done?"

"I'd have done the same thing you did. Why don't you take a seat over there, Peyton? You need some time to calm down."

"Sure." Peyton limped to the chair and sat down to get his breath.

"I'm sorry to have to press you, but can you describe that character?"

Peyton went through the same description Eli had given the sheriff from his jail cell—dungarees, no shirt, straw hat.

"I don't know the boy's name or where he came from. He wasn't kin to nobody around here that I know of."

"That's mighty odd. You hardly ever see a stranger in Belleville, and now we have two—Reese and the thief."

Peyton sat on his chair, trying to slow his breathing, rubbing his hands and trembling.

"I'll let someone in to help you," the sheriff said. "Then I'm going to let Reese out of his cell and go on the hunt for that robber. You'll need to list what he stole as soon as you figure it out. Can you get me a list by morning?"

"I'll try. Thanks, George."

Sheriff McCallum emerged from the store and appointed one of the ladies in the crowd to go in and take care of Peyton.

"Folks, there's been a robbery in the general store," he said. "The store will be closed until I have a chance to investigate. Hopefully, it will be back open in the morning."

Curiosity ran high in the crowd. "Sheriff, is that man in your jail responsible for this?"

"It turns out he's not. I have to go release him and apologize."

Another question popped up. "What all did the thief steal?"

"I'm sorry, there's no time to answer questions right now. You'll have to get all the answers from the paper when it comes out next Tuesday. I need to find the thief."

One of the women in the crowd said, "I'm going to the newspaper office right now to tell Charlie everything I know about this robbery. Anyone want to go with me?"

She whirled around with her skirts swishing and marched toward the newspaper office. Several other ladies followed her.

Sheriff McCallum chuckled, feeling sorry for Charlie. He mounted his horse and rode the short distance to the jail. Pulling the ring of keys off the wall, he unlocked Eli's cell. "You're free to go, with my apologies, sir. It was the customer in the store while you were there."

"Yes, I know. He tried to lure me out of the store before you brought me here."

"We still don't know the extent of the robbery. Anyway, I went out and told Daisy—I mean Mrs. Lloyd—where you are. She was mighty upset with me. She swore you were an honest man. She was yelling at me when I left her house."

Eli grinned at the thought of Mrs. Lloyd's ire, despite his irritation toward the sheriff, and it was contagious. The sheriff caught the humor in it, and a slow smile spread across his face. "I'm awful sorry about the inconvenience. I hope you won't hold it against our fair town."

"No, sir, but I hope it doesn't happen again."

"You can go back to the store and pick up the supplies you ordered for Daisy, but please don't touch anything else while you're there. I still have an investigation to do. The only reason I'm letting you back in there is so I don't have to suffer Daisy's wrath again."

"Mrs. Lloyd and I thank you," said Eli. He walked back to the store, smiling, his haircut forgotten. He went inside to pay for his purchases.

The shopkeeper was red-faced at the sight of the man he had accused. "Mr. Reese, you have my sincere apology. It was an honest mistake."

Eli was tempted to lecture him about making false accusations but held his tongue. "It's behind us, sir. I hope we can be friends."

Peyton helped him carry his purchases to the carriage and shook his hand. Sheriff McCallum was entering the store as Eli drove away. He was hungry and weary but grateful to be free.

Chapter 46: CATCHING THE THIEF

Mrs. Lloyd waited for Eli at the house and spotted him coming from a distance. She went out to the gate, waving at him. "Welcome home, Eli, welcome home. I was sure George would let you out. I told him you were innocent. Come inside and tell me everything."

Eli grinned. "Let me carry these supplies inside for you first."

"All right. I'll take the chicken out of the Dutch oven while you do that. I have a special dinner for you. After the day you had, I figured you might need it."

"That sounds inviting. I could use a hot dinner to help me relax."

He walked out to the carriage for the rest of the supplies. From the corner of his eye, he noticed a horse and rider approaching from the south, traveling at a trot. Eli picked up the twenty pounds of flour in one arm and the five pounds of cornmeal in the other as the rider passed by. He almost dropped his burden when he recognized the rider as the thieving customer from the general store. Fortunately, the young man didn't notice him but kept his eyes straight ahead as he traveled as if lost in thought.

Eli ran back into the house. "Mrs. Lloyd, the thief just passed by on his horse, heading north," he said, panting.

"Good riddance to him," said Mrs. Lloyd.

"Shouldn't I ride into town and tell the sheriff?"

"The fellow will be miles away before you can get back into town. Let him go. Enjoy your dinner," she said, putting the roasted chicken on the table. The skin on the chicken was golden brown. The savory aroma made his mouth water.

"But I can get him myself if I hurry." He turned to leave.

Daisy sighed and returned the chicken to the pot while he ran outside and leaped into the carriage.

He slapped the reins and drove the horse and carriage down the road as a man possessed. He soon caught sight of the thief ahead of him. The rider kept up his steady pace, appearing to be unaware that he was being pursued.

Eli rode hard. The wind blew past him, and the horse's hooves pounded. His heart beat wildly. He reached for the rope under the seat and began twirling it round and round as he approached the thief on his horse. He had never been good at roping, so he breathed a prayer, asking for the Lord's help in catching the thief. The rope went round and round. Eli let fly, and the lariat fell short. Another try. Round and round went the rope a second time. Away it went, looping around the rider's shoulders. Amazing! Eli jerked on his end of the rope before the poor fellow realized what was happening. He slid off his saddle and hit the ground with a thud.

Eli ran and bound his stunned captive, rodeo style. The young man bellowed. "You could have killed me. What do you think you're doing?"

"I'm taking you to the sheriff, you thief."

"I'm not the thief. You were the one with the stolen knife."

"You're lucky I don't beat the tar out of you for what you did to me," said Eli. "I spent the afternoon in jail because of you. You're in a bad position to be making stupid accusations."

With difficulty, Eli pushed the thief into the carriage. There was no need to be gentle. He whistled for the fellow's horse, which had gone a short distance up the road. When the horse returned, Eli paused. There was a duffel tied behind the fellow's saddle. "What's this?"

He searched the duffel and found an assortment of new merchandise. There was a shaving mug, razor, another hunting knife, a pair of shears, a hand spade, some jerky, cinnamon candies, some fishing lures, and the matches and thread he paid for. "I guess we have the evidence here."

The prisoner glared at him. Eli tied the thief's horse to his carriage, then started the slow, tandem walk back to the Lloyd farm.

"I'm back, Mrs. Lloyd," he called as he pulled up. She ran out to meet him and paused to catch her breath.

"So this is the troublemaker? Well, it's too late to take your prisoner back to town before you have dinner. You haven't eaten anything all day. Come on inside. Bring that blighter with you, and we'll feed him before you take him in."

She set an extra place at the table while Eli untied the thief's legs, then helped him down. "You'll be eating dinner here," he said, "then I'm taking you to the sheriff."

The thief hobbled inside with his hands still bound, favoring the left hip that hit the ground first when he flew off his horse. Eli was right behind him, making sure he didn't bolt.

"Sit over there," Mrs. Lloyd said, pointing to a chair. A tasty dinner was on the table—roasted chicken, boiled potatoes, a bowl of fresh corn, and some sliced tomatoes. "Now bow your head," she said. "We're going to pray."

The thief sat quietly while Mrs. Lloyd spoke to the Lord. "Dear Father, thank you for this food we're about to eat. I pray you'll notice our guest and help Eli get him to Sheriff McCallum with no problem. And I pray you'll see that he gets the proper punishment for his crime so he'll turn to you and repent of his sin. Amen."

The thief sat with his head down, glaring at her from the tops of his eyes. Mrs. Lloyd filled his plate with plenty of chicken and vegetables. He managed to eat with his hands bound in front of him.

"What's your name?" she asked.

"Chester."

"Why did you steal from the general store? Don't you have money?"

"Yeah, I got money."

"Then why?"

That ended the conversation. Chester only ate and glared.

"I'll go with you, Eli," Mrs. Lloyd said. "It's getting late, and Sheriff McCallum may have left the jail. I know where he lives. Why don't you put Chester in the carriage? I'll tidy up the kitchen a bit and be right out."

"Yes, ma'am," Eli said. He took Chester outside and deposited him in the carriage, binding his feet. They waited for Mrs. Lloyd. The prisoner pouted but kept his peace.

"All right, let's go," said Mrs. Lloyd, climbing into the carriage beside the captive. With a slight jerk, the carriage started rolling, and they were on their way into town. It would be dark soon, so there was some urgency.

Once in town, they went directly to the jail, but the sheriff had gone home for the night. "Go up to the next street and turn right," Mrs. Lloyd said. "McCallum lives down there about two blocks."

When they arrived at the sheriff's whitewashed one-bedroom cottage, Mrs. Lloyd said, "You stay in the carriage with the prisoner. I'll roust the sheriff."

She charged up the gravel walk and knocked. McCallum was taken by surprise when he opened the door. "What can I do for you, Daisy?" he asked.

"Eli caught your thief for you," she said, pointing to the

carriage. "He claims his name is Chester. He was unlucky enough to pass our house just as Eli was going outside, so he chased after him and roped him like a calf at the county fair. Downed him in no time. We fed him for you, so all he wants now is to be locked up."

The sheriff grinned and sauntered out to the carriage. "Mr. Reese, I can't thank you enough. I would never have caught him if he was headed out of town."

"His duffel is behind my seat," said Eli. "The stolen property is in it."

The sheriff retrieved the duffel. "So, Chester, you didn't get as far as you hoped."

The prisoner scowled at him.

"Daisy, would you and Mr. Reese mind driving this fellow to the jail? I'll follow you and take him off your hands as soon as we get there."

"Yes, we can do that. We have his horse here, too. You'll need to do something with him."

The procession rolled down the street. They arrived at the jail and discharged their prisoner and his horse to the care of McCallum, then Eli and Mrs. Lloyd were free to return home. The sun had dipped below the horizon.

"Mrs. Lloyd, how do you light those lanterns on the carriage?" Eli asked.

"With a match. I'll show you." She found the matches in a compartment behind the seat and touched one to each lantern. Their reflectors sent rays of light onto the road ahead.

"You've been through quite a day, haven't you, Eli?" Mrs. Lloyd asked.

"I've had better."

"God was with you. You won't be a stranger to the Belleville folks anymore. Everyone will know your name. You'll be a hero when they learn you were falsely accused and then apprehended the true thief."

Eli chuckled, then said sadly, "I wish I could tell Mary about this."

When he went to bed that night, he dreamed that Mary and Zach were in the misty distance. When he reached for them, they turned and walked away into the fog. His pillow was covered with tears.

Chapter 47: THE BROKEN AXE

Saturday, August 20, 1892

Eli hadn't accomplished as much work Friday as usual. Mrs. Lloyd had fussed over him all day to help him recover from Thursday's events. He hoped to finish enough work on Saturday to make up for it. As soon as he cared for the animals and collected the eggs, he turned his attention to the fallen trees in the woods at the back of the property. He planned to clear the debris from the forest floor, then chop the fallen limbs and trunks to turn them into fuel for fireplace heat.

Midmorning found him hauling the larger pieces of downed wood into a pile. The area was starting to look much better—more groomed. He was pleased with his progress.

He emerged from the woods and headed for the barn to get Mr. Lloyd's long-handled axe to chop the logs.

It was a sweltering day, and the heat grew more intense with every passing hour. Eli's shirt was drenched in sweat, so he took it off by the barn and left it on a stump in the sun. He balanced the axe over his bare shoulder and strode back into the woods.

As he swung the axe, he enjoyed the surge of power going through his body. He chopped and stacked, chopped and stacked. Slowly, fatigue began to set in. He wished he didn't get tired so quickly. Maybe he needed to do it more often to build his stamina. He took his handkerchief from the pocket of his

Levi's and wiped the sweat from his face.

One more swing of the axe, then he would rest. He maneuvered the log into position and raised the axe over his head when the heavy blade came loose and fell, glancing off his head and slicing into his right shoulder. He dropped the handle and slumped to the ground without moving. Blood ran from his cut shoulder. He didn't wake. Time passed as he lay there in the dirt and leaves. The sun continued in its path.

When Eli finally opened his eyes, he was in pain, unsure of where he was, and didn't know how long he had been there. He was too weak and dizzy to get up.

Mrs. Lloyd had lunch ready at noon and waited for Eli to come in. She assumed he was working hard when he was overdue. She pulled the rope on the dinner bell by the back stoop. The bell swung back and forth, clanging loud enough to raise the neighbors.

That will bring him in for lunch, she thought. But another ten minutes passed, and there was no sign of Eli. She rang the bell again, and he still didn't come. With mounting concern, she went looking for him.

Out by the barn, she spotted his shirt. *He must be in the barn or behind it. Or maybe he's around the chicken coop.* A sense of urgency took over when she didn't find him there. She hurried into the woods and followed the path she thought he would take. There, beside a pile of freshly cut logs, she found his prone body. He had recovered consciousness. The bleeding had stopped, but he was too weak to get up.

"Eli!" Mrs. Lloyd rushed to him to inspect the damage. "What happened?" She studied the lump on his head and the gash on his shoulder and recoiled at the sight. It was a deep cut. She didn't know how to take care of something that bad.

"I think the axe head came loose and fell on me," he said.

"My shoulder hurts."

"I imagine it does," she said. "You stay put. I'm going for the doctor. You have a nasty wound on your shoulder."

"Could I have some water first?"

"Yes. I'll get water and some towels to pillow your head. Then I'll go for the doctor." She put her hand to her mouth, took one more look at him, then hurried off to the house. Her heart pounded so loud that her blood pulsed in her ears. Her hands shook, and she nearly passed out, but she steeled herself and kept going.

In a few minutes, she was back. Eli raised his head just enough to take some water. Even that small effort made him dizzy. Mrs. Lloyd slid a towel under his head to make him more comfortable, then left again to go for the doctor.

Eli's mind wandered as he lay alone in the dirt. How badly was he hurt? Would he get an infection? What if he never saw Mary again? If he died, she would never know. Grief and stress churned around inside him as he lay there helpless.

Then, a quiet voice in his spirit said, "Don't let your heart be troubled. I'm with you."

What? Was that from delirium? No, there it was again. "Don't be afraid. I'm here with you." It wasn't an audible voice, but those words were firmly impressed in his spirit. He marveled. He had never known that gentle voice before but understood who it was without a doubt. Jesus was there with him, watching over him while Mrs. Lloyd went for the doctor. He smiled, closed his eyes, and rested under the protection of the Great Physician.

Meanwhile, Mrs. Lloyd arrived at the doctor's office and told him he was needed for an emergency. He had a patient already, but he was giving him final advice about how to treat his ailment, so he was able to leave quickly. He grabbed his instrument bag, stuffing some extra bandages inside, and some chloroform if he had to do surgery. He went to his closet to retrieve his stretcher. He would need it.

He jumped into his carriage and followed Mrs. Lloyd back to her farm.

"Hurry! Please, hurry."

The poor doctor scrambled to collect his gear. As soon as he was ready, she led him into the woods, where Eli was still lying. The doctor knelt on one knee in the dirt for a better look.

"That's bad, all right," he said. "Eli, open your eyes, son."

Eli opened his eyes, although he preferred to continue his nap despite the pain, which had dulled somewhat.

"We need to move you to the house. I'll pick you up under your arms, and it'll hurt, and Mrs. Lloyd will pick up your feet. We need to transfer you to the stretcher."

The doctor and Mrs. Lloyd got into position. A shot of pain went through Eli's shoulder as the doctor lifted him. He moaned and begged the doctor to stop, but it was already done. He was on the stretcher.

Mrs. Lloyd cried, "Oh, my back," and steadied herself on the closest tree. She tried straightening up but couldn't do it. "I won't be able to carry him into the house," she said. "I strained my back trying to pick up his legs."

"Can you bring my bag of supplies?" the doctor asked. "It's not heavy. I'll pick up the stretcher poles at his head and drag him to the house. I'll pull the stretcher like a sled."

She picked up the bag, and the doctor gripped the poles. He lugged Eli up the long path to the house, with Mrs. Lloyd shuffling behind him, bent over in pain and toting the doctor's bag. It was agony for Eli, who was jostled with every bump.

The doctor dragged Eli through the back door, the kitchen, the parlor, and then into the spare bedroom. With great effort, he manipulated his patient into the bed. The wound had begun to seep again from all the jostling. His flesh was splayed open and needed to be treated quickly.

The doctor gave Eli some chloroform before doing the cleaning and stitching. "Mrs. Lloyd, do you have any ice in the spring house?" he asked. "If you could crush some ice and wrap it in a cloth, we need to get it on that lump on his head."

Ignoring her pain, she was glad to escape the room while he did the stitching. When she returned, his needlework was finished, and he was bandaging the wound.

The doctor placed the icy bundle on Eli's head. "Chill this lump down for a few minutes once an hour today. It will help the swelling to go down."

She agreed to do that.

The doctor asked her to join him in the parlor, away from Eli's hearing. "We need to talk about this injury, Mrs. Lloyd," he said. "This was a deep cut. I cleaned it out, stitched it up, and gave him some morphine for pain. Watch it for infection. And that head injury needs careful tending, too. He may have two black eyes by tomorrow. It's going to take some time for him to heal. You'll need to keep that arm immobile for at least a week, and it will be quite a while before he can do hard work with his right arm. You'll go easy on him, won't you?"

"I'll take good care of him. When will you be coming back to check on him?"

"I'll come Monday to make sure he's on track. He's young and healthy otherwise, so he should be fine. Just watch for infection. And rest that back, Daisy. You can't afford to be laid up, too."

The doctor went on his way. Mrs. Lloyd sat beside Eli on his bed and bowed her head, whispering a prayer. "Lord God, You never blessed me and Mr. Lloyd with a child, but here is Eli, and I can't imagine a finer son. I've become very fond of him. I'm asking you, Father, to heal him quickly and completely, both for his sake and mine. I pray you'll give me the wisdom to care for him, but the healing is up to you."

Eli stirred, half awake.

"Rest, Eli. Just rest."

Chapter 48: DISASTER STRIKES

Saturday, September 3, 1892

It had been two weeks since his accident with the axe. Eli rose early in the morning to feed the chickens and gather eggs. He removed the sling that kept his arm immobile, and it was good to move it as long as he was careful. He was sure he would gain strength quickly.

When he returned to the house, Mrs. Lloyd served him eggs with ham, flapjacks, and hot coffee.

"Eli, you're trying to do too much with that arm," she said. "You need to give it more time."

He chuckled. "That sounds like something my mother would tell me. No, you took me in, and I owe you a great debt." He put a forkful of eggs in his mouth. "I can't waste time when there are things to do around here. I'll be careful, but I won't forget my responsibilities. Besides, moving the arm will make it stronger."

"You don't owe me anything. I'm thankful you're here. I hope we'll still stay in touch when your wife sends for you."

"I've lost hope that will happen, but if it does, I wouldn't think of losing contact with you."

They ate their breakfast with contented hearts, like two people so comfortable with each other that conversation wasn't necessary.

Monday, September 5, 1892

Weeks had passed without receiving a letter from Mary. Eli's spirit was grieved. He prayed every day, knowing he had created the situation himself. He decided to ease the pain in his heart by throwing himself into his work. Before his injury, he had cut a fair amount of wood and stacked it up for the winter, but Mrs. Lloyd would need more. He longed to chop wood again, but his arm wasn't ready.

He searched for work he could do with his good left arm. The kitchen door had become shabby. A coat of paint would do a lot of good, and he believed he could wield a brush with his left hand. He went to the barn and got the paint bucket and a brush. Brushing up and down with his left hand was challenging for a right-handed man, but he kept at it, wiping his drips with a wet rag. Within an hour, the door sported a fresh new look. Eli stepped back and inspected his work.

Mrs. Lloyd joined him in the kitchen to admire his painting job.

"Eli, there are some loose boards in my bedroom floor by the bed. They squeak every time I walk there. How is your arm? Do you think you could fix my floor?"

"Sure, I think so," he said. "I may be able to pry the loose boards with the crowbar, using my foot for pressure. Give me a few minutes to clean the brush and put the paint away."

He returned to the barn to get the tools and supplies for the job. He inserted the crowbar under one of the loose boards and stomped on the crowbar with his foot to protect his shoulder. The work was slow. After every stomp, he had to readjust the crowbar, but he finally had the boards up. Then he had to saw new boards to the correct size with his left hand, but in a couple of hours, he had repaired the floor. These boards wouldn't squeak when stepped on and wouldn't curl up to become a trip hazard.

As he cleaned up the wood scraps and picked up the tools, there was a heavy thump in the parlor.

"Mrs. Lloyd, are you all right?" He expected a quick affirmative answer, but no answer came.

He looked into the parlor. To his horror, Mrs. Lloyd had collapsed on the floor, paralyzed. She tried to speak to him, but it was an unintelligible growling sound. This was a stroke. He had learned about this from his brother William, the medical student. He knew it was life-threatening and jumped into action.

"Mrs. Lloyd," he shouted as if her ears were affected. He rolled her onto her back and straightened her legs. "Hang on! I'm going for the doctor." His eyes darted around, looking for something to cover her. He spotted a knitted throw on the Chesterfield and used it to cover her legs. His heart was pounding in near panic.

He remembered seeing the doctor's office on the way to the general store. He dashed outside, mounted his horse, and took off at a hard gallop. Pain shot through his shoulder as the hooves pounded, so he held his arm tight against his body. He reached Dr. Stevens' office and ran in, shouting, "Doctor, Mrs. Lloyd is having a stroke."

The doctor grabbed his bag and dashed for his horse. "You lead the way. I'll be right behind you."

The two flew down the road, hooves striking the dirt. The horses' heads bobbed in rhythm until they reached the Lloyd home in record time. The doctor ran in to see Mrs. Lloyd lying on the floor. Her eyes were staring into the distance, and she couldn't speak.

"Daisy, talk to me."

Her lips moved.

"We need to get her into bed," the doctor said. The two men

lifted her with incredible difficulty. Eli tried to ignore the pain in his shoulder. They made her comfortable in her bed and covered her with a sheet.

"This isn't good," said the doctor. "It's obvious she's had a bad stroke. See, she's not moving her left side at all, and she can't speak. Her brain has suffered some damage." He sighed and studied Eli with sympathetic eyes. "There's no medical treatment for this, son. You'll have to care for her and see how she progresses. Sometimes, people recover, but mostly they don't. And if they do, there's almost always some lingering disability—trouble keeping their balance, talking or swallowing, or any number of things. You'll need to keep me informed."

"Yes, sir."

"I'll check on her in a couple of days. If she improves, we might be able to help her exercise her legs, but I can tell you now that it will be a long road. She'll need twenty-four-hour care. You probably need to get some help."

"I'm in a lot of trouble, then," said Eli. "I'm just rooming here. I'm not a relative. I don't think she has any relatives. And I don't have any money to pay for help."

"I don't know what to tell you," the doctor said, shaking his head. "She doesn't have anyone else. I think you're it. Let me know if you need anything I can help with."

"Thank you, doctor. I'll do the best I can." Eli's mind was in turmoil. He faced an impossible situation. He sank into the nearest chair with a stunned look on his face.

The doctor paused in his steps and turned around.

"One thing I can do is let the pastor know you need help. Maybe he can get some volunteers to come over." He had been attending the same country church as Mrs. Lloyd.

"That would be a great relief."

The doctor returned to his office by way of the pastor's house, leaving Eli in a panic. How could he care for an aging woman he had only known for a few months? What would he do for money to buy supplies for the house? He would have to cook and feed Mrs. Lloyd if she woke up long enough to eat. He would have to keep her clean and do her laundry. There would be lots of laundry. How could he do all of this?

Again, he prayed, crying out in desperation. "Father, I am in way over my head. I need your help with this. I don't know what Mrs. Lloyd needs or how to help her. But she was there when I needed her, so please help me give her the care she needs."

His head spun, and his heart raced. He walked into the kitchen in a mental fog to see if there was some soup he could heat up.

In the morning, one of the church ladies showed up with some extra bedding and helped Eli change Mrs. Lloyd's bed. She said someone else would be by later in the afternoon with some food. His job that day, and most days, would be washing bedding and tending his patient.

Chapter 49: THE LETTER

Susannah enjoyed having Mary and Zach with her. Her love for both of them was growing. They spent several weeks with her and Christian. The family was dumbfounded that there had been no contact from Eli. Over time, their thinking evolved, and now they wondered if he had fallen into a ditch or a river and was injured or even dead. What else were they to think?

One evening, Christian came home with a little red wagon for Zach. "If you decide to go home, this will be big enough to pull Zach to the general store and even carry your supplies back home. At least you won't feel like a prisoner stuck at the house. But this is not a hint for you to leave. We enjoy having you here."

Mary was delighted. Zach wanted a ride in his wagon right then.

"Mother Wolf, the next time you go to Spencer's Mill," Mary said, "I think I should stop by the house and make sure everything is still in good order. What if Eli got home and didn't know where to find me?"

Susannah chuckled. "I don't blame you for imagining that, dear, but the chances are slim. He would have gone to the bakery and asked John where you were."

"I suppose you're right," said Mary. She wanted so much for Eli to come home.

The next day, Susannah took Mary's desires to heart and decided to travel to Spencer's Mill. After Christian left to pursue his daily schedule, Susannah, Mary, and Zach took off in the carriage. Their first stop was Mary's house so she could check it over.

They pulled up in front and tied the horse to the rail. Mary unlocked the door, walked into the house, and surveyed each room. There was no damage from severe weather or vandalism. Everything was in order except for a layer of dust. She had hoped deep within her heart that she would find Eli there, but that was not to be.

She stepped down to the root cellar to check on the vegetables. Some of the food was rotting. "Do you want to take the good food?" she asked.

Susannah agreed they needed to do that, so they got a basket from the barn and loaded it with some of the produce. Whatever was going bad was thrown into the yard to feed the birds.

Mary sighed deeply. "I'm ready to go now," she told Susannah.

"All right. I'm sorry Eli isn't here." Susannah put a comforting arm around her daughter-in-law's shoulders as they walked to the road. "Oh, did you check the mail?"

"No, I forgot that," Mary said. "There's hardly ever anything important, but maybe I should check it anyway." She turned, trudged back to the letterbox at the front of the house, and pulled out the single letter inside. Her mouth flew open when she read the envelope, and her eyebrows shot up.

"Mother Wolf, it's a letter from Eli." Her pulse quickened.

She ran back to the carriage and ripped the envelope open, her hands shaking. It contained two dollars and a letter.

'My dearest Mary,

First, I want you to know that I miss you and Zach very much. I realize there is no excuse for leaving you the way I did without explanation. There was a battle raging inside me that I have resolved with God's help, and if you would ever think of forgiving me and letting me come back home, I will be there as soon as I can.

I am boarding with Mrs. Lloyd in Belleville, Ohio. She owns a farmhouse outside of town, and I work for her. She and I have been praying that your heart will be tender toward me and take me back, but if you don't, dear Mary, I will understand.

The address of Mrs. Lloyd's house is the return address on this envelope. You can write to me there and let me know your decision.

With all my love,

Eli'

"Mother Wolf, he wants to come home. And this is the address where he's staying." Mary's heart thumped.

Susannah took the envelope and recognized the town of Belleville in the return address. "Oh, my. That's way out past Blackhawk Lake," she said. "It might take almost a week to get a letter to him, but we could get there ourselves in two days. Why don't we go pick him up? Let's talk to Christian about it."

Thank God Eli wasn't dead. Unexpectedly, Susannah's ire rose. She thought she would have a good talk with him about the way a real man treats his family. She would get him straightened out. She never raised a son of hers to behave like that.

Then, a sense of guilt overcame her, so she redirected her thinking. This family needed to heal. Perhaps her best role would be to stay out of the way and let God take care of it. Her heart was at peace with that decision.

At the bakery, they reported the good news that Eli was alive and wanted to come home. Then they went to Matilda's house and told her the same thing. The family rejoiced that the lost sheep was now found.

Susannah could hardly wait for Christian to come home so she could discuss this with him.

He arrived late that evening because of a lengthy consultation with a client in his law office. Susannah explained the situation.

"I'm in favor of going down there and bringing him back, dear," he said, "except it's a good two-day ride, then two days back. That will mean trying to find overnight lodging along the way. What if we can't find an inn? Are you prepared to spend nights in the carriage?"

"Let's take the larger wagon, then," Susannah said. "That would give Zach a little room to play for the hours on the road, and we could spread out quilts to sleep on if we have to."

"That means no covering over our heads to protect us from the sun and rain."

"Yes. I think we can manage that, don't you? The weather has been moderate lately."

Christian agreed to that. "Tomorrow is Wednesday. Most of my clients come early in the week for some reason. So tomorrow, when I get to the office, I will post a sign saying I will be out of the office on Thursday and Friday due to a family emergency. Then we can drive to Belleville and return on Saturday and Sunday. It will be a long, hard trip. Are you sure you're up to it?"

"I should say I am." Susannah was a woman of determination. She spent time Wednesday planning for the trip and packing clothes. She chose food that would travel well since they may not pass any eateries. She also tried to anticipate what they would need if they had to spend the night in the wagon. She asked the caretaker to load tarps, ropes, a hatchet, bales of hay, quilts, and pillows. Maybe she was overdoing the packing, but she would rather have too much than regret leaving something behind.

Chapter 50: A MONUMENTAL DECISION

Wednesday, September 7, 1892

On the second day after her stroke, Mrs. Lloyd opened her eyes. Eli had been caring for her, cringing at doing some of the things that were necessary. But he chose to honor her with the best care he could give her. He tried to spoon some liquid into her mouth. She took a little of the broth, but much of it dribbled down her chin. She had trouble swallowing. Eli wiped her face for her.

"You've had a bad stroke, Mrs. Lloyd. Can you talk?"

Her lips moved silently.

"Don't worry about it," he said with a cheerfulness he didn't feel. "Maybe later today or tomorrow, you'll speak a little. In the meantime, rest. What about your arms? Can you move them?"

Her right arm moved weakly, but her left arm was immobile. Eli hovered over her all day, occasionally trying to feed her and reading her Bible aloud. He cooked a meal and washed her laundry. When he was in the room, her eyes followed him wherever he went. Her mind was active, even though her body was motionless.

That night, Eli made a mat on her bedroom floor and slept there in case she needed him. He was physically and mentally worn out from the situation he found himself in. His arm hadn't yet healed.

His dreams at night were of Mary. He dreamed he and Mary were by the river, holding hands and enjoying the sunlight. But in the morning, when he woke, he was back in Belleville under overwhelming responsibility. His back and arm ached from sleeping on the hard floor.

On Friday afternoon, there was a gentle knock at the door. He was washing bed sheets and dried his arms with a towel as he went to see who was there. Maybe it was one of the church ladies with food.

To his astonishment, he was greeted by his wife, son, mother, and stepfather. His mouth flew open, and his heart overflowed with joy. He threw his arms around Mary and held her tight.

"Mary, Mary," was all he could say. He buried his face in her hair.

"Papa," Zach said and reached up to be held. Eli grabbed him and kissed his cheeks.

"It's good to see you, Eli. May we come in?" Susannah asked.

"Of course, Ma, come in. Have a seat. I'm in the middle of doing some laundry."

Mary and Zach clung to Eli while Susannah and Christian sat on the Chesterfield. They were all weary from the long trip.

"We came to take you home, son. And we all need to hear your explanation."

Eli's face betrayed hesitation. "Ma, I —"

Christian glared at Eli. "What's wrong, Eli? We read your letter to Mary and assumed you wanted to come home."

"Yes, of course, I did, but—"

Susannah's temper flared. "But what?" she demanded. "We've just driven two days—"

"It's Mrs. Lloyd. She had a stroke a few days ago and is completely helpless. I'm doing the best I can, but it's inadequate.

I need help with her. And I certainly can't just walk out and leave her. She has no family, and she took me in when I was desperate."

Susannah and Christian shot glances at each other. "What do we do now? This is an unexpected wrinkle," Susannah said.

"Would you like to meet her?"

Susannah nodded.

Eli led his family into Mrs. Lloyd's bedroom, tiptoeing. "Mrs. Lloyd," he said gently. She opened her eyes. "This is my family. My family is here! This is my wife, Mary; son, Zach; mother, Susannah Wolf; and step-father, Attorney Christian Wolf."

Mrs. Lloyd nodded as much as she could to show she understood. She tried to smile, but one side of her face was paralyzed. It came across as a grimace.

"Mrs. Lloyd has been like an angel to me," said Eli, holding her hand. "She fed me and offered me a place to stay. We've had quite a time together for the past two months." He rubbed her arm.

Susannah took Mrs. Lloyd's hand. "Can you understand what we're saying?"

Mrs. Lloyd nodded.

"Can you move your arms?"

Mrs. Lloyd moved her right arm, but the left arm was useless.

"What about your legs?"

She wiggled her right foot, but the left leg did not move.

Susannah turned to Eli. "Has she improved since the stroke, or is she the same?"

"She hasn't changed at all, except she's awake now. The doctor and I managed to get her into bed, but she's been there ever since. I've been trying to help her . . ."

"Maybe we could take her home with us and care for her

there," Susannah said, looking to Christian for a response.

"I doubt if she could make the trip very well. We need to consult the doctor before we try to move her."

"If you stay with her, I'll go get the doctor," Eli said. "I know where his office is." His mother agreed to watch the patient, so he got his horse and rode to the doctor's office as Mary took Zach into the parlor to play.

Susannah bent over Mrs. Lloyd. "Thank you for caring for my son, Mrs. Lloyd. I can't thank you enough. He went a little crazy there for a while, but he's a good man."

Mrs. Lloyd's eyes flooded with tears, and she nodded her head. Then she lifted her right hand and pointed at Christian.

Christian moved toward her. "What is it?" he asked.

Mrs. Lloyd wiggled her fingers to indicate that she wanted Christian to come closer. When he was right by her bed, she made writing motions in the air.

"You want to write?" Christian asked. Mrs. Lloyd nodded. Susannah searched the room for paper and a pencil and found some in a drawer. She handed the pencil to Mrs. Lloyd.

Christian held the paper near her, and she wrote in a shaky hand, "I NO AIRS." She dropped her hand wearily. After a few seconds, she made writing motions again. Christian held the paper up. She wrote, "GIVE FARM 2 ELI."

Christian's eyes widened, and he took a step back. His mind raced to figure out how to handle this request ethically. He cleared his throat and spoke slowly, still trying to grasp the situation. "Let me make sure I understand what you want, and I beg your pardon in advance if I'm completely off base," he said. "I think you're saying that you have no heirs, and you want your farm to go to Eli when you pass away. Is that right?"

She nodded her head.

"Do you want me to draw up a will for you to sign?"

She nodded.

Christian hesitated. "Since you're now my client, we'll have to write it so it protects you as long as you live. I can make a will saying that your farm goes to Eli upon your death, conditional on his caring for you as long as you live." She nodded.

"To protect Eli, we'll need a local person to witness your signature. I'll get a local attorney to come and act as a witness." She nodded, and the expression on her face relaxed.

"Oh, what about your other possessions—your furnishings, farm implements, livestock, cash assets?"

She pointed to the word "ELI."

Susannah's jaw fell open in amazement. "Christian…"

"It's all right, dear. Can you find some lunch for us while I work?"

She went to the kitchen to look for food for Mrs. Lloyd and the family while Christian went to work drawing up a will. When Eli returned with the doctor, Christian asked where a local attorney could be found. The doctor gave him directions.

Drawing the doctor into another room, Christian said, "We want to know if we can take Mrs. Lloyd back home to better care for her. We live a few miles past Lamar."

The doctor spoke in muted tones. "I'm afraid the old girl might not make a trip like that. She's very frail. If she stays here, she might live a few weeks, or maybe only a few days. I don't look for her to last long. The stroke she had was a bad one. She's had some damage to her brain and can't move the left side of her body. Awfully bad sign." He stared at the floor and shook his head. "She's always been an independent sort of woman. The fact that she can't even move must tear her up inside. She's a prisoner in a worn-out body."

"Thank you, doctor. That tells me what I need to know."

The doctor checked on Mrs. Lloyd one more time. "Goodbye, Daisy. I'll be back in a couple of days."

She lifted her right hand, then dropped it.

Christian left on Eli's horse and went to the local attorney's office in an attractive house on the main street. Attorney Harold Snow was in. Christian explained the situation and showed him Mrs. Lloyd's hand-scrawled notes. He also showed him the will he had drawn up. "Do you think she's in her right mind?" Christian asked. "Could this be what she truly wants to do?"

"I've known her for years," said Mr. Snow. "She's smart enough to know she can't survive long after that stroke. She and Mr. Lloyd never had children, and I don't know of any nieces or nephews. There was a rumor that she had someone staying with her, doing some work on the farm. It sounds like she's bonded with the young man and wants to bless him."

"I'd like someone local to come to Mrs. Lloyd's house to verify this is what she wants, just in case someone disputes it, and then witness her signature."

"I'll be glad to witness her signature when she confirms what you've told me. If we go through with this, there will need to be probate filed when Mrs. Lloyd passes."

"Of course," said Christian, and they rode back to the house.

Christian invited Mr. Snow into Mrs. Lloyd's bedroom.

"Hello, Daisy," said Mr. Snow.

She opened her eyes and acknowledged a friend she and her husband had known for a long time.

He continued. "I was sorry to hear about your stroke."

She tried to nod.

"Mr. Wolf tells me you want to give away your farm."

She managed a weak nod.

Mr. Snow grasped her hand. "Now, these are the terms Mr. Wolf has written in a will for you to sign. You're bequeathing your farm to Eli Reese under the condition that Mr. Reese takes care of you until your death. Is that your intention?"

Mrs. Lloyd made little writing signs in the air with her hand.

Christian handed Mr. Snow a piece of paper. "Here. Hold this up for her to write on."

Mr. Snow held the paper for her. With her right hand, she wrote slowly, "YES DO IT."

Mr. Snow laughed. "She has always been quite sure about what she wants," he said. "Now, Daisy, I'm going to hold this will for you to sign, and you understand that as soon as you complete your signature, you're buying life-long care in exchange for your farm." He held up the will. "Your signature goes right here." He pointed to the line that Christian had drawn for her signature.

She scrawled her name weakly on the line, then on the copy. Her hand dropped in exhaustion.

Mr. Snow signed as a witness, then folded one copy of the will and tucked it into his coat pocket. "Mr. Reese, the farm is now under your control."

Eli was overwhelmed. He stroked Mrs. Lloyd's head gently. "I'll take good care of you, Mrs. Lloyd."

She tried to reach toward him, and he took her hand. They both had tears in their eyes.

After Mr. Snow's departure, Mary turned to Eli, downcast. "What do we do now, Eli? My heart was set on having you back home."

Eli put his arms around her. "Mary, you must have been through a miserable time, more than any wife should endure. You deserve to know everything when we have time for a serious conversation. I'm truly sorry. I'd like you and Zach to stay with Mrs. Lloyd and me. I think we need to sell our house in Spencer's Mill and consider Belleville our new home."

Mary stepped away from Eli, searching his eyes. "This is a lot to accept as suddenly as this. We won't be close to family anymore."

"We haven't been close to family for the past few years, even though we lived near them."

"Lately, I've gotten close to your Ma and Christian. I've been living with them."

Eli blushed when he realized they had taken on a significant role in her life—the role he should have been filling. He turned to his mother. "Ma, I'm sorry. I need to make this up to you somehow. And Christian, thank you for watching over my family." Tears formed in his eyes as his humiliation ran deep. He didn't know how to express what he was feeling. "I'll find a way to pay you back."

Mary grabbed his arm. "I want to see the house, Eli."

She turned and walked through the house with him, running her hand over some of the furnishings and inspecting the kitchen. "There are some things I would change," she whispered to him, "but it's much bigger than our house in Spencer's Mill. And it's on twenty acres of farmland. We have only a little patch of land back home. And look how much room Zach will have to play . . . It's just hard to adjust to such a major change so suddenly. When we came here, I expected to go back to Spencer's Mill tomorrow."

"It's your decision, Mary. I have no right to push you into anything you don't want to do. If you want to return to Spencer's Mill, I can stay here as long as Mrs. Lloyd lives, then sell her farm and move back with you."

"No, I'll stay, Eli," she said. "I'll help you take care of Mrs. Lloyd."

Eli was deeply humbled. Mary was a far better wife than he deserved.

Christian smiled at Susannah. "Well, my dear, it looks like we're going home alone." He turned to Eli. "You'll have to come back at some point and take care of the sale of your house. Or would you rather we tried to find a renter for you?"

"Let's not make any hasty decisions. Mary and I will discuss it and let you know by telegram. Let the house sit unoccupied for a week or two while we decide."

"That will be fine."

"And thank you for caring for Mary and Zach in my absence. I owe you a great debt."

"That's what family is for," said Christian. "Susannah, why don't we stay the night here, then be on our way? Eli, is there a place for us to sleep?"

"There is a second bedroom. You can sleep there. I've been sleeping on the floor in Mrs. Lloyd's room in case she needs something. Zach can sleep with me. Mary, would you mind sleeping on the Chesterfield just this one night?"

She smiled. "Of course not. I'm only glad to be in the same house as you and know you're alive."

Mary and Susannah went into the kitchen, looking for something to prepare for dinner. They all enjoyed one another that evening, looking in on Mrs. Lloyd every few minutes. It was late when they finally decided to turn in for the night.

As soon as Christian and Susannah had gone to bed, Mary turned to her husband and pointed her finger at his face. "I love you, Eli, but don't you ever, ever do that to me again."

Chapter 51: THE LONG RIDE HOME

Saturday, September 10, 1892

It was a long, two-day drive home for Susannah and Christian, but they found traveling much easier without a wiggly two-year-old. Susannah recalled the days in their courtship when they took long rides in the country. "Do you remember those days, Christian? Remember when we took a drive in the country, and that horrible gossiping woman caught us?"

Christian laughed. "Yes, Susannah, I do! Those were adventurous days, weren't they? I was afraid I'd lost you there for a while."

They traveled on, listening to the wind in the trees and the rattle of the wagon wheels, savoring their solitude. The breeze was cool. No children or grandchildren, no caretaker, and no housekeeper. Just the two of them.

The light level changed gradually as clouds crept across the sun. Susannah lifted her eyes to the sky. "It looks like it might rain. We're still hours from home. What will we do if a storm comes?"

"I'm not worried about a hard storm. We're past the summer storm season, but we might get some rain. I'm glad you had Jesse put that canvas in the wagon. Good thinking. That will keep the raindrops off."

They traveled until twilight, knowing from prior experience that there wouldn't be an inn along the way. They would be sleeping in the wagon under the threat of rain. Christian pulled off the road into a tree-sheltered area. He broke open another bale of hay and spread it in the wagon's bed, covering the hay with quilts. With a sweep of his arm, he faked a grand bow as if it were the royal suite. "Mrs. Wolf, would you like to join me in our bed chamber?" Then he paused, shaking his head, and chuckled. "This is no way for people our age to live, my dear. There's no dignity in it."

"It's quite a fine bed, Mr. Wolf," she replied. "We'll sleep well as long as the rain holds off." She gazed skyward. Most of the stars were hidden by clouds.

Christian considered their situation. "Why don't I get the canvas out and make a tent over us? Even if it rains, we'll stay dry."

She laughed with delight. "This will be another adventure to remember."

Christian pulled out the canvas. Then he searched the edge of the woods and found slender tree limbs. He used them to build a makeshift tent frame over the top of the wagon, lashing them in place with ropes.

Susannah pulled food out of her basket while he worked. "We don't have much food left, Christian. Just beef jerky, Thursday's rolls, raw green beans, apples, and strawberries."

"It's not a gourmet meal, but it's nutritious. We can be grateful for that," he said.

"We'll save the apples for breakfast."

They sat on a hay bale and ate their meal together as the last edge of the sun dropped below the western horizon. The moon rose to take its place. They laughed and talked together as they had done during their courtship. It was a memory Susannah would have for the rest of her life.

Sunday, September 11, 1892

There must have been a light rain during the night because the canvas over them was wet in the morning. They had slept surprisingly well on their hay mattress despite the damp air. They roused themselves and ate their apples as the sun rose over a partly cloudy sky. Christian made a small fire in a clearing, and Susannah brewed a pot of coffee. With sugar, the hot brew was weak but satisfying going down, renewing their spirits for the long ride ahead.

"Christian, do you smell that? Doesn't the aroma of coffee and wood smoke remind you of breakfasts in your childhood?"

He smiled and nodded. He pulled the canvas off their makeshift tent, and they started home. "We can probably make it home in another five or six hours. It will take a little longer if we stop at the Tea Room in Lamar to get a decent meal," he said.

"I don't know about you, but I'm getting road-weary. It will be good to stop and have a hot meal."

The two of them traveled on, carefree and enjoying life. The dark clouds gathered overhead, but they had their canvas to keep them dry, so they were unconcerned.

Somewhere south of Lamar, the wind picked up. It got stronger as time passed, so they decided to forego the Tea Room to reach home more quickly. The wind swirled heavily as they finally passed through Lamar, blowing Susannah's hair wildly, loose strands whipping her face. They still had two hours of travel to get home. Christian urged the horses on as fast as he dared. The afternoon sky grew black, and the temperature dropped.

"I hope it holds off until we get home," Susannah said later, scanning the dark, heavy clouds. "We still have over an hour to go. We probably should have stopped at the hotel in Lamar."

Now, she was worried.

Christian glanced up at the sky overhead. "Why don't you get that canvas out and prepare for rain?"

Susannah stepped unsteadily to the back of the moving wagon, dropping to her knees, hanging on to the side to keep from falling, and retrieved the heavy canvas. She struggled to unfold it. Should the weather worsen, she could tug the edge over their heads for shelter.

They were about a mile from home when the rain started. At first, it was a light sprinkle blowing in the wind. Susannah pulled the canvas over their heads as best she could, but it was cumbersome and difficult to control, especially with the wind whipping it. She gripped it with all her might. The rain began to pour down steadily in large drops. Lightning flashed, and thunder rolled, coming closer. It had become a dangerous situation, but there was no escaping it. There was no shelter anywhere. They could either stop, or they could continue. Stopping didn't make any sense.

The horses were skittish and hard to control.

As they headed up their driveway, the rain pelted down in earnest. Susannah struggled to hold one edge of the flapping canvas over their heads, but a heavy gust of wind tore it from her grip, and it flew off to the side of the driveway like a giant kite, exposing them to the torrential rain.

"Christian, I'm sorry!" she shouted over the roaring of the wind. "I couldn't hold it."

"I know, Susannah. We'll be in the barn in just a few seconds."

She sneezed. "We'll catch our death in this weather."

The sky was nearly black, the rain cold. Both of them shivered from the force of the wind and the water running over their bodies. Christian drove the wagon directly into the barn and unhitched the horses, giving them their feed while the storm raged outside. He and Susannah hugged their arms for warmth and tried to figure out how to get into the house without risking a fall.

"Christian, the ground is covered with flowing water, so we can't see any uneven spots where we might trip. We could break our ankles. Or we could even get struck by lightning out there."

Christian tried to calm his wife. "Susannah, I've never known you to be so jittery. We're stuck in a hard place, that's true, but our only options are staying out here in the cold or running to the house. Which would you rather do?"

Susannah took a deep breath and shivered. "We can't stay here."

They waited for a moment, hoping for a lull in the storm that didn't come. They had no choice. "I'm going for it," Christian shouted over the storm's roar. "Are you ready?"

"There's no sign of it letting up," she shouted. "Let's go."

Christian grabbed his wife's hand. They ran for the veranda, sloshing through puddles all the way in. They finally found themselves standing in the warm foyer of their home in dripping wet clothing. The caretaker had a fire going in the fireplace. The warmth of the flames had never been so appreciated; the snapping and crackling of the hot embers were delightful to their ears.

The storm continued to rage outside. Together, they left their muddy shoes in the foyer and ran up the stairs as fast as they could in their drenched clothing. Susannah's soaked skirts left a trail of water behind them.

The wind and rain raged through the night. Bursts of lightning and the deep roll of thunder kept Susannah awake and tense. Outside, the water level rose in the yard. Christian woke in the middle of the night and nudged her. "Do we have anything outside that needs to be brought in? We're going to have a real flood problem soon."

Susannah giggled nervously. “You must be half asleep. We couldn’t go out to rescue anything now.” She rose from the bed and pulled a chair to the window to watch the storm in horrified fascination. Every flash of lightning revealed the trees bending to the wind and the torrential rain pouring down. She twisted her handkerchief in her shaking hands.

“This is the worst storm I’ve ever seen. I have an awful sense of foreboding. Do you think the horses will be all right?”

“I hope so. There’s nothing we can do for them now.”

Christian tried to go back to sleep, but Susannah kept watch. The wind roared on through the night.

Chapter 52: THE STORM

A few miles to the west in Spencer's Mill, the storm became even more violent. John and Kate huddled in the kitchen of their house. They were safer downstairs than upstairs in the bedrooms. The children shook with fright. Kate was proud of how Steven and Grace maintained calm despite their fear. Davy clutched her leg. She knelt to hug and comfort her youngest.

The wind raged heavily around the windows, rattling the glass and whooshing through cracks around the casings, making the curtains billow into the room. They heard a rumble in the distance. It sounded like a Nickel Plate locomotive getting closer and closer, but there was no train track that close.

"I know about this," John shouted above the screaming of the wind. "A tornado is headed our way. Everybody, get under the stairs. Now." The family dashed for the closet under the stairs, where they would be protected from flying glass should some debris blow through a window. The rumbling sound became louder and louder, finally reaching a deafening level, so loud it vibrated their bodies and numbed their ears as if a train were roaring right through their parlor.

"Listen to me, Steven," shouted John through the roar. "If you feel like something is trying to pull us apart, hold Ma and Gracie as tight as you can. Don't let go."

Standing beside him, Steven didn't hear him because of the

raging storm. It wasn't necessary, anyway. Steven tightened his grip on his sister and mother. John wrapped his arms around Steven and Gracie while Kate held Davy closer. She pressed into John.

They experienced a drop in pressure and the funny sensation of being lighter. John had a horrible premonition of disaster. Nothing mattered at that moment except his family. Not the bakery, not his bank account, not his reputation. Only his family. All five were huddled together, trembling and praying for God's mercy to protect them. Steven was as pale as a sheet, and Gracie began to cry. Still, they held onto each other.

There was a crash of broken glass from somewhere close, followed by a heavy thud that shook the house. Then, the rumbling sound moved off into the distance, and suddenly, it was over. A steady rain still came down, but the terror had passed. Kate opened the closet door, peered out from under the stairs, and cautiously ventured into the parlor. A large tree limb had been blown through their front window. She circled the invading branch to reach the door and stared into the dim light outside.

"John, we were fortunate," she said. "Look at all the tree branches lying about in the street. Only one of them came flying through our windows. I hope it doesn't ruin the rug."

The yard and the street were full of debris—leafy branches, pieces of wood from neighbors' houses, and miscellaneous baskets and gardening tools the neighbors must have left outside. She spotted dead chickens in the chaos, possibly from their chicken coop.

"We'll have to check the store and find out what was damaged there," John said. "I'll go as soon as I can get that branch out of our house." He stepped out onto the porch, wrapped his arms around the tree branch in the window, and tried to lug it onto the lawn.

"Steven, come help me with this tree," he said. Father and son both tugged on the limb. With Kate pushing from the other end, they made slow progress and finally got it out of the parlor. "We'll have to clean up the wet dirt and leaves from the rug. It will be easier to clean when it dries. Don't walk on it."

"If you're going to the store, we'll all go together, John. I'm so thankful we survived; I don't want us to be separated yet." She was still trembling.

He nodded. "I'll bring the carriage around."

By some miracle, the horses were still in their stalls but frightened, whinnying and stamping. John took a few minutes to stroke their necks, reassuring them, and hitched them to the carriage.

The light rain was barely noticeable as the family drove to the store in the weak evening light, concentrating on the downed limbs everywhere. They had to stop several times to pull away branches in the road so the carriage could pass.

As they approached the bakery, Steven said, "Look, Ma. Our Crust and Crumb sign is on the ground."

"Oh, no, John, we'll have to put the sign back up tomorrow. Steven, will you help Pa take it inside for the night?"

Steven hopped out of the carriage with John. They lugged the wet, heavy sign into the bakery. Miraculously, their windows had survived the wind, and there didn't seem to be any other damage except for loose shingles. Some of the other businesses on the street had not fared so well.

John worried about his brother. "Ma and Christian were bringing Eli and his family back today," he said. "We need to be sure they're safe. I'll take you back home, and then I'll check on Eli."

"No, John, not tonight. Please."

"It will be all right," he said, patting her knee. "I want to make sure Eli and Mary are safe. I'll bring them home with me if they're in any need. We'll have to find a place for them."

Kate relented. "You're right. Just be careful."

They turned toward home, and John dropped off his family in the relative safety of the house. As he put the carriage in the barn, night approached.

He struck out on horseback, carrying his lantern high, and picked his way through fallen debris to Eli's house. The closer he got, the more damage became visible. Glass was blown out of windows, tree limbs breached solid walls, and splintered lumber was scattered everywhere. When Eli's house came into view, he gasped in disbelief. The roof of their home had lifted off cleanly and smashed against the house across the street.

John ran into his brother's home. "Eli? Mary? Are you hurt?" He ran from one room to another. Standing in the parlor and looking up at stars peeking between the fragmented storm clouds was surreal. Everything was drenched. The beds were thrown against the walls and puddled with dirty water. All the furniture was soaked and thrown into disarray. The plaster walls were blistered. John didn't know if the house would ever be the same, but his main concern was where his brother and family were. They were nowhere to be found. He was powerless and sick with dread.

John waded to the backyard, where the chicken coop was flattened. The chickens were gone—somewhere. The horse was gone. The outhouse was overturned. By some quirk of the twisting wind, the barn had survived unscathed. He continued calling, "Eli? Mary?" But there was no answer.

John was grief-stricken. How cruel that Eli had just been found after a long absence, only to be lost again. John was in tears when he reasoned that his brother must have been killed in the storm. Getting to Ma's house in the dark tonight would be too difficult and dangerous, so all he could do was return home. He would resume his search tomorrow, and if he couldn't find

Eli's family, he would have to go out and tell Ma. How he dreaded that. He went home sobbing to tell Kate that Eli and his family were probably dead.

Kate took the news in shock. She sucked in deep gulps of air and held onto John, trying to deal with the horror. He took her hand, and they prayed together, not knowing how to pray.

"Let's try to get some sleep," John said. "Tomorrow is going to be tough. We'll close the bakery and restaurant for the day." He lowered his voice. "We need to look for bodies."

The clouds had cleared in the morning, and the sun shone brightly. The air was muggy and unseasonably warm, the water in the streets still ankle-deep. John and Kate left their children at home while searching for Eli's family, leaving them with strict instructions to stay in the house.

"Steven," John said, "you're in charge. Take care of your brother and sister." They did not want their children to go through the unspeakable trauma of seeing the bodies of their relatives lying on the ground—or, heaven forbid, up in a tree somewhere.

They picked their way through the trash on the roads and finally reached Eli's street. Kate burst into tears at the sight of the house with no roof. Even John was startled at the sight of it in the daylight, without the veil of darkness to diminish its horror. Kate's hands shook, and John's eyes darted about frantically as they ran for the house, sloshing through the mud and water, searching from room to room. They searched Eli's house and the surrounding neighborhood but could not find them.

"We'll have to go back and pick up the children, then go and tell Ma that the whole family is missing," John said. "I wish I didn't have to be the one to give her the awful news."

"The sooner, the better," Kate said, her voice quivering. "She needs to know."

At home, they herded the children into the carriage and took off for Susannah and Christian's house. The children were in tears over losing their uncle, aunt, and little cousin. It didn't seem real. Steven had been especially fond of Uncle Eli.

Traveling the seven miles took extra time. The road was mostly washed out, muddy, and full of obstacles. After four tense hours on the road, they finally made the trip that, in more favorable weather, took less than two hours by carriage.

In the aftermath of the storm, Christian was at home since the road to Lamar was unsafe for travel. He and Susannah welcomed John's family, barely observing their grim expressions. Susannah was still upset from the storm the day before and had not been able to sleep. Her nerves were raw.

"Ma, could we all sit down?" John asked. "We have some hard news. Please sit down."

Christian whispered, "John, whatever you tell us, please go gently with your mother. I've never seen her such a wreck. She didn't sleep at all last night."

Susannah stood and peered into her son's face. "Oh, no, John, have the bakery and restaurant been destroyed? You'll be ruined financially. Please, give me all the details." She braced herself for the worst.

"Ma," said John quietly. "It's even worse than that. Please sit down."

"What could be worse?"

Christian put his arm around Susannah and pulled her down onto the Chesterfield. She couldn't stop talking long enough to give John a chance. The words kept coming out. "That storm was one of the worst I've ever been through. We were in the open wagon, riding through it when it started. Lightning flashing, thunder crashing—we were completely exposed. It's a wonder we didn't catch pneumonia in that cold downpour. We still may get sick. Look, my hands are still shaking. So what do you have to tell us?"

John folded his hands and averted his eyes, forcing himself to say what needed to be said. "Ma, there was a tornado in Spencer's Mill last night, and the roof was ripped off Eli's house. And Eli, and Mary, and Zach —they're gone. They're not at the house anywhere. We searched for their bodies around the neighborhood but couldn't find them there, either."

When Susannah heard that news, the stress she had built up during the hours of the storm was relieved like a dam bursting. Her shoulders began to shake. Then she began to giggle and ended up laughing loudly despite herself. Christian stared at her in amusement, but John was speechless at her wildly inappropriate reaction. He quickly recovered and raised his voice.

"What's wrong with you? I'm telling you that your son and his family are dead or missing."

Susannah continued laughing as she reached for a handkerchief in Christian's pocket and wiped the tears from her eyes. "I'm sorry to shock you by laughing, John, but they're not dead. They weren't there last night—thank God for His mercy. They're still in Belleville, where Eli has a farm. They're going to be living there. It's a long story."

"What?" John's brow knitted. Nothing made sense.

"Let me speak to Hannah first. Then we'll explain this whole thing to you without interruption."

It was lunchtime, so Susannah asked the housekeeper to make some sandwiches. "Now, let's all find places to sit and get this ironed out," she said. She and Christian explained what happened, interrupting each other with details. Finally, the whole story came out—the story of Mrs. Lloyd, the stroke, and the will she signed.

John and Katie listened patiently to the entire story. "So … Eli won't be coming back to Spencer's Mill?" John paused. "I'm sorry we couldn't mend our relationship before he left. I guess I've lost a brother for good."

"Maybe not," said Christian. "He was a different man when we were there. That dark attitude was gone. And he'll have to come back to collect their belongings and put the house up for sale … although the storm might have made that simpler for him."

"They hardly have any possessions left," said Kate. "And the house is practically worthless now that it has no roof, and the walls are ruined. Who would buy a property like that? They'll have to tear it down and start over."

"Oliver Hardin," said John. "That's the kind of property he likes to snatch up—something he can buy cheap, then fix up for resale. We should contact him. I'm sorry the value of the house has tumbled overnight. That's a real blow to Eli."

"Not nearly as hard a blow as it would have been if God hadn't been watching over him," said Susannah. "He provided Eli with a new home and twenty-acre farm to replace the little house he just lost, and He did it before the storm. Now that's a miracle."

John's eyebrows raised, and his jaw dropped as he realized what a miracle it was. "I should say," he agreed, nodding.

Chapter 53: RECOVERY

John's family drove their carriage home, splashing through the debris-laden water, guiding the horses around fallen limbs and potholes. The storm had hit their little village the hardest. The tornado had bounced up and down, choosing which houses to strike and which to spare. From a human standpoint, there was no warning, sense, or predictability to it.

On arrival at Spencer's Mill, they all went to work at the bakery. Gracie cleaned up wet leaves and dirt while Kate started a batch of dough. Davy occupied himself by carrying bowls and utensils for his mother. John and Steven brought a ladder to the front of the building and then tried to figure out how to hang a long, heavy sign. Fortunately, Mr. Link recognized their dilemma from the general store window and volunteered his ladder. He and John hung the sign as a team, one on each end. It was heartening to have neighbors working together.

"Grace, you sweep out the salesroom while I work in the kitchen," Kate said. "Then go see if Mr. Link needs help cleaning up. Steven, when you're finished helping your father, go help Mr. Link."

A customer weary from cleaning came in the door, hoping to find bread. All that was left was day-old stale bread. "I need to find something for my neighbors," she said. "They have five children. A falling oak tree smashed into one end of their house. They were lucky that none of them were injured badly, but the end of the house that was hit was the kitchen and pantry. They don't have anything to eat."

That story broke Kate's heart. "Wait, let me give you the leftover bread. It's dry, but it might help fill their stomachs. I'll go into the root cellar and get some vegetables, too. They need more than bread." She came back with a basket full of fruits and vegetables. "Please give them this."

The customer thanked her profusely and left with the food for her neighbors.

Another customer came in. This time, it was Agatha Brown, the town gossip. She was unusually agitated. "Do you have any bread left, Mrs. Reese?"

"No, Mrs. Brown, I'm sorry. I gave it to a family who lost half of their house. I'll have some in the morning."

"I don't know what I'm going to do." Agatha was sincerely distressed and wringing her hands. "During the storm, a limb from a tree was thrown at my house with such force that it came right through my wooden door. It was terrifying. Now, anyone can get in, and I live there alone. I don't know what I'm going to do. I'm not safe there." Her tears flowed as she spoke.

Just then, Steven came back into the store. "Mr. Link is in pretty good shape," he said. "Grace is helping to sweep some wet leaves and stuff off his floor; then he'll be ready to reopen."

"Go get your father, Steven. He's at the butcher shop helping clean up broken glass. Tell him we need him here."

"On my way," Steven said.

"We'll see what John can do for you, Mrs. Brown. Please come into the kitchen, and I'll make you a nice cup of tea."

Mrs. Brown began to weep in earnest but followed Kate into the kitchen and found a chair. The two women were drinking their tea when John returned. He recognized Mrs. Brown and cringed. Her presence always meant trouble. She had been spreading malicious gossip for years. What did she want?

"I'm here, Kate. What do you need?"

"Mrs. Brown is in trouble, John. Last night, a limb crashed through her front door, and now anyone can get in. She's afraid to stay there by herself."

John studied Mrs. Brown's face. She didn't look like the same hateful woman who sashayed around town with her nose in the air, ready to whisper a juicy tidbit of gossip. Today she was a pathetic old lady who needed a friend.

"Where do you live, Mrs. Brown? I'll go take a look."

"It's not far. Only about four blocks from here. We can walk."

"No, there's no time for walks on a day like today. We'll take the carriage. Steven, go to the barn. You'll find a couple of boards out there. Please put them in the carriage and get hammers, nails, and a saw. Depending on the damage, maybe we can fix it while we're there."

"I'll stay here and bake pies," Kate said. "Grace can slice peaches for me when she's finished helping Mr. Link."

John, Steven, and Mrs. Brown took the carriage to her house with the wood and tools in the back.

I hope she doesn't start to talk or give us instructions, thought John. *She's never said a helpful thing. Better if she remains silent.*

All the twisted gossip she told about him flooded his mind, especially the rumor that Kate was forced to support the family in the bakery because he couldn't earn a living. He began to feel defensive and angry. *Why am I doing this?*

But another voice in his head objected. He remembered the words from Ephesians about "walking worthy"--he couldn't remember all of it-- "endeavoring to keep the unity of the Spirit in the bond of peace."

John glanced at Mrs. Brown again, sitting beside him, sniffling and dabbing her red nose with a handkerchief. His conscience urged him to overlook her faults and to try his best to keep the unity of the Spirit in the bond of peace. His heart wasn't in it, but he decided to do what was right.

The door of her house was closed, just as she said, but there was a substantial hole right in the middle, big enough for a slender thief to wiggle through with no difficulty. The limb still rested in the splintered hole.

"I can't do a professional job of fixing your door, Mrs. Brown, but I can give you a patch to keep you safe until you get a new one," John said.

She nodded. "I'd be very grateful."

John and Steven pulled the wet, heavy limb out of the door, then measured and cut the board into two lengths to cover the hole. They nailed them firmly to her door. It took about an hour. No one was going to get through that hole without a crowbar.

"We're finished, Mrs. Brown," said John as he loaded his tools into the wagon. "You should be safe now."

"Mr. Reese," she said and sucked in a breath. "That was the kindest thing anyone has done for me in a long time. I can't thank you enough. If I can ever return the favor…."

"You can pray for our family and our bakery, Mrs. Brown. That will be enough."

She extended her hand in the first warm gesture she had made in years. He took it, and she laid her other hand over his. "Thank you again, Mr. Reese."

He smiled. "You can call me John." He and Steven waved at her and drove away.

"Let's go to Uncle Eli's house on our way home," said John. "We'll get whatever furniture can be salvaged and bring whatever food we can from their flooded root cellar. We'll find room to store it in our cellar until they come to Spencer's Mill to get it."

They pulled up to the roofless, storm-scarred house and tied the horses to the rail.

Father and son went through the house quickly, pulling out whatever little could be salvaged. Then they packed the kitchen supplies into crates and stored them in the barn.

"There aren't many crates left in the barn, Pa. We should use them to get the food out of the root cellar." They turned their backs to the task and salvaged everything they could. Their carriage was too small to hold everything.

"We'll leave our carriage here and take Eli's wagon home," John said. "You take the reins, boy. I'm stiff and sore from all our work today."

Steven had never driven a team of horses before, but he had seen his Pa drive the carriage many times. He grinned, mounted the wagon's seat, and slapped the reins like an experienced coachman. He needed some help rounding corners but soon got the hang of it. Steven ran inside at top speed when they reached the bakery, nearly tripping over the threshold. "Ma, Ma—Pa let me drive Uncle Eli's wagon."

Kate emerged from the kitchen, wiping her hands on her apron. "Well, Steven, congratulations. I guess you're not a boy anymore. You're a young man now." Steven's shoulders went back, and his chest puffed out in pride. He was walking a little taller.

John winked at Kate, and she grinned.

The next day, the bakery and restaurant were back in business, crowded with customers. Supplies were getting low by the middle of the day. Kate and her workers put bread in the ovens as quickly as they emptied the last batch.

One disappointed customer, Mrs. Palmer, who hadn't been able to buy the cinnamon rolls she wanted, left the store frustrated and upset. Agatha Brown came up the street with her basket over her arm, planning to buy bread. Mrs. Palmer recognized her as she approached and thought she would get a sympathetic ear. She grumbled to Mrs. Brown, "I came all this way to get cinnamon rolls, and they didn't even make any today. How can you run a bakery like that?"

Agatha Brown pulled herself up. "You'll have to give them some allowances for the tornado. These people, especially John Reese himself, are the finest in town. Excuse me. I need to go inside and buy bread."

Mrs. Palmer stood slack-jawed, staring at her back as she walked away.

Sunday, September 18, 1892

On Sunday, John and Kate were relieved to have a day off to rest. It was a special Sunday, giving thanks for protection from the tornado.

There had been very few casualties in town, primarily cuts, scrapes, and one broken arm. Considering the extent of the property damage, it was a miracle that no lives were lost.

The congregation at Trinity Chapel joined their voices, singing, "Praise God from whom all blessings flow—." It was a delight to hear Mr. LaRue still singing loudly and off-key. Kate smiled, and tears of gratitude flowed down her face. She had her family beside her, unharmed.

That morning, Pastor Waverly's sermon was on God's protection and provision. He began reading from Psalm 91, ". . . I will say of the Lord, He is my refuge and my fortress: my God; in him will I trust." Those were words of special meaning after the past few days' events.

After the sermon, Agatha Brown gathered a few friends around her in the parking lot, whispering and glancing at Kate and John. What could she be telling them now?

Kate spotted Susannah and Christian. "Mother, has Eli contacted you yet?"

"No, dear, but we expect to hear something soon. We said we would stay in touch once a week or so."

After that short conversation with her mother-in-law, Kate's friend Cloris approached her. "Kate, you'll never believe what Agatha Brown is telling people." She giggled.

"What now? It could be anything."

"She says how wonderful John is and how everyone should buy their baked goods at your bakery."

Kate was speechless. "Well . . ." she said, with a grin. Maybe all Agatha needed all along was some friendship.

Chapter 54: THE ANGELS VISIT

Thursday, September 29, 1892

A few days later in Belleville, Eli and Mary tended to Mrs. Lloyd, who showed no improvement. "Mary, I found some money in Mrs. Lloyd's cookie jar. I can use it to buy food. Can you watch Mrs. Lloyd while I go?"

"Yes…Please don't be gone too long. I may not know what to do if she runs into trouble."

Eli smiled. "Don't worry. I'll be back soon." He kissed his wife and took off on his horse.

Mary stayed at the house with the patient and little Zach. Eli was deeply grateful for the blessing of having Mary there to help with Mrs. Lloyd. Her presence gave him the freedom to run other necessary errands.

Mary brought some broth to Mrs. Lloyd's room and tried to coax some into her mouth, but it ran down her face and had to be mopped up gently with a cloth. She sat by the bed and read the Bible for several minutes in her soft voice. When she came to a particular passage, she stopped and read it three times, her voice getting stronger each time. "The God of my rock; in him will I trust: he is my shield, and the horn of my salvation, my high tower, and my refuge, my saviour…."

Mrs. Lloyd opened her eyes, then closed them again. Mary put down the Bible, patted Mrs. Lloyd's hand, and left the room.

Zach sat on the parlor floor, playing with two chunks of

wood that he lined up like train cars. "Mama, can you play trains with me?"

"I'll play trains with you if you play laundry with me first," Mary said. "We need to dunk the sheets up and down in the water."

Zach's eyes lit up. "Okay, Mama." He jumped up and ran to the kitchen with her. Mary pumped a tub full of water and submerged the sheets. Zach helped her dunk them up and down, up and down. The boy was soaked up to his shoulders and all over the front of his shirt. He giggled and enjoyed it thoroughly. His giggling lightened Mary's heart. The two of them were still having fun when Eli returned.

Eli walked in the door with his food purchases and smiled to see his wife and son having a good splash in the sudsy water. "How's Mrs. Lloyd?"

"There was no change as of about twenty minutes ago. I tried feeding her a little broth, but she couldn't swallow it. Then I read the Bible to her for a while. She's sleeping now."

"I'll go look in on her," Eli said. He went into her room. She was peaceful, but something had changed. He checked for the rise and fall of her chest as she breathed, but there was no movement. He squeezed her wrist to get a pulse, but there was nothing.

"Mary," he called quietly. "Come in here." He realized he was standing on holy ground. When Mary came in, wondering why he had called, he said, "The angels have just been here. They took her with them." Tears ran down his cheeks, and he shook his head. "I'm sorry I wasn't here when she took her last breath. She was a great lady, a true follower of Jesus. She saved me from myself when I was drowning in self-doubt." He leaned over and kissed her forehead.

Mary slipped an arm around Eli's waist, and he wrapped

his arm around her shoulder. They held onto each other for a minute, gazing at Mrs. Lloyd's peaceful face. Eli broke the moment by saying quietly, "I guess I'd better get the doctor to confirm that she's gone. He'll tell me what to do next."

It didn't take Eli long to return with the doctor. Doc Stevens confirmed that she had passed. "I'll call on the undertaker when I get back in town. He'll come to measure for the coffin. Do you know where you would like to bury her?"

Eli thought quickly. "Mr. Lloyd is buried near the woods on a rise. I think she'd like to be next to him where she can stay on the farm she loved," he said. "I'll make it special, with stones and hedges, and put up a nice monument."

The doctor nodded, put on his hat, and slipped out quietly.

Eli went to the barn to look for a shovel and chose a shaded spot on the rise, where he began to dig.

Chapter 55: ELI AND MARY GO HOME

Friday, September 30, 1892

Christian came home from work, weary from consulting with a problematic client that Friday. "Susannah, I got a telegram at the office from Eli today. Mrs. Lloyd passed away yesterday. After they bury her, he'll bring Mary and Zach back to Spencer's Mill to take care of the house."

"That's good . . . good for everyone. Mrs. Lloyd is no longer suffering. She's rejoicing in heaven, and Eli and Mary have been released from their responsibility," Susannah said. "What shall we do to make their trip easier?"

"We'll ask them to stay here with us. They don't have a home of their own here."

"Of course, Christian. Please send them a telegram tomorrow."

Susannah counted the days until Eli's arrival. She cleaned the extra bedroom and changed the bed so everything would be fresh, adding a pallet on the floor for little Zach.

Monday, October 3, 1892

Three days later, Susannah thought there was a light tapping at the door. A little voice on the other side called, "Grandma, Grandma, let us in."

Susannah ran to the door and threw it open. She tried to hug all of them at one time. "Come in, come in." Zach held up his chubby arms to be picked up, and she obliged him.

"Eli, Mary, it's so good to see you. Come inside and take a rest. I know it's been a long trip."

"Good to be back, Ma, even if it's for a little while. We have our bags in the wagon. Let me go out and get them."

"You rest, Eli. We can get them later. Let me look at you." They went into the parlor and found places to sit. "What are your plans while you're here?"

"We'd like to get a good night's sleep, for one thing," Mary said, laughing. "It was quite a trip with a two-year-old. Two long days in the wagon. You remember about that, don't you?"

Susannah grinned and nodded.

"Tomorrow," said Eli, "we'll look at the house. I dread seeing it. Then we'll need to go to Lamar and talk to Oliver Hardin. I hope he'll want to buy it."

"You'll probably get a shock when you first see it. It certainly isn't the same. John and Steven packed up your dishes and other kitchen equipment in crates. They're in your barn. And they set aside whatever food from your flooded root cellar they could salvage. There wasn't much else left."

Eli stared down at his boots, stuffing his hands in his pockets. "I appreciate it. He didn't have to do that."

"You might tell him that."

"I will, Ma."

Mary spoke up. "We have plenty of dishes and kitchen equipment in Belleville. I'll tell Kate she can have whatever's in our barn."

"She'll be glad to have them," Susannah said. "She's always looking for more."

Mary continued, "We want to see Kate and John while we're in town. And we'll visit Matilda and Josh."

"We're thinking of going through Wapeka on our way home to see the family there. But then we'll have to get back to Belleville," Eli interrupted. "Mrs. Lloyd's will is in probate, and I want to be there when the deed and her bank account are signed over to me. The judge is in Logan County this month, so I expect everything will happen quickly."

"You have certainly been blessed. Well . . . Christian will be home soon. Do you want to bring your bags in now, son? We'll have dinner when he gets here."

Tuesday, October 4, 1892

Christian was obliged to go to his office the next day, so Susannah climbed into Eli's wagon with Mary and Zach. The roads were partially dried out, leaving deep ruts. Most of the debris had been pulled off to the side, but Eli still had to pick their way carefully. It took extra time.

Their first stop was at their old house. As they approached, all Eli could say was, "Oh, no." Mary was wide-eyed at the sight of it, clapping her hand over her mouth. They walked through the door and went from room to room in a daze. There was nothing left.

"We'll have to throw out all of the upholstered furniture," Mary said. "It's still soaked and beginning to smell."

Chunks of plaster had fallen off the walls, and some of the wood floors were still wet. Mud and leaves coated whatever window glass hadn't been blown out.

"I'm most shocked that the roof was lifted right off," Eli said. "Did you see the neighbor across the street dismantling it and storing the lumber in his barn?"

"Yes. Someone needs to get some good out of it."

They inspected the kitchen and bedrooms once more.

"If we had been here when this happened, I don't think we

would have made it," Mary said. She was trembling. "God has been looking out for us in more ways than we realized."

They found their kitchen equipment in the barn where John and Steven put it. Eli and Mary carried it to the wagon, one crate at a time, while Susannah kept Zach busy. They said a sad goodbye to their house and went to the Crust and Crumb Bakery.

Inside the store, the fragrance of cinnamon, peaches, and hot sourdough bread filled the air. Kate appeared from the kitchen, untying her apron. "Hello, everyone." She threw her arms around her sister-in-law. "Mary, it's so good to see you."

"Hello, Kate. I love the smell of this bakery. It's heavenly." Mary took a deep breath, savoring the aromas. "We brought all of our kitchen equipment for you. I don't need it in Belleville."

"Wonderful. Thank you. John's in his office. Eli, you can go on in while the women talk."

"I don't want to disturb John while he's working. I'll bring in the crates of supplies and wait until we have enough time to talk after the bakery closes."

Kate thought he was probably dreading an awkward greeting but didn't try to change his mind. She turned back to Mary and Susannah.

"Steven and Grace are still at school, and Davy is at the house with the nanny. Steven will be beside himself to see you both."

"Katie, can you bring your family to our house for dinner this evening?" Susannah asked. "We're going to invite Matilda and Josh, too. Hannah is cooking for all of us."

"We'd love to come, Mother. Thank you. It will be a treat for me not to cook. Mary, you have some food in our root cellar. You'll want to take that with you."

"I'll take a look. Much of it might not make a two-day trip, so we'll leave those things here for you to use. I'll take some of it for lunch on the road, maybe apples, celery, and carrots. But you might as well keep the rest. We have plenty back in Belleville, anyway."

"Well, I can give you enough bread and a nice pie for your journey. That brings up something else. What did I hear about Eli inheriting a farm?"

Mary's eyes sparkled. "Let me tell you the whole story…."

It was a superb dinner at Susannah and Christian's house that evening. Matilda, John, and Eli had their families there. It was a rare time, all enjoying one another's companionship, chatting and laughing without any undercurrent of anger. There was only a little awkwardness between John and Eli.

Afterward, Eli drew Steven aside.

"Steven, would you like to take a walk out back?" he asked.

"Sure, Uncle Eli."

Man and boy disappeared into the back lawn, walking as far back as possible to have some privacy. Along the way, Eli picked up some leftover debris from the storm and tossed it to the side of the yard. "Steven, the last time we walked together, I said some things I shouldn't have said."

"Ma told me you were telling me the truth," Steven said. "But then she told me the rest of the story, about how Pa repented and became a changed man."

"Yes, he did. I didn't tell you that because I was still hurting from the embarrassment he had caused me. I had other embarrassing things, too, making me want to run away from my family for a little while. That was stupid."

"Everybody sure was upset."

"Well, they had a right to be. But God was watching over me, so I chose the same path your Pa took. I repented, and God has forgiven me. So has my family."

Steven nodded his head, looking thoughtful. "I hope I never do anything stupid that my family has to forgive me for."

"I hope so, too, Steven." Eli slowly shook his head. The boy was only eleven, so the possibilities of his falling into stupidity were infinite. Eli decided he would pray for Steven every day.

Chapter 56: THE RECONCILIATION

Wednesday, October 5, 1892

It was a typically busy day for Kate. Her instructions to the bakery staff included baking forty loaves of bread, eight dozen rolls, seven pies, and six cakes. After leaving the instructions, she consulted with the restaurant's cook about what products he might need to order for Thursday.

As they planned the day's menu, a stranger walked in. He was a tall, sinewy man dressed in rough work clothes, carrying a straw hat in his worn hands. He shifted his weight from one foot to the other, betraying his impatience. Kate didn't recognize him.

"I'd like to speak to the owner, please," he said.

She went to fetch John. "A customer in the bakery would like to speak to you. He didn't say what he wanted."

John went to talk to him. He thought he recognized him from somewhere but couldn't place him.

"I'm John Reese. May I help you, sir?"

"I hope so." He reached out and shook John's hand as he introduced himself. "My name is Tibbs. You've been by my vegetable stand outside of town a ways."

"Oh, yes, that's where I've seen you, Mr. Tibbs."

"We just received word that my wife's mother has died in

Delphos. Mrs. Tibbs is packing for us to travel to be with the family. We need to go today, so we don't miss the funeral. My problem is that I have the vegetable stand stocked full, and it'll sit there and rot unless I can find someone to buy it all at a discount. I wondered if you would be interested since you have the restaurant."

"I'm sorry to hear about your mother-in-law. As for the vegetables, I don't think I can use that much before it spoils."

"You could use it better than anyone else in town. If you'd be interested, could you come with me now and take a look? I'm sure we can come to an agreement. I'll discount it."

"All right. Give me a minute to hitch up my wagon and tell my wife where I'm going."

In a few minutes, the two men were ready to go. Tibbs led the way, and John followed in the wagon. It was about a half-hour drive to the east.

Arriving at the vegetable stand, John stared at it with dismay.

"You have a lot of produce here, Mr. Tibbs, much more than I can use. My restaurant budget for produce is only six dollars per day. This will only last maybe two days. I can't use it all."

"Mr. Reese, if you give me twelve dollars, it's all yours. Please, take it all, so I don't come back to rotten vegetables in a week."

John hesitated. That meant spending two days' budget, loading all of the produce, taking it home, then unloading it. Manual labor wasn't the way he wanted to spend his day. On the other hand, this man was in a real jam. If he were in the same situation, he would like someone to help him. He decided to take the vegetables.

"Here you are," he said, pulling the twelve dollars out of his pocket. "Would you do me one favor?"

"If it doesn't take me too long, begging your pardon. My

wife is in a real hurry."

"My mother lives about fifteen minutes from here. Do you know the big house on the left with the long tree-lined driveway? The name is Wolf."

"Yes, I know the house."

"My brother Eli is visiting there. Would you stop and ask Eli if he would come to help me?"

"Yes, I can do that. Well, thanks, Mr. Reese. You've taken a big load off my mind."

"Good luck, Mr. Tibbs. I'll be praying for your family."

Tibbs headed down the road at a gallop. John didn't know if Eli would help him. He wasn't even sure his relationship with Eli was that solid yet. Since his brother returned from Belleville, there hadn't been as much time to talk with him privately as he had wanted. Their conversation yesterday was easier than in the past but still a little awkward. He hoped Eli's heart had changed and he would be willing to help.

The mountain of vegetables stood there under the trees, waiting for him. Someone had come by and done some shopping because there was a quarter on the rack beside the bell peppers. John slid it into his pocket.

He realized he had left the store so fast that he only had one basket in the wagon. He could have planned better. There was nothing to do but fill up the single basket with vegetables, climb into the wagon, unpack the basket, climb out of the wagon with the empty basket, and start all over. It could take quite a long time.

He was through about a fourth of it when he thought he spotted a rider approaching him, raising dust as he came. "Eli," he shouted, waving his hands.

Eli pulled up on the reigns. "Wow, you have bought yourself enough vegetables to feed an army, haven't you?"

John grinned with relief. "Almost. Are you willing to give

me a hand with this?"

"That's what I'm here for. Tell you what, stay in the wagon, and I'll hand the vegetables to you. Just give me that basket so I can fill it."

John was grateful to have help, but the biggest blessing was seeing that Eli's heart had healed. They worked together like a well-rehearsed team and had everything loaded in short order.

"I'm so grateful for your help, Eli. I want to spend some time talking, but I need to get back to town now. I was in the middle of ordering my supplies when Tibbs interrupted me."

"You're not going alone, John. I'll go with you and help unload. Ma said she would come later with Mary and Zach. They're bringing dinner."

John sighed with relief. "This is a real blessing, Eli. I can't thank you enough."

Eli tied his horse to the back of the wagon and crawled up on the seat beside John.

"John, I need to talk to you about how I behaved over the past few years."

"No need, Eli."

"Yes, there is a need. John, I was so hurt about that courtroom mess and angrier than I thought—well, I reacted without thinking. And the things I told Steven—that was wrong, and I knew it when I told him. I couldn't stop myself; I was so angry. And then you were successful, and I wasn't—that rubbed me the wrong way. But it was because you were a hard worker, and I wasn't putting much effort into it, especially after settling Pa's estate. That was my fault, and I'm ready to make up for it now."

"I'm sorry you went through all that, Eli. I'm still blaming myself."

"Well, I'm sorry for what I did to you. And I'm sorry for what I did to Steven. He and I have already talked about it, but

I wanted to have the same talk with you. Can you forgive me? And can we go back to being brothers like we used to be?"

John thought that men shouldn't cry, but his eyes were leaking. "There's nothing I would like more, Eli." John put his arm around his brother's shoulders. "None of this would have happened if I hadn't done wrong first. I'm so sorry."

Eli patted John's knee. The two of them grinned at each other. It was like old times.

"All right, then." That was all Eli could say.

Back at the shop, John and Eli unloaded the produce until it overflowed the root cellar.

"Give me those apples and pumpkins," Kate told them. "They're going into pies and tarts. Some of the carrots can go into cakes. And John, why don't you make some fliers to pass around town saying that there will be a half-price salad with the purchase of a bowl of soup for the next two days at the restaurant? Maybe we can pull more customers in."

"That's my girl," John said appreciatively. "Beets, potatoes, and onions will keep, but the rest can go into a salad buffet. We can give an empty bowl to each customer and let them make their salad."

"There's an idea. You're a genius, John. I'll put serving bowls of different ingredients on the buffet. We'll have to make up extra salad dressing and get out more cruets."

John was deeply grateful that the cracks in the family were healing. Of lesser importance, the wholesale vegetables wouldn't go to waste. Some of them were sent home with his mother, and what they didn't use in the bakery or restaurant went to neighbors and needy folks in the village.

Friday, October 7, 1892

Two days later, after selling their house to Oliver Hardin, it was time for Eli and Mary to return to their new life in Belleville. John and Kate left the store in the care of their staff early in the morning and took their children to Susannah's house to say goodbye to Eli's family. They bustled around in front of the house, helping the travelers get their belongings into the wagon. Finally, their departure could no longer be delayed, and it was time to go.

The two brothers embraced in a bittersweet farewell.

"Eli – Eli, God bless you and your family. Have a good life."

"And the same to you, John. I couldn't ask for a better man to call my brother."

Both of them had tears running down their cheeks. Eli dabbed at his face with his handkerchief while John wiped his face with the back of his hand.

Susannah stood near the veranda and saw the drama between her sons with an overflowing heart.

Eli and Mary climbed into their wagon with Zach, and the horses pulled them down the long driveway with the few possessions they could rescue from their ruined house. They were going home. As they rounded the bend, they turned around for one last wave. John's eyes followed them until they were out of sight. "I will miss them," he whispered in a hoarse voice. Kate nodded.

It would be three years before they would see each other again, but the critical work of forgiveness and reconciliation had been done. The post office was their only point of contact. Letters traveled back and forth three or four times a year. The letters were unfolded, read, then lovingly re-folded and put in the desk where they could be retrieved and revisited from time to time. Yes, it would be years . . . but whenever John and Eli thought of one another, it was with fondness and longing.

***

A NOTE FROM THE AUTHOR

Thank you for reading "The Rippling Effect." To show my appreciation, I'd like to offer free downloads from my website:

- Downloadable short stories for easy evening reading
- Resources for your book club

Also:

- Articles of interest
- Updates on upcoming books

You'll get information on my next book,
"The Phineas Fletcher Mysteries."
After Phineas investigates the villain who harassed
John and Kate in "The Rippling Effect,"
he goes on to solve more mysteries.
You'll want to read about his adventures.

Visit my website:
www.CherieHarbridgeWilliams.com

Thanks again for choosing "The Rippling Effect!"

- *Cherie*

OTHER BOOKS BY THIS AUTHOR

TEACUPS AND LIES

The first book in the "Spencer's Mill" series. Susannah Reese is a wife and mother in 1886 who experiences the worst crisis possible - the sudden death of her husband and the loss of her income. She relies on her faith and the help of some of her sons to make it through. But just as she thinks her life is about to improve, she is sabotaged by an unlikely source.

"Teacups and Lies" is a story of God's strength, faithfulness, and provision in desperate times. It is about the triumph of love and the power of family.

THE PHINEAS FLETCHER MYSTERIES

Phineas Fletcher first appeared in "Teacups and Lies" as the father-in-law of Danny Reese and the annoying would-be suitor of Susannah Reese. He was hailed as a hero in "The Rippling Effect" when he helped find and capture the criminal harassing John Reese's family. Now, he comes into his own as an investigator of all sorts of crimes. He's the finder of perpetrators, missing victims, and stolen objects. In this book, he solves seven unique mysteries, each with its twist.

FREE PHINEAS FLETCHER STORY

You can download a free Phineas Fletcher short story,
"The Unlikely Jewel Thief"

Go to

www.CherieHarbridgeWilliams.com

and enter the email address where you would like to receive the download.

Jewelry is coming up missing in the home of a well-to-do resident of Spencer's Mill, Ohio. They aren't stolen all at once; a piece is taken every few days. The owner is baffled. How is the thief getting in right under her nose and doing it so often? Phineas checks out the various suspects in inventive ways and finally fingers the culprit.

This is an easy-reading story you will enjoy in one sitting .Read it yourself, and share it with your friends.

WHAT'S NEXT?

A new novel named "The Man With A Mask" will be released in the winter of 2023-2024. You'll experience romance, danger, and intrigue as you watch the clash of good vs. evil and the progression of a soul without an anchor.

Watch for upcoming news on the website:

www.CherieHarbridgeWilliams.com

ATTENTION: BOOK CLUBS

As of this writing, we have developed resources for your book club on two books:

TEACUPS AND LIES

THE RIPPLING EFFECT

There is no charge for these resources. Log on to our website,

www.CherieHarbridgeWilliams.com

to get the free downloads. You'll find information on the author, puzzles, a coloring page, suggested topics of discussion, and recipes for book club refreshments.

Happy reading!

Made in United States
North Haven, CT
22 December 2023

46508535R00196